The Windup Girl

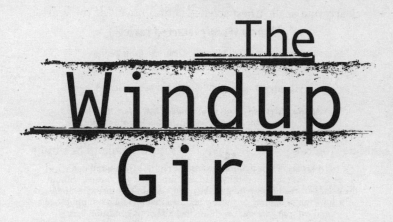

The Windup Girl

Paolo Bacigalupi

orbit

www.orbitbooks.net

ORBIT

First published in Great Britain in 2010 by Orbit
First publishing in the United States in 2009 by Night Shade Books

19 21 23 24 22 20

A CIP catalogue record for this book
is available from the British Library.

ISBN 978-0-356-50053-9

Typeset in Minion by M Rules
Printed and bound in Great Britain by
Clays Ltd, St Ives plc

Papers used by Orbit are from well-managed forests
and other responsible sources.

MIX
Paper from
responsible sources
FSC www.fsc.org FSC® C104740

Orbit
An imprint of
Little, Brown Book Group
Carmelite House
50 Victoria Embankment
London EC4Y 0DZ

An Hachette UK Company
www.hachette.co.uk

www.orbitbooks.net

For Anjula

1

'No! I don't want the mangosteen.' Anderson Lake leans forward, pointing. 'I want that one, there. *Kaw pollamai nee khap.* The one with the red skin and the green hairs.'

The peasant woman smiles, showing teeth blackened from chewing betel nut, and points to a pyramid of fruits stacked beside her. '*Un nee chai mai kha?*'

'Right. Those. *Khap.*' Anderson nods and makes himself smile. 'What are they called?'

'*Ngaw.*' She pronounces the word carefully for his foreign ear, and hands across a sample.

Anderson takes the fruit, frowning. 'It's new?'

'*Kha.*' She nods an affirmative.

Anderson turns the fruit in his hand, studying it. It's more like a gaudy sea anemone or a furry puffer fish than a fruit. Coarse green tendrils protrude from all sides, tickling his palm. The skin has the rust-red tinge of blister rust, but when he sniffs he doesn't get any stink of decay. It seems perfectly healthy, despite its appearance.

'*Ngaw,*' the peasant woman says again, and then, as if reading his mind. 'New. No blister rust.'

Anderson nods absently. Around him, the market *soi* bustles with Bangkok's morning shoppers. Mounds of durians fill the alley in reeking piles and water tubs splash with snakehead fish and red-fin *plaa*. Overhead, palm-oil polymer tarps sag under the blast furnace heat of the tropic sun, shading the market with hand-painted images of clipper ship trading companies and the face of the revered Child Queen. A man jostles past, holding vermilion-combed chickens high as they flap and squawk outrage on their way to slaughter, and women in brightly colored *pha sin* bargain and smile with the vendors, driving down the price of pirated U-Tex rice and new-variant tomatoes.

None of it touches Anderson.

'*Ngaw*,' the woman says again, seeking connection.

The fruit's long hairs tickle his palm, challenging him to recognize its origin. Another Thai genehacking success, just like the tomatoes and eggplants and chiles that abound in the neighboring stalls. It's as if the Grahamite Bible's prophecies are coming to pass. As if Saint Francis himself stirs in his grave, restless, preparing to stride forth onto the land, bearing with him the bounty of history's lost calories.

'*And he shall come with trumpets, and Eden shall return . . .*'

Anderson turns the strange hairy fruit in his hand. It carries no stink of cibiscosis. No scab of blister rust. No graffiti of genehack weevil engraves its skin. The world's flowers and vegetables and trees and fruits make up the geography of Anderson Lake's mind, and yet nowhere does he find a helpful signpost that leads him to identification.

Ngaw. A mystery.

He mimes that he would like to taste and the peasant woman takes back the fruit. Her brown thumb easily tears away the hairy rind, revealing a pale core. Translucent and veinous, it resembles nothing so much as the pickled onions served in martinis at research clubs in Des Moines.

She hands back the fruit. Anderson sniffs tentatively. Inhales floral syrup. *Ngaw*. It shouldn't exist. Yesterday, it didn't. Yesterday, not a single stall in Bangkok sold these fruits, and yet now they sit in pyramids, piled all around this grimy woman where she squats on the ground under the partial shading of her tarp. From around her neck, a gold glinting amulet of the martyr Phra Seub winks at him, a talisman of protection against the agricultural plagues of the calorie companies.

Anderson wishes he could observe the fruit in its natural habitat, hanging from a tree or lurking under the leaves of some bush. With more information, he might guess genus and family, might divine some whisper of the genetic past that the Thai Kingdom is trying to excavate, but there are no more clues. He slips the *ngaw's* slick translucent ball into his mouth.

A fist of flavor, ripe with sugar and fecundity. The sticky flower bomb coats his tongue. It's as though he's back in the HiGro fields of Iowa, offered his first tiny block of hard candy by a Midwest Compact agronomist when he was nothing but a farmer's boy, barefoot amid the corn stalks. The shell-shocked moment of flavor – real flavor – after a lifetime devoid of it.

Sun pours down. Shoppers jostle and bargain, but nothing touches him. He rolls the *ngaw* around in his mouth, eyes closed, tasting the past, savoring the time when this fruit must once have flourished, before cibiscosis and Nippon genehack weevil and blister rust and scabis mold razed the landscape.

Under the hammer heat of tropic sun, surrounded by the groan of water buffalo and the cry of dying chickens, he is one with paradise. If he were a Grahamite, he would fall to his knees and give ecstatic thanks for the flavor of Eden's return.

Anderson spits the black pit into his hand, smiling. He has read travelogues of history's botanists and explorers, the men and women who pierced the deepest jungle wildernesses of the earth in search of new species – and yet their discoveries cannot compare to this single fruit.

Those people all sought discoveries. He has found a resurrection.

The peasant woman beams, sure of a sale. '*Ao gee kilo kha?*' How much?

'Are they safe?' he asks.

She points at the Environment Ministry certificates laid on the cobbles beside her, underlining the dates of inspection with a finger. 'Latest variation,' she says. 'Top grade.'

Anderson studies the glinting seals. Most likely, she bribed the white shirts for stamps rather than going through the full inspection process that would have guaranteed immunity to eighth-generation blister rust along with resistance to cibiscosis 111.mt7 and mt8. The cynical part of him supposes that it hardly matters. The intricate stamps that glitter in the sun are more talismanic than functional, something to make people feel secure in a dangerous world. In truth, if cibiscosis breaks out again, these certificates will do nothing. It will be a new variation, and all the old tests will be useless, and then people will pray to their Phra Seub amulets and King Rama XII images and make offerings at the City Pillar Shrine, and they will all cough up the meat of their lungs no matter how many Environment Ministry stamps adorn their produce.

Anderson pockets the *ngaw*'s pit. 'I'll take a kilo. No. Two. *Song.*'

He hands over a hemp sack without bothering to bargain. Whatever she asks, it will be too little. Miracles are worth the world. A unique gene that resists a calorie plague or utilizes nitrogen more efficiently sends profits sky-rocketing. If he looks around the market right now, that truth is everywhere displayed. The alley bustles with Thais purchasing everything from generipped versions of U-Tex rice to vermilion-variant poultry. But all of those things are old advances, based on previous genehack work done by AgriGen and PurCal and Total Nutrient Holdings. The fruits of old science, manufactured in the bowels of the Midwest Compact's research labs.

The *ngaw* is different. The *ngaw* doesn't come from the Midwest. The Thai Kingdom is clever where others are not. It thrives while countries like India and Burma and Vietnam all fall like dominoes, starving and begging for the scientific advances of the calorie monopolies.

A few people stop to examine Anderson's purchase, but even if Anderson thinks the price is low, they apparently find it too expensive and pass on.

The woman hands across the *ngaw,* and Anderson almost laughs with pleasure. Not a single one of these furry fruits should exist; he might as well be hefting a sack of trilobites. If his guess about the *ngaw's* origin is correct, it represents a return from extinction as shocking as if a Tyrannosaurus were stalking down Thanon Sukhumvit. But then, the same is true of the potatoes and tomatoes and chiles that fill the market, all piled in such splendid abundance, an array of fecund nightshades that no one has seen in generations. In this drowning city, all things seem possible. Fruits and vegetables return from the grave, extinct flowers blossom on the avenues, and behind it all, the Environment Ministry works magic with the genetic material of generations lost.

Carrying his sacked fruit, Anderson squeezes back down the *soi* to the avenue beyond. A seethe of traffic greets him, morning commuters clogging Thanon Rama IX like the Mekong in flood. Bicycles and cycle rickshaws, blue-black water buffaloes and great shambling megodonts.

At Anderson's arrival, Lao Gu emerges from the shade of a crumbling office tower, carefully pinching off the burning tip of a cigarette. Nightshades again. They're everywhere. Nowhere else in the world, but here they riot in abundance. Lao Gu tucks the remainder of the tobacco into a ragged shirt pocket as he trots ahead of Anderson to their cycle rickshaw.

The old Chinese man is nothing but a scarecrow, dressed in

rags, but still, he is lucky. Alive, when most of his people are dead. Employed, while his fellow Malayan refugees are packed like slaughter chickens into sweltering Expansion towers. Lao Gu has stringy muscle on his bones and enough money to indulge in Singha cigarettes. To the rest of the yellow card refugees he is as lucky as a king.

Lao Gu straddles the cycle's saddle and waits patiently as Anderson clambers into the passenger seat behind. 'Office,' Anderson says. '*Bai khap.*' Then switches to Chinese. '*Zou ba.*'

The old man stands on his pedals and they merge into traffic. Around them, bicycle bells ring like cibiscosis chimes, irritated at their obstruction. Lao Gu ignores them and weaves deeper into the traffic flow.

Anderson reaches for another *ngaw*, then restrains himself. He should save them. They're too valuable to gobble like a greedy child. The Thais have found some new way to disinter the past, and all he wants to do is feast on the evidence. He drums his fingers on the bagged fruit, fighting for self-control.

To distract himself, he fishes for his pack of cigarettes and lights one. He draws on the tobacco, savoring the burn, remembering his surprise when he first discovered how successful the Thai Kingdom had become, how widely spread the nightshades. And as he smokes, he thinks of Yates. Remembers the man's disappointment as they sat across from one another with resurrected history smoldering between them.

'Nightshades.'

Yates' match flared in the dimness of SpringLife's offices, illuminating florid features as he touched flame to a cigarette and drew hard. Rice paper crackled. The tip glowed and Yates exhaled, sending a stream of smoke ceilingward to where crank fans panted against the sauna swelter.

'Eggplants. Tomatoes. Chiles. Potatoes. Jasmine. Nicotiana.' He held up his cigarette and quirked an eyebrow. 'Tobacco.'

He drew again, squinting in the cigarette's flare. All around, the shadowed desks and treadle computers of the company sat silent. In the evening, with the factory closed, it was just possible to mistake the empty desks for something other than the topography of failure. The workers might have only gone home, resting in anticipation of another hard day at their labors. Dust-mantled chairs and treadle computers put the lie to it – but in the dimness, with shadows draped across furniture and moonlight easing through mahogany shutters, it was possible to imagine what might have been.

Overhead, the crank fans continued their slow turns, Laotian rubber motorbands creaking rhythmically as they chained across the ceiling, drawing a steady trickle of kinetic power from the factory's central kink-springs.

'The Thais have been lucky in their laboratories,' Yates said, 'and now here you are. If I were superstitions, I'd think they conjured you along with their tomatoes. Every organism needs a predator, I understand.'

'You should have reported how much progress they were making,' Anderson said. 'This factory wasn't your only responsibility.'

Yates grimaced. His face was a study in tropic collapse. Broken blood vessels mapped rosy tributaries over his cheeks and punctuated the bulb of his nose. Watery blue eyes blinked back at Anderson, as hazy as the city's dung-choked air. 'I should have known you'd cut my niche.'

'It's not personal.'

'Just my life's work.' He laughed, a dry rattling reminiscent of early onset cibiscosis. The sound would have had Anderson backing out of the room if he didn't know that Yates, like all of

AgriGen's personnel, had been inoculated against the new strains.

'I've spent years building this,' Yates said, 'and you tell me it's not personal.' He waved toward the office's observation windows where they overlooked the manufacturing floor. 'I've got kink-springs the size of my fist that hold a gigajoule of power. Quadruple the capacity-weight ratio of any other spring on the market. I'm sitting on a revolution in energy storage, and you're throwing it away.' He leaned forward. 'We haven't had power this portable since gasoline.'

'Only if you can produce it.'

'We're close,' Yates insisted. 'Just the algae baths. They're the only sticking point.'

Anderson said nothing. Yates seemed to take this as encouragement. 'The fundamental concept is sound. Once the baths are producing in sufficient quantities—'

'You should have informed us when you first saw the nightshades in the markets. The Thais have been successfully growing potatoes for at least five seasons. They're obviously sitting on top of a seedbank, and yet we heard nothing from you.'

'Not my department. I do energy storage. Not production.'

Anderson snorted. 'Where are you going to get the calories to wind your fancy kink-springs if a crop fails? Blister rust is mutating every three seasons now. Recreational generippers are hacking into our designs for TotalNutrient Wheat and SoyPRO. Our last strain of HiGro Corn only beat weevil predation by sixty percent, and now we suddenly hear you're sitting on top of a genetic gold mine. People are starving—'

Yates laughed. 'Don't talk to me about saving lives. I saw what happened with the seedbank in Finland.'

'We weren't the ones who blew the vaults. No one knew the Finns were such fanatics.'

'Any fool on the street could have anticipated. Calorie companies do have a certain reputation.'

'It wasn't my operation.'

Yates laughed again. 'That's always our excuse, isn't it? The company goes in somewhere and we all stand back and wash our hands. Pretend like we weren't the ones responsible. The company pulls SoyPRO from the Burmese market, and we all stand aside, saying intellectual property disputes aren't our department. But people starve just the same.' He sucked on his cigarette, blew smoke. 'I honestly don't know how someone like you sleeps at night.'

'It's easy. I say a little prayer to Noah and Saint Francis, and thank God we're still one step ahead of blister rust.'

'That's it then? You'll shut the factory down?'

'No. Of course not. The kink-spring manufacturing will continue.'

'Oh?' Yates leaned forward, hopeful.

Anderson shrugged. 'It's a useful cover.'

The cigarette's burning tip reaches Anderson's fingers. He lets it fall into traffic. Rubs his singed thumb and index finger as Lao Gu pedals on through the clogged streets. Bangkok, City of Divine Beings, slides past.

Saffron-robed monks stroll along the sidewalks under the shade of black umbrellas. Children run in clusters, shoving and swarming, laughing and calling out to one another on their way to monastery schools. Street vendors extend arms draped with garlands of marigolds for temple offerings and hold up glinting amulets of revered monks to protect against everything from infertility to scabis mold. Food carts smoke and hiss with the scents of frying oil and fermented fish while around the ankles of their customers, the flicker-shimmer shapes of cheshires twine, yowling and hoping for scraps.

Overhead, the towers of Bangkok's old Expansion loom, robed in vines and mold, windows long ago blown out, great bones picked clean. Without air conditioning or elevators to make them habitable, they stand and blister in the sun. The black smoke of illegal dung fires wafts from their pores, marking where Malayan refugees hurriedly scald *chapatis* and boil *kopi* before the white shirts can storm the sweltering heights and beat them for their infringements.

In the center of the traffic lanes, northern refugees from the coal war prostrate themselves with hands upstretched, exquisitely polite in postures of need. Cycles and rickshaws and megodont wagons flow past them, parting like a river around boulders. The cauliflower growths of *fa' gan* fringe scar the beggars' noses and mouths. Betel nut stains blacken their teeth. Anderson reaches into his pocket and tosses cash at their feet, nodding slightly at their *wais* of thanks as he glides past.

A short while later, the whitewashed walls and alleys of the *farang* manufacturing district come into view. Warehouses and factories all packed together along with the scent of salt and rotting fish. Vendors scab along the alley lengths with bits of tarping and blankets spread above to protect them from the hammer blast of the sun. Just beyond, the dike and lock system of King Rama XII's seawall looms, holding back the weight of the blue ocean.

It's difficult not to always be aware of those high walls and the pressure of the water beyond. Difficult to think of the City of Divine Beings as anything other than a disaster waiting to happen. But the Thais are stubborn and have fought to keep their revered city of Krung Thep from drowning. With coal-burning pumps and leveed labor and a deep faith in the visionary leadership of their Chakri Dynasty, they have so far kept at bay that thing which has swallowed New York and Rangoon, Mumbai and New Orleans.

Lao Gu forges down an alley, ringing his bell impatiently at the coolie laborers who clot the artery. WeatherAll crates rock on brown backs. Logos for Chaozhou Chinese kink-springs, Matsushita anti-bacterial handlegrips, and Bo Lok ceramic water filters sway back and forth, hypnotic with shambling rhythm. Images of the Buddha's teachings and the revered Child Queen splash along the factory walls, jostling with hand-painted pictures of *muay thai* matches past.

The SpringLife factory rises over the traffic press, a high-walled fortress punctuated by huge fans turning slowly in its upper story vents. Across the *soi* a Chaozhou bicycle factory mirrors it, and between them, the barnacle accretion of jumbled street carts that always clog around the entrances of factories, selling snacks and lunches to the workers inside.

Lao Gu brakes inside the SpringLife courtyard and deposits Anderson before the factory's main doors. Anderson climbs down from the rickshaw, grabs his sack of *ngaw*, and stands for a moment, staring up at the eight-meter wide doors that facilitate megodont access. The factory ought to be renamed Yates' Folly. The man was a terrible optimist. Anderson can still hear him arguing the wonders of genehacked algae, digging through desk drawers for graphs and scrawled notes as he protested.

'You can't prejudge my work just because the Ocean Bounty project was a failure. Properly cured, the algae provides exponential improvements in torque absorption. Forget its calorie potential. Focus on the industrial applications. I can deliver the entire energy storage market to you, if you'll just give me a little more time. Try one of my demo springs at least, before you make a decision . . .'

The roar of manufacturing envelops Anderson as he enters the factory, drowning out the last despairing howl of Yates' optimism.

Megodonts groan against spindle cranks, their enormous heads hanging low, prehensile trunks scraping the ground as they tread slow circles around power spindles. The genehacked animals comprise the living heart of the factory's drive system, providing energy for conveyor lines and venting fans and manufacturing machinery. Their harnesses clank rhythmically as they strain forward. Union handlers in red and gold walk beside their charges, calling out to the beasts, switching them occasionally, encouraging the elephant-derived animals to greater labor.

On the opposite side of the factory, the production line excretes newly packaged kink-springs, sending them past Quality Assurance and on to Packaging where the springs are palletized in preparation for some theoretical time when they will be ready for export. At Anderson's arrival on the floor, workers pause in their labors and *wai*, pressing their palms together and raising them to their foreheads in a wave of respect that cascades down the line.

Banyat, his head of QA, hurries over smiling. He *wais*.

Anderson gives a perfunctory *wai* in return. 'How's quality?'

Banyat smiles. '*Dee khap.* Good. Better. Come, look.' He signals up the line and Num, the day foreman, rings the warning bell that announces full line stop. Banyat motions Anderson to follow. 'Something interesting. You will be pleased.'

Anderson smiles tightly, doubting that anything Banyat says will be truly pleasing. He pulls a *ngaw* out of the bag and offers it to the QA man. 'Progress? Really?'

Banyat nods as he takes the fruit. He gives it a cursory glance and peels it. Pops the semi-translucent heart into his mouth. He shows no surprise. No special reaction. Just eats the damn thing without a second thought. Anderson grimaces. *Farang* are always the last to know about changes in the country, a fact that Hock Seng likes to point out when his paranoid mind begins to suspect that Anderson intends to fire him. Hock Seng probably already knows about this fruit as well, or will pretend when he asks.

Banyat tosses the fruit's pit into a bin of feed for the megodonts and leads Anderson down the line. 'We fixed a problem with the cutting press,' he says.

Num rings his warning bell again and workers step back from their stations. On the third sounding of the bell, the union *mahout* tap their charges with bamboo switches and the megodonts shamble to a halt. The production line slows. At the far end of the factory, industrial kink-spring drums tick and squeal as the factory's flywheels shed power into them, the juice that will restart the line when Anderson is done inspecting.

Banyat leads Anderson down the now silent line, past more *wai*-ing workers in their green and white livery, and pushes aside the palm oil polymer curtains that mark the entrance to the fining room. Here, Yates' industrial discovery is sprayed with glorious abandon, coating the kink-springs with the residue of genetic serendipity. Women and children wearing triple-filter masks look up and tear away their breathing protection to *wai* deeply to the man who feeds them. Their faces are streaked with sweat and pale powder. Only the skin around their mouths and noses remains dark where the filters have protected them.

He and Banyat pass through the far side and into the swelter of the cutting rooms. Temper lamps blaze with energy and the tide pool reek of breeding algae clogs the air. Overhead, tiered racks of drying screens reach the ceiling, smeared with streamers of generipped algae, dripping and withering and blackening into paste in the heat. The sweating line techs are stripped to nearly nothing – just shorts and tanks and protective head gear. It is a furnace, despite the rush of crank fans and generous venting systems. Sweat rolls down Anderson's neck. His shirt is instantly soaked.

Banyat points. 'Here. See.' He runs his finger along a disassembled cutting bar that lies beside the main line. Anderson kneels to inspect the surface. 'Rust,' Banyat murmurs.

'I thought we inspected for that.'

'Saltwater.' Banyat smiles uncomfortably. 'The ocean is close.'

Anderson grimaces at the dripping algae racks overhead. 'The algae tanks and drying racks don't help. Whoever thought we could just use waste heat to cure the stuff was a fool. Energy efficient my ass.'

Banyat gives another embarrassed smile, but says nothing.

'So you've replaced the cutting tools?'

'Twenty-five percent reliability now.'

'That much better?' Anderson nods perfunctorily. He signals to the tool leader and the man shouts out through the fining room to Num. The warning bell rings again and the heat presses and temper lamps begin to glow as electricity pours into the system. Anderson shies from the sudden increase in heat. The burning lamps and presses represent a carbon tax of fifteen thousand baht every time they begin to glow, a portion of the Kingdom's own global carbon budget that SpringLife pays handsomely to siphon off. Yates' manipulation of the system was ingenious, allowing the factory to use the country's carbon allocation, but the expense of the necessary bribes is still extraordinary.

The main flywheels spin up and the factory shivers as gears beneath the floor engage. The floorboards vibrate. Kinetic power sparks through the system like adrenaline, a tingling anticipation of the energy about to pour into the manufacturing line. A megodont screams protest and is lashed into silence. The whine of the flywheels rises to a howl, and then cuts off as joules gush into the drive system.

The line boss' bell rings again. Workers step forward to align the cutting tools. They're producing two-gigajoule kink-springs, and the smaller size requires extra care with the machinery. Further down the line, the spooling process begins and the cutting press with its newly repaired precision blades rises into the air on hydraulic jacks, hissing.

'*Khun*, please.' Banyat motions Anderson behind a protection cage.

Num's bell rings a final time. The line grinds into gear. Anderson feels a brief thrill as the system engages. Workers crouch behind their shields. Kink-spring filament hisses out from alignment flanges and threads through a series of heated rollers. A spray of stinking reactant showers the rust-colored filament, greasing it in the slick film that will accept Yates' algae powder in an even coat.

The press slams down. Anderson's teeth ache with the crush of weight. The kink-spring wire snaps cleanly and then the severed filament is streaming through the curtains and into the fining room. Thirty seconds later it re-emerges, pale gray and dusty with the algae-derived powder. It threads into a new series of heated rollers before being tortured into its final structure, winding in on itself, torquing into a tighter and tighter curl, working against everything in its molecular structure as the spring is tightened down. A deafening shriek of tortured metal rises. Lubricants and algae residue shower from the sheathing as the spring is squeezed down, spattering workers and equipment, and then the compressed kink-spring is being whisked away to be installed in its case and sent on to QA.

A yellow LED flashes all-clear. Workers dash out from their cages to reset the press as a new stream of rust-colored metal hisses out of the bowels of the tempering rooms. Rollers chatter, running empty. Stoppered lubricant nozzles cast a fine mist into the air as they self-cleanse before the next application. The workers finish aligning the presses then duck again behind their barriers. If the system breaks, the kink-spring filament will become a high energy blade, whipping uncontrollably through the production room. Anderson has seen heads carved open like soft mangoes, the shorn parts of people and the Pollack-spatter of blood that comes from industrial system failures –

The press slams down, clipping another kink-spring among the forty per hour that now, apparently, will have only a seventy-five percent chance of ending up in a supervised disposal fill at the Environment Ministry. They're spending millions to produce trash that will cost millions more to destroy – a double-edged sword that just keeps cutting. Yates screwed something up, whether by accident or by spiteful sabotage, and it's taken more than a year to realize the depths of the problem, to examine the algae baths that breed the kink-springs' revolutionary coatings, to rework the corn resins that enclose the springs' gear interfaces, to change the QA practices, to understand what a humidity level that hovers near 100% year-round does to a manufacturing process conceptualized in drier climes.

A burst of pale filtering dust kicks into the room as a worker stumbles through the curtains from the fining chamber. His dark face is a sweat-streaked combination of grit and palm-oil spray. The swinging curtains reveal a glimpse of his colleagues encased in pale dust clouds, shadows in a snowstorm as the kink-spring fil-ament is encased in the powder that keeps the springs from locking under intense compression. All that sweat, all those calo-ries, all that carbon allotment – all to present a believable cover for Anderson as he unravels the mystery of nightshades and *ngaw*.

A rational company would shut down the factory. Even Anderson, with his limited understanding of the processes involved in this next-generation kink-spring manufacture would do so. But if his workers and the unions and the white shirts and the many listening ears of the Kingdom are to believe that he is an aspiring entrepreneur, the factory must run, and run hard.

Anderson shakes Banyat's hand and congratulates him on his good work.

It's a pity, really. The potential for success is there. When Anderson sees one of Yates' springs actually work, his breath catches. Yates was a madman, but he wasn't stupid. Anderson has watched joules pour out of tiny kink-spring cases, ticking along contentedly for hours when other springs wouldn't have held a quarter of the energy at twice the weight, or would simply have constricted into a single molecularly bound mass under the enormous pressure of the joules being dumped into them. Sometimes, Anderson is almost seduced by the man's dream.

Anderson takes a deep breath and ducks back through the fining room. He comes out on the other side in a cloud of algae powder and smoke. He sucks air redolent with trampled megodont dung and heads up the stairs to his offices. Behind him one of the megodonts shrieks again, the sound of a mistreated animal. Anderson turns, gazing down on the factory floor, and makes a note of the *mahout*. Number Four spindle. Another problem in the long list that SpringLife presents. He opens the door to the administrative offices.

Inside, the rooms are much as they were when he first encountered them. Still dim, still cavernously empty with desks and treadle computers sitting silent in shadows. Thin blades of sunlight ease between teak window shutters, illuminating smoky offerings to whatever gods failed to save Tan Hock Seng's Chinese clan in Malaya. Sandalwood incense chokes the room, and more silken streamers rise from a shrine in the corner where smiling golden figures squat over dishes of U-Tex rice and sticky fly-covered mangoes.

Hock Seng is already sitting at his computer. His bony leg ratchets steadily at the treadle, powering the microprocessors and the glow of the 12cm screen. In its gray light, Anderson catches the flicker of Hock Seng's eyes, the twitch of a man fearing bloody slaughter every time a door opens. The old man's flinch is as hallucinogenic as a cheshire's fade – one moment there, the next gone and doubted – but Anderson is familiar enough with yellow card refugees to recognize the suppressed terror. He shuts the door, muting the manufacturing roar, and the old man settles.

Anderson coughs and waves at the swirling incense smoke. 'I thought I told you to quit burning this stuff.'

Hock Seng shrugs, but doesn't stop treadling or typing. 'Shall I open the windows?' His whisper is like bamboo scraping over sand.

'Christ, no.' Anderson grimaces at the tropic blaze beyond the shutters. 'Just burn it at home. I don't want it here. Not any more.'

'Yes. Of course.'

'I mean it.'

Hock Seng's eyes flick up for a moment before returning to his screen. The jut of his cheek bones and the hollows of his eyes show in sharp relief under the glow of the monitor. His spider fingers continue tapping at the keys. 'It's for luck,' he murmurs. A low wheezing chuckle follows. 'Even foreign devils need luck. With all the factory troubles, I think maybe you would appreciate the help of Budai.'

'Not here.' Anderson dumps his newly acquired *ngaw* on his desk and sprawls in his chair. Wipes his brow. 'Burn it at home.'

Hock Seng inclines his head slightly in acknowledgment. Overhead, the rows of crank fans rotate lazily, bamboo blades panting against the office's swelter. The two of them sit marooned, surrounded by the map of Yates' grand design. Ranks of empty desks and workstations sit silent, the floor plan that should have held sales staff, shipping logistics clerks, HR people, and secretaries.

Anderson sorts through the *ngaw*. Holds up one of his green-haired discoveries for Hock Seng. 'Have you ever seen one of these before?'

Hock Seng glances up. 'The Thai call them *ngaw*.' He returns to his work, treadling through spreadsheets that will never add and red ink that will never be reported.

'I know what the Thai call them.' Anderson gets up and crosses to the old man's desk. Hock Seng flinches as Anderson sets the *ngaw* beside his computer, eyeing the fruit as if it is a scorpion. Anderson says, 'The farmers in the market could tell me the Thai name. Did you have them down in Malaya, too?'

'I—' Hock Seng starts to speak, then stops. He visibly fights for self-control, his face working through a flicker-flash of emotions. 'I—' Again, he breaks off.

Anderson watches fear mold and re-mold Hock Seng's features. Less than one percent of the Malayan Chinese escaped the Incident. By any measure, Hock Seng is a lucky man, but Anderson pities him. A simple question, a piece of fruit, and the old man looks as if he's about to flee the factory.

Hock Seng stares at the *ngaw*, breath rasping. Finally he murmurs, 'None in Malaya. Only Thais are clever with such things.' And then he is working again, eyes fixed on his little computer screen, memories locked away.

Anderson waits to see if Hock Seng will reveal anything more but the old man doesn't raise his eyes again. The puzzle of the *ngaw* will have to wait.

Anderson returns to his own desk and starts sifting through the mail. Receipts and tax papers that Hock Seng has prepared sit at one corner of his desk, demanding attention. He begins working through the stack, adding his signature to Megodont Union paychecks and the SpringLife chop to waste disposal approvals. He tugs at his shirt, fanning himself against the increasing heat and humidity.

Eventually Hock Seng looks up. 'Banyat was looking for you.'

Anderson nods, distracted by the forms. 'They found rust on

the cutting press. The replacement improved reliability by five percent.'

'Twenty-five percent, then?'

Anderson shrugs, flips more pages, adds his chop to an Environment Ministry carbon assessment. 'That's what he says.' He folds the document back into its envelope.

'Still not a profitable statistic. Your springs are all wind and no release. They keep joules the way the Somdet Chaopraya keeps the Child Queen.'

Anderson makes a face of irritation but doesn't bother defending the erratic quality.

'Did Banyat also tell you about the nutrient tanks?' Hock Seng asks. 'For the algae?'

'No. Just the rust. Why?'

'They have been contaminated. Some of the algae is not producing the . . .' Hock Seng hesitates. 'The skim. It is not productive.'

'He didn't mention it to me.'

Another slight hesitation. Then, 'I'm sure he tried.'

'Did he say how bad it was?'

Hock Seng shrugs. 'Just that the skim does not meet specifications.'

Anderson scowls. 'I'm firing him. I don't need a QA man who can't actually tell me the bad news.'

'Perhaps you were not paying close attention.'

Anderson has a number of words for people who try to raise a subject and then somehow fail, but he's interrupted by a scream from the megodont downstairs. The noise is loud enough to make the windows shake. Anderson pauses, listening for a follow-up cry.

'That's the Number Four power spindle,' he says. 'The *mahout* is incompetent.'

Hock Seng doesn't look up from his typing. 'They are Thai. They are all incompetent.'

Anderson stifles a laugh at the yellow card's assessment. 'Well, that one is worse.' He goes back to his mail. 'I want him replaced. Number Four spindle. Remember that.'

Hock Seng's treadle loses its rhythm. 'This is a difficult thing, I think. Even the Dung Lord must bow before the Megodont Union. Without the labor of the megodonts, one must resort to the joules of men. Not a powerful bargaining position.'

'I don't care. I want that one out. We can't afford a stampede. Find some polite way to get rid of him.' Anderson pulls over another stack of paychecks waiting for his signature.

Hock Seng tries again. '*Khun,* negotiating with the union is a complicated thing.'

'That's why I have you. It's called delegating.' Anderson continues flipping the papers.

'Yes, of course.' Hock Seng regards him drily. 'Thank you for your management instruction.'

'You keep telling me I don't understand the culture here,' Anderson says. 'So take care of it. Get rid of that one. I don't care if you're polite or if everyone loses face, but find a way to axe him. It's dangerous to have someone like that in the power train.'

Hock Seng's lips purse, but he doesn't protest any more. Anderson decides to assume that he will be obeyed. He flips through the pages of another permit letter from the Environment Ministry, grimacing. Only Thais would spend so much time making a bribe look like a service agreement. They're polite, even when they're shaking you down. Or when there's a problem with the algae tanks. Banyat . . .

Anderson shuffles through the forms on his desk. 'Hock Seng?'

The old man doesn't look up. 'I will take care of your *mahout*,' he says as he keeps typing. 'It will be done, even if it costs you when they come to bargain again for bonuses.'

'Nice to know, but that's not my question.' Anderson taps his desk. 'You said Banyat was complaining about the algae skim. Is he having problems with the new tanks? Or the old ones?'

'I . . . He was unclear.'

'Didn't you tell me we had replacement equipment coming off the anchor pads last week? New tanks, new nutrient cultures?'

Hock Seng's typing falters for a moment. Anderson pretends puzzlement as he shuffles through his papers again, already knowing that the receipts and quarantine forms aren't present. 'I should have a list here somewhere. I'm sure you told me it was arriving.' He looks up. 'The more I think about it, the more I think I shouldn't be hearing about any contamination problems. Not if our new equipment actually cleared Customs and got installed.'

Hock Seng doesn't answer. Presses on with his typing as though he hasn't heard.

'Hock Seng? Is there something you forgot to tell me?'

Hock Seng's eyes remain fixed on the gray glow of his monitor. Anderson waits. The rhythmic creak of the crank fans and the ratchet of Hock Seng's treadle fills the silence.

'There is no manifest,' the old man says, finally. 'The shipment is still in Customs.'

'It was supposed to clear last week.'

'There are delays.'

'You told me there wouldn't be any problem,' Anderson says. 'You were certain. You told me you were expediting the Customs personally. I gave you extra cash to be sure of it.'

'The Thai keep time in their own method. Perhaps it will be this afternoon. Perhaps tomorrow.' Hock Seng makes a face that resembles a grin. 'They are not like we Chinese. They are lazy.'

'Did you actually pay the bribes? The Trade Ministry was supposed to get a cut, to pass on to their pet white shirt inspector.'

'I paid them.'

'Enough?'

Hock Seng looks up, eyes narrowed. 'I paid.'

'You didn't pay half and keep half for yourself?'

Hock Seng laughs nervously. 'Of course I paid everything.'

Anderson studies the yellow card a moment longer, trying to determine his honesty, then gives up and tosses down the papers. He isn't even sure why he cares, but it galls him that the old man thinks he can be fooled so easily. He glances again at the sack of *ngaw*. Perhaps Hock Seng senses just how secondary the factory is ... He forces the thought away and presses the old man again. 'Tomorrow then?'

Hock Seng inclines his head. 'I think this is most likely.'

'I'll look forward to it.'

Hock Seng doesn't respond to the sarcasm. Anderson wonders if it even translates. The man speaks English with an extraordinary facility, but every so often they reach an impasse of language that seems more rooted in culture than vocabulary.

Anderson returns to the paperwork. Tax forms here. Paychecks there. The workers cost twice as much as they should. Another problem of dealing with the Kingdom. Thai workers for Thai jobs. Yellow card refugees from Malaya are starving in the street, and he can't hire them. By rights, Hock Seng should be out in the job lines starving with all the other survivors of the Incident. Without his specialized skills in language and accountancy and Yates' indulgence, he would be starving.

Anderson pauses on a new envelope. It's posted to him, personally, but true to form the seal is broken. Hock Seng has a hard time respecting the sanctity of other people's mail. They've discussed the problem repeatedly, but still the old man makes 'mistakes.'

Inside the envelope, Anderson finds a small invitation card. Raleigh, proposing a meeting.

Anderson taps the invitation card against his desk, thoughtful.

Raleigh. Flotsam of the old Expansion. An ancient piece of drift-wood left at high tide, from the time when petroleum was cheap and men and women crossed the globe in hours instead of weeks.

When the last of the jumbo jets rumbled off the flooded runways of Suvarnabhumi, Raleigh stood knee-deep in rising seawater and watched them flee. He squatted with his girlfriends and then outlived them and then claimed new ones, forging a life of lemongrass and baht and fine opium. If his stories are to be believed, he has survived coups and counter-coups, calorie plagues and starvation. These days, the old man squats like a liver-spotted toad in his Ploenchit 'club,' smiling in self-satisfaction as he instructs newly arrived foreigners in the lost arts of pre-Contraction debauch.

Anderson tosses the card on the desk. Whatever the old man's intentions, the invitation is innocuous enough. Raleigh hasn't lived this long in the Kingdom without developing a certain paranoia of his own. Anderson smiles slightly, glancing up at Hock Seng. The two would make a fine pair: two uprooted souls, two men far from their homelands, each of them surviving by their wits and paranoia...

'If you are doing nothing other than watching me work,' Hock Seng says, 'the Megodont Union is requesting a renegotiation of their rates.'

Anderson regards the expenses piled on his desk. 'I doubt they're so polite.'

Hock Seng's pen pauses. 'The Thai are always polite. Even when they threaten.'

The megodont on the floor below screams again.

Anderson gives Hock Seng a significant look. 'I guess that gives you a bargaining chip when it comes to getting rid of the Number Four *mahout*. Hell, maybe I just won't pay them anything at all until they get rid of that bastard.'

'The union is powerful.'

Another scream shakes the factory, making Anderson flinch. 'And stupid!' He glances toward the observation windows. 'What the hell are they doing to that animal?' He motions at Hock Seng. 'Go check on them.'

Hock Seng looks as if he will argue, but Anderson fixes him with a glare. The old man gets to his feet.

A resounding trumpet of protest interrupts whatever complaint the old man is about to voice. The observation windows rattle violently.

'What the—'

Another trumpeted wail shakes the building, followed by a mechanical shriek: the power train, seizing. Anderson lurches out of his chair and runs for the window but Hock Seng reaches it ahead of him. The old man stares through the glass, mouth agape.

Yellow eyes the size of dinner plates rise level with the observation window. The megodont is up on its hind legs, swaying. The beast's four tusks have been sawn off for safety, but it is still a monster, fifteen feet at the shoulder, ten tons of muscle and rage, balanced on its hind legs. It pulls against the chains that bind it to the winding spindle. Its trunk lifts, exposing a cavernous maw. Anderson jams his hands over his ears.

The megodont's scream hammers through the glass. Anderson collapses to his knees, stunned. 'Christ!' His ears are ringing. 'Where's that *mahout*?'

Hock Seng shakes his head. Anderson isn't even sure the man has heard. Sounds in his own ears are muffled and distant. He staggers to the door and yanks it open just as the megodont crashes down on Spindle Four. The power spindle shatters. Teak shards spray in all directions. Anderson flinches as splinters fly past and his skin burns with needle slashes.

Down below, the *mahouts* are frantically unchaining their beasts and dragging them away from the maddened animal, shouting encouragement, forcing their will on the elephantine creatures. The megodonts shake their heads and groan protest, tugging against their training, overwhelmed by the instinctual urge to aid their cousin. The rest of the Thai workers are fleeing for the safety of the street.

The maddened megodont launches another attack on its winding spindle. Spokes shatter. The *mahout* who should have controlled the beast is a mash of blood and bone on the floor.

Anderson ducks back into his office. He dodges around empty desks and jumps another, sliding over its surface to land before the company's safes.

His fingers slip as he spins combination dials. Sweat drips in his eyes. 23-right. 106-left … His hand moves to the next dial as he prays that he won't screw up the pattern and have to start again. More wood shatters out on the factory floor, accompanied by the screams of someone who got too close.

Hock Seng appears at his elbow, crowding.

Anderson waves the old man away. 'Tell the people to get out of here! Clear everyone out! I want everyone out!'

Hock Seng nods but lingers as Anderson continues to struggle with the combinations.

Anderson glares at him. 'Go!'

Hock Seng ducks acquiescence and runs for the door, calling out, his voice lost in the screams of fleeing workers and shattering hardwoods. Anderson spins the last of the dials and yanks the safe open: papers, stacks of colorful money, eyes-only records, a compression rifle … a spring pistol.

Yates.

He grimaces. The old bastard seems to be everywhere today, as if his *phii* is riding on Anderson's shoulder. Anderson pumps the handgun's spring and stuffs it in his belt. He pulls out the compression rifle. Checks its load as another scream echoes behind. At least Yates prepared for this. The bastard was naïve, but he wasn't stupid. Anderson pumps the rifle and strides for the door.

Down on the manufacturing floor, blood splashes the drive systems and QA lines. It's difficult to see who has died. More than just the one *mahout*. The sweet stink of human offal permeates the air. Gut streamers decorate the megodont's circuit around its spindle. The animal rises again, a mountain of genetically engineered muscle, fighting against the last of its bonds.

Anderson levels his rifle. At the edge of his vision, another megodont rises onto its hind legs, trumpeting sympathy. The *mahouts* are losing control. He forces himself to ignore the expanding mayhem and puts his eye to the scope.

His rifle's crosshairs sweep across a rusty wall of wrinkled flesh. Magnified with the scope, the beast is so vast he can't miss. He switches the rifle to full automatic, exhales, and lets the gas chamber unleash.

A haze of darts leaps from the rifle. Blaze orange dots pepper the megodont's skin, marking hits. Toxins concentrated from AgriGen research on wasp venom pump through the animal's body, gunning for its central nervous system.

Anderson lowers the rifle. Without the scope's magnification, he can barely make out the scattered darts on the beast's skin. In another few moments it will be dead.

The megodont wheels and fixes its attention on Anderson, eyes flickering with Pleistocene rage. Despite himself, Anderson is impressed by the animal's intelligence. It's almost as if the animal knows what he has done.

The megodont gathers itself and heaves against its chains. Iron links crack and whistle through the air, smashing into conveyor lines. A fleeing worker collapses. Anderson drops his useless rifle and yanks out the spring gun. It's a toy against ten tons of enraged animal, but it's all he has left. The megodont charges and Anderson fires, pulling the trigger as quickly as his finger can convulse. Useless bladed disks spatter against the avalanche.

The megodont slaps him off his feet with its trunk. The prehensile appendage coils around his legs like a python. Anderson scrabbles for a grip on the door jam, trying to kick free. The trunk squeezes. Blood rushes into his head. He wonders if the monster simply plans to pop him like some blood-bloated mosquito, but then the beast is dragging him off the balcony. Anderson scrabbles for a last handhold as the railing slides past and then he's airborne. Flying free.

The megodont's exultant trumpeting echoes as Anderson sails through the air. The factory floor rushes up. He slams into concrete. Blackness swallows him. *Lie down and die.* Anderson fights unconsciousness. *Just die.* He tries to get up, to roll away, to do anything at all, but he can't move.

Colorful shapes fill his vision, trying to coalesce. The megodont is close. He can smell its breath.

Color blotches converge. The megodont looms, rusty skin and ancient rage. It raises a foot to pulp him. Anderson rolls onto his side but can't get his legs to work. He can't even crawl. His hands scrabble against the concrete like spiders on ice. He can't move quickly enough. *Oh Christ, I don't want to die like this. Not here. Not like this . . .* He's like a lizard with its tail caught. He can't get up, he can't get away, he's going to die, jelly under the foot of an oversized elephant.

The megodont groans. Anderson looks over his shoulder. The beast has lowered its foot. It sways, drunken. It snuffles about with its trunk and then abruptly its hindquarters give out. The monster settles back on its haunches, looking ridiculously like a dog. Its expression is almost puzzled, a drugged surprise that its body no longer obeys.

Slowly its forelegs sprawl before it and it sinks, groaning, into straw and dung. The megodont's eyes sink to Anderson's level. They stare into his own, nearly human, blinking confusion. Its trunk stretches out for him again, slapping clumsily, a python of muscle and instinct, all uncoordinated now. Its maw hangs open, panting. Sweet furnace heat gusts over him. The trunk prods at him. Rocks him. Can't get a grip.

Anderson slowly drags himself out of reach. He gets to his knees, then forces himself upright. He sways, dizzy, then manages to plant his feet and stand tall. One of the megodont's yellow eyes tracks his movement. The rage is gone. Long-lashed eyelids blink. Anderson wonders what the animal is thinking. If the neural havoc tearing through its system is something it can feel. If it knows its end is imminent. Or if it just feels tired.

Standing over it, Anderson can almost feel pity. The four ragged ovals where its tusks once stood are grimy foot-diameter ivory patches, savagely sawed away. Sores glisten on its knees and scabis growths speckle its mouth. Close up and dying, with its muscles paralyzed and its ribs heaving in and out, it is just an ill-used creature. The monster was never destined for fighting.

The megodont lets out a final gust of breath. Its body sags.

People are swarming all around Anderson, shouting, tugging at him, trying to help their wounded and find their dead. People are everywhere. Red and gold union colors, green SpringLife livery, the *mahouts* clambering over the giant corpse.

For a second, Anderson imagines Yates standing beside him, smoking a nightshade and gloating at all the trouble. '*And you said you'd be gone in a month.*' And then Hock Seng is beside him, whisper voice and black almond eyes and a bony hand that reaches up to touch his neck and comes away drenched red.

'You're bleeding,' he murmurs.

2

'Lift!' Hock Seng shouts. Pom and Nu and Kukrit and Kanda all lean against the shattered winding spindle, drawing it from its cradle like a splinter pulled from the flesh of a giant, dragging it up until they can send the girl Mai down underneath.

'I can't see!' she shouts.

Pom and Nu's muscles flex as they try to keep the spindle from reseating itself. Hock Seng kneels and slides a shakelight down to the girl. Her fingers brush his and then the LED tool is gone, down into the darkness. The light is worth more than she is. He hopes they won't drop the spindle back into its seat while she's down there.

'Well?' he calls down a minute later. 'Is it cracked?'

No answer comes from below. Hock Seng hopes she isn't caught, trapped somehow. He settles into a squat as he waits for her to finish her inspection. All around, the factory is a hive of activity as workers try to put the place back in order. Men swarm over the megodont's corpse, union workers with bright machetes and four-foot bone saws, their hands red with their work as they render down a mountain of flesh. Blood runs off the beast as its hide is stripped away revealing marbled muscle.

Hock Seng shudders at the sight, remembering his own people

similarly disassembled, other bloodlettings, other factory wreckage. Good warehouses destroyed. Good people lost. It's all so
reminiscent of when the Green Headbands came with their
machetes and his warehouses burned. Jute and tamarind and kink-
springs all going up in fire and smoke. Slick machetes gleaming in
the blaze. He turns his eyes away, forcing down memories. Forces
himself to breathe.

As soon as the Megodont Union heard one of their own was
lost, they sent their professional butchers. Hock Seng tried to get
them to drag the carcass outside and finish their work in the
streets, to make room for the power train repairs, but the union
people refused and so now in addition to the buzz of activity and
cleanup, the factory is full of flies and the increasing reek of
death.

Bones protrude from the corpse like coral rising from an ocean
of deep red meat. Blood runs from the animal, rivers of it, rushing toward the storm drains and Bangkok's coal-driven
flood-control pumps. Hock Seng watches sourly as blood flows
past. The beast held gallons of it. Untold calories rushing away.
The butchers are fast, but it will take them most of the night to dis-
member the animal completely.

'Is she done yet?' Pom gasps. Hock Seng's attention returns to
the problem at hand. Pom and Nu and their compatriots are all
straining against the spindle's weight.

Hock Seng again calls down into the hole. 'What do you see,
Mai?'

Her words are muffled.

'Come up, then!' He settles back on his haunches. Wipes sweat
off his face. The factory is hotter than a rice pot. With all the
megodonts led back to their stables, there is nothing to drive the
factory's lines or charge the fans that circulate air through the
building. Wet heat and death stench swaddle them like a blanket.

They might as well be in the slaughter grounds of Khlong Toey. Hock Seng fights the urge to gag.

A shout rises from the union butchers. They've cut open the megodont's belly. Intestines gush out. Offal gatherers – the Dung Lord's people, all – wade into the mass and begin shoveling it into handcarts, a lucky source of calories. With such a clean source, the offal will likely go to feed the pigs of the Dung Lord's perimeter farms, or stock the yellow card food lines feeding the Malayan Chinese refugees who live in the sweltering old Expansion towers under the Dung Lord's protection. Whatever pigs and yellow cards won't eat will be dumped into the methane composters of the city along with the daily fruit rind and dung collections, to bake steadily into compost and gas and eventually light the city streets with the green glow of approved-burn methane.

Hock Seng tugs at a lucky mole, thoughtful. A good monopoly, that. The Dung Lord's influence touches so many parts of the city, it's a wonder that he hasn't been made Prime Minister. Certainly, if he wanted it, the godfather of godfathers, the greatest *jao por* to ever influence the Kingdom could have anything he wanted.

But will he want what I have to offer? Hock Seng wonders. *Will he appreciate a good business opportunity?*

Mai's voice finally filters up from underneath, interrupting his ruminations. 'It's cracked!' she shouts. A moment later she claws her way out of the hole, dripping sweat and covered with dust. Nu and Pom and the rest release their hemp ropes. The spindle crashes back into its cradle and the floor shakes.

Mai glances behind her at the noise. Hock Seng thinks he catches a glimpse of fear, the realization that the spindle could have truly crushed her. The look is gone as quickly as it came. A resilient child.

'Yes?' Hock Seng asks. 'Go on? Is it the core that has split?'

'Yes, *Khun,* I can slide my hand into the crack this far.' She shows him, touching her hand nearly at her wrist. 'And another on the far side, just the same.'

'*Tamade*,' Hock Seng curses. He's not surprised, but still. 'And the chain drive?'

She shakes her head. 'The links I could see were bent.'

He nods. 'Get Lin and Lek and Chuan—'

'Chuan is dead.' She waves toward the smears where the megodont trampled two workers.

Hock Seng grimaces. 'Yes of course.' Along with Noi and Kapiphon and unfortunate Banyat the QA man who will never now hear Mr. Anderson's irritation that he allowed line contamination in the algae baths. Another expense. A thousand baht to the dead workers' families and two thousand for Banyat. He grimaces again. 'Find someone else then, someone small from the cleaning gang like you. You will be going underground. Pom and Nu and Kukrit, get the spindle out. All the way out. We will need to inspect the main drive system, link by link. We cannot even consider starting again until it has been checked.'

'What's the rush?' Pom laughs. 'It will be a long time before we run again. The *farang* will have to pay the union bags and bags of opium before they're willing to come back. Not after he gunned down Hapreet.'

'When they do return, we won't have Number Four Spindle,' Hock Seng snaps. 'It will take time to win an approval from the crown to cut another tree of this diameter, and then to float the log down from the North – assuming the monsoon comes at all this year – and all that time we will be running under constrained power. Think about that. Some of you will not be working at all.' He nods at the spindle. 'The ones who work hardest will be the ones who stay.'

Pom smiles apologetically, hiding his anger, and *wais*. '*Khun*, I was loose with my words. I meant no offense.'

'Good then.' Hock Seng nods and turns away. He keeps his face sour, but privately, he agrees. It will take opium and bribes and a renegotiation of their power contract before the megodonts once again make their shuffling revolutions around the spindle cranks. Another red item for the balance sheets. And it doesn't even include the cost of the monks who will need to chant, or the Brahmin priests, or the *feng shui* experts, or the mediums who must consult with the *phii* so that workers will be placated and continue working in this bad luck factory—

'*Tan Xiansheng!*'

Hock Seng looks up from his calculations. Across the floor, the *yang guizi* Anderson Lake is sitting on a bench beside the workers' lockers, a doctor tending his wounds. At first, the foreign devil wanted to have her sew him upstairs, but Hock Seng convinced him to do it down on the factory floor, in public, where the workers could see him, with his white tropical suit covered with blood like a *phii* out of a graveyard, but still alive at least. And unafraid. A lot of face to be gained from that. The foreigner is fearless.

The man drinks from a bottle of Mekong whiskey that he sent Hock Seng out to buy as if Hock Seng was nothing more than a servant. Hock Seng sent Mai, who came back with a bottle of fake Mekong with an adequate label and enough change to spare that he tipped her a few baht extra for her cleverness, while looking into her eyes and saying, 'Remember that I did this for you.'

In a different life, he would have believed that he had bought a little loyalty when she nodded solemnly in response. In this life, he only hopes that she will not immediately try to kill him if the Thais suddenly turn on his kind and decide to send the yellow card Chinese all fleeing into the blister-rusted jungle. Perhaps he has bought himself a little time. Or not.

As he approaches, Doctor Chan calls out in Mandarin, 'Your foreign devil is a stubborn one. Always moving around.'

She's a yellow card, like him. Another refugee forbidden from feeding herself except by wits and clever machinations. If the white shirts discovered she was taking rice from a Thai doctor's bowl ... He stifles the thought. It's worth it to help someone from the homeland, even if it is only for a day. An atonement of sorts for all that has gone before.

'Please try to keep him alive.' Hock Seng smiles slightly. 'We still need him to sign our pay stubs.'

She laughs. '*Ting mafan*. I'm rusty with a needle and thread, but for you, I'd bring this ugly creature back from the dead.'

'If you're that good, I'll call for you when I catch cibiscosis.'

The *yang guizi* interjects in English, 'What's she complaining about?'

Hock Seng eyes him. 'You move about too much.'

'She's damn clumsy. Tell her to hurry up.'

'She also says you are very very lucky. Another centimeter difference and the splinter cuts your artery. Then your blood is on the floor with all the rest.'

Surprisingly, Mr. Lake smiles at this news. His eyes go to the mountain of meat being rendered down. 'A splinter. And I thought it was the megodont that was going to get me.'

'Yes. You nearly died,' Hock Seng says. And that would have been disastrous. If Mr. Lake's investors were to lose heart and give up the factory ... Hock Seng grimaces. It is so much harder to influence this *yang guizi* than Mr. Yates, and yet this stubborn foreign devil must be kept alive, if only so that the factory will not close.

It's an irritating realization, that he was once so close to Mr. Yates, and now so far from Mr. Lake. Bad luck and a stubborn *yang guizi*, and now he must come up with a new plan to cement his long-term survival and the revival of his clan.

'You should celebrate your survival, I think,' Hock Seng

suggests. 'Make offerings to Kuan Yin and Budai for your very good luck.'

Mr. Lake grins, his pale blue eyes on Hock Seng. Twin watery devil pools. 'You're damn right I will.' He holds up the bottle of fake Mekong, already half gone. 'I'll be celebrating all night long.'

'Perhaps you would like me to arrange a companion?'

The foreign devil's face turns to stone. He looks at Hock Seng with something akin to disgust. 'That's not your business.'

Hock Seng curses himself, even as he keeps his face immobile. He has apparently pushed too far, and now the creature is angry again. He makes a quick *wai* of apology. 'Of course. I do not mean to insult you.'

The *yang guizi* looks out across the factory floor. The pleasure of the moment seems drained from him. 'How bad is the damage?'

Hock Seng shrugs. 'You are right about the spindle core. It is cracked.'

'And the main chain?'

'We will inspect every link. If we are lucky, it will only be the sub-train that is affected.'

'Not likely.' The foreign devil offers him the whiskey bottle. Hock Seng tries to hide his revulsion as he shakes his head. Mr. Lake grins knowingly and takes another pull. Wipes his lips on the back of his arm.

A new shout rises from the union's butchers as more blood gushes from the megodont. Its head lies at an angle now, half-severed from the rest of the body. More and more, the carcass is taking on the appearance of separated parts. Not an animal at all, more a child's playset for building a megodont from the ground up.

Hock Seng wonders if there is a way to force the union to cut him in on the profits they get from selling the untainted meat. It seems unlikely, given how quickly they staked out their space, but perhaps when their power contract is renegotiated, or when they demand their reparations.

'Will you take the head?' Hock Seng asks. 'You can make a trophy of it.'

'No.' The *yang guizi* looks offended.

Hock Seng forces himself not to grimace. It's maddening to work with the creature. The devil's moods are mercurial, and always aggressive. Like a child. One moment joyful, the next petulant. Hock Seng forces down his irritation; Mr. Lake is what he is. His karma has made him a foreign devil, and Hock Seng's karma has brought them together. It's no use complaining about the quality of U-Tex when you are starving.

Mr. Lake seems to catch Hock Seng's expression and explains himself. 'This wasn't a hunt. It was just an extermination. As soon as I hit it with the darts, it was dead. There's no sport in that.'

'Ah. Of course. Very honorable.' Hock Seng stifles his disappointment. With the foreign devil demanding the head, he could have replaced the stumpy tusk remainders with coconut oil composites and sold the ivory to the doctors near Wat Boworniwet. Now, even that money will be gone. A waste. Hock Seng considers explaining the situation to Mr. Lake, explaining the value of meat and calories and ivory lying before them, then decides against it. The foreign devil would not understand, and the man is too easy to anger as it is.

'The cheshires are here,' Mr. Lake comments.

Hock Seng looks to where the *yang guizi* indicates. At the periphery of the bloodletting, shimmering feline shapes have appeared; twists of shadow and light summoned by the carrion scent. The *yang guizi* makes a face of distaste, but Hock Seng has a measure of respect for the devil cats. They are clever, thriving in places where they are despised. Almost supernatural in their tenacity. Sometimes it seems that they smell blood before it is even spilled. As if they can peer a little way into the future and know precisely where their next meal will appear. The feline shimmers stealth toward the sticky pools of blood. A butcher kicks one away, but there are too many to really fight, and his attack is desultory.

Mr. Lake takes another pull of whiskey. 'We'll never get them out.'

'There are children who will hunt them,' Hock Seng says. 'A bounty is not expensive.'

The *yang guizi* makes a face of dismissal. 'We have bounties back in the Midwest, too.'

Our children are more motivated than yours.

But Hock Seng doesn't contest the foreigner's words. He'll put out the bounty, regardless. If the cats are allowed to stay, the workers will start rumors that Phii Oun the cheshire trickster spirit has caused the calamity. The devil cats flicker closer. Calico and ginger, black as night – all of them fading in and out of view as their bodies take on the colors of their surroundings. They shade red as they dip into the blood pool.

Hock Seng has heard that cheshires were supposedly created by a calorie executive – some PurCal or AgriGen man, most likely – for a daughter's birthday. A party favor for when the little princess turned as old as Lewis Carroll's Alice.

The child guests took their new pets home where they mated with natural felines, and within twenty years, the devil cats were on every continent and *Felis domesticus* was gone from the face of the world, replaced by a genetic string that bred true ninety-eight percent of the time. The Green Headbands in Malaya hated Chinese people and cheshires equally, but as far as Hock Seng knows, the devil cats still thrive there.

The *yang guizi* flinches as Doctor Chan sticks him again and he gives her a dirty look. 'Finish up,' he says to her. 'Now.'

She *wais* carefully, hiding her fear. 'He moved again,' she whispers to Hock Seng. 'The anesthetic is not good. Not as good as what I am used to.'

'Don't worry.' Hock Seng replies. 'That's why I gave him the whiskey. Finish your work. I will deal with him.' To Lake *Xiansheng* he says, 'She is almost finished.'

The foreigner makes a face but doesn't threaten her anymore, and at last the doctor completes her sewing. Hock Seng takes her aside and hands her an envelope with her payment. She *wais* her thanks but Hock Seng shakes his head. 'There is a bonus in it. I wish you to deliver a letter as well.' He hands her another envelope. 'I would like to speak with the boss of your tower.'

'Dog Fucker?' She makes a face of distaste.

'If he heard you call him that, he'd destroy whatever is left of your family.'

'He's a hard one.'

'Just deliver the note. That will be enough.'

Doubtfully, she takes the envelope. 'You've been good to our family. All the neighbors also speak of your kindness. Make offerings to your . . . loss.'

'What I do is too little.' Hock Seng forces a smile. 'Anyway, we Chinese must stick together. Perhaps in Malaya we were still Hokkien, or Hakka or Fifth Wave, but here we are all yellow cards. I am embarrassed I cannot do more.'

'It is more than anyone else.' She *wais* to him, emulating the manners of their new culture, and departs.

Mr. Lake watches her go. 'She's a yellow card, isn't she?'

Hock Seng nods. 'Yes. A doctor in Malacca. Before the Incident.'

The man is quiet, seeming to digest this information. 'Was she cheaper than a Thai doctor?'

Hock Seng glances at the *yang guizi*, trying to decide what he wants to hear. Finally he says, 'Yes. Much cheaper. Just as good. Maybe better. But much cheaper. They do not allow us to take Thai

niches here. So she has very little work except for yellow cards –
who of course have too little to pay. She is happy for the work.'

Mr. Lake nods thoughtfully and Hock Seng wonders what he is
thinking. The man is an enigma. Sometimes, Hock Seng thinks
yang guizi are too stupid to have possibly taken over the world
once, let alone twice. That they succeeded in the Expansion and
then – even after the energy collapse beat them back to their own
shores – that they returned again, with their calorie companies and
their plagues and their patented grains . . . They seem protected by
the supernatural. By rights, Mr. Lake should be dead, a bit of
human offal mingled with the bodies of Banyat and Noi and the
nameless stupid Number Four Spindle megodont handler who
caused the beast to panic in the first place. And yet here the foreign
devil sits, complaining about the tiny prick of a needle, but completely unconcerned that he has destroyed a ten-ton animal in the
blink of an eye. The *yang guizi* are strange creatures indeed. More
alien than he suspected, even when he traded with them regularly.

'The *mahout* will have to be paid off again. Bribed to come back
to work,' Hock Seng observes.

'Yes.'

'And we will have to hire monks to chant for the factory. To
make the workers happy again. *Phii* must be placated.' Hock Seng
pauses. 'It will be expensive. People will say that your factory has
bad spirits in it. That it is sited wrong, or that the spirit house is
not large enough. Or that you cut down a *phii's* tree when it was
built. We will have to bring a fortune teller, perhaps a *feng shui*
master to get them to believe the place is good. And then the
mahout will demand hazard pay—'

Mr. Lake interrupts. 'I want to replace the *mahout*,' he says. 'All
of them.'

Hock Seng sucks air through his teeth. 'It is impossible. The
Megodont Union controls all of the city's power contracts. It is a

government mandate. The white shirts award the power monopoly. There is nothing we can do about the unions.'

'They're incompetent. I don't want them here. Not anymore.'

Hock Seng tries to tell if the *farang* is joking. He smiles hesitantly. 'It is Royal Mandate. One might as well wish to replace the Environment Ministry.'

'There's a thought.' Mr. Lake laughs. 'I could team up with Carlyle & Sons and start complaining every day about taxes and carbon credit laws. Get Trade Minister Akkarat to take up our cause.' His gaze rests on Hock Seng. 'But that's not the way you like to operate, is it?' His eyes become abruptly cold. 'You like the shadows and the bargaining. The quiet deal.'

Hock Seng swallows. The foreign devil's pale skin and blue eyes are truly horrific. As alien as a devil cat, and just as comfortable in a hostile land. 'It would be unwise to enrage the white shirts.' Hock Seng murmurs. 'The nail that stands up will be pounded down.'

'That's yellow card talk.'

'As you say. But I am alive when others are dead, and the Environment Ministry is very powerful. General Pracha and his white shirts have survived every challenge. Even the December 12 attempt. If you wish to poke at a cobra, be ready for its bite.'

Mr. Lake looks as if he will argue, but instead shrugs. 'I'm sure you know best.'

'It is why you pay me.'

The *yang guizi* stares at the dead megodont. 'That animal shouldn't have been able to break out of its harness.' He takes another drink from his bottle. 'The safety chains were rusted; I checked. We aren't going to pay a cent of reparations. That's final. That's my bottom line. If they had secured their animal, I wouldn't have had to kill it.'

Hock Seng inclines his head in tacit agreement, though he will not speak it out loud. '*Khun*, there is no other option.'

Mr. Lake smiles coldly. 'Yes, of course. They're a monopoly.' He makes a face. 'Yates was a fool to locate here.'

Hock Seng experiences a chill of anxiety. The *yang guizi* suddenly looks like a petulant child. Children are rash. Children do things to anger the white shirts or the unions. And sometimes they pick up their toys and run away home. A disturbing thought indeed. Anderson Lake and his investors must not run away. Not yet.

'What are our losses, to date?' Mr. Lake asks.

Hock Seng hesitates, then steels himself to deliver bad news. 'With the loss of the megodont, and now the cost of placating the unions? Ninety million baht, perhaps?'

A shout comes from Mai, waving Hock Seng over. He doesn't have to look to know it is bad news. He says, 'There will be damage below as well, I think. Expensive to repair.' He pauses, touches the delicate subject. 'Your investors, the Misters Gregg and Yee, will have to be notified. It is likely that we do not have the cash to do repairs and also to install and calibrate the new algae baths when they arrive.' He pauses. 'We will require new funds.'

He waits anxiously, wondering what the *yang guizi*'s reaction will be. Money flows through the company so quickly sometimes Hock Seng thinks of it as water, and yet he knows this will not be pleasant news. The investors sometimes become balky at expenses. With Mr. Yates, the fights over money were common. With Mr. Lake, less so. The investors do not complain so much now that Mr. Lake has arrived, yet it is still a fantastic amount of money to spend on a dream. If Hock Seng ran the company, he would have shut it down more than a year ago.

But Mr. Lake doesn't blink at the news. All he says is, 'More money.' He turns to Hock Seng. 'And when will the algae tanks and nutrient cultures clear Customs?' he asks. 'When, really?'

Hock Seng blanches. 'It is difficult. Parting the bamboo curtain is not something done in a day. The Environment Ministry likes to interfere.'

'You said you paid to keep the white shirts off our backs.'

'Yes.' Hock Seng inclines his head. 'All the appropriate gifts have been given.'

'So why was Banyat complaining about contaminated baths? If we've got live organisms breeding—'

Hock Seng hurries to interrupt. 'Everything is at the anchor pads. Delivered by Carlyle & Sons last week . . .' He makes a decision. The *yang guizi* needs to hear good news. 'Tomorrow the shipment will clear Customs. The bamboo curtain will part, and your shipment will arrive on the backs of megodonts.' He makes himself smile. 'Unless you wish to fire the Union right now?'

The devil shakes his head, even smiles a little at the joke, and Hock Seng feels a flush of relief.

'Tomorrow then. For certain?' Mr. Lake asks.

Hock Seng steels himself and inclines his head in agreement, willing it to be the truth. Still the foreigner holds him with his blue eyes. 'We spend a lot of money here. But the one thing the investors can't tolerate is incompetence. I won't tolerate it, either.'

'I understand.'

Mr. Lake nods, satisfied. 'Good then. We'll wait to talk with the home office. After we've got the new line equipment out of Customs, we'll call. Give them some good news with the bad. I don't want to ask for money with nothing to show at all.' He looks at Hock Seng again. 'We wouldn't want that, would we?'

Hock Seng makes himself nod. 'As you say.'

Mr. Lake takes another drink from his bottle. 'Good. Find out how bad the damage is. I'll want a report in the morning.'

With this dismissal, Hock Seng heads across the factory floor to the waiting spindle crew. He hopes that he is right about the shipment. That it will be truly released. That he will be proven right by events. It is a gamble, but not a bad one. And the devil would not have wanted to hear too much bad news at once, in any case.

When Hock Seng arrives at the winding spindle, Mai is dusting herself off from another foray into the hole. 'How does it look?' Hock Seng asks. The winding spindle is fully disengaged from the line. Now drawn forth, it lies on the ground, a massive spike of teak. The cracks are large and obvious. He calls down the hole. 'A lot of damage?'

A minute later, Pom crawls out covered in grease. 'Those tunnels are tight.' he gasps. 'I can't fit down some of them.' He wipes the sweat and grime with an arm. 'It's the sub-train for certain, and we won't know about the rest until we send children down along the links. If the main chain is damaged, we'll have to pull up the floor.'

Hock Seng peers into the revealed spindle hole with a grimace, flashing back to tunnels and rats and cowering survival in the jungles of the south. 'We'll have Mai find some of her friends.'

He surveys the damage again. He owned buildings like this, once. Whole warehouses filled with goods. And now look what he is, a factotum for *yang guizi*. An old man with a body that's falling apart and a clan that has been filed down to his single head. He sighs and forces down frustration. 'I want to know everything about how bad the damage is, before I talk to the *farang* again. No surprises.'

Pom *wais*. 'Yes, *Khun*.'

Hock Seng turns for the offices, limping slightly for the first few steps before forcing himself not to favor the leg. With all the activity, his knee aches, a reminder of an encounter of his own with the monsters that drive the factory. He can't help stopping at the top of the steps to study the megodont carcass, the places where the workers died. Memories scratch and peck at him, swirling like black crows, hungry to take over his head. So many friends dead.

So much family gone. Four years ago, he was a big name. Now? Nothing.

He pushes through the door. The offices are silent. Empty desks, expensive treadle computers, the treadmill and its tiny communications screen, the company's massive safes. As he scans the room, religious fanatics in green headbands leap from the shadows, machetes whirling, but they are only memories.

He closes the door behind him, shutting out the sounds of butchery and repair. Forces himself not to go to the window and look down again on the blood and carcass. Not to dwell on memories of blood running down the gutters of Malacca, of Chinese heads stacked like durians for sale.

This is not Malaya, he reminds himself. *You are safe.*

Still, the images are there. As bright as photographs and spring festival fireworks. Even with the Incident four years in the past, he must perform calming rituals. When the feeling is bad, almost any object reminds him of menace. He closes his eyes, forces himself to breathe deeply, to remember the blue ocean and his clipper fleets white upon the waves ... He takes another deep breath and opens his eyes. The room is safe again. Nothing but empty desks set in careful rows and dusty treadle computers. Shutters blocking out the blaze of tropic sunlight. Dust motes and incense.

Across the room, deep in shadows, the twinned vaults of SpringLife's safes gleam dully, iron and steel, squatting there, taunting him. Hock Seng has keys to one, the petty cash safe. But the other, the great safe, only Mr. Lake can open.

So close, he thinks.

The blueprints are there. Just inches away. He has seen them laid out. The DNA samples of the genehacked algae, their genome maps on solid state data cubes. The specifications for growing and processing the resulting skim into lubricants and powder. The necessary tempering requirements for the kink-spring filament to accept the new coatings. A next generation of energy storage sits within his grasp. And with it, a hope of resurrection for himself and his clan.

Yates mumbled and drank and Hock Seng filled his *baijiu* glass and listened to his rambles and encouraged his trust and dependence for more than a year. And it was all a waste. Now it comes down to this safe that he cannot open because Yates was foolish enough to raise the investors' ire, and too incompetent to bring his dream to fruition.

There are new empires waiting to be built, if only Hock Seng can reach the documents. All he has are incomplete copies from when they used to sit in the open, splashed across Yates' desk, before the drunken fool bought the cursed office safe.

Now there is a key and a combination, and a wall of iron between him and the blueprints. A good safe. Hock Seng is familiar with its sort. Benefited from its security when he too was a big name and had files he needed to protect. It is irritating – perhaps more irritating than anything else – that the foreign devils use the same brand of safe as he used for his own trading empire in Malaya: YingTie. A Chinese tool, twisted to foreign purposes. He has spent days staring at that safe. Meditating on the knowledge that it contains—

Hock Seng cocks his head, suddenly thoughtful.

Did you close it, Mr. Lake? In all the excitement, did you forget perhaps to lock it closed once again?

Hock Seng's heart beats faster.

Did you lapse?

Mr. Yates sometimes did.

Hock Seng tries to control growing excitement. He limps across to the safe. Stands before it. A shrine, an object of worship. A monolith of forged steel, impervious to everything except patience and diamond drills. Every day he sits across from it, feels it mocking him.

Could it be as simple as this? Is it possible that in the rush of disaster that Mr. Lake simply forgot to close it?

Hock Seng reaches out hesitantly and puts his hand on the lever. He holds his breath. Prays to his ancestors, prays to the elephant-headed Phra Kanet, the Thai people's remover of obstacles, to every god he knows. He leans on the handle.

One thousand *jin* of steel push back, every molecule resisting his pressure.

Hock Seng lets out his breath and steps back, forcing down his disappointment.

Patience. Every safe has a key. If Mr. Yates had not been so incompetent, if he had not somehow angered the investors, he would have been the perfect key. Now it must be Mr. Lake instead.

When Mr. Yates installed the safe, he joked that he had to keep the family jewels safe, and laughed. Hock Seng had made himself nod and *wai* and smile, but all he could think about was how valuable the blueprints were, and how stupid he had been not to copy faster, when they had been easily available.

And now Yates is gone, and in his place a new devil. A devil truly. Blue-eyed and gold-haired and hard-edged where Yates was soft. This dangerous creature who double-checks everything Hock Seng does and makes everything so much harder, and who must somehow be convinced to give up the secrets of his company. Hock Seng purses his lips. *Patience. You must be patient. Eventually the foreign devil will make a mistake.*

'Hock Seng!'

Hock Seng goes to the door and waves down to Mr. Lake, acknowledging the summons, but instead of going downstairs immediately, he goes to his shrine.

He prostrates himself before the image of Kuan Yin and begs that she will have mercy on him and his ancestors. That she will give him a chance to redeem himself and his family. Beneath the golden character for good fortune, suspended upside down so that it will gush down upon him, Hock Seng places U-Tex rice and cuts open a blood orange. The juice runs down his arm; a ripe one, clean of contamination, and expensive. One cannot cut too close to the bone with gods; they like the fat, not the lean. He lights incense.

As smoke streams into the still air, filling the office once again, Hock Seng prays. He prays that the factory will not close, and that his bribes will bring the new line equipment through the bamboo curtain without difficulty. That the foreign devil Mr. Lake will lose his head and trust him too much, and that the cursed safe will open and reveal its secrets to him.

Hock Seng prays for luck. Even an old Chinese yellow card needs luck.

3

Emiko sips whiskey, wishing she were drunk, and waits for the signal from Kannika that it is time for her humiliation. A part of her still struggles against it but the rest of her – the part that sits with her midriff-baring mini-jacket and tight *pha sin* skirt and a glass of whiskey in her hand – doesn't have the energy to fight.

And then she wonders if she has it backwards, if the part that struggles to maintain her illusions of self-respect is the part intent upon her destruction. If her body, this collection of cells and manipulated DNA – with its own stronger, more practical needs – is actually the survivor: the one with will.

Isn't that why she sits here, listening to the throb of beating sticks and the wail of *pi klang* as girls writhe under glow worms and men and whores shout their encouragement? Is it because she lacks the will to die? Or because she is too stubborn to allow it?

Raleigh says that all things come in cycles, like the rise and fall of the tides along the beaches of Koh Samet, or the rise and fall of a man's prick when he has a pretty girl. Raleigh slaps his girls on their bare bottoms and laughs at the jokes of the new wave *gaijin* and tells Emiko that whatever they want to do with her, money is money, and nothing is new under the sun. And perhaps he is right. Nothing that Raleigh demands has not been demanded before. Nothing that Kannika conceives to hurt her and make her cry out is truly different. Except that she draws cries and moans from a windup girl. This, at least, is novelty.

Look! She is almost human!

Gendo-sama used to say that she was more than human. He used to stroke her black hair after they had made love and say that he thought it a pity New People were not more respected, and really it was too bad her movements would never be smooth. But still, did she not have perfect eyesight and perfect skin and disease- and cancer-resistant genes, and who was she to complain? At least her hair would never turn gray, and she would never age as quickly as he, even with his surgeries and pills and ointments and herbs that kept him young.

He had stroked her hair and said, 'You are beautiful, even if you are New People. Do not be ashamed.'

And Emiko had snuggled into his embrace. 'No. I am not ashamed.'

But that had been in Kyoto, where New People were common, where they served well, and were sometimes well-respected. Not human, certainly, but also not the threat that the people of this savage basic culture make her out to be. Certainly not the devils that the Grahamites warn against at their pulpits, or the soulless creatures imagined out of hell that the forest monk Buddhists claim; not a creature unable to ever achieve a soul or a place in the cycles of rebirth and striving for Nirvana. Not the affront to the Q'ran that the Green Headbands believe.

The Japanese were practical. An old population needed young workers in all their varieties, and if they came from test tubes and grew in crèches, this was no sin. The Japanese were practical.

And isn't that why you sit here? Because the Japanese are so very practical? Though you look like one, though you speak their tongue, though Kyoto is the only home you knew, you were not Japanese.

Emiko puts her head in her hands. She wonders if she will find a date, or if she will be left alone at the end of the night, and then wonders if she knows which she prefers.

Raleigh says there is nothing new under the sun, but tonight, when Emiko pointed out that she was New People, and there had never been New People before, Raleigh laughed, and said she was right and special and who knows, maybe that meant anything was possible. And then he slapped her bottom and told her to get up on stage and show how special she was going to be tonight.

Emiko traces her fingers through the wetness of bar rings. Warm beers sit and sweat wet slick rings, as slick as girls and men, as slick as her skin when she oils it to shine, to be soft like butter when a man touches her. As soft as skin can be, and perhaps more so, because even if her physical movements are all stutter-stop flash-bulb strange, her skin is more than perfect. Even with her augmented vision she barely spies the pores of her flesh. So small. So delicate. *So optimal.* But made for Nippon and a rich man's climate control, not for here. Here, she is too hot and sweats too little.

She wonders if she were a different kind of animal, some mindless furry cheshire, say, if she would feel cooler. Not because her pores would be larger and more efficient and her skin not so painfully impermeable, but simply because she wouldn't have to think. She wouldn't have to know that she had been trapped in this suffocating perfect skin by some irritating scientist with his test tubes and DNA confetti mixes who made her flesh so so smooth, and her insides too too hot.

Kannika grabs her by the hair.

Emiko gasps at the sudden attack. She searches for help but none of the other patrons are interested in her. They are watching the girls on stage. Emiko's peers are servicing the guests, plying them with Khmer whiskey and pressing their bottoms to their laps and running their hands over the men's chests. And anyway, they have no love for her. Even the good-hearted ones – the ones with *jai dee,* who somehow manage to care for a windup like herself – will not step in.

Raleigh is talking with another *gaijin,* smiling and laughing with the man, but his ancient eyes are on Emiko, watching for what she will do.

Kannika yanks her hair again. '*Bai!*'

Emiko obeys, climbing down from her bar stool and tottering in her windup way toward the circle stage. The men all laugh and point at the Japanese windup and her broken unnatural steps. A freak of nature transplanted from her native habitat, trained from birth to duck her head and bow.

Emiko tries to distance herself from what is about to happen. She is trained to be clinical about such things. The crèche in which she was created and trained had no illusions about the many uses a New Person might be put to, even a refined one. New People serve and do not question. She moves toward the stage with the careful steps of a fine courtesan, stylized and deliberate movements, refined over decades to accommodate her genetic heritage, to emphasize her beauty and her difference. But it is wasted on the crowd. All they see are stutter-stop motions. A joke. An alien toy. A windup.

They have her strip off her clothes.

Kannika flicks water onto her oiled skin. Emiko glistens with water jewels. Her nipples harden. The glow-worms twist and writhe overhead, sending out phosphorescent mating light. The men laugh at her. Kannika slaps her hip and makes her bow. Slaps her ass hard enough to burn, tells her to bow lower, to make obeisance to these small men who imagine themselves to be the vanguard of some new Expansion.

The men laugh and wave and point and order more whiskey. Raleigh grins from his place in the corner, the fond elder uncle, happy to teach these newcomers – these small corporate men and women high on fantasies of multinational profiteering – the ways of the old world. Kannika motions that Emiko should kneel.

A black-bearded *gaijin* with the deep tan of a clipper ship sailor watches from inches away. Emiko meets the man's eyes. He stares intently, as if he is examining an insect under a magnifying glass: fascinated, and yet also repulsed. She has the urge to snap at him, to try to force him to look at her, to see her instead of simply evaluating her as a piece of genetic trash. But instead she bows and knocks her head against the teak stage in subservience while Kannika speaks in Thai and tells them Emiko's life story. That she was once a rich Japanese plaything. That she is theirs now: a toy for them to play with, to break even.

And then she grabs Emiko's hair and yanks her up. Emiko gasps as her body arches. She catches a glimpse of the bearded man staring in surprise at the sudden violent gesture, at her abasement. A flash of the crowd. The ceiling with its glow-worm cages. Kannika drags her further back, bending her like willow, forcing her to thrust her breasts out to the crowd, to arch further still, to spread her thighs as she struggles not to topple sideways. Her head touches the teak of the stage. Her body forms a perfect arc. Kannika says something and the crowd laughs. The pain in Emiko's back and neck is extreme. She can feel the crowd's eyes on her, a physical thing, molesting her. She is utterly exposed.

Liquid gushes over her.

She tries to rise, but Kannika presses her down and dumps more beer in her face. Emiko gags and splutters, drowning. Finally Kannika releases her and Emiko jerks upright, coughing. Liquid foams down her chin, spills down her neck and breasts, trickles to her crotch.

Everyone is laughing. Saeng is already offering the bearded man a fresh beer, and he is grinning and tipping Saeng and everyone is laughing at how Emiko's body twitches and jerks now that she is in a panic, coughing the liquid from her lungs. She is nothing but a silly marionette creature now, all stutter-stop motion – herky-jerky *heechy-keechy* – with no trace of the stylized grace that her mistress Mizumi-sensei trained into her when she was a girl in the crèche. There is no elegance or care to her movements now; the telltales of her DNA are violently present for all to see and mock.

Emiko continues coughing, almost retching at the beer in her lungs. Her limbs twitch and flail, giving everyone a chance to see her true nature. Finally she gets a full breath. Controls her flailing movements. She reverts to stillness, kneeling, waiting for the next assault.

In Japan she was a wonder. Here, she is nothing but a windup. The men laugh at her strange gait and make faces of disgust that she exists at all. She is a creature forbidden to them. The Thai men would happily mulch her in their methane composting pools. If they met her or an AgriGen calorie man, it is hard to say which they would rather see mulched first. And then there are the *gaijin*. She wonders how many of them claim membership in the Grahamite Church, dedicated to destroying everything that she represents: her affront to niche and nature. And yet they sit contentedly and enjoy this humiliation of her even still.

Kannika grabs her again. She has disrobed now and has a jadeite cock in her hands. She shoves Emiko down, pushing her onto her back. 'Hold her hands,' she says, and the men reach out eagerly, grip her wrists.

Kannika pries her legs wide and then Emiko cries out as Kannika takes her. Emiko turns her face aside, waiting out the assault, but Kannika sees her avoidance. She pinches Emiko's face in one hand and forces her to show her features so that the men can see the effect of Kannika's ministrations.

The men urge Kannika on. Begin to chant. Count in Thai. *Neung! Song! Sam! Si!*

Kannika indulges them with a building rhythm. The men sweat

and watch and shout for more for the price of their admission. More men are holding her down, hands on her ankles and wrists, freeing Kannika for her abuse. Emiko writhes, her body shaking and jerking, twitching in the ways that windups do, in the ways that Kannika excels at bringing out. The men laugh and comment on the freakish movements, the stutter-stop motions, flash-bulb strange.

Kannika's fingers join the jade between Emiko's legs, play at Emiko's core. Emiko's shame builds. Again she tries to turn her face aside. Men are gathered around, close, staring. More crowd behind, straining for a glimpse. Emiko moans. Kannika laughs, low and knowing. She says something to the men and increases her tempo. Her fingers play in Emiko's folds. Emiko moans again as her body betrays her. She cries out. Arches. Her body performs just as it was designed – just as the scientists with their test tubes intended. She cannot control it no matter how much she despises it. The scientists will not allow her even this small disobedience. She comes.

The audience roars approval, laughing at the bizarre convulsions that orgasm wrings from her DNA. Kannika gestures at her movements as if to say, 'You see? Look at this animal!' and then she is kneeling above Emiko's face and hissing to Emiko that she is nothing, and will always be nothing, and for once the dirty Japanese get what is coming to them.

Emiko wants to tell her that no self-respecting Japanese would do these things. Wants to tell her that all Kannika plays with is a disposable Japanese toy – a triviality of Japanese ingenuity, like Matsushita's disposable cellulose handlegrips for a cycle-rickshaw – but she has said it before and it only makes things worse. If she remains silent the abuse will end soon.

Even if she is New People, there is nothing new under the sun.

Yellow card coolies crank at wide-bore fans, driving air through the club. Sweat drips from their faces and runs in gleaming rivulets down their backs. They burn calories as quickly as they consume them and yet still the club bakes with the memory of the afternoon sun.

Emiko stands beside a fan, letting it cool her as much as she can, pausing in her labors of ferrying drinks for customers and hoping that Kannika will not catch sight of her again.

Whenever Kannika gets hold of her, she drags her out to where the men can all examine her. Makes her walk in the traditional Japanese windup way, emphasizing the stylized motions of her kind. Makes her turn this way and that, and the men joke about her aloud even as they silently consider buying her once their friends have gone away.

In the center of the main room, men invite young girls in their *pha sin* and cropped jackets out onto the dance floor and make slow turns around the parquet as the band plays Contraction mixes, songs that Raleigh has dredged from his memory and translated for use on traditional Thai instruments, strange melancholy amalgamations of the past, as exotic as his children with their turmeric hair and their wide round eyes.

'Emiko!'

She flinches. It's Raleigh, motioning her toward his office. Men's gazes follow her stutter-stop movements as she passes the bar. Kannika looks up from her date where they twine hands and nuzzle close. She smiles slightly as Emiko goes by. When Emiko first came to the country, she was told that the Thais have thirteen kinds of smile. She suspects that Kannika's denotes no good will.

'Come on.' Raleigh says, impatient. He leads her through a curtain and down the hall past where the girls change into their work clothes, then through another door.

The memorabilia of three lifetimes lines his office's walls, everything from yellowed photographs of a Bangkok lit entirely by electricity to an image of Raleigh wearing the traditional dress of some savage hilltribe in the North. Raleigh invites Emiko to recline on a cushion on the raised platform where he does his private business. Another man is already sprawled there, a pale tall creature with blue eyes and blond hair and an angry scar on his neck.

The man startles when she comes into the room. 'Jesus and Noah, you didn't tell me she was a windup,' he says.

Raleigh grins and settles on his own cushion. 'Didn't know you were a Grahamite.'

The man almost smiles at the taunt. 'Keeping something this risky . . . You're playing with blister rust, Raleigh. The white shirts could be all over you.'

'The Ministry doesn't give a damn as long I pay the bribes. The guys who patrol around here aren't the Tiger of Bangkok. They just want to make a buck and sleep through the night.' He laughs. 'Buying her ice is more expensive than paying the Environment Ministry to look the other way.'

'Ice?'

'Wrong pore structure. She overheats.' He scowls. 'If I'd known beforehand, I wouldn't have bought her.'

The room reeks of opium and Raleigh busies himself filling the pipe again. He claims that opium has kept him young, vital through the years, but Emiko suspects that he sails for Tokyo and the same aging treatments Gendo-sama used. Raleigh holds the opium over its lamp. It heats and sizzles, and he turns the ball on its needles, working the tar until it turns viscous, then he quickly rolls it back into a ball and presses it into his pipe. He extends the pipe to the lamp and breathes deeply as the tar turns to smoke. He closes his eyes. Blindly offers it to the pale man.

'No, thank you.'

Raleigh's eyes open. He laughs. 'You should try it. It's the one thing the plagues didn't get. Lucky for me. Can't imagine going through withdrawal at my age.'

The man doesn't answer. Instead, his pale blue eyes study Emiko. She has the uncomfortable feeling of being taken apart, cell by cell. Not so much that he undresses her with his gaze – this she experiences every day: the feel of men's eyes darting across her skin, clasping at her body, hungering and despising her – instead his study is clinically detached. If there is hunger there, he hides it well.

'She's the one?' he asks.

Raleigh nods. 'Emiko, tell the gentleman about our friend from the other night.'

Emiko glances at Raleigh, discomfited. She is fairly certain that she has never seen this pale blond *gaijin* at the club before, at least, that he has never attended any special performance. She has never served him a whiskey ice. She wracks her memories. No, she would remember. He has a sunburn, obvious despite the dim flicker of the candles and opium lamp. And his eyes are too strangely pale, unpleasantly so. She would remember him.

'Go on.' Raleigh urges. 'Tell him what you told me. About the white shirt. The kid you went with.'

Raleigh is normally fanatic about the privacy of guests. He has even talked about building a separate stairwell for patrons, simply so they will not be seen entering and leaving Ploenchit tower at all, an access passage that would allow them to enter from a block away, under the street. And yet now he wants her to reveal so much.

'The boy?' she asks, stalling for time, unnerved by Raleigh's eagerness to expose a guest, and a white shirt, at that. She glances at the stranger again, wondering who he is, and what sort of hold he has on her papa-san.

'Go on,' Raleigh motions impatiently, the opium pipe gripped in his teeth. He leans into the opium lamp to smoke again.

'He was a white shirt,' Emiko begins. 'He came with a group of other officers . . .'

A new one. Brought around by his friends. All of them laughing and egging him on. All of them drinking free because Raleigh knows better than to charge, their good will worth more than the liquor. The young man, drunk. Laughing and making jokes about her in the bar. And then stealthily returning later, in privacy, hidden from his colleagues' prying eyes.

The pale man makes a face. 'They'll go with you? With your kind?'

'*Hai*.' Emiko nods, showing nothing of what she thinks of his contempt. 'White shirts and Grahamites.'

Raleigh laughs softly. 'Sex and hypocrisy. They go together like coffee and cream.'

The stranger glances sharply at Raleigh, and Emiko wonders if the old man can see the disgust in those pale blue eyes or if he is too stoned on opium to care. The pale man leans forward, cutting Raleigh out of the conversation. 'And what did this white shirt tell you?'

Is there a flicker of fascination there? Does she intrigue him? Or is it simply her story that interests him?

Despite herself, Emiko feels a stirring of her genetic urge to please, an emotion that she hasn't felt since her abandonment. Something about the man reminds her of Gendo-sama. Even though his blue *gaijin* eyes are like pools of chemical bath acid and his face is kabuki pale, he has presence. The air of authority is palpable, and strangely comforting.

Are you a Grahamite? she wonders. *Would you use me and then mulch me?* She wonders if she cares. He is not beautiful. He is not Japanese. He is nothing. And yet his horrifying eyes hold her with the same power that Gendo-sama used to exercise.

'What do you wish to know?' she whispers.

'Your white shirt said something about generipping,' the *gaijin* says. 'Do you remember?'

'*Hai.* Yes. I think perhaps he was very proud. He came with a bag of newly designed fruits. Gifts for all of the girls.'

More interest from the *gaijin.* It warms her. 'And what did the fruit look like?' he asks.

'It was red, I think. With ... threads. Long threads.'

'Green hairs? About so long?' He indicates a centimeter with his fingers. 'Thickish?'

She nods. 'Yes. That's right. He called them *ngaw.* And his aunt had made them. She was going to be recognized by the Child Queen's Protector, the Somdet Chaopraya, for her contribution to the Kingdom. He was very proud of his aunt.'

'And he went with you,' the man prompts.

'Yes. But later. After his friends were gone.'

The pale man shakes his head impatiently. He doesn't care about the details of the liaison: the boy's nervous eyes, the way he approached the mama-san and how Emiko was sent up to wait for him to follow a safe time later, so that no one would make the connection. 'What else did he say about this aunt?' he asks.

'Just that she rips for the Ministry.'

'Nothing else? Not where she rips? Where they have test fields? Nothing of that sort?'

'No.'

'That's it?' The *gaijin* glances at Raleigh, irritated. 'This is what you dragged me here for?'

Raleigh rouses himself. 'The *farang,*' he prompts. 'Tell him about the *farang.*'

Emiko can't help but show her confusion. 'Sorry?' She remembers the white shirt boy, bragging about his aunt. How his aunt would be given a prize and a promotion for her work with *ngaw* ... nothing of *farang.* 'I don't understand.'

Raleigh puts down his pipe, scowling. 'You told me he talked about *farang* generippers.'

'No.' She shakes her head. 'He said nothing about foreigners. I am sorry.'

The scarred *gaijin* makes a face of irritation. 'Let me know when you've got something worth my time, Raleigh.' He reaches for his hat, makes to stand.

Raleigh glares at her. 'You said there was a *farang* generipper!'

'No . . .' Emiko shakes her head. 'Wait!' She puts out a hand to the *gaijin*. 'Wait. *Khun*, please wait. I know what Raleigh-san is talking about.' Her fingers brush his arm. The *gaijin* jerks away from her touch. He steps out of reach with a look of disgust.

'Please,' she begs. 'I did not understand. The boy said nothing about *farang*. But he used a name . . . it could have been *farang*.' She looks to Raleigh for confirmation. 'Is this what you mean? The strange name? It could have been foreign, yes? Not Thai. Not Chinese or Hokkien . . .'

Raleigh interrupts, 'Tell him what you told me, Emiko. That's all I want. Tell him everything. Every single detail. Just like you're talking to me after a date.'

And so she does. As the *gaijin* sits again, listening suspiciously, she tells everything. About the boy's nervousness, how he couldn't look at her, and then how he couldn't look away. How he talked because his erection would not come. How he watched her undress. How he talked about his aunt. Trying to make himself seem important to a whore and a New People whore at that, and how strange and silly that had seemed to her, and how she hid her thoughts of him. And then finally the part that makes Raleigh smile in satisfaction and the pale scarred man's eyes widen.

'The boy said the man Gi Bu Sen gives them blueprints, but he betrays them more often than not. But his aunt discovered a trickery. And then they made the successful rip of the *ngaw*. Gi Bu Sen did hardly anything for them with the *ngaw*. It was all his aunt's work, in the end.' She nods. 'That is what he said. This Gi Bu Sen tricks them. But his aunt is too brilliant to be tricked.'

The scarred man studies her closely. Cold blue eyes. Pale skin like a corpse. 'Gi Bu Sen,' the man murmurs. 'You're sure that was the name?'

'Gi Bu Sen. I am sure.'

The man nods, thoughtful. The lamp that Raleigh uses for his opium crackles in the silence. Far below on the street, a late-night water seller calls out, his voice floating up through the open shutters and mosquito screens. The noise seems to break the *gaijin* from his reverie. His pale eyes focus on her again. 'I would be very interested to know if your friend returned for another visit.'

'He was ashamed, afterward.' Emiko touches her cheek, where she hides a fading bruise with makeup. 'I think he will not—'

Raleigh interrupts. 'Sometimes they come back. Even if they feel guilty.' He shoots her a dark look. She makes herself nod in confirmation. The boy will not be coming back, but it will make the *gaijin* happy to think so. And it will make Raleigh happy. Raleigh is her patron. She should agree. Should agree with conviction.

'Sometimes.' It's all she can manage. 'Sometimes they come back, even if they are ashamed.'

The *gaijin* eyes them both. 'Why don't you go get her some ice, Raleigh?'

'It's not time for her next round. And she's got a show coming up.'

'I'll cover the loss.'

Raleigh clearly wants to stay, but he's smart enough not to protest. He forces a smile. 'Of course. Why don't you two talk?' He looks at her significantly as he leaves. Emiko knows Raleigh wants her to seduce this *gaijin*. To entice him with herky-jerky sex and the promise of transgression. And then to listen to him and report, as all the girls are asked to.

She leans closer, letting the *gaijin* see her exposed skin. His eyes trace across her flesh, following the line of her thigh where it slips beneath her *pha sin*, the way her hip presses against fabric. He looks away. Emiko hides her irritation. Is he attracted? Nervous? Disgusted? She cannot tell. With most men, it is easy. Obvious. They fit such simple patterns. She wonders if he finds a New Person too disgusting, or if perhaps he prefers boys.

'How do you survive here?' the *gaijin* asks. 'The white shirts should have mulched you by now.'

'The payments. As long as Raleigh-san is willing to pay, they will ignore.'

'And you live somewhere, too? Raleigh pays for that as well?' When she nods, he says, 'Expensive, I suppose?'

She shrugs. 'Raleigh-san keeps a tally of my debts.'

As if summoned, Raleigh returns with her ice. The *gaijin* pauses as Raleigh comes through the door, waits impatiently as Raleigh sets down the glass on the low table. Raleigh hesitates, and when the scarred man ignores him, he mumbles something about enjoying themselves and leaves again. She watches the old man's departure thoughtfully, wondering at the hold this man has over Raleigh. Before her, the glass of icy water sweats, seductive. At the man's nod she reaches for it and drinks. Convulsive. Before she knows it, it is gone. She presses the cold glass against her cheek.

The scarred man watches. 'So you're not engineered for the tropics,' he says. He leans forward, studying her, his eyes moving across her skin. 'It's interesting that your designers modified your pore structure.'

She fights the urge to recoil from his interest. She steels herself. Leans closer. 'It is to make my skin more attractive. Smooth.' She draws her *pha sin* above her knees, lets it slide up her thighs. 'Would you like to touch?'

He glances at her, questioning.

'Please.' She nods permission.

He reaches out and his hand slips along her flesh. 'Lovely,' he murmurs. She feels a flush of satisfaction as his voice catches. His eyes have gone wide, like a child unmoored. He clears his throat.

'Your skin is burning,' he says.

'*Hai*. As you say, I was not designed for this climate.'

Now he's examining every bit of her. Eyes roaming across her, starving, as if he will feed upon her with his gaze. Raleigh will be pleased. 'It makes sense,' he says. 'Your model must only sell to elites . . . they'd have climate control.' He nods to himself, studying her. 'It would be worth the trade-off, to them.'

He looks up at her. 'Mishimoto? Were you one of Mishimoto's then? You can't be diplomatic. The government would never bring a windup into the country, not with the palace's religious stance—' His eyes lock with hers. 'You were dumped by Mishimoto, weren't you?'

Emiko fights the sudden flood of shame. It's as though he has sliced her open and gone rooting through her entrails, impersonal and insulting, like some cibiscosis medical technician making an autopsy. She sets her drink down carefully. 'Are you a generipper?' she asks. 'Is this how you know so much about me?'

His expression shifts in an instant, from wide-eyed fascination to smirking slyness. 'More like a hobbyist,' he says. 'A genespotter, if you will.'

'Really?' She lets him see some of the contempt she feels for him. 'Not, maybe, a man from the Midwest Compact, perhaps? Not a company man?' She leans forward. 'Not a *calorie man*, possibly?'

She whispers the last words, but they have their effect. The man jerks back. His smile remains, frozen, but his eyes now evaluate her the way a mongoose evaluates a cobra. 'What an interesting thought,' he says.

She welcomes the guarded gaze after her own feelings of shame.

If she's lucky, perhaps this *gaijin* will slaughter her and be done with it. At least then she can rest.

She waits, expecting him to strike her. No one tolerates impudence from New People. Mizumi-sensei made sure that Emiko never showed a trace of rebellion. She taught Emiko to obey, to kowtow, to bend before the desires of her superiors, and to be proud of her place. Even though Emiko is ashamed by the *gaijin's* prying into her history and by her own loss of control, Mizumi-sensei would say this is no excuse to prod and bait the man. It hardly matters. It is done, and Emiko feels dead enough in her soul that she will happily pay whatever price he chooses to extract.

Instead, the man says, 'Tell me again about the night with the boy.' The anger has left his eyes, replaced by an expression as implacable as Gendo-sama's once was. 'Tell me everything,' he says. '*Now.*' His voice whips her with command.

She wills herself to resist, but the in-built urge of a New Person to obey is too strong, the feeling of shame at her rebellion too overwhelming. *He is not your patron*, she reminds herself, but even so at the command in his voice she's nearly pissing herself with her need to please him.

'He came last week...' She returns again to the details of her night with the white shirt. She spins out the story, telling it for this *gaijin's* pleasure much as she once played *samisen* for Gendo-sama, a dog desperate to serve. She wishes she could tell him to eat blister rust and die, but that is not her nature and so instead she speaks and the *gaijin* listens.

He makes her repeat things, asks more questions. Returns to threads she thought he had forgotten. He is relentless, pecking at her story, forcing explanations. He is very good with his questions. Gendo-sama used to question underlings this way, when he wanted to know why a clipper ship was not completed on schedule. He bored through the excuses like a genehack weevil.

Finally the *gaijin* nods, satisfied. 'Good,' he says. 'Very good.'

Emiko feels a wash of pleasure at his compliment, and despises herself for it. The *gaijin* finishes his whiskey. Reaches into his pocket and pulls out a wad of cash, peels off several bills as he stands.

'These are for you, only. Don't show them to Raleigh. I'll settle with him before I leave.'

She supposes she should feel grateful, but she instead feels used. As used by this man with his questions and his words as those others, the hypocritical Grahamites and the Environment Ministry's white shirts, who wish to transgress with her biological oddity, who all slaver for the pleasure of intercourse with an unclean creature.

She holds the bills between her fingers. Her training tells her to be polite, but his self-satisfied largesse irritates her.

'What does the gentleman think I will do with his extra baht?' she asks. 'Buy a pretty piece of jewelry? Take myself out to dinner? I am property, yes? I am Raleigh's.' She tosses the money at his feet. 'It makes no difference if I am rich or poor. I am owned.'

The man pauses, one hand on the sliding door. 'Why not run away, then?'

'To where? My import permits have expired.' She smiles bitterly. 'Without Raleigh-san's patronage and connections, the white shirts would mulch me.'

'You wouldn't run for the North?' the man asks. 'For the windups there?'

'What windups?'

The man smiles slightly. 'Raleigh hasn't mentioned them to you? Windup enclaves in the high mountains? Escapees from the coal war? Released ones?'

At her blank expression he goes on. 'There are whole villages up there, living off the jungles. It's poor country, genehacked half to death, out beyond Chiang Rai and across the Mekong, but the windups there don't have any patrons and they don't have any owners. The coal war's still running, but if you hate your niche so much, it's an alternative to Raleigh.'

'Is it true?' She leans forward. 'This village, is it real?'

The man smiles slightly. 'You can ask Raleigh, if you don't believe me. He's seen them with his own eyes.' He pauses. 'But then, I suppose he wouldn't see much benefit in telling you. Might encourage you to slip your leash.'

'You're telling the truth?'

The pale strange man tips his hat. 'At least as much truth as you've told me.' He slides the door aside and slips out, leaving Emiko alone with a pounding heart and a sudden urge to live.

4

'500, 1000, 5000, 7500 . . .'

Protecting the Kingdom from all the infections of the natural world is like trying to catch the ocean with a net. One can snare a certain number of fish, sure, but the ocean is always there, surging through.

'10,000, 12,500, 15,000 . . . 25,000 . . .'

Captain Jaidee Rojjanasukchai is more than aware of this as he stands under the vast belly of a *farang* dirigible in the middle of the sweltering night. The dirigible's turbofans gust and whir overhead. Its payload lies scattered, crates and boxes splintered open, their contents spilled across the anchor pad as though a child has reck-lessly strewn his toys. Sundry valuables and interdicted items lie everywhere.

'30,000, 35,000 . . . 50,000 . . .'

Around him, Bangkok's newly renovated airfield spreads in all directions, lit by high-intensity methane lamps mounted on mirror towers: a vast green-bathed expanse of anchor pads dotted with the massive balloons of the *farang* floating high overhead, and, at its edges, the thickly grown walls of HiGro Bamboo and spun barbed wire that are supposed to define the international boundaries of the field.

'60,000, 70,000, 80,000 ...'

The Thai Kingdom is being swallowed. Jaidee idly surveys the wreckage his men have wrought, and it seems obvious. They are being swallowed by the ocean. Nearly every crate holds something of suspicion. But really, the crates are symbolic. The problem is ubiquitous: gray-market chemical baths are sold in Chatachuk Market and men pole their skiffs up the Chao Phraya in the dead of night with hulls full of next-gen pineapples. Pollen wafts down the peninsula in steady surges, bearing AgriGen and PurCal's latest genetic rewrites, while cheshires molt through the garbage of the *sois* and jingjok2 lizards vandalize the eggs of nightjars and peafowl. Ivory beetles bore through the forests of Khao Yai even as cibiscosis sugars, blister rust, and *fa' gan* fringe bore through the vegetables and huddled humanity of Krung Thep.

It is the ocean they all swim in. The very medium of life.

'90 ... 100,000 ... 110 ... 125 ...'

Great minds like Premwadee Srisati and Apichat Kunikorn may argue over best practices for protection or debate the merits of UV sterilization barriers along the Kingdom's borders versus the wisdom of pre-emptive genehack mutation, but in Jaidee's view they are idealists. The ocean always flows through.

'126 ... 127 ... 128 ... 129 ...'

Jaidee leans over Lieutenant Kanya Chirathivat's shoulder and watches as she counts bribe money. A pair of Customs inspectors stand stiffly aside, waiting for their authority to be returned to them.

'130 ... 140 ... 150 ...' Kanya's voice is a steady chant. A paean to wealth, to greasing the skids, to new business in an ancient country. Her voice is clear and meticulous. With her, the count will always be correct.

Jaidee smiles. Nothing wrong with a little gift of good will.

At the next anchor pad, 200 meters away, megodonts scream as they drag cargo out of a dirigible's belly and pile the shipment for sorting and Customs approval. Turbofans gust and surge, stabilizing the vast airship anchored overhead. The balloon lists and spins. Gritty winds and megodont dung scour across Jaidee's arrayed white shirts. Kanya places a hand over the baht she is counting. The rest of Jaidee's men wait, impassive, their hands on machetes as the winds whip against them.

The turbofan gusts subside. Kanya continues her chant. '160 ... 170 ... 180 ...'

The Customs men are sweating. Even in the hot season, there's no reason to sweat so. Jaidee isn't sweating. But then, he's not the one who has been forced to pay twice for protection that was probably expensive the first time.

Jaidee almost pities them. The poor men don't know what lines of authority may have changed: if payments have been rerouted; if Jaidee represents a new power, or a rival one; don't know where he ranks in the layers of bureaucracy and influence that run through the Environment Ministry. And so they pay. He's surprised that they managed to find the cash at all, on such short notice. Almost as surprised as they must have been when his white shirts smashed the doors of the Customs Office and secured the field.

'Two hundred thousand.' Kanya looks up at him. 'It's all here.'

Jaidee grins. 'I told you they'd pay.'

Kanya doesn't return the smile, but Jaidee doesn't let it damp his glee. It's a good hot night and they've made a lot of money and as a bonus they've watched the Customs Service sweat. Kanya always has difficulty accepting good fortune when it comes her way. Somewhere during her young life she lost track of how to take pleasure. Starvation in the North-east. The loss of her parents and siblings. Hard travels to Krung Thep. Somewhere she lost her capacity for joy. She has no appreciation for *sanuk*, for fun, even such intense fun, such *sanuk mak* as successfully shaking down the

Trade Ministry or the celebration of Songkran. And so when Kanya takes 200,000 baht from the Trade Ministry and doesn't bat an eye except to wipe away the scouring dust of the anchor pads, and certainly doesn't smile, Jaidee doesn't let it hurt his feelings. Kanya has no taste for fun, that is her *kamma*.

Still, Jaidee pities her. Even the poorest people smile sometimes. Kanya, almost never. It's quite unnatural. She doesn't smile when she is embarrassed, when she is irritated, when she is angry or when she has joy. It makes others uncomfortable, her complete lack of social grace, and it is why she landed at last in Jaidee's unit. No one else can stand her. The two of them make a strange pair. Jaidee who always finds something to smile at, and Kanya, whose face is so cold it might as well be carved from jade. Jaidee grins again, sending goodwill to his lieutenant. 'Let's pack it up, then.'

'You've overstepped your authority,' one of the Customs men mutters.

Jaidee shrugs complacently. 'The Environment Ministry's jurisdiction extends to every place where the Thai Kingdom is threatened. It is the will of Her Royal Majesty the Queen.'

The man's eyes are cold, even though he forces himself to smile pleasantly. 'You know what I mean.'

Jaidee grins, shrugging off the other's ill will. 'Don't look so forlorn. I could have taken twice this much, and you still would have paid.'

Kanya begins packaging up the money as Jaidee sifts through the wreckage of a crate with the tip of his machete. 'Look at all this important cargo that must be protected!' He flips over a bundle of kimonos. Probably shipped to a Japanese manager's wife. He stirs through lingerie worth more than his month's salary. 'We wouldn't want some grubby official rifling through all of this, would we?' He grins and glances at Kanya. 'Do you want any of this? It's made of real silk. The Japanese still have silk worms, you know.'

Kanya doesn't look up from her work with the money. 'It's not my size. Those Japanese manager wives are all fat on genehack calories from their deals with AgriGen.'

'You would steal, too?' The Customs official's face is a mask of controlled rage behind a polite, gritted smile.

'Apparently not.' Jaidee shrugs. 'My lieutenant seems to have better taste than the Japanese. Anyway, your profits will return, I'm sure. This will be but a minor inconvenience.'

'And what about the damage? How will that be explained?' The other Customs man waves at a folding screen in the Sony style that lies half-torn.

Jaidee studies the artifact. It shows what he supposes must be the equivalent of a samurai family for the late twenty-second century: A Mishimoto Fluid Dynamics manager overseeing some kind of windup workers in a field and . . . Are those *ten* hands on each worker that he sees? Jaidee shudders at the bizarre blasphemy. The small natural family pictured at the edge of the field doesn't seem perturbed, but then, they are Japanese: they even let their children be entertained by a windup monkey.

Jaidee makes a face. 'I'm sure you'll find some excuse. Perhaps the freight megodonts stampeded.' He claps the Customs men on their backs. 'Don't look so glum! Use your imagination! You should think of this as building merit.'

Kanya finishes packing up the money. She secures the woven satchel and slings it over her shoulder.

'We're done,' she says.

Downfield, a new dirigible is slowly descending, its massive kink-spring fans using up the last of their joules to maneuver the beast over its anchors. Cables snake down from its belly, dragged by lead weights. Anchor pad workers wait with upraised hands to secure the floating monster to their megodont teams, as though praying to some massive god. Jaidee watches with interest. 'In any case, the Benevolent Association of Retired Royal Environment Ministry Officers appreciates this. You've built merit with them, regardless.' He hefts his machete and turns to his men.

'*Khun* officers!' He shouts over the drone of the dirigible fans and the scream of freight megodonts. 'I have a challenge for you!' He points to the descending dirigible with his machete. 'I have two hundred thousand baht for the first man who searches a crate from that new vessel over there! Come on! That one! Now!'

The Customs men stare, dumbstruck. They start to speak, but their voices are drowned out by the roar of dirigible fans. They mouth protestations: '*Mai tum! Mai tum! Mai tawng tum!* No no nonono!' as they wave their arms and object, but Jaidee is already dashing across the airfield, brandishing his machete and howling after this new prey.

Behind him, his white shirts follow in a wave. They dodge crates and laborers, leap over anchor cables, duck under megodont bellies. His men. His loyal children. His sons. The foolish followers of ideals and the Queen, joining his call, the ones who cannot be bribed, the ones who hold all of the honor of the Environment Ministry in their hearts.

'That one! That one!'

They speed like pale tigers across the landing field, leaving the carcasses of Japanese freight containers littered behind them like so much debris after a typhoon. The Customs men's voices fade. Jaidee is already far distant from them, feeling the joy of his legs pumping under him, the pleasure of clean and honorable pursuit, running faster ever faster, his men following, covering the distance with the adrenaline sprint of pure warrior purpose, raising their machetes and axes to the giant machine as it comes down from the sky, looming over them like the demon king Tosacan ten thousand feet tall, settling over them. The megodont of all megodonts, and on its side, in *farang* lettering, the words: CARLYLE & SONS.

Jaidee is unaware that a shriek of joy has escaped his lips. Carlyle & Sons. The irritating *farang* who speaks so casually about changing pollution credit systems, of removing quarantine inspections, of streamlining everything that has kept the Kingdom alive as other countries have collapsed, the foreigner who curries so much favor with Trade Minister Akkarat and the Somdet Chaopraya, the Crown Protector. This is a true prize. Jaidee is all pursuit. He stretches for the landing cables as his men surge past, younger and faster and fanatically dedicated, all of them reaching out to secure their quarry.

But this dirigible is smarter than the last.

At the sight of the white shirts swarming under its landing position, the pilot reorients his turbofans. The wash gushes over Jaidee. The fans scream and rev as the pilot wastes gigajoules in an attempt to push away from the ground. The dirigible's landing cables whip inward, winding on spindle cranks like an octopus yanking in its limbs. The turbofans shove Jaidee to the ground as they spin to full power.

The dirigible rises.

Jaidee pushes himself up, squinting into the hot winds as the dirigible shrinks into night blackness. He wonders if the disappearing monster was warned by the control towers or the Customs Service or if the pilot was simply clever enough to realize that a white shirt inspection was of no benefit to his masters.

Jaidee grimaces. Richard Carlyle. Too clever by half, that one. Always in meetings with Akkarat, always at public benefits for cibiscosis victims, tossing money about, always talking about the positives of free trade. He is just one of dozens of *farang* who have returned to the shores like jellyfish after a bitter water epidemic, but Carlyle is the loudest. The one whose smiling face annoys Jaidee most.

Jaidee pushes himself fully upright and brushes off the white hemp weave of his uniform. It doesn't matter; the dirigible will return. Like the ocean rushing onto the beach, it is impossible to keep the *farang* away. Land and sea must intersect. These men with profits in their beating hearts have no choice, they must rush in no matter the consequence, and he must always meet them.

Kamma.

Jaidee slowly returns to the cracked contents of the inspected shipping crates, wiping his face of sweat, breathing from the exertion of his run. He waves at his men to continue their labor. 'There! Break those open over there! I don't want a single crate uninspected.'

The Customs men are waiting for him. He pokes through a new crate's wreckage with the point of his machete as the two men approach. They're like dogs. Impossible to be rid of unless you feed them. One of them tries to prevent Jaidee from swinging his machete into another crate.

'We paid! We will be filing protests. There will be investigations. This is international soil!'

Jaidee makes a face. 'Why are you still here?'

'We paid you a fair price for protection!'

'More than fair.' Jaidee shoulders past the men. 'But I am not here to debate these things. It is your *damma* to protest. It is mine to protect our borders, and if that means I must invade your 'international soil' to save our country, so be it.' He swings his machete and another crate crackles open. WeatherAll wood bursts wide.

'You've overstepped yourself!'

'Probably. But you will have to send someone from the Ministry of Trade to tell me himself. Someone more much powerful than you.' He spins his machete thoughtfully. 'Unless you wish to debate me now, with my men?'

The two flinch. Jaidee thinks he catches a flicker of a smile on Kanya's lips. He glances over, surprised, but already his lieutenant is again the face of blank professionalism. It is pleasant to see her smile. Jaidee briefly wonders if there is something more he can do to encourage a second flash of teeth from his dour subordinate.

Sadly, the Customs men seem to be reconsidering their position; they are backing away from his machete.

'Do not think that you can insult us in this way, without consequence.'

'Of course not.' Jaidee chops at the shipping crate again, shattering it fully. 'But I appreciate your monetary donation, even so.' He looks up at them. 'When you complain, make sure you tell them it was me, Jaidee Rojjanasukchai who did this work.' He grins again. 'And make sure you tell them that you actually tried to bribe the Tiger of Bangkok.'

Around him, his men all laugh at the joke. The Customs men step back, surprised at this new revelation, the dawning comprehension of their opponent.

Jaidee surveys the destruction around him. Splinters of the balsa crate material lie everywhere. The crates are engineered for strength and weightlessness and their lattice works well enough to hold goods – as long as no one applies a machete.

The work goes quickly. Materials are pulled from crates and laid out in careful rows. The Customs men hover, taking the names of his white shirts until his men finally raise their machetes and give chase. The officers retreat, then stop and observe from a safer distance. The scene reminds Jaidee of animals fighting over a carcass. His men feeding on the offal of foreign lands while the scavengers probe and test, the ravens and cheshires and dogs all waiting their own chance to converge on the carrion. The thought depresses him a little.

The Customs men hang back, watching.

Jaidee inspects the line of sorted contents. Kanya follows close behind. Jaidee asks, 'What do we have, Lieutenant?'

'Agar solutions. Nutrient cultures. Some kind of breeding tanks.

PurCal cinnamon. A papaya seedstock we don't recognize. A new iteration of U-Tex that probably sterilizes any rice varietal it meets.' She shrugs. 'About what we expected.'

Jaidee flips open a shipping container's lid and peers inside. Checks the address. A company in the *farang* manufacturing district. He tries sounding out the foreign letters, then gives up. He tries to remember if he's seen the logo before, but doesn't think so. He fingers through the materials inside, sacks of some sort of protein powder. 'Nothing of wonderful interest, then. No new version of blister rust leaping out of a box from AgriGen or PurCal.'

'No.'

'It's a pity we couldn't catch that last dirigible. They ran quite quickly. I would have liked to search the cargo of *Khun* Carlyle.'

Kanya shrugs. 'They will return.'

'They always do.'

'Like dogs to a carcass,' she says.

Jaidee follows Kanya's gaze to the Customs men, watching from their safe distance. He is saddened that they see the world so similarly. Does he influence Kanya? Or does she influence him? He used to have much more fun at this work. But then, work used to be so much more clear-cut. He's not accustomed to stalking the gray landscapes that Kanya walks. But at least he has more fun.

His reverie is broken by the arrival of one of his men. Somchai, sauntering over, his machete swinging casually. He's a fast one, as old as Jaidee but hard-edged from losses when blister rust swept the North for the third time in a single growing season. A good man, and loyal. And clever.

'There's a man watching us,' Somchai mumbles as he draws close to the two of them.

'Where?'

Somchai jerks his head subtly. Jaidee lets his eyes roam the bustle of the landing fields. Beside him, Kanya stiffens.

Somchai nods. 'You see him, then?'

'*Kha.*' She nods affirmative.

Jaidee finally catches sight of the man, standing a good distance away, watching both the white shirts and the Customs men. He has on a simple orange sarong and purple linen shirt, as if he might be a laborer, and yet he carries nothing. He does nothing. And he seems well-fed. Not showing ribs and hollow cheeks the way most laborers do. He watches, casually leaning against an anchor hook. 'Trade?' Jaidee asks.

'Army?' Kanya guesses. 'He's a confident one.'

As though he senses Jaidee's eyes, the man turns. His eyes lock with Jaidee for moment.

'Shit.' Somchai frowns. 'He's seen us.' He and Kanya join Jaidee in an open study of the man. The man is unperturbed. He spits a stream of red betel and turns and saunters away, disappearing into the bustle of freight movements.

Somchai asks, 'Should I go after him? Question him?'

Jaidee cranes his neck, trying to catch another glimpse of the man where he has been swallowed by the bustle. 'What do you think, Kanya?'

She hesitates. 'Haven't we prodded enough cobras for one night?'

Jaidee smiles slightly. 'The voice of wisdom and restraint speaks.'

Somchai nods agreement. 'Trade will be furious as it is.'

'One hopes so.' Jaidee motions to Somchai to return to his inspections. As they watch him go, Kanya says, 'We may have overstepped this time.'

'You mean *I* may have overstepped.' Jaidee grins. 'You're losing your nerve?'

'Not my nerve.' Her gaze travels back to where their observer disappeared. 'There are bigger fish than us, *Khun* Jaidee. The anchor pads ...' Kanya trails off. Finally, after visibly working to choose her words, she says, 'It's an aggressive move.'

'You're sure you're not afraid?' he teases her.

'No!' She stops short, swallows her outburst, masters her composure.

Privately, Jaidee admires her ability to speak with a cool heart. He was never so careful with his words, or his actions. He was always the sort to charge in like a megodont and try to right the trampled rice shoots after. *Jai rawn*, rather than *jai yen*. A hot heart, rather than a cool one. Kanya, though ...

Finally she says, 'This may not have been the best place to strike.'

'Don't be a pessimist. The anchor pads are the best of all possible places. Those two weevils over there coughed up 200,000 baht, no trouble at all. Too much money to be involved in anything honest.' Jaidee grins. 'I should have come here a long time ago and taught these *heeya* a lesson. Better than wandering the river with a kink-spring skiff, arresting children for generip smuggling. At least this is honest work.'

'But it will get Trade involved for certain. By law, it's their turf.'

'By any sane law, none of this should be imported at all.' Jaidee waves a hand, dismissive. 'Laws are confusing documents. They get in the way of justice.'

'Justice is always lost where Trade is concerned.'

'We're both more than aware of that. In any case, it's my head. You won't be touched a bit. You couldn't have stopped me, even if you had known where we were going tonight.'

'I wouldn't—' Kanya starts.

'Don't worry about it. It's time that Trade and its pet *farang* felt a sting here. They were complacent, and needed a reminder that they still must perform the occasional *khrab* to the idea of our laws.' Jaidee pauses, surveying the wreckage again. 'There's truly nothing else on the black lists?'

Kanya shrugs. 'Just the rice. Everything else is innocuous enough, on paper. No breeding specimens. No genetics in suspension.'

'But?'

'Much of it will be misused. Nutrient cultures can't have any good purpose.' Kanya is back to her blank and depressed expression. 'Should we pack it all back up?'

Jaidee grimaces, finally shakes his head. 'No. Burn it.'

'I'm sorry?'

'Burn it. We both know what is happening here. Give the *farang* something to claim against their insurance companies. Let them know that their activity is not free.' Jaidee grins. 'Burn it all. Every last crate.'

And for the second time that night, as shipping crates crackle with fire and WeatherAll oils rush and ignite and kick sparks into the air like prayers going up to heaven, Jaidee has the satisfaction of seeing Kanya smile again.

It is nearly morning by the time Jaidee returns home. The *ji ji ji* of jingjok lizards punctuates the creak of cicadas and the high whine of mosquitoes. He slips off his shoes and climbs the steps, teak creaking under his feet as he steals into his stilt-house, feeling the smooth wood under his soles, soft and polished against his skin.

He opens the screened door and slips inside, closing the door quickly behind him. They're close to the *khlong*, only meters away, and the water is brackish and thick. The mosquitoes swarm close.

Inside, a single candle burns, illuminating Chaya where she lies on a floor couch, asleep, waiting. He smiles tenderly and slips into the bathroom to quickly disrobe and pour water over his shoulders. He tries to be quick and quiet about his bath, but water spatters flatly on the wood. He dips water again and spills it over his back. Even in the dead of night the air is warm enough that he doesn't mind the water's slight chill. In the hot season, everything is a relief.

When he comes out of his bath with a sarong wrapped around his waist, Chaya is awake, looking up at him with thoughtful brown eyes. 'You're very late,' she says. 'I was worried.'

Jaidee grins. 'You should know better than to worry. I'm a tiger.' He nuzzles close to her. Kisses her gently.

Chaya grimaces and pushes him away. 'Don't believe everything the newspapers say. A tiger.' She makes a face. 'You smell like smoke.'

'I just bathed.'

'It's in your hair.'

He rocks back on his heels. 'It was a very good night.'

She smiles in the darkness, her white teeth flashing, mahogany skin a dull sheen in the black. 'Did you strike a blow for our Queen?'

'I struck a blow against Trade.'

She flinches. 'Ah.'

He touches her arm. 'You used to be happy when I made important people angry.'

She pushes away from him and stands, starts straightening the cushions. Her movements are abrupt, irritated. 'That was before. Now I worry about you.'

'You shouldn't.' Jaidee moves out of her way as she finishes with the couch. 'I'm surprised you bother to wait up. If I were you, I would go to sleep and dream beautiful dreams. Everyone has given up on controlling me. I'm just a line-item expense for them, now. I'm too popular with the people to do anything about. They put spies on me to watch me, but they do nothing to stop me anymore.'

'A hero to the people, and a thorn for the Ministry of Trade. I would rather have Trade Minister Akkarat as a friend and the people as your enemy. We'd all be safer.'

'You didn't think so when you married me. You liked that I was a fighter. That I had so many victories in Lumphini Stadium. You remember?'

She doesn't answer. Instead begins rearranging the cushions again, refusing to turn around. Jaidee sighs and puts a hand on her shoulder, pulls her up to face him, so that he can see her eyes. 'Anyway, why is it that you bring this up, now? Am I not here? And perfectly fine?'

'When they shot you, you weren't so fine.'

'That's in the past.'

'Only because they put you behind a desk, and General Pracha paid reparations.' She holds up her hand, showing her own missing fingers. 'Don't tell me you're safe. I was there. I know what they can do.'

Jaidee makes a face. 'We aren't safe in any case. If it's not Trade, it's blister rust or cibiscosis or something else, something worse. We aren't living in a perfect world anymore. This isn't the Expansion.'

She opens her mouth to respond, then closes it and turns away. Jaidee waits, letting her master herself. When she turns back, her emotions are under control again. 'No. You're right. None of us are safe. I wish, though.'

'You might as well run to Ta Prachan market and get an amulet, for all the good wishing does.'

'I did. The one with Phra Seub. But you don't wear it.'

'Because it's just superstition. Whatever happens to me is my *kamma*. A magic amulet isn't going to change that.'

'Still, it doesn't hurt.' She pauses. 'I would feel better if you wore it.'

Jaidee smiles and starts to make a joke of it, but something in her expression makes him change his mind. 'Fine. If it makes you happy. I'll wear your Phra Seub.'

From the sleeping rooms, a noise echoes, a wet coughing. Jaidee stiffens. Chaya shifts and looks over her shoulder to the noise. 'It's Surat.'

'Did you take him to Ratana?'

'It's not her job to examine sick children. She has real work to do. Real genehacks to worry over.'

'Did you take him or not?'

Chaya sighs. 'She said it's not an upgrade. Nothing to worry about.'

Jaidee tries not to let his relief show. 'Good.' The coughing comes again. It reminds him of Num, dead and gone. He fights off sadness.

Chaya touches his chin, pulls his attention back to her. Smiles up at him. 'So what is it that left you smelling of smoke, noble warrior, defender of Krung Thep? Why so pleased with yourself?'

Jaidee smiles slightly. 'You can read it in the whisper sheets tomorrow.'

She purses her lips. 'I'm worried about you. Really.'

'That's because you have a good heart. But you shouldn't worry. They're done with heavy-handed measures against me. It went badly the last time. The papers and whisper sheets liked the story too much. And our most revered Queen has registered her own support for what I do. They'll keep their distance. Her Majesty the Queen, at least, they still respect.'

'You were lucky that she was allowed to hear of you at all.'

'Even that *heeya* the Crown Protector can't blind her.'

Chaya stiffens at his words. 'Jaidee, please. Not so loud. The Somdet Chaopraya has too many ears.'

Jaidee makes a face. 'You see? This is what we've come to. A Crown Protector who spends his time meditating on how to take the inner apartments of the Grand Palace. A Trade Minister who conspires with *farang* to destroy our trade and quarantine laws. And meanwhile, we all try not to speak too loudly.'

'I'm glad I went to the anchor pads tonight. You should have seen how much money those Customs officers were raking in, just standing aside and letting anything at all pass through. The next mutation of cibiscosis could have been sitting in vials right in front of them, and they would have held out a hand for a bribe. Sometimes, I think we're living the last days of old Ayutthaya all over again.'

'Don't be melodramatic.'

'History repeats itself. No one fought to protect Ayutthaya, either.'

'And so what does that make you? Some villager of Bang Rajan, reincarnated? Holding back the *farang* tide? Fighting to the last man? That sort of thing?'

'At least they fought! Which would you rather be? The farmers who held off the Burmese army for a month, or the ministers of the Kingdom who ran away and let their capital be sacked?' He grimaces. 'If I were smart, I'd go to the anchor pads every night and teach Akkarat and the *farang* a real lesson. Show them that someone's still willing to fight for Krung Thep.'

He expects Chaya to try to shut him up again, to cool his hot-hearted talk, but instead, she is silent. Finally she asks, 'Do you think our lives are always reborn here, in this place? Do we have to come back and face all of this again, no matter what?'

'I don't know,' Jaidee says. 'That's the sort of question Kanya would ask.'

'She's a dour one. I should get her an amulet, too. Something that would make her smile for once.'

'She is a bit strange.'

'I thought Ratana was going to propose to her.'

Jaidee pauses, considering Kanya and pretty Ratana, with her breathing mask and her underground life in the Ministry's biological containment labs. 'I don't pry into her private life.'

'She'd smile more if she had a man.'

'If someone as good as Ratana couldn't make her happy, then no man has a hope.' Jaidee grins. 'Anyway, if she had a man, he'd spend all his time being jealous of the men she commands in my unit. All the handsome men . . .' He leans forward and tries to kiss Chaya but she pulls away too quickly.

'Ugh. You smell like whiskey, too.'

'Whiskey and smoke. I smell like a real man.'

'Go off to bed. You'll wake up Niwat and Surat. And mother.'

Jaidee pulls her close, puts his lips to her ear. 'She wouldn't mind another grandchild.'

Chaya pushes him away, laughing. 'She will if you wake her up.'

His hands slip along her hips. 'I'll be very quiet.'

She slaps his hands away, but doesn't try very hard. He catches her hand. Feels the stumps of her missing fingers, caresses their ridges. Suddenly they're both solemn again. She takes a ragged breath. 'We've all lost too many things. I can't bear to lose you, too.'

'You won't. I'm a tiger. And I'm no fool.'

She holds him close. 'I hope so. I truly do.' Her warm body presses against him. He can feel her breathing, steady, full of concern for him. She draws back and looks at him solemnly, her eyes dark and full of care.

'I'll be fine,' he says again.

She nods but doesn't seem to be listening. Instead she seems to be studying him, following the lines of his brow, of his smiles, of his scars and pocks. The moment seems to stretch forever, her dark eyes on him, memorizing, solemn. At last she nods, as though listening to something she tells herself, and her worried expression lifts. She smiles and pulls him close, pressing her lips to his ear. 'You are a tiger,' she whispers, as if she is a fortune teller pronouncing, and her body relaxes into him, pressing to him fully. He feels a rush of relief as they come together, finally.

He clasps her to him more tightly. 'I've missed you,' he whispers.

'Come with me.' She slips free and takes him by the hand. Leads him toward their bed. She pulls aside the mosquito netting and slips under its tenting gossamer. Clothing rustles, falling away. A shadow woman teases him from within.

'You still smell like smoke,' she says.

Jaidee pulls aside the nets. 'And whiskey. Don't forget the whiskey.'

5

The sun peers over the rim of the earth, casting its blaze across Bangkok. It rushes molten over the wrecked tower bones of the old Expansion and the gold-sheathed *chedi* of the city's temples, engulfing them in light and heat. It ignites the sharp high roofs of the Grand Palace where the Child Queen lives cloistered with her attendants, and flames from the filigreed ornamentation of the City Pillar Shrine where monks chant 24-7 on behalf of the city's seawalls and dikes. The blood warm ocean flickers with blue mirror waves as the sun moves on, burning.

The sun hits Anderson Lake's sixth-floor balcony and pours into his flat. Jasmine vines at the edge of the veranda rustle in the hot breeze. Anderson looks up, blue eyes slitted against the glare. Sweat jewels pop and gleam on his pale skin. Beyond the rail, the city appears as a molten sea, glinting gold where spires and glass catch the full blaze of the sun.

He's naked in the heat, seated on the floor, surrounded by open books: flora and fauna catalogs, travel notes, an entire history of the South-east Asian peninsula scattered across teak. Moldy, crumbling tomes. Scraps of paper. Half-torn diaries. The excavated memories of a time when tens of thousands of plants lofted pollen and spores and seeds into the air. He has spent all night at work, and yet he barely remembers the many varietals he has examined.

Instead, his mind returns to flesh exposed – a *pha sin* sliding up a girl's legs, the memory of peacocks on a shimmering purple weave riding high, smooth thighs damply parted.

In the far distance, the towers of Ploenchit stand tall, backlit. Three shadow fingers spiking skyward in a yellow haze of humidity. In the daylight they just look like more Expansion-era slums, without a hint of the pulsing addictions contained within.

A windup girl.

His fingers on her skin. Her dark eyes solemn as she said, 'You may touch.'

Anderson takes a shuddering breath, forcing away the memories. She is the opposite of the invasive plagues he fights every day. A hothouse flower, dropped into a world too harsh for her delicate heritage. It seems unlikely that she will survive for long. Not in this climate. Not with these people. Perhaps it was that vulnerability that moved him, her pretended strength when she had nothing at all. Seeing her fight for a semblance of pride even as she hiked up her skirt at Raleigh's order.

Is that why you told her about the villages? Because you pitied her? Not because her skin felt as smooth as mango? Not because you could hardly breathe when you touched her?

He grimaces and turns his attention again to his open books, forcing himself to attend to his true problem, the question that has brought him across the world on clipper ship and dirigible: Gi Bu Sen. The windup girl said Gi Bu Sen.

Anderson shuffles through his books and papers, comes up with a photograph. A fat man, sitting with other Midwest scientists at an AgriGen-sponsored conference on blister rust mutation. He is looking away from the camera, bored, the wattles of his neck showing.

Are you still fat? Anderson wonders. *Do the Thais feed you as well as we did?*

There were only three possibilities: Bowman, Gibbons and Chaudhuri. Bowman, who disappeared just before the SoyPRO monopoly broke. Chaudhuri, who walked off a dirigible and disappeared into the Indian Estates, either kidnapped by PurCal or run off, or dead. And Gibbons. Gi Bu Sen. The smartest of them all, and the one deemed least likely. Dead, after all. His seared body recovered from the ashes of his home by his children . . . and then entirely cremated before the company could perform an autopsy. But dead. And when the children were questioned with lie detectors and drugs, all they could say was that their father had always insisted that he not be autopsied. That he couldn't abide anyone cutting into his corpse and pumping it with preservatives. But the DNA matched. It was him. Everyone was sure it was him.

Except that it's easy to doubt when all you have are a few genetic clippings from the supposed corpse of the finest generipper in the world.

Anderson shuffles through more papers, hunting up the transcripts of the calorie man's final days, culled from bugging devices they kept in the labs. Nothing. Not a hint of his plans. And then he was dead. And they were forced to believe that it was true.

In that way, the *ngaw* almost makes sense. The nightshades as well. Gibbons always enjoyed flaunting his expertise. An egotist. Every colleague said so. Gibbons would delight in playing with the full range of a complete seedbank. An entire genus resurrected and then a bit of local lore to top it off. *Ngaw*. At least, Anderson assumes the fruit is local. But who knows? Perhaps it is an entirely new creation. Something sprung complete from Gibbons' mind, like Adam's rib spawning Eve.

Anderson idly thumbs through the books and notes before him. None of them mention the *ngaw*. All he has is the Thai word and its singular appearance. He doesn't even know if '*ngaw*' is the traditional moniker for the red and green fruit, or something newly

named. He had hoped that Raleigh would have his own recollec-
tions, but the man is old, and addled on opium – if he knew an
Angrit word for the historical fruit, it is lost to him now. In any
case, there's no obvious translation. It will be at least a month
before Des Moines can examine the samples. And there's no telling
if it will be in their catalogues even then. If it's sufficiently altered,
there may be no shortcut to a DNA match.

One thing is certain: the *ngaw* is new. A year ago, none of the
inventory agents described anything of the sort in their ecosystem
surveys. Between one year and the next, the *ngaw* appeared. As if
the soil of the Kingdom had simply decided to birth up the past
and deposit it in the markets of Bangkok.

Anderson thumbs through another book, hunting. Since his
arrival, he has been creating a library, a historical window into the
City of Divine Beings, tomes drawn from before the calorie wars
and plagues, before the Contraction. He has pillaged through
everything from antiquities shops to the rubble of Expansion
towers. Most of the paper of that time has already burned or rotted
in the humid tropics, but he has found pockets of learning even so,
families that valued their books more than as a quick way to start
a fire. The accumulated knowledge now lines his walls, volume
after volume of mold-fringed information. It depresses him.
Reminds him of Yates, that desperate urge to excavate the corpse
of the past and reanimate it.

'Think of it!' Yates had crowed. 'A new Expansion! Dirigibles,
next-gen kink-springs, fair trade winds . . .'

Yates had books of his own. Dusty tomes he'd stolen from
libraries and business schools across North America, the neglected
knowledge of the past – a careful pillaging of Alexandria that had
gone entirely unnoticed because everyone knew global trade was
dead.

When Anderson arrived, the books had filled the SpringLife

offices and ranged around Yates' desk in stacks: *Global Management in Practice, Intercultural Business, The Asian Mind, The Little Tigers of Asia, Supply Chains and Logistics, Pop Thai, The New Global Economy, Exchange Rate Considerations in Supply Chains, Thais Mean Business, International Competition and Regulation.* Anything and everything related to the history of the old Expansion.

Yates had pointed to them in his final moments of desperation and said, 'But we can have it again! All of it!' And then he had wept, and Anderson finally felt pity for the man. Yates had invested his life in something that would never be.

Anderson flips through another book, examining ancient photographs in turn. Chiles. Piles of them, laid out before some long dead photographer. Chiles. Eggplants. Tomatoes. All those wonderful nightshades again. If it hadn't been for the nightshades, Anderson wouldn't have been dispatched to the Kingdom by the home office, and Yates might have had a chance.

Anderson reaches for his package of Singha hand-rolled cigarettes, lights one, and sprawls back, contemplative, examining the smoke of ancients. It amuses him that the Thais, even amid starvation, have found the time and energy to resurrect nicotine addiction. He wonders if human nature ever really changes.

The sun glares in at him, bathing him with light. Through the humidity and haze of burning dung, he can just make out the manufacturing district in the distance, with its regularly spaced structures so different from the jumble tile and rust wash of the old city. And beyond the factories, the rim of the seawall looms with its massive lock system that allows the shipment of goods out to sea. Change is coming. The return to truly global trade. Supply lines that circle the world. It's all coming back, even if they're slow at relearning. Yates had loved kink-springs, but he'd loved the idea of resurrected history even more.

'You aren't AgriGen here, you know. You're just another grubby *farang* entrepreneur trying to make a buck along with the jade prospectors and the clipper hands. This isn't India, where you can walk around flashing AgriGen's wheat crest and requisitioning whatever you want. The Thais don't roll over like that. They'll cut you to pieces and send you back as meat if they find out what you are.'

'You're out on the next dirigible flight,' Anderson said. 'Be glad the main office even approved that.'

But then Yates had pulled the spring gun.

Anderson draws again on his cigarette, irritated. He becomes aware of the heat. Overhead, his room's crank fan has come to a halt. The winding man, who is supposed to arrive every day at four in the afternoon, apparently didn't load enough joules. Anderson grimaces and rises to pull the shades, blocking out the blaze. The building is a new one, built on thermal principles that allow cool ground air to circulate easily through the building, but it is still difficult to withstand the direct blaze of equatorial sun.

Now in shadow, Anderson returns to his books. Turns pages. Flips through yellowed tomes and cracked spines. Crumbling paper ill-treated by humidity and age. He opens another book. He pinches his cigarette between his lips, squinting through the smoke, and stops.

Ngaw.

Piles of them. The little red fruits with their strange green hairs sit before him, mocking him from within a photo of a *farang* bargaining for food with some long ago Thai farmer. All around them, brightly colored, petroleum-burning taxis blur past, but just to their side, a huge pyramidal pile of *ngaw* stares out of the photo, taunting.

Anderson has spent enough time poring over ancient pictures that they seldom affect him. He can usually ignore the foolish confidence of the past – the waste, the arrogance, the absurd wealth –

but this one irritates him: the fat flesh hanging off the *farang*, the astonishing abundance of calories that are so obviously secondary to the color and attractiveness of a market that has thirty varieties of fruit: mangosteens, pineapples, coconuts, certainly ... but there are no oranges, now. None of these ... these ... dragon fruits, none of these pomelos, none of these yellow things ... *lemons*. None of them. So many of these things are simply gone.

But the people in the photo don't know it. These dead men and women have no idea that they stand in front of the treasure of the ages, that they inhabit the Eden of the Grahamite Bible where pure souls go to live at the right hand of God. Where all the flavors of the world reside under the careful attentions of Noah and Saint Francis, and where no one starves.

Anderson scans the caption. The fat, self-contented fools have no idea of the genetic gold mine they stand beside. The book doesn't even bother to identify the *ngaw*. It's just another example of nature's fecundity, taken entirely for granted because they enjoyed so damn much of it.

Anderson briefly wishes that he could drag the fat *farang* and ancient Thai farmer out of the photograph and into his present, so that he could express his rage at them directly, before tossing them off his balcony the way they undoubtedly tossed aside fruit that was even the slightest bit bruised.

He flips through the book but finds no other images, nor mentions of the kinds of fruits available. He straightens, agitated, and goes to the balcony again. Steps out into the sun's blaze and stares out across the city. From below, the calls of water sellers and the cry of megodonts echo up. The chime of bicycle bells streaming across the city. By noon, the city will be largely stilled, waiting for the sun to begin its descent.

Somewhere in this city a generipper is busily toying with the building blocks of life. Re-engineering long-extinct DNA to fit post-Contraction circumstances, to survive despite the assaults of blister rust, Nippon genehack weevil and cibiscosis.

Gi Bu Sen. The windup girl was certain of the name. It has to be Gibbons.

Anderson leans on the balcony's rail squinting into the heat, surveying the tangled city. Gibbons is out there, hiding. Crafting his next triumph. And wherever he hides, a seedbank will be close.

6

The problem with keeping money in a bank is that in the blink of a tiger's eye it will turn on you: what's yours becomes theirs, what was your sweat and labor and sold off portions of a lifetime become a stranger's. This problem – this banking problem – gnaws at the forefront of Hock Seng's mind, a genehack weevil that he cannot dig out and cannot pinch into pus and exoskeleton fragments.

Imagined in terms of the time – time spent earning wages that a bank then holds – a bank can own more than half of a man. Well, at least a third, even if you are a lazy Thai. And a man without one third of his life, in truth, has no life at all.

Which third can a man lose? The third from his chest to the top of his balding skull? From his waist to his yellowing toenails? Two legs and an arm? Two arms and a head? A quarter of a man, cut away, might still hope to survive, but a third is too much to tolerate.

This is the problem with a bank. As soon as you place your money in its mouth, it turns out that the tiger has gotten its teeth locked around your head. One third, or one half, or just a liver-spotted skull, it might as well be all.

But if a bank cannot be trusted, what can? A flimsy lock on a door? The ticking of a mattress, carefully unstuffed? The ravaged tiles of a rooftop lifted up and wrapped in banana leaves? A cutaway in the bamboo beams of a slum shack, cleverly sliced open and hollowed to hold the fat rolls of bills that he shoves into them?

Hock Seng digs into bamboo.

The man who rented him the room called it a flat, and in a way, it is. It has four walls, not just a tenting of coconut polymer tarps. It has a tiny courtyard behind, where the outhouse lies and which he shares – along with the walls – with six other huts. For a yellow card refugee, this is not a flat but a mansion. And yet all around he hears the groaning complaining mass of humanity.

The WeatherAll wooden walls are frankly an extravagance even if they don't quite touch the ground, even if the jute sandals of his neighbors peek underneath, and even if they reek with the embedded oils that keep them from rotting in the humidity of the tropics. But they are necessary, if only to provide places to store his money other than in the bottom of his rain barrel wrapped in three layers of dog hide that he prays may still be waterproof after six months of immersion.

Hock Seng pauses in his labors, listening.

Rustling comes from the next room but nothing indicates that anyone eavesdrops on his mouselike burrowing. He returns to the process of loosening a disguised bamboo panel at its joint, carefully saving the sawdust for later.

Nothing is certain – that is the first lesson. The *yang guizi* foreign devils learned this in the Contraction when their loss of oil sent them scuttling back to their home shores. He himself finally learned it in Malacca. Nothing is certain, nothing is secure. A rich man becomes a poor man. A noisy Chinese clan, fat and happy during Spring Festival, fed well on pork strips, *nasi goreng* and Hainan-style chicken becomes a single emaciated yellow card. Nothing is eternal. The Buddhists understand this much, at least.

Hock Seng grins mirthlessly and continues his quiet burrowing, following a line across the top of the panel, digging out more packed sawdust. He now lives in the height of luxury, with his patched mosquito net and his little burner that can ignite green methane twice a day, if he's willing to pay the local *pi lien* elder brother for an illegal tap into the city lamp-post delivery pipes. He has his own set of clay rain urns sitting in the tiny courtyard, an astounding luxury in itself, protected by the honor and uprightness of his neighbors, the desperately poor, who know that there must be limits to anything, that every squalor and debauch has limits, and so he has rain barrels full of green slime mosquito eggs that he can assure himself will never be stolen from, even if he may be murdered outside his door, or the neighbor's wife may be raped by any *nak leng* who takes a fancy to her.

Hock Seng pries at the tiny panel in the bamboo strut, holding his breath, trying to make no scraping sound. He chose this place for its exposed joists and the tiles overhead in the low dark ceiling. For the nooks and crannies and opportunities. All around him the slum inhabitants wake and groan and complain and light their cigarettes as he sweats with the tension of opening this hiding place. It's foolish to keep so much money here. What if the slum burns? What if the WeatherAll catches fire from some fool's candle overturned? What if the mobs come and attempt to trap him inside?

Hock Seng pauses, wipes the sweat off his brow. *I am crazy. No one is coming for me. The Green Headbands are across the border in Malaya and the Kingdom's armies will keep them well away.*

And even if they do come, I have an archipelago's worth of distance to prepare for their arrival. Days of travel on a kink-spring train, even if the rails aren't blown by the Queen's Army generals. Twenty-four hours at least, even if they use coal for their attack. And otherwise? Weeks of marching. Plenty of time. I am safe.

The panel comes open completely in his shaking hand, revealing the bamboo's hollow interior. The tube is watertight, perfected by nature. He sends his skinny arm questing into the hole, feeling blind.

For a moment, he thinks someone has taken it, robbed him while he was gone but then his fingers touch paper, and he fishes up rolls of cash one by one.

In the next room, Sunan and Mali are discussing her uncle, who wants them to smuggle cibi.11.s.8 pineapples, sneaking them in on a skiff from the *farang* quarantine island of Koh Angrit. Quick money, if they're willing to take the risk of bringing in banned foodstock from the calorie monopolies.

Hock Seng listens to them mutter as he stuffs his own cash into an envelope, then tucks it inside his shirt. Diamonds, baht, and jade pit his walls all around, but still, it hurts to take this money now. It goes against his hoarding instinct.

He presses the bamboo panel closed again. Takes spit and mixes it with the meager sawdust that remains, and presses the compound into the visible cracks. He rocks back on his heels and examines the bamboo pole. It is nearly invisible. If he didn't know to count upwards four joints, he wouldn't know where to look, or what to look for.

The problem with banks is that they cannot be trusted. The problem with secret caches is that they are hard to protect. The problem with a room in a slum is that anyone can take the money when he is gone. He needs other caches, safe places to hide the opium and jewels and cash he procures. He needs a safe place for everything. For himself as well, and for that, any amount of money is worth spending.

All things are transient. Buddha says it is so, and Hock Seng, who didn't believe in or care about karma or the truths of the dharma when he was young, has come in his old age to understand his grandmother's religion and its painful truths. Suffering is his lot. Attachment is the source of his suffering. And yet he cannot stop himself from saving and preparing and striving to preserve himself in this life which has turned out so poorly.

How is it that I sinned to earn this bitter fate? Saw my clan whittled by red machetes? Saw my businesses burned and my clipper ships sunk? He closes his eyes, forcing memories away. Regret is suffering.

He takes a deep breath and climbs stiffly to his feet, surveys the room to ascertain that nothing is out of place, then turns and shoves his door open, wood scraping on dirt, and slips out in the squeezeway that is the slum's thoroughfare. He secures the door with a bit of leather twine. A knot, and nothing else. The room has been broken into before. It will be broken into again. He plans on it. A big lock would attract the wrong attention, a poor man's bit of leather entices no one.

The way out of the Yaowarat slum is full of shadows and squatting bodies. The heat of the dry season presses down on him, so intense that it seems no one can breathe, even with the looming presence of the Chao Phraya dikes. There is no escape from the heat. If the seawall gave way, the entire slum would drown in nearly cool water, but until then, Hock Seng sweats and stumbles through the maze of squeezeways, rubbing up against scavenged tin walls.

He jumps across open gutters of shit. Balances on planks and slips past women sweating over steaming pots of U-Tex glass noodles and reeking sun-dried fish. A few kitchen carts, ones who have bribed either the white shirts or the slum's *pi lien*, burn small dung fires in public, choking the alleys with thick smoke and frying chile oil.

He squeezes around triple-locked bicycles, stepping carefully. Clothes and cook pots and garbage spill out from under tarp walls, encroaching on the public space. The walls rustle with the movement of people within: a man coughing through the last stages of lung water; a woman complaining about her son's *lao-lao* rice wine habit; a little girl threatening to hit her baby brother. Privacy is not something for a tarp slum, but the walls provide polite illusion. And certainly it is better than the Expansion tower internments of the yellow cards. A tarp slum is luxury for him. And with native Thais all around, he has cover. Better protection than he ever enjoyed in Malaya. Here, if he doesn't open his mouth and betray his foreigner's accent, he can be mistaken for a local.

Still, he misses that place where he and his family were alien and yet had forged a life. He misses the marble-floored halls and red lacquer pillars of his ancestral home, ringing with the calls of his children and grandchildren and servants. He misses Hainan chicken and *laksa asam* and good sweet *kopi* and *roti canai*.

He misses his clipper fleet and the crews (And isn't it true that he hired even the brown people for his crews? Even had them as captains?) who sailed his Mishimoto clippers to the far side of the world, sailing even as far as Europe, carrying tea strains resistant to genehack weevil and returning with expensive cognacs that had not been seen since the days of the Expansion. And in the evenings, he returned to his wives and ate well and worried only that a son was not diligent or that a daughter would find a good husband.

How silly and ignorant he had been. He fancied himself a sea trader, and yet understood so little of the turning tides.

A young girl emerges from under a tarp flap. She smiles at him, too young to know him for a stranger, and too innocent yet to care. She is alive, burning with the limber vitality that an old man can only envy with every aching bone. She smiles at him.

She could be his daughter.

Malaya's night was black and sticky, a jungle filled with the squawks of night birds and the pulse and whir of insect life. Dark harbor waters lapped before them. He and Fourth Daughter, that useless waif, the only one he could preserve, hid among piers and rocking boats, and when darkness fell completely, he guided her down to the water, to where waves rushed onto the beach in steady surges and the stars overhead were pinpricks of gold in blackness.

'Look, Ba. Gold,' she whispered.

There were times when he'd told her that every star was a bit of gold that was hers for the taking, because she was Chinese and with hard work and attendance to her ancestors and traditions, she would prosper. And now, here they were under a blanket of gold dust, the Milky Way spread over them like some great shifting blanket, the stars so thick that if he were tall enough he could reach up and squeeze them and have them run down his arms.

Gold, all around, and all of it untouchable.

Amid the lapping of fishing boats and little spring craft, he found a rowboat and pulled for deep water, aiming for the bay, following the currents, a black speck on the shifting reflections of the ocean.

He would have preferred a cloudy night, but at least there was no moon, and so he pulled and pulled, while all around them sea carp surfaced and rolled, showing the fat pale bellies that people of his clan had engineered to feed a starving nation. He pulled on the oars and the carp surrounded them, showing bloated stomachs now thickened on the blood and gristle of their creators.

And then his little boat was alongside the object of his search, a trimaran anchored in the deep. The place where Hafiz's boat people slept. He climbed aboard and slipped silent among them. Studying them all as they slept soundly, protected by their religion. Safe and alive while he had nothing.

His arms and shoulders and back ached from the strain of rowing. An old man's aches. A soft man's pains.

He slipped among them, searching, too old for the nonsense survival, and yet unable to give it up. He might still survive. The one daughter mouth might survive. Even if she was a girl child. Even if she would do nothing for her ancestors, at least she was of his clan. A clipping of DNA that still might be saved. Finally he found the body he wanted, leaned down and touched it gently, covered the man's mouth.

'Old friend,' he whispered.

The man's eyes went wide as he awoke. '*Encik* Tan?' He nearly saluted, even half-naked and lying on his back. And then, as if recognizing the change in their fortunes, his hand fell back, and he addressed Hock Seng as he had never dared in real life. 'Hock Seng? You're still alive?'

Hock Seng pursed his lips. 'This useless daughter mouth and I need to go north. I need your help.'

Hafiz sat up, rubbing his eyes. He glanced furtively at the rest of his sleeping clan. He whispered, 'If I turned you in, I would make a fortune. The head of Three Prosperities. I would be rich.'

'You were not poor when you worked with me.'

'Your head is worth more than all the Chinese skulls stacked in the streets of Penang. And I would be safe.'

Hock Seng started to respond angrily but Hafiz put his hand up, indicating silence. He ushered Hock Seng to the edge of the deck, against the rail. He leaned close, his lips nearly touching Hock Seng's ear. 'Do you not know the danger you bring on me? Some of my own family wear green headbands now. My own sons! It is not safe here.'

'You think this is something I just learned now?'

Hafiz had the grace to look away, embarrassed. 'I cannot help you.'

Hock Seng grimaced. 'Is this what my kindness to you has earned? Did I not attend your wedding? Gift you and Rana well?

Fete you for ten days? Did I not pay for Mohammed's admission to college in K.L.?'

'You did that and more. My debts to you are great.' Hafiz bowed his head. 'But we are not the men we were before. The Green Headbands are everywhere among us, and those of us who loved the yellow plague can only suffer. Your head would buy my family security. I'm sorry. It is true. I don't know why I don't strike you now.'

'I have diamonds, jade.'

Hafiz sighed and turned away, showing his broad muscled back. 'If I took your jewels, I would just as quickly be tempted to take your life. If we speak of money, then your head must always be the most valuable prize. Best not to discuss the temptations of wealth.'

'So this is how we end?'

Hafiz turned back to Hock Seng, pleading. 'Tomorrow I will give your clipper ship *Dawn Star* to them and foreswear you utterly. If I were smart I would turn you in as well. All the ones who have aided the yellow plague are suspected now. We who fattened on Chinese industry and thrived under your generosity are the most hated in our new Malaya. The country is not the same as it was. People are hungry. They are angry. They call us all calorie pirates, profiteers, and yellow dogs. There is nothing to quell it. Your blood is already shed, but they have yet to decide what to do with us. I cannot risk my family for you.'

'You could come north with us. Sail together.'

Hafiz sighed. 'The Green Headbands already sail the coasts searching for refugees. Their net is wide and deep. And they slaughter those they catch.'

'But we are clever. More clever than they. We could slip past.'

'No, it is impossible.'

'How do you know?'

Hafiz looked away, embarrassed. 'My sons boast to me.'

Hock Seng scowled bitterly, holding his daughter's hand. Hafiz said, 'I'm sorry. My shame will go with me until I die.' He turned abruptly and hurried for the galley. He returned with unspoiled mangoes and papaya. A bag of U-Tex. A PurCal cibi melon. 'Here, take these. I'm sorry I can do no more. I'm sorry. I have to think of my own survival as well.' And with that he ushered Hock Seng off the boat and out into the waves.

A month later, Hock Seng crossed the border alone, crawling through leech-infested jungle after being abandoned by the snake-heads who betrayed them.

Hock Seng has heard that those who helped the yellow people later died in droves, plunging from cliffs into the sea to swim as best they could for the shore's smashing rocks, or shot where they floated. He wonders often if Hafiz was one of those to die, or if his gift of the last of Three Prosperities' unscuttled clippers was enough to save his family. If his Green Headband sons spoke for him, or if they watched coldly as their father suffered for his many, many sins.

'Grandfather? Are you well?'

The little girl touches Hock Seng gently on the wrist, watching him with wide black eyes. 'My mother can get you boiled water if you need to drink.'

Hock Seng starts to speak, then simply nods and turns away. If he speaks to her, she will know him for a refugee. Best that he simply blend in. Best not to reveal that he lives amongst them at the whim of white shirts and the Dung Lord and a few faked stamps on his yellow card. Best to trust no one, even if they seem friendly. A smiling girl one day is a girl with a stone bashing in the brains of a baby the next. This is the only truth. One can think there are such things as loyalty and trust and kindness but they are devil cats. In the end they are only smoke and cannot be grasped.

Another ten minutes of twisting passages carries him close to the city's seawalls where hovels attach themselves like barnacles to the ramparts of revered King Rama XII's blueprint for the survival of his city. Hock Seng finds Laughing Chan sitting beside a *jok* cart eating a steaming bowl of U-Tex rice porridge with small bits of unidentifiable meat buried in the paste.

In his last life, Laughing Chan was a plantation overseer, tapping the trunks of rubber trees to capture latex drippings, a crew of one hundred and fifty under him. In this life, his flair for organization has found a new niche: running laborers to unload megodonts and clipper ships down on the docks and out on the anchor pads when Thais are too lazy or thick, or slow, or he can bribe someone higher up to let his yellow card crew have the rice. And sometimes, he does other work as well. Moves opium and the amphetamine *yaba* from the river into the Dung Lord's very own towers. Slips AgriGen's SoyPRO in from Koh Angrit, despite the Environment Ministry's blockades.

He's missing an ear and four teeth but that doesn't stop him from smiling. He sits and grins like a fool, and shows the gaps in his teeth, and all the while his eyes roam over the passing pedestrian traffic. Hock Seng sits and another bowl of steaming *jok* is set before him, and they eat the U-Tex gruel with coffee that is almost as good as what they used to drink down south, and all the while both of them watch the people all around, their eyes following the woman who serves them from her pot, the men crouched at the other tables in the alley, the commuters squeezing past with their bicycles. The two of them are yellow cards, after all. It is as much in their nature as a cheshire's search for birds.

'You're ready?' Laughing Chan asks.

'A little longer, yet. I don't want your men to be seen.'

'Don't worry. We almost walk like Thais, now.' He grins and his gaps show. 'We're going native.'

'You know Dog Fucker?'

Laughing Chan nods sharply and his smile disappears. 'And Sukrit knows me. I will be below the seawall, village side. Out of sight. I have Ah Ping and Peter Siew to watch close.'

'Good then.' Hock Seng finishes his *jok* and pays for Laughing Chan's food as well. With Laughing Chan and his men nearby, Hock Seng feels a little better. But still, it is a risk. If this thing goes wrong Laughing Chan will be too far away to do much more than effect vengeance. And really, when Hock Seng thinks about it, he isn't sure he has paid enough for that.

Laughing Chan saunters off, slipping between tarp structures. Hock Seng continues on through the stagnant heat to the steep, rough path that runs up the side of the seawall. He climbs up through the slums, his knee aching with every step. Eventually, he reaches the high broad embankment of the city's tidal defenses.

After the sheltered stink of the slums, the sea breeze rushing over him and tugging at his clothes is a relief. The bright blue ocean reflects like a mirror. Others stand on the embankment's promenade, taking the fresh air. In the distance one of King Rama XII's coal pumps squats like a massive toad on the embankment's edge. The symbol for Korakot, the crab, is visible in its metal hide. Steam and smoke gout from its stacks in steady puffs.

Somewhere, deep underground, organized by the genius of the King, the pumps send their tendrils and suck water from beneath so that the city will not drown. Even in the hot season, seven pumps run steadily, keeping Bangkok from being swallowed. In the rainy season, all twelve of the zodiac signs run as the rain drenches down and everyone poles the thoroughfares of the city in skiffs, skin soaked, grateful that the monsoon hasn't failed and that the seawalls haven't broken.

He makes his way down the other side and out on a dock. A farmer with a skiff full of coconuts offers him one, slashing open the green top for Hock Seng to drink. Across the waters the drowned buildings of Thonburi poke up through the waves. Skiffs and fishing nets and clipper ships slip back and forth in the water. Hock Seng takes a deep breath, sucking the smell of salt and fish and seaweed deep into his lungs. The life of the ocean.

A Japanese clipper slides past, palm-oil polymer hull and high white sails like a gull's. The hydrofoil package below it is still hidden, but once it's out in the water, it will use its spring cannon to launch its high sails, and then the ship will leap up from the water like a fish.

Hock Seng remembers standing on the deck of his own first clipper, its high sails flying, slashing across the ocean like a stone skipped by a child, laughing as they tore over the waves, as spray rushed and blasted him. He had turned to his number one wife and told her that all things were possible, that the future was theirs.

He settles himself on the shoreline and drinks the rest of the green coconut water while a beggar boy watches. Hock Seng beckons. This one is smart enough, he supposes. He likes to reward the smart ones, the ones who are patient enough to linger and see what he will do with a coconut husk. He hands it to the boy. The boy takes it with a *wai* and goes to smash it on the mortared stones at the top of the seawall. Then he squats and uses a scrap of oyster shell to scrape the slimy tender meat from the interior, starving.

Eventually, Dog Fucker arrives. His real name is Sukrit Kamsing, but Hock Seng seldom hears the man's true name on the lips of yellow cards. There is too much bile and history built up. Instead, it's always Dog Fucker, and the words drip with hate and fear. He's a squat man, full of calories and muscle. As perfect for his work as a megodont is for converting calories into joules. The scars on his hands and arms show pale. The slits where his nose once stood stare at Hock Seng, two dark vertical nostril slashes that give him a porcine appearance.

There is some argument among yellow cards about whether Dog Fucker let *fa' gan* run too long, allowing its cauliflower growths to send enough tendrils deep into his flesh that doctors were forced to chop the whole thing off to save his life, or if the Dung Lord simply took his nose to teach him a lesson.

Dog Fucker squats beside Hock Seng. Hard black eyes. 'Your Doctor Chan came to me. With a letter.'

Hock Seng nods. 'I want to meet with your patron.'

Dog Fucker laughs slightly. 'I broke her fingers and fucked her dead for interrupting my nap.'

Hock Seng keeps his face impassive. Maybe Dog Fucker is lying. Maybe he is telling the truth. It is impossible to know. Regardless, it is a tease. To see if Hock Seng will flinch. To see if he will bargain. Perhaps Doctor Chan is gone. Another name to weigh him down when he finally reincarnates. Hock Seng says, 'Your patron will look favorably on the offer, I think.'

Dog Fucker scratches absently at the slit of a nostril. 'Why not meet me at my office, instead?'

'I like open places.'

'You have people around here? More yellow cards? You think they'll make you safe?'

Hock Seng shrugs. He looks out at the ships and their sails. At the wide world beckoning. 'I want to offer you and your patron a deal. A mountain of profit.'

'Tell me what it is.'

Hock Seng shakes his head. 'No. I must speak with him in person. Him only.'

'He doesn't talk to yellow cards. Maybe I'll just feed you to the red-fin *plaa* out there. Just like the Green Headbands did with your kind down south.'

'You know who I am.'

'I know who your letter says you were.' Dog Fucker rubs at the edges of his nose slits, studying Hock Seng. 'Here, you're just another yellow card.'

Hock Seng doesn't say anything. He hands the hemp sack of money across to Dog Fucker. Dog Fucker eyes it suspiciously, doesn't take it. 'What is it?'

'A gift. Look and see.'

Dog Fucker is curious. But also cautious. It's a good thing to know. He isn't the sort to put his hand in a bag and come up with a scorpion. Instead, he loosens the sack and dumps it. Bundles of cash spill out, roll in the shells and dirt of low tide. Dog Fucker's eyes widen. Hock Seng keeps himself from smiling.

'Tell the Dung Lord that Tan Hock Seng, head of the Three Prosperities Trading Company has a business proposal. Deliver my note to him and you will also profit greatly.'

Dog Fucker smiles. 'I think perhaps that I'll simply take this money, and my men will beat you until you tell me where you hide all your paranoid yellow card cash.'

Hock Seng doesn't say anything. Keeps his face impassive.

Dog Fucker says, 'I know all about Laughing Chan's people here. He owes me for his disrespect.'

Hock Seng is surprised that he feels no fear. He lives in fear of all things, but thuggish *pi lien* like Dog Fucker are not what fill his nights with terror. In the end, Dog Fucker is a businessman. He is not a white shirt, puffed on national pride or hungry for a little more respect. Dog Fucker works for money. Acts for money. He and Hock Seng are different parts of the economic organism, but underneath everything, they are brothers. Hock Seng smiles slightly as confidence builds.

'This is just a gift, for your trouble. What I propose will provide much more. For all of us.' He takes out the last two items. One, a letter. 'Give it to your master, sealed.' The other, he hands across: a small box with its familiar universal spindle and braces, a palm-oil polymer casing in a dull shade of yellow.

Dog Fucker takes the object, turns it over. 'A kink-spring?' He makes a face. 'What's the point of this?'

Hock Seng smiles. 'He'll know when he reads the letter.' He stands and turns away, without even waiting for Dog Fucker to respond, feeling stronger and more assured than any time since the Green Headbands came and his warehouses went up in smoke and his clipper ships went sliding down into the ocean depths. In this moment, Hock Seng feels like a man. He walks straighter, his limp forgotten.

It's impossible to know if Dog Fucker's people will follow him and so he walks slowly, knowing that both Dog Fucker's and Laughing Chan's men surround him, a floating ring of surveillance as he works his way down the alleys and cuts into deeper slums, until, at last, Laughing Chan is there, waiting for him, smiling.

'They let you go,' he says.

Hock Seng pulls out more money. 'You did well. He knows it was your men, though.' He gives Laughing Chan an extra roll of baht. 'Pay him off with this.'

Laughing Chan smiles at the pile of money. 'This is twice what I need for that. Even Dog Fucker likes to use us when he doesn't want to risk smuggling SoyPRO over from Koh Angrit.'

'Take it anyway.'

Laughing Chan shrugs and pockets it. 'It's very kind of you. With the anchor pads shut down, we can use the extra baht.'

Hock Seng is turning away, but at Laughing Chan's words he turns back.

'What did you say about the anchor pads?'

'They're shut down. The white shirts raided them last night. Everything's locked tight.'

'What happened?'

Laughing Chan shrugs. 'I heard they burned everything. Sent it all up in smoke.'

Hock Seng doesn't pause to ask any more. He turns and runs, as fast as his old bones will carry him. Cursing himself all the way. Cursing that he was a fool and didn't put his nose to the wind, that he let himself be distracted from bare survival by the urgent wish to do something more, to reach ahead.

Every time he makes plans for his future, he seems to fail. Every time he reaches forward, the world leans against him, pressing him down.

On Thanon Sukhumvit, in the sweat of the sun, he finds a news vendor. He fumbles through newspapers and the hand-cranked whisper sheets of rumor, through luck pages advertising good numbers for gambling and the names of predicted *muay thai* champions.

He tears them open, one after another, more frantic with every copy.

All of them show the smiling face of Jaidee Rojjanasukchai, the incorruptible Tiger of Bangkok.

7

'Look! I'm famous!'

Jaidee holds the whisper sheet picture up beside his own face, grinning at Kanya. When she doesn't smile, he puts it back in its rack, along with all the rest of his pictures.

'Eh, you're right. It's not really a good likeness. They must have bribed it out of our records department.' He sighs wistfully. 'But I was young then.'

Still, Kanya doesn't respond, just stares morosely at the water of the *khlong*. They've spent the day hunting for skiffs smuggling PurCal and AgriGen crops up the river, sailing back and forth across the river mouth, and Jaidee still thrums with a certain exhilaration.

The prize of the day was a clipper ship anchored just off the docks. Ostensibly an Indian trading vessel sailed north from Bali, it turned out to be brimming with cibiscosis-resistant pineapples. It was satisfying to see the harbormaster and the ship's captain both stammering excuses while Jaidee's white shirts poured lye over the entire shipment, crate after crate rendered sterile and inedible. All that smuggling profit gone.

He flips though the other papers attached to the display board, finds a different image of himself. This one from his time as a *muay thai* competitor, laughing after a fight in Lumphini Stadium. *The Bangkok Morning Post.*

'My boys will like this one.'

He opens the paper and scans the story. Trade Minister Akkarat is spitting mad. The quotes from the Trade Ministry call Jaidee a vandal. Jaidee is surprised they don't just call him a traitor or a terrorist. That they restrain themselves tells him just how impotent they really are.

Jaidee can't help smiling over the pages at Kanya. 'We really hurt them.'

Again, Kanya doesn't respond.

There's a certain trick to ignoring her bad moods. The first time Jaidee met Kanya, he almost thought she was stupid, the way her face remained so impassive, so impervious to any hint of fun, as though she were missing an organ, a nose for smell, eyes for sight, and whatever curious organ makes a person sense *sanuk* when it is right in front of them.

'We should be getting back to the Ministry,' she says, and turns to scan the boat traffic along the *khlong*, looking for a possible ride.

Jaidee pays the whisper sheet man for his paper as a canal taxi glides into view.

Kanya flags it and it slides up beside them, its flywheel whining with accumulated power, waves sloshing the *khlong* embankment as its wake catches up. Huge kink-springs crowd half its displacement. Wealthy Chaozhou Chinese business people cram the covered prow of the boat like ducks on their way to slaughter.

Kanya and Jaidee jump aboard and stand on the running board outside the seating compartment. The ticket child ignores their white uniforms, just as they ignore her. She sells a 30-baht ticket to another man who boards with them. Jaidee grabs a safety line as the boat accelerates away from the dock. Wind caresses his face as they make their way down the *khlong*, aiming for the heart of the city. The boat moves quickly, zipping around small paddled skiffs and long tail boats in the canal. Blocks of dilapidated houses and shopfronts slide past, *pha sin* and blouses and sarong hang colorful in the sun. Women bathe their long black hair in the brown waters of the canal. The boat slows abruptly.

Kanya looks forward. 'What is it?'

Up ahead, a tree has fallen, blocking much of the canal. Boats jam around it, trying to squeeze past.

'A *bo* tree,' Jaidee says. He looks around for landmarks. 'We'll have to let the monks know.'

No one else will move it. And despite the shortage of wood, no one will harvest it either. It would be unlucky. Their boat wallows as the *khlong* traffic tries to slip through the tiny gap left in the canal, where the sacred tree has not blocked movement.

Jaidee makes a noise of impatience and then calls ahead. 'Clear out, friends! Ministry business. Clear the way!' He waves his badge.

The sight of the badge and his bright white uniform is enough to get boats and skiffs poling aside. The pilot of their taxi flashes Jaidee a grateful look. Their kink-spring craft slips into the press, jostling for space.

As they ease around the bare branches of the tree, the *khlong* taxi's passengers all make deep *wais* of respect to the fallen trunk, pressing their palms together and touching them to their foreheads.

Jaidee makes his own *wai*, then reaches out to touch the wood, letting his fingers slide over the riddled surface as they pass. Small boreholes speckle it. If he were to peel away the bark, a fine net of grooves would describe the tree's death. A *bo* tree. Sacred. The tree under which the Buddha attained enlightenment. And yet they could do nothing to save it. Not a single varietal of fig survived, despite their best efforts. The ivory beetles were too much for them. When the scientists failed, they prayed to Phra Seub

Nakhasathien, a last desperate effort, but even the martyr couldn't save them in the end.

'We couldn't save everything,' Kanya murmurs, seeming to read his thoughts.

'We couldn't save even one thing.' Jaidee lets his fingers slide along the grooves where the ivory beetle did its work. 'The *farang* have so much to answer for, and yet still Akkarat seeks to treat with them.'

'Not with AgriGen.'

Jaidee smiles bitterly and pulls his hand away from the fallen tree. 'No, not with them. But their ilk, nonetheless. Generippers. Calorie men. Even PurCal when the famines are worst. Why else do we let them squat out on Koh Angrit? In case we need them. In case we fail, and must go begging for their rice and wheat and soy.'

'We have our own generippers, now.'

'Thanks to His Royal Majesty King Rama XII's foresight.'

'And Chaopraya Gi Bu Sen.'

'Chaopraya.' Jaidee makes a face. 'No one that evil should be graced with such a respectful title.'

Kanya shrugs, but doesn't bait him. Soon the *bo* tree is behind them. At Srinakharin Bridge they disembark. The smell of food stalls calls to Jaidee. He motions Kanya to follow as he makes his way into a tiny *soi*. 'Somchai says there's a good *som tam* cart down here. Good clean papayas, he tells me.'

'I'm not hungry,' Kanya says.

'That's why you're always in such a terrible mood.'

'Jaidee . . .' Kanya starts, then stops.

Jaidee glances back at her, catches the worried expression on her face. 'What is it? Come on then.'

'I'm worried about the anchor pads.'

Jaidee shrugs. 'Don't be.'

Up ahead, food carts and tables cluster along the walls of the alley, all jammed together. Small bowls of *nam plaa prik* sit tidily in the centers of the scavenged table planks. 'You see? Somchai was right.' He finds the salad cart he wants and examines the spices and fruit, starts ordering for both of them. Kanya comes up beside, a compact cloud of dark mood.

'Two hundred thousand baht is a lot of money for Akkarat to lose,' she mutters as Jaidee tells the *som tam* vendor to add more chiles.

Jaidee nods thoughtfully as the woman stirs the threads of green papaya into the mix of spices. 'It's true. I had no idea there was so much money being made out there.'

It's enough to finance a new lab for generip research, or put five hundred white shirts on inspection in the tilapia farms of Thonburi ... He shakes his head. And this was just one raid. It's amazing to him.

There are times when he thinks he understands how the world works, and then, every so often, he lifts the lid of some new part of the divine city and finds roaches scuttling where he never expected. Something new, indeed.

He goes to the next food cart, stacked with trays of chile-laden pork and RedStar bamboo tips. Fried snakehead *plaa*, battered and crisp, pulled from the Chao Phraya River that day. He orders more food. Enough for both of them, and Sato for drinking. He settles at an open table as the food is brought out.

Teetering on a bamboo stool at the end of his day, with rice beer warming his belly, Jaidee can't help smiling at his dour subordinate.

As usual, even with good food before her, Kanya remains herself. '*Khun* Bhirombhakdi was complaining about you at headquarters,' she says. 'He said he would go to General Pracha, and have your smiling lips ripped off.'

Jaidee scoops chiles into his mouth. 'I'm not afraid of him.'

'The anchor pads were supposed to be his territory. His protection racket, his bribe money.'

'First you worry about Trade, now you worry about Bhirombhakdi. That old man is afraid of his own shadow. He makes his wife taste every dish for him to make sure he won't get blister rust.' He shakes his head. 'Stop being so sour. You should smile more. Laugh a little. Here, drink this.' Jaidee pours more Sato for his lieutenant. 'We used to call our country the Land of Smiles.' Jaidee demonstrates. 'And there you sit, sad-faced, as though you are eating limes all day.'

'Perhaps we had more to smile about, then.'

'Well, that might be true.' Jaidee sets his Sato back on the splintered tabletop and stares at it thoughtfully. 'We must have done something terrible in our previous lives to have earned these ones. It's the only thing I can think of that explains it all.'

Kanya sighs. 'I sometimes see my grandmother's spirit, wandering around the *chedi* near my house. She told me one time that she couldn't reincarnate until we made a better place for her to arrive.'

'Another of the Contraction *phii*? How did she find you? Wasn't she Isaan people, too?'

'She found me anyway.' Kanya shrugs. 'She is very unhappy with me.'

'Yes, well, I suppose we'll be unhappy, too.'

Jaidee has seen these ghosts as well, walking the boulevards sometimes, sitting in the trees. *Phii* are everywhere, now. Too many to count. He has seen them in the graveyards and leaning against the bones of riddled *bo* trees, all of them looking at him with some irritation.

Mediums all speak of how crazy with frustration the *phii* are, how they cannot reincarnate and thus linger, like a great mass of people at Hualamphong Station hoping for a train ride down to the beaches. All of them waiting for a reincarnation that they cannot have because none of them deserve the suffering of this particular world.

Monks like Ajahn Suthep say this is nonsense. He sells amulets to ward off these *phii* and says that they are nothing but hungry ghosts, created by the unnatural death of eating from blister rust-tainted vegetables. Anyone can go to his shrine and make a donation, or else go to the Erawan shrine and make an offering to Brahma – perhaps have the temple dancers perform for a little while – and buy a hope that the spirits may be put to rest to travel on to their next incarnation. It is possible to hope for such things.

Still, the ghosts are all around. Everyone agrees on that. The victims of AgriGen and PurCal and all their ilk.

Jaidee says, 'I wouldn't take it personally, about your grandmother. On the full moon, I've seen the *phii* crowding the roads around the Environment Ministry, too. Many dozens of them.' He smiles sadly. 'It's really impossible to fix, I think. When I think about Niwat and Surat growing up with this ...' He takes a breath, fighting back more emotion than he cares to show before Kanya. Takes another drink. 'Anyway, the fight is good. I just wish we could get hold of some AgriGen or PurCal executives and throttle them. Maybe give them a taste of blister rust AG134.s. Then my life would be complete. I could die happy.'

'You probably won't reincarnate, either,' Kanya observes. 'You're too good to end up in this hell again.'

'If I'm lucky I'll be reborn in Des Moines, and bomb their generip labs.'

'If only.'

Jaidee looks up at Kanya's tone. 'What's bothering you? Why so sad? We'll both be reborn somewhere beautiful, I'm sure. Both of us. Think of all the merit we earned just last night. I thought those

Customs *heeya* were going to shit themselves when we burned the cargo.'

Kanya makes a bitter face. 'They've probably never met a white shirt they couldn't bribe.'

And as quick as that, she kills his attempt at good humor. No wonder no one likes her at the Ministry. 'No. That's true. Everyone takes bribes, now. It's not like before. People don't remember the worst times. They aren't afraid the way they were before.'

'And now you dive down the cobra's throat with Trade.' Kanya says, 'After the December 12 coup, it seems as if General Pracha and Minister Akkarat are always circling one another, looking for a new excuse to fight. They never finished their feud, and now you do something to further anger Akkarat. It makes things unstable.'

'Well, I was always too *jai rawn* for my own good. Chaya complains about it, too. That's why I keep you around. I wouldn't worry about Akkarat, though. He'll spit for a while, then he'll calm down. He may not like it, but General Pracha has too many allies in the Army for another coup attempt. With Prime Minister Surawong dead, Akkarat really has nothing left. He's isolated. Without megodonts and tanks to back up his threats, Akkarat may be rich, but he is a paper tiger. This is a good lesson for him.'

'He's dangerous.'

Jaidee looks at her seriously. 'So are cobras. So are megodonts. So is cibiscosis. We're surrounded by dangers. Akkarat . . .' Jaidee shrugs. 'Anyway, it's already done. There's nothing you can do to change it. Why worry now? *Mai pen rai.* Never mind.'

'Still, you should be careful.'

'You're thinking of that man at the anchor pads? The one Somchai saw? Did he frighten you?'

Kanya shrugs. 'No.'

'I'm surprised. He frightened me.' Jaidee watches Kanya, wondering how much he should say, how much he should reveal that he knows about the world around him. 'I have a very bad feeling about him.'

'Really?' Kanya looks distressed. 'You're frightened? Of one stupid man?'

Jaidee shakes his head. 'Not afraid so that I will run and hide behind Chaya's *pha sin*, but still, I've seen him before.'

'You didn't tell me.'

'I wasn't sure at first. Now I am. I think he is with Trade.' He pauses, testing. 'I think they are hunting me again. Maybe considering another assassination. What do you think of that?'

'They wouldn't dare touch you. Her Majesty the Queen has spoken in your favor.'

Jaidee touches his neck where the old spring gun scar still shows light on his dark skin. 'Not even after what I did to them at the anchor pads?'

Kanya bridles. 'I'll assign a bodyguard.'

Jaidee laughs at her fierceness and is warmed and reassured by it. 'You're a good girl, but I'd be a fool to take a bodyguard. Then everyone would know that I can be frightened. That's not the way of a tiger. Here, eat this.' He scoops more snake head *plaa* onto Kanya's plate.

'I'm full.'

'Don't be so polite. Eat.'

'You should have a bodyguard. Please.'

'I'll trust you to guard my back. You should be more than enough.'

Kanya flinches. Jaidee hides a smile at her discomfort. *Ahh, Kanya,* he thinks. *We all have choices we must face in life. I've made mine. But you have your own* kamma. He speaks gently. 'Go on and eat more, you look skinny. How will you find a special friend if you're only bones?'

Kanya pushes her plate away. 'I don't eat much these days, it seems.'

'People are starving everywhere, and you can't eat.'

Kanya makes a face and scoops a sliver of fish onto her spoon.

Jaidee shakes his head. He sets down his own fork and spoon. 'What is it? You're even more glum than usual. I feel like we've just put one of our brothers in a funeral urn. What's bothering you?'

'It's nothing. Really. Just not hungry.'

'Speak up, Lieutenant. I want straight talk from you. It's an order. You're a good officer. I can't stand having your sad face. I don't like any of my people to be sad-faced, even the ones from Isaan.'

Kanya grimaces. Jaidee watches as his lieutenant mulls what she will say. He wonders if he was ever so tactful as this young woman. He doubts it. He has always been too brash, too easily angered. Not like Kanya, dour Kanya, all *jai yen* all the time. Not *sanuk* at all, but certainly *jai yen*.

He waits, thinking that at last he will hear her story, her full story in all its painful humanity, but when Kanya finally summons the words, she surprises him. She speaks in a near whisper. Almost too embarrassed to form the words at all.

'Some of the men complain that you don't take enough gifts of goodwill.'

'What?' Jaidee sits back, goggles at her. 'We won't participate in that sort of thing. We're different than the rest. And proud of it.'

Kanya nods readily. 'And the newspapers and whisper sheets love you for it. And the people love you for it.'

'But?'

Her miserable look returns. 'But you don't get promoted anymore, and the men who are loyal to you get no help from your patronage, and they lose heart.'

'But look what we accomplish!' Jaidee taps the sack of money between his legs that they confiscated off the clipper ship. 'They all know that if they have a need, they will be helped. We have more than enough for anyone in need.'

Kanya looks down at the table and mumbles, 'Some say you like to keep the money.'

'What?' Jaidee stares at her, dumbstruck. 'Do you think this?'

Kanya shrugs miserably. 'Of course not.'

Jaidee shakes his head, apologizing. 'No, of course you wouldn't. You've been a good girl. You've done great things here.' He smiles at his lieutenant, almost overwhelmed with compassion for the young woman who came to him starving, idolizing him and his years as a champion, wanting so much to emulate him.

'I do what I can to squash the rumors, but ...' Kanya shrugs again, miserable. 'Cadets say that being under Captain Jaidee is like starving of *akah* worms. You work and work and get skinnier and skinnier. These are good boys we have, but they can't help but feel ashamed when they have old uniforms and their comrades have new crisp ones. When they ride a bicycle two at a time, and their comrades ride kink-spring scooters.'

Jaidee sighs. 'I remember a time when the white shirts were loved.'

'Everyone needs to eat.'

Jaidee sighs again. He pulls the satchel out from between his legs and shoves it across to Kanya. 'Take the money. Divide it equally amongst them. For their bravery and hard work yesterday.'

She looks at him surprised. 'You're sure?'

Jaidee shrugs and smiles, hiding his own disappointment, knowing that this is the best way, and yet saddened immeasurably by it. 'Why not? They're good boys, as you say. And it's not as though the *farang* and the Ministry of Trade aren't reeling at this very moment. They did good work.'

Kanya *wais* deep respect, ducking her head low and raising her pressed palms to her forehead.

'Oh, stop that nonsense.' Jaidee pours more Sato into Kanya's glass, finishing the bottle. '*Mai pen rai*. Never mind. These are small things. Tomorrow we'll have new battles to fight. And we'll need good loyal boys to follow us. How will we ever overcome the AgriGens and PurCals of the world if we don't feed our friends?'

8

'I lost 30,000.'

'Fifty,' Otto mutters.

Lucy Nguyen stares at the ceiling. 'One-Eighty Five? Six?'

'Four hundred.' Quoile Napier sets his warm glass of Sato down on the low table. 'I lost four hundred thousand blue bills on Carlyle's goddamn dirigible.'

The entire table falls silent, stunned. 'Christ.' Lucy sits up, bleary with drink in the middle of the afternoon. 'What were you smuggling in, cibi-resistant seedstock?'

The conversationalists sprawl on the veranda of Sir Francis Drake's, all five together, the '*Farang* Phalanx' as Lucy has styled them, all of them staring out at the dry season blast furnace and drinking themselves into a stupor.

Anderson reclines with them, half-listening to their slurred complaints as he turns the problem of the *ngaw*'s origins over in his mind. He's got another bag of the fruit between his feet, and he can't help thinking that the answer to his puzzle lies close, if only he had sufficient ingenuity to suss it out. He drinks warm Khmer whiskey and ponders.

Ngaw: apparently impervious to blister rust and cibiscosis even when directly exposed; obviously resistant to Nippon genehack weevil and leafcurl, or it could never have grown. A perfect product. The fruit of access to different genetic material than AgriGen and the rest of the calorie companies use for their generipping.

Somewhere in this country a seedbank is hidden. Thousands, perhaps hundreds of thousands, of carefully preserved seeds, a treasure trove of biological diversity. Infinite chains of DNA, each with their own potential uses. And from this gold mine, the Thais are extracting answers to their knottiest challenges of survival. With access to the Thai seedbank, Des Moines could mine genetic code for generations, beat back plague mutations. Stay alive a little longer.

Anderson shifts in his seat, stifling irritation, wiping away sweat. He's so close. Nightshades have been reborn, and now *ngaw*. And Gibbons is running loose in South-east Asia. If it weren't for that illegal windup girl he wouldn't even know about Gibbons. The Kingdom has been singularly successful at maintaining its operational security. If he could just ascertain the seedbank's location, a raid might even be possible ... They've learned since Finland.

Beyond the veranda, nothing with any intelligence is moving. Tantalizing beads of sweat run down Lucy's neck and soak her shirt as she complains about the state of the coal war with the Vietnamese. She can't hunt for jade if the Army is busy shooting anything that moves. Quoile's sideburns are matted. No breezes blow.

Out in the street, rickshaw men huddle in thin pools of shade. Their bones and joints protrude from bare taut skin, skeletons with flesh stretched tight on their frames. At this time of day they only sullenly emerge from shadow when they are called, and then only for double fee.

The entire ramshackle structure of the bar is scabbed to the outer wall of a wrecked Expansion tower. A hand-painted sign leans against one of the stairs up to the veranda, with the scrawled words: SIR FRANCIS DRAKE'S. The sign is a recent addition, relative to the decay and wreckage around it, painted by a handful of *farang* determined to name their surroundings. The fools who did the naming long ago disappeared up country, either swallowed in the jungle as blister rust rewrites swept over them, or torn apart in the tangle of war lines over coal and jade. Still, the sign remains, either because it amuses the owner, who has taken the name on as a nickname, or because no one can summon the energy to paint over it. In the meantime, it peels in the heat.

Regardless of provenance, Drake's is perfectly placed between the seawall shipping locks and the factories. Its dilapidated wreckage faces off across from the Victory Hotel so the *Farang* Phalanx can drink itself stupid and watch to see if any new foreigners of interest have washed up on the shores.

There are other, lower, dives for those sailors who manage to pass Customs and quarantine and washdown, but it is here, with the snapping white tablecloths of the Victory on one side of the cobbled street, and Sir Francis' bamboo slum on the other, where those foreigners who settle in Bangkok for any length of time eventually sink.

'What were you shipping?' Lucy asks again, prodding Quoile to explain his losses.

Quoile leans forward and lowers his voice, encouraging all of them to rouse themselves. 'Saffron. From India.'

A pause, and then Cobb laughs. 'Good airlift product. I should have thought of that.'

'Ideal for a dirigible. Low weight. More profitable than opium on the uplift,' Quoile says. 'The Kingdom still hasn't figured out how to crack the seedstock, and all the politicians and generals want it for their household kitchens. Lots of face, if they can get it. I had solid pre-orders. I was going to be rich. Unbelievably rich.'

'Are you ruined then?'

'Maybe not. I'm negotiating with Sri Ganesha Insurance, they might cover some.' Quoile shrugs. 'Well, eighty percent. But all the bribes to get it into the country? All the payoffs to the Customs agents?' He makes a face. 'That's a complete loss. Still, I might get out with my skin.

'In a way, I got lucky. The shipment only falls under insurance guidelines because it was still on Carlyle's dirigible. I ought to toast that damn pilot for getting himself drowned in the ocean. If they'd unloaded the cargo and the white shirts had burned it on the ground, it would have been classified contraband. Then I'd be out there on the street with the *fa' gan* beggars and the yellow cards.'

Otto scowls. 'That's about the only thing to be said for Carlyle. If he wasn't so interested in touching politics, none of this would have happened.'

Quoile shrugs. 'We don't know that.'

'It's damn certain,' Lucy interjects. 'Carlyle spends half his energy complaining about the white shirts and the other half cozying up with Akkarat. It's a message from General Pracha to Carlyle and the Trade Ministry. We're just the carrier pigeons.'

'Carrier pigeons are extinct.'

'You think we won't be? General Pracha would be happy to throw every one of us into Khlong Prem prison if he thought it would send the right message to Akkarat.' Her gaze swings to Anderson. 'You're awfully quiet, Lake. You didn't lose anything at all?'

Anderson stirs himself. 'Manufacturing materials. Replacement parts for my line. Probably a hundred fifty thousand blue bills. My secretary's still evaluating the damage.' He glances at Quoile. 'Our stuff was on the ground. No insurance.'

The memory of his conversation with Hock Seng is still fresh. Hock Seng first played at denial, complaining of incompetence at the anchor pads, before finally confessing that everything was lost, and that he had failed to pay all the bribe money in the first place. An ugly confessional, almost hysterical, the old man terrified of losing his job and Anderson pressing him further and further into his fear, humiliating him and shouting at him, making the old man cower, making a point of his displeasure. Still, he can't help wondering if the lesson has been learned, or if Hock Seng will try to be tricky again. Anderson grimaces. If the old man didn't free up so much of Anderson's time for more important work, he'd ship the old bastard back to the yellow card towers.

'I told you this was a stupid place to run a factory,' Lucy says.

'The Japanese do it.'

'Only because they have special arrangements with the palace.'

'The Chaozhou Chinese do just fine, too.'

Lucy makes a face. 'They've been here for generations. Practically Thai at this point. We're more like yellow cards than Chaozhou, if you want to make comparisons. A smart *farang* knows not to keep too much invested in this place. The ground's always shifting. It's too damn easy to lose everything in a crackdown. Or another coup.'

'We all work with the hands we're dealt.' Anderson shrugs. 'Anyway, Yates chose the site.'

'I told Yates it was stupid, too.'

Anderson recalls Yates, eyes bright with the possibilities of a new global economy. 'Maybe not stupid. But definitely an idealist.' He finishes his drink. The bar owner is nowhere in sight. He waves for the waiters, who all ignore him. One of them, at least, is asleep, standing.

'You're not worried you'll get yanked the way Yates did?' Lucy asks.

Anderson shrugs. 'Wouldn't be the worst thing that could happen. It's damn hot.' He touches his sunburned nose. 'I'm more of a northern wastes sort.'

Nguyen and Quoile, dark-skinned both, laugh at that, but Otto just nods grimly, his own peeling nose a testament to his inability to adapt to the burn of the equatorial sun.

Lucy pulls out a pipe and pushes a couple of flies away before setting down her smoking tools and an accompanying ball of opium. The flies hobble away, but don't take to the air. Even the bugs seem stunned by the heat. Down an alley, near the rubble of an old Expansion tower, children are playing next to a freshwater pump. Lucy watches them as she tamps her pipe. 'Christ, I wish I was a kid again.'

Everyone seems to have lost the energy for conversation. Anderson pulls the sack of *ngaw* out from between his feet. Takes one out and peels it. Pries the translucent fruit from the *ngaw's* interior and tosses the hairy hollow rind on the table. Pops the fruit into his mouth.

Otto cocks his head, curious. 'What's that you've got?'

Anderson digs more out of his sack, distributes them. 'Not sure. Thais call them *ngaw.*'

Lucy stops tamping her pipe. 'I've seen them. They're all over the market. They don't have blister rust?'

Anderson shakes his head. 'Not so far. The lady who sold them said they were clean. Had the certificates.'

Everyone laughs, but Anderson shrugs off their cynicism. 'I let them sit for a week. Nothing. They're cleaner than U-Tex.'

The others follow his lead and eat their own fruits. Eyes widen. Smiles appear. Anderson opens the sack wide and sets it on the table. 'Go ahead. I've been eating too many as it is.'

They all rifle the bag. A pile of rinds grows in the center of the table. Quoile chews thoughtfully. 'It sort of reminds me of lychee.'

'Oh?' Anderson controls his interest. 'Never heard of it.'

'Sure. I had a drink that tasted a bit like it. Last time I was in

India. Kolkata. A PurCal sales rep took me to one of his restaurants, when I first started looking at shipping saffron.'

'So you think it's this . . . leechee?'

'Could be. Lychee was what he called the drink. Might not have been the fruit at all.'

'If it's a PurCal product, I don't see how it would show up here,' Lucy says. 'These should all be out on Koh Angrit, under quarantine while the Environment Ministry finds ten thousand different ways to tax the thing.' She spits the pit into her palm and tosses it off the balcony into the street. 'I'm seeing these everywhere. They've got to be local.' She reaches into the sack and takes another. 'You know who might know about them, though . . .' She leans back and calls into the dimness of the bar. 'Hagg! You still there? You awake back in there?'

At the man's name, the others stir and try to straighten themselves, like children caught by a strict parent. Anderson forces down an instinctive chill. 'I wish you hadn't done that,' he mutters.

Otto grimaces. 'I thought he died.'

'Blister rust never gets the chosen ones, don't you know?'

Everyone stifles a laugh as a form shambles out of the gloom. Hagg's face is flushed, and sweat speckles his face. He surveys the Phalanx solemnly. 'Hello, all.' He nods his head to Lucy. 'Still trafficking with these sort, then?'

Lucy shrugs. 'I make do.' She nods at a chair. 'Don't just stand there. Have a drink on us. Tell us your stories.' She lights her opium pipe and draws on it as the man pulls up the chair beside her and sags into it.

Hagg is a solid man, well-fleshed. Not for the first time, Anderson thinks how interesting it is that Grahamite priests, of all their flock, are always the ones whose waistlines overflow their niche. Hagg waves for whiskey, and surprises everyone when a waiter appears at his elbow almost immediately.

'No ice,' the waiter says on arrival.

'No, no ice. Of course not.' Hagg shakes his head emphatically. 'Don't want the damn calories spent, anyway.'

When the waiter returns, Hagg takes the drink and downs it instantly, then sends the waiter back for a second. 'It's good to be back in from the countryside,' he says. 'You start missing the pleasures of civilization.' He toasts them all with his second glass and downs it as well.

'How far out were you?' Lucy asks around the pipe clamped in her teeth. She's starting to look a little glassy from the burning tar.

'Near the old border with Burma, Three Pagodas pass.' He looks sourly at them all as if they are guilty of the sins he researches. 'Looking into ivory beetle spread.'

'Not safe up there, I heard.' Otto says. 'Who's the *jao por?*'

'A man named Chanarong. And he was no trouble at all. Far easier to work with him than the Dung Lord or any of the small *jao por* in the city. Not all of the godfathers are so focused on profits and power.' Hagg looks back pointedly. 'For those of us who aren't interested in pillaging the Kingdom of coal or jade or opium, the countryside is safe enough.' He shrugs. 'In any case, I was invited by Phra Kritipong to visit his monastery. To observe the changes in ivory beetle behavior.' He shakes his head. 'The devastation is extraordinary. Whole forests with not a leaf on them. Kudzu, and nothing else. The entire overstory is gone, timber fallen everywhere.'

Otto looks interested. 'Anything salvageable?'

Lucy gives him a look of disgust. 'It's ivory beetle, you idiot. No one around here wants that.'

Anderson asks, 'You say the monastery invited you up? Even though you're a Grahamite?'

'Phra Kritipong is enlightened enough to know that neither Jesus Christ nor the Niche Teachings are anathema to his kind.

Buddhist and Grahamite values overlap in many areas. Noah and the martyr Phra Seub are entirely complementary figures.'

Anderson stifles a laugh. 'If your monk saw how Grahamites operate back home, he might see it differently.'

Hagg looks offended. 'I am not some preacher of field burnings. I am a scientist.'

'Didn't mean any offense.' Anderson pulls out a *ngaw*, offers it to Hagg. 'This might interest you. We just found them in the market.'

Hagg eyes the *ngaw*, surprised. 'The market? Which one?'

'All over,' Lucy supplies.

'They showed up while you were gone,' Anderson says. 'Try it, they're not bad.'

Hagg takes the fruit, studying it closely. 'Extraordinary.'

'You know what they are?' Otto asks.

Anderson peels another fruit for himself, but even as he does, he listens closely. He would never directly ask the question of a Grahamite, but he's perfectly willing to let others do the work.

'Quoile thought it was a leechee,' Lucy says. 'Is he right?'

'No, not a lychee. That's for certain.' Hagg turns it in his hand. 'It looks like it could be something the old texts called a rambutan.' Hagg is thoughtful. 'Though, if I recall correctly, they're somewhat related.'

'Rambootan?' Anderson keeps his expression friendly and neutral. 'That's a funny name. The Thais all call them *ngaw*.'

Hagg eats the fruit, spits the fat pit into his palm. Examines the black seed, wet with his saliva. 'I wonder if it will breed true.'

'You could put it in a flower pot and find out.'

Hagg gives him an irritated look. 'If it doesn't come from a calorie company, it will breed. The Thais don't make sterile generips.'

Anderson laughs. 'I didn't think the calorie companies made tropical fruits.'

'They make pineapples.'

'Right. Forgot.' Anderson waits. 'How do you know so much about fruits?'

'I studied biosystems and ecology at Alabama New University.'

'That's your Grahamite college, right? I thought all you studied was how to start a field burning.'

The others suck in their breath at the provocation, but Hagg just looks back coldly. 'Don't bait me. I'm not that sort. If we're ever going to restore Eden, it will take the knowledge of ages to accomplish it. Before I came over, I spent a year immersed in Pre-Contraction Southeast Asian Ecosystems.' He reaches across and takes another fruit. 'This must gall the calorie companies.'

Lucy fumbles for another fruit. 'You think we could fill a clipper ship with these and send them back across the water? You know, play calorie company in reverse? People would pay a fortune for them, I'll bet. New flavor and all? Sell it as a luxury.'

Otto shakes his head. 'You'd have to convince them it's not blister-rust tainted; the red skin will make people nervous.'

Hagg nods agreement. 'It's a route best not pursued.'

'But the calorie companies do it.' Lucy points out. 'They ship seeds and food wherever they want. They're global. Why shouldn't we try the same?'

'Because it goes against all the Niche Teachings,' Hagg says gently. 'The calorie companies have already earned their place in hell. There's no reason you should be eager to join them.'

Anderson laughs. 'Come on, Hagg. You can't seriously be against a little entrepreneurial spirit. Lucy's on to something. We could even put your face on the side of the crates.' He makes a sign of Grahamite blessing. 'You know, approved by the Holy Church and all that. Safe as SoyPRO.' He grins. 'What do you think of that?'

'I would never participate in such blasphemy.' Hagg scowls. 'Food should come from the place of its origin, and stay there. It shouldn't spend its time crisscrossing the globe for the sake of profit. We went down that path once, and it brought us to ruin.'

'More Niche Teachings.' Anderson peels another fruit. 'There must be a niche for money somewhere in Grahamite orthodoxy. Your cardinals are fat enough.'

'The teachings are sound, even if the flock strays.' Hagg stands abruptly. 'Thank you for the company.' He frowns at Anderson, but reaches across the table and grabs one more fruit before stalking away.

As soon as he's gone, everyone relaxes. 'Christ, Lucy, why'd you do that?' Otto asks. 'That man creeps me out. I left the Compact so I could get away from Grahamite priests looking over my shoulder. And you have to call one over?'

Quoile nods morosely. 'I heard there's another priest here at the joint embassy now.'

'They're everywhere. Like maggots.' Lucy waves at them. 'Toss me another fruit.'

They return to their gorging. Anderson watches them, curious to see if these well-travelled creatures will have any other ideas about its provenance. The rambutan is an interesting possibility, though. Already, despite the bad news about the destroyed algae tanks and nutrient cultures, the day is turning out better than expected. Rambutan. A word to send back to Des Moines and the researchers. A route of investigation into the origins of this mysterious botanic object. Somewhere, there will be a historical record of it. He'll have to go back to his books and see if he can find—

'Look who's here,' Quoile mutters.

Everyone turns. Richard Carlyle, in a perfectly pressed linen suit, is climbing the stairs. He takes off his hat as he reaches the shade, fanning himself.

'I fucking hate that man,' Lucy mutters. She lights another pipe, draws hard.

'What's he smiling about?' Otto asks.

'Hell if I know. He lost a dirigible, didn't he?'

Carlyle pauses in the shade, scans the patrons across the room, nods at all of them. 'Pretty hot one,' he calls out.

Otto stares at him, red-faced and bullet-eyed, and mutters, 'If it hadn't been for his fucking politicking, I'd be a rich man today.'

'Don't be dramatic.' Anderson pops another *ngaw* into his mouth. 'Lucy, give the man a puff of your pipe. I don't feel like having Sir Francis kick us out into the heat for brawling.'

Lucy's eyes have gone glassy with opium, but she waves the pipe in Otto's general direction. Anderson reaches across and plucks it from her fingers and gives it to Otto, before standing and picking up his empty glass. 'Anyone else want something?' Desultory shakes of the head.

Carlyle grins as he arrives at the bar. 'You get poor old Otto sorted out?'

Anderson glances back. 'Lucy smokes serious opium. I doubt he'll be able to walk, let alone fight anyone.'

'Devil's drug, that.'

Anderson toasts him with his empty glass. 'That, and booze.' He peers over the edge of the bar. 'Where the hell's Sir Francis?'

'I thought you were here to answer that question.'

'I guess not,' Anderson says. 'You lose much?'

'Some.'

'Really? You don't seem bothered.' Anderson gestures back at the rest of the Phalanx. 'Everyone else is pissing and moaning about how you keep interfering with politics, cozying up with Akkarat and the Trade Ministry. But here you are smiling ear to ear. You could be a Thai.'

Carlyle shrugs. Sir Francis, elegantly dressed, carefully coiffed, emerges from a back room. Carlyle asks for whiskey and Anderson holds up his own empty glass.

'No ice,' Sir Francis says. 'The mulie men want more money to run the pump.'

'Pay them, then.'

Sir Francis shakes his head as he takes Anderson's glass. 'If you bargain when they squeeze your balls, they will only squeeze again. And I cannot bribe the Environment Ministry to give me access to the coal grid like you *farang*.'

He turns away and pulls down a bottle of Khmer whiskey, pours an immaculate shot. Anderson wonders if any of the rumors about the man are true.

Otto, now mumbling incoherently about 'fugging dribigles,' claims that Sir Francis was an old *Chaopraya*, a high assistant to the crown, forced out of the palace in a power play. This theory has as much merit as the idea that he is former servant of the Dung Lord, retired, or that he is a Khmer prince, displaced and living incognito ever since the Thai Kingdom was enlarged to swallow the East. Everyone agrees he must have been of high rank – it's the only thing that explains his disdain for his patrons.

'Pay now,' he says as he sets the shots on the bar.

Carlyle laughs. 'You know our credit's good.'

Sir Francis shakes his head. 'You both lost plenty at the anchor pads. Everyone knows it. Pay now.'

Carlyle and Anderson shell out coins. 'I thought we had a better relationship than that,' Anderson complains.

'This is politics.' Sir Francis smiles. 'Maybe you are here tomorrow. Maybe you are swept away like Expansion plastic on a beach. There are whisper sheets on all the street corners, calling for Captain Jaidee to be made a *chaopraya* advisor to the palace. If he rises, then all you *farang* . . .' he makes a shooing motion with his hand, 'all gone.' He shrugs. 'General Pracha's radio stations are calling Jaidee a tiger and hero, and the student associations have been calling for the Trade Ministry to be closed down and placed under the white shirts. The Trade Ministry lost face. *Farang* and Trade are close like *farang* and fleas.'

'Nice.'

Sir Francis shrugs. 'You do smell.'

Carlyle scowls. 'Everyone smells. It's the goddamn hot season.'

Anderson intercedes. 'I suppose Trade is seething, losing face like that.' He takes a sip of the warm whiskey and grimaces. He used to like room-temperature liquor, before he came here.

Sir Francis counts their coins into his cash box. 'Minister Akkarat is still smiling, but the Japanese want reparations for their losses and the white shirts will never give them. So either Akkarat will pay to make up for what the Tiger of Bangkok has done, or he will lose face to the Japanese as well.'

'You think the Japanese will leave?'

Sir Francis makes a face of disgust. 'The Japanese are like the calorie companies, always looking for a way in. They will never go away.' He moves to the other end of the bar, leaving them once again isolated.

Anderson pulls out a *ngaw* and offers it Carlyle. 'Want one?'

Carlyle takes the fruit and holds it up for examination. 'What the hell is this?'

'*Ngaw*.'

'It reminds me of cockroaches.' He makes a face. 'You're an experimental bastard. I'll give you that.' He pushes the *ngaw* back across to Anderson and carefully wipes his hand on his trousers.

'Afraid?' Anderson goads.

'My wife liked eating new things, too. Couldn't stop herself. Had the madness for flavor. Just couldn't resist trying new foods.' Carlyle shrugs. 'I'll wait and see if you're spitting up blood next week.'

They lean back on their stools and gaze across the dust and

heat to where the Victory Hotel gleams white. Down an alley a washing woman has set out laundry in pans near the rubble of an old high-rise. Another is washing her body, carefully scrubbing under her sarong, its fabric clinging to her skin. Children run naked through the dirt, jumping over bits of broken concrete that were laid down more than a hundred years ago in the old Expansion. Far down the street the levees rise, holding back the sea.

'How much did you lose?' Carlyle finally asks.

'Plenty. Thanks to you.'

Carlyle doesn't respond to the jab. He finishes his shot and waves for another. 'Really no ice?' he asks Sir Francis. 'Or is this just because you think we'll be gone tomorrow?'

'Ask me tomorrow.'

'If I'm still here tomorrow will you have ice then?' Carlyle asks.

Sir Francis flashes a grin. 'Depends how much you keep paying mulies and megodonts for unloading freight. Everyone talks about getting rich burning calories for *farang* . . . so no ice for Sir Francis.'

'But if we're gone, no drinkers. Even if Sir Francis has got all the ice in the world.'

Sir Francis shrugs. 'As you say.'

Carlyle scowls at the Thai man's back. 'Megodont unions, white shirts, Sir Francis. Everywhere you turn, there's another open hand.'

'Price of doing business,' Anderson says. 'Still, the way you were smiling when you came in, I thought you hadn't lost anything at all.'

Carlyle takes his new whiskey. 'I just like seeing all of you on the veranda looking like your dogs died from cibiscosis. Anyway, even if we've had losses, no one's chained us in a Khlong Prem sweat cell. No reason not to smile about that.' He leans close. 'This isn't the last of the story. Not by a long shot. Akkarat's still got some tricks up his sleeve.'

'If you push hard enough on the white shirts, they always bite back.' Anderson warns. 'You and Akkarat made a lot of noise, talking about tariff and pollution credit changes. Windups, even. And now my assistant is telling me the same things that Sir Francis just said: all the Thai newspapers are calling our friend Jaidee a Queen's Tiger. Celebrating him.'

'Your assistant? You mean that paranoid yellow card spider you keep in your offices?' Carlyle laughs. 'That's the problem with you. You all sit around, bitching and wishing, and meanwhile I'm changing the rules of the game. You're all Contraction thinkers.'

'I'm not the one who lost a dirigible.'

'Cost of doing business.'

'I'd think losing a fifth of your fleet would be more than just a cost.'

Carlyle makes a face. He leans close and lowers his voice. 'Come on, Anderson. This tiff with the white shirts isn't what it seems. Some people have been waiting for them to go too far.' He pauses, making sure his words are understood. 'Some of us have been working toward it, even. I've just come from speaking with Akkarat himself, and I can assure you the news is about to turn in our favor.'

Anderson almost laughs, but Carlyle wags an admonishing finger. 'Go ahead, shake your head now, but before I'm done you'll be kissing my ass and thanking me for the new tariff structures, and we'll all have reparations in our bank accounts.'

'The white shirts never pay reparations. Not when they burn a farm, not when they confiscate a cargo. Never.'

Carlyle shrugs. He looks out toward the hot light of the veranda and observes, 'The monsoons are coming.'

'Not likely.' Anderson gives the blazing day a sour look. 'They're already late by two months.'

'Oh, they're coming all right. Maybe not this month. Maybe not next, but they're coming.'

'And?'

'The Environment Ministry is expecting replacement equipment for the city's levee pumps. Critical equipment. For seven pumps.' He pauses. 'Now, where do you think that equipment is sitting?'

'Enlighten me.'

'All the way across the Indian Ocean.' Carlyle flashes a sudden shark-like smile. 'In a certain Kolkata hanger that I happen to own.'

The air seems to have left the bar. Anderson glances around, making sure no one is close. 'Christ, you silly bastard. Are you serious?'

It all makes sense, now. Carlyle's bragging, his certainty. The man has always had a freebooter's willingness to take risks. But it's difficult to distinguish bluster from sincerity with Carlyle. If he says he has Akkarat's ear, perhaps he only speaks with secretaries. It's all talk. But this . . .

Anderson starts to speak but sees Sir Francis approaching and turns away instead, grimacing. Carlyle's eyes sparkle with mischief. Sir Francis sets a new whiskey beside his hand, but Anderson doesn't care about drinks anymore. As soon as Sir Francis retreats, he leans forward.

'You're holding the city hostage?'

'The white shirts seem to have forgotten they need outsiders. We're in the middle of a new Expansion and every string is connected to every other string, and yet they're still thinking like a Contraction ministry. They don't understand how dependent they've already become on *farang*.' He shrugs. 'At this point, they're just pawns on a chess board. They have no idea who moves them, and couldn't stop us even if they tried.'

He tosses back another shot of whiskey, grimaces and slaps it down on the bar. 'We should all send flowers to that Jaidee white shirt bastard. He's done his job perfectly. With half the city's coal pumps offline ...' He shrugs. 'The nice thing about dealing with the Thais is that they're really a very sensitive people. I won't even have to make a threat. They'll figure it out all on their own, and make things right.'

'Quite a gamble.'

'Isn't everything?' Carlyle favors Anderson with a cynical smile. 'Maybe we're all dead tomorrow from a blister rust rewrite. Or maybe we're the richest men in the Kingdom. It's all a gamble. The Thais play for keeps. So should we.'

'I'd just put a spring gun to your head and trade your brains for the pumps.'

'That's the spirit!' Carlyle laughs. 'Now you're thinking like a Thai. But I've got myself covered there, too.'

'What? With the Trade Ministry?' Anderson makes a face. 'Akkarat doesn't have the muscle to protect you.'

'Better than that. He's got generals.'

'You're drunk. General Pracha's friends run every part of the military. The only reason the white shirts don't run the entire country already is because the old King stepped in before Pracha could squash Akkarat the last time.'

'Times change. Pracha's white shirts and his payoffs have made a lot of people angry. People want a change.'

'You're talking revolution, now?'

'Is it revolution if the palace asks for it?' Carlyle reaches non-chalantly across the bar for the bottle of whiskey and pours. He upends it and gets less than half a shot from the bottle. He raises an eyebrow to Anderson. 'Ah. Now you're paying attention.' He points to Anderson's tumbler. 'Are you going to drink that?'

'How far does this go?'

'You want in on the deal?'

'Why would you offer?'

'You have to ask?' Carlyle shrugs. 'When Yates set up your factory, he tripled the Megodont Union's fees for joules. Threw money everywhere. Hard not to notice that kind of funding.'

He nods at the other expatriates, now playing a listless game of poker and waiting for the heat of the day to abate so that they can go on with their work or their whoring or their passive wait for the next day. 'Everyone else, they're children. Little kids wearing adult clothes. You're different.'

'You think we're rich?'

'Oh stop the theatrics. My dirigibles haul your cargo.' Carlyle regards him. 'I've seen where your supply shipments originate from,' he looks at Anderson significantly, 'before they arrive in Kolkata.'

Anderson pretends nonchalance. 'So?'

'An awful lot of material coming from Des Moines.'

'You think I'm worth talking to because I've got Midwestern investors? Doesn't everyone get their investors where the money is? So what if a rich widow wants to experiment with kink-springs. You read too much into small things.'

'Do I?' Carlyle looks around the bar and leans close. 'People are talking about you.'

'How so?'

'They say you're quite interested in seeds.' He looks significantly at the rind of the *ngaw* between them. 'We're all genespotters, these days. But you're the only one who pays for your intelligence. The only one who asks about white shirts and generippers.'

Anderson smiles coldly. 'You've been talking to Raleigh.'

Carlyle inclines his head. 'If it's any consolation, it wasn't easy. He didn't want to talk about you. Not at all.'

'He should have thought a little harder.'

'He can't get his aging treatments without me.' Carlyle shrugs.

'We have shipping representatives in Japan. You weren't offering him another decade of easy living.'

Anderson forces a laugh. 'Of course.' He smiles, but inside he is seething. He'll have to deal with Raleigh. And now perhaps Carlyle as well. He's been sloppy. He eyes the *ngaw* with disgust. He's been waving his latest interest in front of everyone. Grahamites, even, and now this. It's too easy to get comfortable. To forget all the lines of exposure. And then one day in a bar, someone slaps you in the face.

Carlyle is saying, 'If I could just speak with certain people. Discuss certain propositions . . .' he trails off, brown eyes hunting for a sign of agreement in Anderson's expression. 'I don't care which company you're working for. If I understand your interests correctly, then we might find our goals lie in similar directions.'

Anderson drums his fingers on the bar, thoughtful. If Carlyle were to disappear, would it rouse any interest at all? He might even be able to blame it on overzealous white shirts . . .

'You think you've got a chance?' Anderson asks.

'It wouldn't be the first time the Thais have reformed their government with force. The Victory Hotel wouldn't exist if Prime Minister Surawong hadn't lost his head and his mansion in the December 12 coup. Thai history is littered with changes in administration.'

'I'm a little concerned that if you're talking to me, you're talking to others. Maybe too many others.'

'Who else would I talk to?' Carlyle jerks his head toward the rest of the *Farang* Phalanx. 'They're nothing. Wouldn't consider them for a second. Your people though . . .' Carlyle trails off, considering his words, then leans forward.

'Look, Akkarat has some experience with these matters. The white shirts have created a number of enemies. And not just *farang.* All our project requires is a bit of help gathering momentum.' He takes a sip of his whiskey, considers the taste for a moment before setting the glass down. 'The consequences would be quite favorable for us if it succeeds.' He locks eyes with Anderson. 'Quite favorable for you. For your friends in the Midwest.'

'What do you get out of it?'

'Trade, of course.' Carlyle grins. 'If the Thais face outward instead of living in this absurd defensive crouch of theirs, my company expands. It's just good business. I can't imagine that your people enjoy cooling their heels on Koh Angrit, begging to be allowed to sell a few tons of U-Tex or SoyPRO to the Kingdom when there's a crop failure. You could have free trade, instead of sitting out on that quarantine island. I'd think that would be attractive to you. It certainly would benefit me.'

Anderson studies Carlyle, trying to decide how much to trust the man. For two years they have drunk together, have whored occasionally, have closed shipping contracts on a handshake, but Anderson knows only a little about him. The home office has a portfolio, but it's thin. Anderson mulls. The seedbank is out there, waiting. With a pliable government . . .

'Which generals are backing you?'

Carlyle laughs. 'If I told you that, you'd just think I was foolish and unable to keep secrets.'

The man is all talk, Anderson decides. He'll have to make sure Carlyle disappears, soon, quietly, before his cover gets blown. 'It sounds interesting. Maybe we should meet to talk a little more about our mutual goals.'

Carlyle opens his mouth to respond then pauses, studying Anderson. He smiles and shakes his head. 'Oh no. You don't believe me.' He shrugs. 'Fair enough. Just wait then. In two days time, I think you'll be more impressed. We'll talk then.' He looks significantly at

Anderson. 'And we'll talk at a place of my choosing.' He finishes his drink.

'Why wait? What's going to change between now and then?'

Carlyle settles his hat on his head and smiles. 'Everything, my dear *farang*. Everything.'

9

Emiko wakes to afternoon swelter. She stretches, breathing shallowly in the oven bake of her five-by.

There is a place for windups. The knowledge tingles within her. A reason to live.

She presses a hand up against the WeatherAll planks that divide her sleeping slot from the one above. Touching the knots. Thinking of the last time she felt so content. Remembering Japan and the luxuries that Gendo-sama bequeathed: her own flat; climate control that blew cool through humid summer days; *dangan* fish that glowed and changed colors like chameleons, iridescent and changeable dependent on their speed: blue slow fish, red fast ones. She used to tap the glass of their tank and watch them streak red through dark waters, their windup nature in brightest bloom.

She, too, used to glow brightly. She was built well. Trained well. Knew the ways of pillow companion, secretary, translator and observer, services for her master that she performed so admirably that he honored her like a dove, and released her into the bright blue arc of the sky. She had been so honored.

The WeatherAll knots stare down at her, the only decoration on the divider that separates her sleeping slot from the one above and keeps the garbage of her neighbors from raining down. Linseed reek billows off the wood, nauseating in the five-by's hot confines. In Japan there were rules about using such wood for human habitation. Here in the tower slums, no one cares.

Emiko's lungs burn. She breathes shallowly, listening to the grunt and snore of the other bodies. No sound filters down from the slot above. Puenthai must not be back. Otherwise, she would have suffered already, would have been kicked or fucked by now. It's not often that she survives a whole day without abuse. Puenthai is not yet home. Perhaps he is dead. The *fa' gan* fringe on his neck was certainly thick enough the last time she saw him.

She squirms out of her slot and straightens in the narrow gap between the five-by and the door. Stretches again, then reaches in and fumbles for her plastic bottle, yellowed and thinned with age. Drinks blood-warm water. She swallows convulsively, wishing she had ice.

Two flights up, a splintered door gives way and she spills out onto the roof. Sunlight and heat envelop her. Even with the sun hammering down, it is cooler than her five-by.

All around her, clotheslines draped with rustling *pha sin* and trousers rustle in the sea breeze. The sun is sinking, glistening from the tips of *wats* and *chedi*. The water of the *khlongs* and the Chao Phraya glistens. Kink-spring skiffs and trimaran clipper ships glide across red mirrors.

To the north, the distance is lost in the orange haze of dung burn and humidity, but somewhere out there, if the pale scarred *farang* is to be believed, windups dwell. Somewhere beyond the armies that war for shares of coal and jade and opium, her own lost tribe awaits her. She was never Japanese; she was only ever a windup. And now her true clan awaits her, if only she can find a way.

She stares north a moment longer, hungering, then goes to the bucket she stowed the night before. There is no water on the upper levels, no pressure to reach so high, and she cannot risk bathing at the public pumps – so every night she struggles up the stairs with her water bucket, and leaves it here in anticipation of the day.

In the privacy of the open air and the setting sun, she bathes. It is a ritual process, a careful cleansing. The bucket of water, a fingerling of soap. She squats beside the bucket and ladles the warm water over herself. It is a precise thing, a scripted act as deliberate as *Jo No Mai*, each move choreographed, a worship of scarcity.

She pours a ladleful over her head. Water courses down her face, runs over breasts and ribs and thighs, trickles onto hot concrete. Another ladleful, soaking her black hair, coursing down her spine and curling around her buttocks. Again a ladle of water, sheeting over her skin like mercury. And then the soap, rubbing it into her hair and then her skin, scouring herself of the previous night's insults until she wears a pale sheen of suds. And again the bucket and ladle, rinsing herself as carefully as with the first wetting.

Water sluices away soap and grime, even some of the shame comes with it. If she were to scrub for a thousand years she would not be clean, but she is too tired to care and she has grown accustomed to scars she cannot scour away. The sweat, the alcohol, the humid salt of semen and degradation, these she can cleanse. It is enough. She is too tired to scrub harder. Too hot and too tired, always.

At the end of her rinsing, she is happy to find a little water left in the bucket. She dips one ladleful and drinks it, gulping. And then in a wasteful, unrestrained gesture, she upends the bucket over her head in one glorious cathartic rush. In that moment, between the touch of the water, and the splash as it pools around her toes, she is clean.

*

Out on the streets, she tries to blend into the daylight street activity. Mizumi-sensei trained her to walk in certain ways, to accent and make beautiful the stutter motion of her body. But if Emiko is very careful, and fights her nature and training – if she wears *pha sin*, and does not swing her arms – she almost passes.

Along the sidewalks, seamstresses lounge beside treadle sewing machines, waiting for evening trade. Snack sellers stack the remains of their wares in tidy piles, awaiting the day's final shoppers. Night market food stalls are setting out little bamboo stools and tables in the street, the ritual encroachment on the thoroughfares that signals the end of day and the beginning of life in a tropic city.

Emiko tries not to stare; it's been a long time since she risked walking streets in daylight. When Raleigh acquired her five-by, he gave her strict instructions. He could not keep her in Ploenchit itself – even whores and pimps and drug addicts had limits – so he installed her in a slum where bribes were cheaper and the neighbors were not so picky about the neighboring offal. But his instructions were strict: walk only at night, keep to shadows, come directly to the club, and return directly home. Anything else and there was little hope of survival.

Her nape prickles as she makes her way through the daylit crowds. Most of these people will not care about her. The benefit of the daytime is that people are far too busy with their own lives to worry about a creature like her, even if they catch sight of her odd movements. In the deep night of green methane flicker, there are fewer eyes, but they are idle ones, high on *yaba* or *laolao*, eyes with the time and opportunity to pursue.

A woman selling Environment Ministry-certified sticks of sliced papaya watches her suspiciously. Emiko forces herself not to panic. She continues down the street with her mincing steps, trying to convince herself that she appears eccentric, rather than genetically transgressive. Her heart pounds against her ribs.

Too fast. Slow down. You have time. Not so much as you would like, but still, enough to ask questions. Slowly. Patiently. Do not betray yourself. Do not overheat.

Her palms are wet with sweat, the only part of her body that ever really feels cool. She keeps them open wide like fans, trying to absorb comfort. She pauses at a public pump to splash water on her skin and drink deep, glad that New People fear little in the way of bacterial or parasitic infection. She is an inhospitable host. That, at least, is benefit.

If she were not a New Person, she would simply strut into Hualamphong Railway Station, and purchase a ticket on a kink-spring train, ride it as far as the wastes of Chiang Mai, and then proceed into the wilderness. It would be easy. Instead she must be clever. The roads will be guarded. Anything that leads to the Northeast and the Mekong will be clogged with military personnel transferring between the eastern front and the capital. A New Person would excite attention, particularly given that New People military models sometimes fight on behalf of the Vietnamese.

But there is another way. From her time with Gendo-sama she remembers that much of the Kingdom's freight moves by river.

Emiko turns down Thanon Mongkut toward the docks and levees, and stops short. White shirts. She cringes against a wall as the pair stalks past. They don't even look at her – she blends if she does not move – but still, as soon as they are out of sight, she has the urge to scuttle back to her tower. Most of the white shirts there have been bribed. These ones ... She shivers.

At last, the *gaijin* warehouses and trading stations rise before her, the newly built commercial blocks. She makes her way up the seawall. At its top, the ocean spreads before her, bustling with clipper ships unloading, dock workers and coolies hauling freight, *mahout* coaxing megodonts to greater labor as pallets come off the clippers and are loaded on huge Laotian-rubber-wheeled wagons for transit to the warehouses. Reminders of her former life litter the view.

A smudge on the horizon marks the quarantine zone of Koh Angrit, where *gaijin* traders and agricultural executives squat amid stockpiles of calories, all of them waiting patiently for a crop failure or plague to beat aside the Kingdom's trade barriers. Gendo-sama once led her to that floating island of bamboo rafts and warehouses. Stood on its gently rolling decks and had her translate as he confidently sold the foreigners on advances in sailing technologies that would speed a shipment of patented SoyPRO around the world.

Emiko sighs and ducks under the draped lines of *saisin* that top the levee. The sacred thread runs down the seawall in both directions, disappearing into the distance. Every morning the monks of a different temple bless the thread, adding spiritual support to the physical defenses that push back the hungry sea.

In her former life, when Gendo-sama provided her with permits and indulgences to move inside the city with impunity, Emiko had the opportunity to see the yearly blessing ceremonies of the dikes and pumps and the *saisin* that connects it all. As the first monsoon rains poured down on the assembled people, Emiko watched Her Revered Majesty the Child Queen pull the levers that set the divine pumps roaring to life, her delicate form dwarfed by the apparatus that her ancestors had created. Monks chanted and stretched fresh *saisin* from the city pillar, the spiritual heart of Krung Thep, to all of the twelve coal-driven pumps that ringed the city, and then they had all prayed for the continued life of their fragile city.

Now, in the dry season, the *saisin* looks ragged and the pumps are largely silent. The floating docks and their barges and skiffs bob softly in red sunlight.

Emiko makes her way down into the bustle, watching faces, hoping to spy someone who seems kind. She watches people pass, keeping her body still so that she does not betray her nature. Finally steels herself. She calls out to a passing day laborer, '*Kathorh kha*. Please, *Khun*. Can you tell me where I might purchase ferry tickets north?'

The man is covered with the powder and sweat of his work but he smiles, friendly. 'How far north?'

She hazards a city name, unsure even if it will be close enough to the place that the *gaijin* has described. 'Phitsanulok?'

He makes a face. 'There's nothing going that far, not much past Ayutthaya. The rivers have gotten too low. Some people are using mulies to pull their way north, but that is all. Some kink-spring skiffs. And the war ...' He shrugs. 'If you need to go north, the roads will be dry for a while yet.'

She masks her disappointment and *wais* carefully. No river then. By road or nothing. If she could go by river, then she would also have a way to cool herself. By road ... she imagines the long distance through the tropic blaze of the dry season. Perhaps she should wait for the rainy season. With the monsoon, the temperatures will fall and the rivers rise ...

Emiko starts back over the seawall and down through the slums that house dock families and de-quarantined sailors on shore leave. By road then. It was foolish even for her to go looking. If she could get aboard a kink-spring train – but that would require permits. Many, many permits, just to get aboard. But if she could bribe someone, stow away ... She grimaces. All roads lead to Raleigh. She will have to speak with him. To beg the old crow for things he has no reason to give.

A man with dragon tattoos on his stomach and a *takraw* ball tattooed on his shoulder gawks at her as she walks past. '*Heechy-keechy*,' he murmurs.

Emiko doesn't slow, doesn't turn at the words, but her skin prickles.

The man follows her. '*Heechy-keechy*,' he says again.

She glances back. His face is unfriendly. He's missing a hand as well, she's horrified to notice. He reaches out with the stump and prods her shoulder. She jerks away, stutter-stop reaction, betraying her nature. He smiles, and his teeth are black with betel nut.

Emiko turns down a *soi*, hoping to escape his attention. Again he calls after her. '*Heechy-keechy*.'

Emiko ducks into another winding squeezeway, breaks into a faster walk. Her body warms. Her hands become slick with sweat. She pants rapidly, trying to expel the increasing heat. Still the man follows. He doesn't call out again but she hears his footsteps. She makes another turn. Cheshires scatter before her, shimmers of light flushed like cockroaches. If only she could evaporate as they do, fade against a wall and let this man slide past.

'Where are you going, windup?' the man calls. 'I just want to get a look at you.'

If she were still with Gendo-sama she would face this man. Would stand confident, protected by import stamps and owner-ship permits and consulates and the awful threat of her master's retribution. A piece of property, true, but respected nonetheless. She could even go to a white shirt or the police for protection. With stamps and a passport, she was not a transgression against niche and nature, but an exquisite valued object.

The alley opens onto a new street, full of *gaijin* warehouses and trading fronts, but the man grabs her arm before she can reach it. She's hot. Already flushed with her rising panic. She stares at the street longingly but it is all shacks and dry goods and a few *gaijin*, who will be no help for her. Grahamites are the last people she wishes to encounter.

The man drags her back into the alley. 'Where do you think you're going, windup?'

His eyes are bright and hard. He's chewing something – an amphetamine stick. *Yaba.* Coolie laborers use them to keep working, to burn calories that they do not have. His eyes sparkle as he grips her wrist. He pulls her deeper into the alley, out of sight. She's too hot to run. There is nowhere to go, even if she did.

'Stand against the wall.' he says. 'No.' He shoves her around. 'Don't look at me.'

'Please.'

A knife appears in his good hand, glinting. 'Shut up,' he says. 'Stay there.'

His voice has the power of command, and despite her better instincts she finds herself obeying. 'Please. Just let me go,' she whispers.

'I fought your kind. In the jungles in the north. Windups everywhere. *Heechy-keechy* soldiers.'

'I am not that kind.' She whispers. 'Not military.'

'Japanese, same as you. I lost a hand because of your kind. And a lot of good friends.' He shows her the stump where his hand is missing, pushes it against her cheek. His breath gusts hot on her nape as he wraps his arm around her neck, pressing the knife to her jugular. Indenting the skin.

'Please. Just let me go.' She presses back against his crotch. 'I'll do anything.'

'You think I'd soil myself that way?' He shoves her hard against the wall, making her cry out. 'With an animal like you?' A pause, then. 'Get down on your knees.'

Out on the street, cycle rickshaws clatter over cobbles. People call out, asking about the price of hemp rope and whether anyone

knows the time of the Lumphini *muay thai* fight. The knife hooks
around her neck again, finds her pulse with its point. 'I saw my
friends all die in the forests because of Japanese windups.'

She swallows, and repeats softly, 'I am not that kind.'

He laughs. 'Of course not. You're some other creature. Another
one of their devils like they keep in their shipyard across the river.
Our people are starving, and your kind take their rice.'

The blade presses against her throat. He will kill her. She is sure
of it. His hatred is great, and she is nothing but trash. He is high
and angry and dangerous and she is nothing. Even Gendo-sama
couldn't have protected her from this. She swallows, feeling the
blade press against her Adam's apple.

*Is this how you will die? Is this what you were meant for? To
simply be bled out like a pig?*

A spark of rage flickers, an antidote to despair.

*Will you not even try to survive? Did the scientists make you too
stupid even to consider fighting for your own life?*

Emiko closes her eyes and prays to Mizuko Jizo Bodhisattva,
and then the *bakeneko* cheshire spirit for good measure. She takes
a breath, and then with all her strength she slams her hand against
the knife. The blade slices past her neck, a searing line.

'*Arai wa?!*' the man shouts.

Emiko shoves hard against him and ducks under his flailing
knife. Behind her, she hears a grunt and thud as she bolts for the
street. She doesn't look back. She plunges into the street, not caring
that she shows herself as a windup, not caring that in running she
will burn up and die. She runs, determined only to escape the
demon behind her. She will burn, but she will not die passive like
some pig led to slaughter.

She flies down the street, dodging pyramids of durian and hur-
dling over coiled hemp ropes. This suicidal flight is pointless, yet
she will not stop. She shoves aside a *gaijin* haggling over burlap

sacks of local U-Tex rice. He jerks away, crying out in alarm as she flashes past.

All around, the traffic of the street seems to have slowed to a crawl. Emiko weaves under the bamboo scaffolding of a construction site. Running is strangely easy. People move as if they're suspended in honey. Only she is moving. When she glances behind her, she sees that her pursuer has fallen far behind. He's astonishingly slow. Amazing that she even feared him. She laughs at the absurdity of this suspended world –

She slams into a laborer and goes sprawling, taking him down as well. The man shouts, '*Arai wa!* Watch where you're going!'

Emiko forces herself up to her knees, hands numb with abrasions. She tries to stand but the world tilts, blurry. She collapses. Pushes upright again, drunken, overwhelmed by the furnace heat within her. The ground tilts and rotates, but she manages to stand. Leans against a sun-baked wall as the man she hit shouts at her. His rage washes over her, meaningless. Darkness and heat are closing in on her. She's burning up.

Out in the street, in the tangle of mulie carts and bicycles, she catches sight of a *gaijin* face. She blinks away the closing darkness, stumbles forward a step. Is she mad? Does the *bakeneko* cheshire toy with her? She clutches the shoulder of the man who is shouting at her, staring into the traffic, searching to confirm what her boiling brain has hallucinated. The laborer cries out and recoils from her touch, but she barely notices.

Another flash of the face in the traffic. It's the *gaijin*, the scarred pale one from Raleigh's place. The one who told her to go north. His rickshaw shows briefly before disappearing behind a megodont. And then he's there again, on the other side, looking toward her. Their eyes lock. The same man. She's sure of it.

'Grab her! Don't let that *heechy-keechy* get away!'

Her attacker, shouting and waving his knife as he clambers

through bamboo scaffolding. She's amazed that he's so slow, so much slower than she would have expected. She watches, puzzled. Perhaps he is also crippled from his time in the war? But no, his gait is correct, it's just that everything around her is slow: the people, the traffic. Odd. Surreal and slow.

The laborer seizes her. Emiko lets herself be dragged, scanning the traffic for another glimpse of the *gaijin*. Did she hallucinate?

There! The *gaijin* again. Emiko throws off the laborer's grasp and lunges into traffic. With the last of her energy, she ducks under the belly of a megodont, nearly crashing into its great columnar legs and then she's on the other side, pacing the *gaijin's* rickshaw, reaching up to him like a beggar . . .

He observes her with cold eyes, completely detached. She stumbles and grabs at the rickshaw to steady herself, knowing he will shove her back. She is nothing but a windup. She was a fool. She was stupid to hope that he would see her as a person, a woman, as anything other than offal.

Abruptly he grabs her hand and pulls her aboard. The *gaijin* shouts at his driver to ride, to ride – *gan cui chi che, kuai kuai kuai!* – to hurry up. He spews words in three different languages and then they are accelerating, but slowly.

Her attacker leaps onto the rickshaw. He slashes her shoulder. Emiko watches as her blood sprays the seat. Jewel droplets suspended in sunlight. He raises the knife again. She tries to lift a hand to defend herself, to fight him off, but she's too tired. She's limp with exhaustion and heat. The man slashes again, screaming.

Emiko watches the knife descend, a movement as slow as honey poured in winter. So slow. So far away. Her flesh tears. Heat blur and exhaustion. She's fading. The knife descends again.

Suddenly the gaijin lunges between them. A spring gun gleams in his hand. Emiko watches, vaguely intrigued that the man carries a weapon, but the fight between the gaijin and the yaba addict is so very small and far away. So very very dark ... Heat swallows her.

10

The windup girl does nothing to defend herself. She cries out, but barely flinches as the knife bites. '*Bai!*' Anderson shouts to Lao Gu. '*Kuai kuai kuai!*'

He shoves the attacker away as the cycle lurches forward. The Thai man hacks clumsily at Anderson, then goes after the windup girl again, slashing. She does nothing to escape. Blood spatters. Anderson yanks a spring pistol from beneath his shirt and shoves it into the man's face. The man's eyes widen.

He drops off the rickshaw, running for cover. Anderson follows him with the barrel, trying to decide if he should put a disk in the man's head or let him escape, but the man ducks behind a megodont wagon, robbing him of the decision.

'Goddamnit.' Anderson peers through the traffic, making sure the man is truly gone, then shoves his pistol back under his shirt. He turns to the slumped girl. 'You're safe now.'

The windup lies inert, clothes slashed and disarrayed, eyes closed, panting rapidly. When he presses his palm to her flushed forehead, she flinches and her eyelids flutter. Her skin is scalding. Listless black eyes stare up at him. 'Please,' she murmurs.

The heat in her skin is overwhelming. She's dying. Anderson yanks her jacket open, trying to vent her. She's burning up, overheated by her flight and poor genetic design. Absurd that anyone would do this to a creature, hobble it so.

He shouts over his shoulder, 'Lao Gu! Go to the levees!' Lao Gu glances back, uncomprehending. '*Shui*! Water! *Nam*! The ocean, damn it!' Anderson motions toward the dike walls. 'Quickly! *Kuai, kuai kuai!*'

Lao Gu nods sharply. He stands on his pedals and accelerates again, forcing the bike through the clotted traffic, calling out warnings and curses at obstructing pedestrians and draft animals. Anderson fans the windup girl with his hat.

At the levee walls, Anderson throws the windup girl over his shoulder and hauls her up uneven stairs. Guardian *naga* flank the stairs, their long undulating snake bodies guiding him upward. Their faces watch impassive as he staggers higher. Sweat drips in his eyes. The windup is a furnace against his skin.

He tops the levee. Red sun burns against his face, silhouetting drowned Thonburi across the waters. The sun is almost as hot as the body draped over his shoulder. He stumbles down the other side of the embankment and heaves the girl into the sea. The splash soaks him with saltwater.

She sinks like a stone. Anderson gasps and lunges after her sinking form. *You fool. You stupid fool.* He catches a limp arm and drags her body up from the depths. Holds her so that her face floats above the waves, bracing himself to keep her from sinking again. Her skin burns. He half expects the sea to boil around her. Her black hair fans out like a net in the lapping waves. She dangles in his grasp. Lao Gu jostles down beside him. Anderson waves him over. 'Here. Hold her.'

Lao Gu hesitates.

'Hold her, damn it. *Zhua ta.*'

Reluctantly, Lao Gu slides his hands under her arms. Anderson touches her neck, feeling for a pulse. Is her brain already cooked? He could be trying to revive a vegetable.

The windup's pulse whirs like a hummingbird's, faster than any creature her size should run. Anderson leans down to listen to her breathing.

Her eyes snap open. He jerks away. She thrashes and Lao Gu loses his grip. She disappears under water.

'No!' Anderson lunges after her.

She surfaces again, thrashing and coughing and reaching for him. Her hand locks on his and he pulls her to the bank. Her clothes swirl about her like tangled seaweed and her black hair glistens like silk. She stares up at Anderson with dark eyes. Her skin is suddenly blessedly cool.

'Why did you help me?'

Methane lamps flicker on the streets, turning the city ethereal shades of green. Darkness has fallen and the lamp-posts hiss against the blackness. Humidity reflects on cobbles and concrete, gleams on people's skin as they lean close around candles in the night markets.

The windup girl asks again. 'Why?'

Anderson shrugs, glad the darkness hides his expression. He doesn't have a good answer himself. If her attacker complains of a *farang* and a windup girl, it will trigger questions and attract white shirts to him. A foolish risk, considering how exposed he already finds himself. He's far too easy to describe, and it's not far from where he found the girl to Sir Francis', and from there to more uncomfortable questions.

He forces down his paranoia. He's as bad as Hock Seng. The *nak leng* was obviously high on *yaba*. He won't go to the white shirts. He'll slink away and lick his wounds.

Still, it was foolish.

When she fainted in the rickshaw he was sure that she was about to die, and a part of him had been glad. Relieved that he could take back that moment when he recognized her, and against all his training, tied his fate to hers.

He glances over at her. Her skin has lost its terrifying flush and furnace heat. She holds the remnants of slashed clothes around her, keeping her modesty. It's pitiable, really, that a creature so utterly owned clings to modesty.

'Why?' she asks again.

He shrugs again. 'You needed help.'

'No one helps a windup.' Her voice is flat. 'You are a fool.' She pushes damp hair away from her face. A surreal stutter-stop motion, the genetic bits of her unkinking. Her smooth skin shines between the edges of her slashed blouse, the gentle promise of her breasts. What would she feel like? Her skin gleams, smooth and inviting.

She catches him staring. 'Do you wish to use me?'

'No.' he looks away, uneasy. 'It's not necessary.'

'I would not fight you,' she says.

Anderson feels a sudden revulsion at the acquiescence in her voice. On another day, at another time, he probably would have taken her for the novelty. Thought nothing of it. But the fact that she expects so little fills him with distaste. He forces a smile. 'Thank you. No.'

She nods shortly. Looks out again at the humid night and the green glow of the street lamps. It's impossible to say if she is grateful or surprised, or if his decision even matters to her. However her mask might have slipped in the heat of terror and relief of escape, her thoughts are carefully locked away now.

'Is there someplace I should take you?'

She shrugs. 'Raleigh. He is the only one who will keep me.'

'But he wasn't the first, was he? You weren't always . . .' He trails off. There's no polite word and, looking at the girl, he doesn't have the appetite to call her a toy.

She glances over at him, then out again at the passing city. Gas lights puddle the street with low green pockets of phosphor, separated by deep canyons of shadow. They pass under a lamp and Anderson catches her face, dimly illuminated, humidity-sheened and pensive, before it disappears again in darkness.

'No. I was not always this way. Not . . .' she trails off. 'Not like this.' She falls quiet, thoughtful. 'Mishimoto employed me. I had . . .' she shrugs, 'an owner. An owner at the company. I was owned. Gen— my owner acquired a temporary foreign business exemption to bring me to the Kingdom. A ninety-day permit. Extendible by palace waiver because of the Japanese Friendship. I was his Personal Secretary: translation, office management and . . . companion.' Another shrug, more felt than seen. 'But it is expensive to return to Japan. A dirigible ticket for a New Person is the same as for your kind. My owner concluded that leaving his secretary in Bangkok was more economical. When his assignment here ended, he decided to upgrade new in Osaka.'

'Jesus and Noah.'

She shrugs. 'I was given my final pay at the anchor pad and he went away. Up and away.'

'And now Raleigh?' he asks.

Again the shrug. 'No Thai wants a New Person for secretary, or translation. In Japan, okay. Common, even. Too few babies born, too much working needed. Here . . .' She shakes her head. 'Calorie markets are controlled. Everyone is jealous for U-Tex. Everyone protects their rice. Raleigh does not care. Raleigh . . . likes novelty.'

The clouded scent of fish frying washes over them, greasy and cloying. A night market, full of people dining by candlelight, hunched over noodles and skewers of octopus and plates of *laap*. Anderson stifles an urge to raise the rickshaw's rain hood and close the privacy curtain, to hide the evidence of her company. Woks flame brightly with the telltale green sparkles of Environment

Ministry-taxed methane. The sweat sheen on the people's dark skins is barely lit. At their feet, cheshires circle, alert for charity scraps and opportunities for theft.

A cheshire shadow bleeds across the darkness, causing Lao Gu to swerve. He curses softly in his own language. Emiko laughs, a small surprised sound as she claps her hands in delight. Lao Gu glares back at her.

'You like cheshires?' Anderson asks.

Emiko looks at him in surprise. 'You do not?'

'Back home, we can't kill them fast enough,' he says. 'Even Grahamites offer blue bills for their skins. Probably the only thing they've ever done that I agreed with.'

'Mmm, yes.' Emiko's brow wrinkles thoughtfully. 'They are too much improved for this world, I think. A natural bird has so little chance, now.' She smiles slightly. 'Just think if they had made New People first.'

Is it mischief in her eyes? Or melancholy?

'What do you think would have happened?' Anderson asks.

Emiko doesn't meet his gaze, looks out instead at the circling cats amongst the diners. 'Generippers learned too much from cheshires.'

She doesn't say anything else, but Anderson can guess what's in her mind. If her kind had come first, before the generippers knew better, she would not have been made sterile. She would not have the signature tick-tock motions that make her so physically obvious. She might have even been designed as well as the military windups now operating in Vietnam – deadly and fearless. Without the lesson of the cheshires, Emiko might have had the opportunity to supplant the human species entirely with her own improved version. Instead, she is a genetic dead end. Doomed to a single life cycle, just like SoyPRO and TotalNutrient Wheat.

Another shadow cat bolts across the street, shimmering and

shading through darkness. A high-tech homage to Lewis Carroll, a few dirigible and clipper ship rides, and suddenly entire classes of animals are wiped out, unequipped to fight an invisible threat.

'We would have realized our mistake,' Anderson observes.

'Yes. Of course. But perhaps not soon enough.' She changes the subject abruptly. Nods at a temple rising against the night skyline. 'It's very pretty, yes? You like their temples?'

Anderson wonders if she has changed the subject to avoid conflict and argument, or if she is actually afraid that he will successfully refute her fantasy. He studies the rising *chedi* and *bot* of the temple. 'It's a lot nicer than what the Grahamites are building back home.'

'Grahamites.' She makes a face. 'So concerned with niche and nature. So focused on their Noah's ark, after the flood has already happened.'

Anderson thinks of Hagg, sweating and distressed at the destruction caused by ivory beetle. 'If they could, they'd keep us all on our own continents.'

'It is impossible, I think. People like to expand. To fill new niches.'

The temple's golden filigree shines dully under the moon. The world truly is shrinking again. A few dirigible and clipper rides and Anderson clatters through darkened streets on the far side of the planet. It's astounding. In his grandparents' time, even the commute between an old Expansion suburb and a city center was impossible. His grandparents used to tell stories of exploring abandoned suburbs, scavenging for the scrap and leavings of whole sprawling neighborhoods that were destroyed in the petroleum Contraction. To travel ten miles had been a great journey for them, and now look at him . . .

Ahead of them, white uniforms materialize at the mouth of an alley.

Emiko blanches and leans close. 'Hold me.'

Anderson tries to shake her off, but she clings. The white shirts have stopped, are watching them approach. The windup clings more tightly. Anderson fights an urge to shove her from the rickshaw and flee. This is the last thing he needs.

She whispers, 'I am against quarantine now, like Nippon genehack weevil. If they see my movement, they will know. They will mulch me.' She nestles close. 'I am sorry. Please.' Her eyes beg.

In a sudden rush of pity he wraps his arms around her, enfolding her in whatever protection a calorie man can offer a piece of illegal Japanese trash. The Ministry men call out to them, smiling. Anderson smiles back and gives a bob of the head, even as his skin prickles. The white shirts' eyes linger. One of them smiles and says something to the other as he twirls the baton that dangles from his wrist. Emiko shivers uncontrollably beside Anderson, her smile a forced mask. Anderson pulls her closer.

Please don't ask for a bribe. Not this time. Please.

They slide past.

Behind them, the white shirts start laughing, either about the *farang* and the girl clutched together or about something else completely unrelated and it doesn't matter really because they are disappearing into the distance and he and Emiko are safe again.

She draws away, shaking. 'Thank you,' she whispers. 'I was careless to come out. Stupid.' She pushes her hair away from her face and looks back. The Ministry men are quickly receding. Her fists clench. 'Stupid girl,' she murmurs. 'You are not a cheshire who disappears as you please.' She shakes her head, angry, driving home her own lesson. 'Stupid. Stupid. Stupid.'

Anderson watches, transfixed. Emiko is adapted for a different sort of world, not this brutal sweltering place. The city will swallow her eventually. It's obvious.

She becomes aware of his gaze. Shares a small melancholy smile. 'Nothing lasts forever, I think.'

'No.' Anderson's throat is tight.

They stare at one another. Her blouse has fallen open again, showing the line of her throat, the inner curve of her breasts. She doesn't move to hide herself, just looks back at him, solemn. Is it deliberate? Does she mean to encourage him? Or is it simply her nature to entice? Perhaps she cannot help herself at all. A set of instincts as ingrained in her DNA as the cheshire's clever stalking of birds. Anderson leans close, unsure.

Emiko doesn't pull away, moves instead to meet him. Her lips are soft. Anderson runs his hand up her hip, pushes her blouse open and quests inside. She sighs and presses closer, her lips opening to him. Does she wish this? Or only acquiesce? Is she even capable of refusing? Her breasts press against him. Her hands slip down his body. He's shaking. Trembling like a sixteen-year-old boy. Did the geneticists embed her DNA with pheromones? Her body is intoxicating.

Mindless of the street, of Lao Gu, of everything, he pulls her to him, running his hand up to cup her breast, to hold her perfect flesh.

The windup girl's heart speeds like a hummingbird's under his palm.

11

Jaidee has a certain respect for the Chaozhou Chinese. Their factories are large and well-run. They have generations rooted in the Kingdom, and they are intensely loyal to Her Majesty the Child Queen. They are utterly unlike the pathetic Chinese refugees who have flooded in from Malaya, fleeing to his country in hopes of succor after they alienated the natives of their own. If the Malayan Chinese had been half as clever as the Chaozhou, they would have converted to Islam generations ago, and woven themselves fully into the tapestry of that society.

Instead, the Chinese of Malacca and Penang and the Western Coast arrogantly held themselves apart, thinking the rising tide of fundamentalism would not affect them. And now they come begging to the Kingdom, hoping that their Chaozhou cousins will aid them when they were not clever enough to help themselves.

The Chaozhou are smart, where the Malayan Chinese are stupid. They are practically Thai themselves. They speak Thai. They took Thai names. They may have Chinese roots somewhere in their distant past, but they are Thai. And they are loyal. Which, when Jaidee thinks about it, is more than can be said about some of his own race, certainly more than can be said of Akkarat and his brood at the Trade Ministry.

So Jaidee feels a certain sympathy when a Chaozhou business-man in a long white shirt, loose cotton trousers and sandals strides back and forth in front of him on the factory floor, complaining that his factory has been shut down because some coal ration has been exceeded, when he paid every white shirt who came through his door, and that Jaidee has no right – *no right* – to shut down the entire factory.

Jaidee even has sympathy when the man calls him a turtle's egg – which is certainly an annoying thing to hear, knowing that it is a terrible insult in Chinese. Yet still, he remains tolerant of the emotional explosions on the part of this businessman. It's in the Chinese nature to be a bit hot-hearted. They are given to explo-sions of emotion that a Thai would never indulge in.

All in all, Jaidee has sympathy for the man.

But he doesn't have sympathy for a man who shoves a finger into his chest repeatedly while he curses, and so Jaidee is sitting atop that man's chest now – with a black baton over his wind-pipe – explaining the finer points of respect due a white shirt.

'You seem to have mistaken me for another Ministry man,' Jaidee observes.

The man gurgles and tries to get free, but the baton crushing his throat prevents him. Jaidee watches him carefully. 'You of course understand that we have coal rationing because we are a city under-water. Your carbon allocation was exceeded many months ago.'

'Ghghhaha.'

Jaidee considers the response. Shakes his head sadly. 'No. I think that we cannot allow it to continue. King Rama XII decreed, and Her Royal Majesty the Child Queen now supports that we shall never abandon Krung Thep to the invasions of the rising sea. We will not flee from our City of Divine Beings the way the cowards of Ayutthaya fled from the Burmese. The ocean is not some marching army. Once we accede to the waters, we will never again throw it out.' He regards the sweating Chinese man. 'And so we must all do our part. We must all fight together, like the villagers of Bang Rajan, to keep this invader from our streets, don't you think?'

'Gghhghghhghhhh . . .'

'Good.' Jaidee smiles. 'I'm glad we're making progress.'

Someone clears his throat.

Jaidee looks up, stifling his annoyance. 'Yes?'

A young private in new whites stands respectfully, waiting. '*Khun* Jaidee' He *wais*, lowering his head to his pressed palms. Holds the pose. 'I am very sorry for my interruption.'

'Yes?'

'*Chao Khun* General Pracha requests your presence.'

'I'm busy,' Jaidee says. 'Our friend here finally seems willing to communicate with a cool heart and a reasonable demeanor.' He smiles kindly down at the businessman.

The boy says, 'I was to tell you . . . I was told to, to . . .'

'Go ahead.'

'To tell you that you should get your, your – so sorry – 'glory-seeking ass' – so sorry – back to the Ministry. Immediately if not before.' He winces at the words. 'If you have no cycle you were supposed to take mine.'

Jaidee grimaces. 'Ah. Yes. Well then.' He gets up off the businessman. Nods to Kanya. 'Lieutenant? Perhaps you can reason with our friend here?'

Kanya makes a face of puzzlement. 'Is something wrong?'

'It seems Pracha is finally ready to rant and rave at me.'

'Should I come with you?' Kanya glances at the businessman. 'This lizard can wait for another day.'

Jaidee grins at her concern. 'Don't worry about me. Finish here. I'll let you know whether we're being exiled south to guard yellow card internments for the rest of our careers when you get back.'

As they head for the door, the businessman musters new bravery. 'I'll have your head for this, *heeya!*'

The sound of Kanya's club connecting and a yelp are the last things Jaidee hears as he exits the factory.

Outside, the sun glares down. He's already sweating from the exertion of working on the businessman, and the sun burns uncomfortably. He stands under the shade of a coconut palm until the messenger can bring the bike around.

The boy eyes Jaidee's sweating face with concern. 'You wish to rest?'

Jaidee laughs. 'Don't worry about me, I'm just getting old. That *heeya* was a troublesome one, and I'm not the fighter I used to be. In the cool season I wouldn't be sweating so.'

'You won a lot of fights.'

'Some.' Jaidee grins. 'And I trained in weather hotter than this.'

'Your lieutenant could do such work,' the boy says. 'No need for you to work so hard.'

Jaidee wipes his brow and shakes his head. 'And then what would my men think? That I'm lazy.'

The boy gasps. 'No one would think such a thing of you. Never!'

'When you're a captain, you'll understand better.' Jaidee smiles indulgently. 'Men are loyal when you lead from the front. I won't have a man wasting his time winding a crank fan for me, or waving a palm frond just to keep me comfortable like those *heeya* in the Trade Ministry. I may lead, but we are all brothers. When you're a captain, promise me you'll do the same.'

The boy's eyes shine. He *wais* again. 'Yes, *Khun.* I won't forget. Thank you!'

'Good boy.' Jaidee swings his leg over the boy's bike. 'When Lieutenant Kanya is finished here, she'll give you a ride back on our tandem.'

He steers out into traffic. In the hot season, without rain, not many except the insane or the motivated are out in the direct heat, but covered arches and paths hide markets full of vegetables and cooking implements and clothing.

At Thanon Na Phralan, Jaidee takes his hands off the handlebars to *wai* to the City Pillar Shrine as he passes, whispering a prayer for the safety of the spiritual heart of Bangkok. It is the place where King Rama XII first announced that they would not abandon the city to the rising seas. Now, the sound of monks chanting for the city's survival filters out onto the street, filling Jaidee with a sense of peace. He raises his hands to his forehead three times, one of a river of other riders who all do the same.

Fifteen minutes later, the Environment Ministry appears, a series of buildings, red-tiled, with steeply sloping roofs peering out of bamboo thickets and teak and rain trees. High white walls and Garuda and Singha images guard the Ministry's perimeter, stained with old rain marks and fringed with growing ferns and mosses.

Jaidee has seen the compound from the air, one of a handful taken up for a dirigible overflight of the city when Chaiyanuchit still ran the Ministry and white shirt influence was absolute, when the plagues that swept the earth were killing crops at such a fantastic rate that no one knew if anything at all would survive.

Chaiyanuchit remembered the beginning of the plagues. Not many could claim that. And when Jaidee was just a young draftee, he was lucky enough to work in the man's office, bringing dispatches.

Chaiyanuchit understood what was at stake, and what had to be done. When the borders needed closing, when ministries needed isolating, when Phuket and Chiang Mai needed razing, he did not hesitate. When jungle blooms exploded in the north, he burned and burned and burned, and when he took to the sky in His Majesty the King's dirigible, Jaidee was blessed to ride with him.

By then, they were only mopping up. AgriGen and PurCal and

the rest were shipping their plague-resistant seeds and demanding exorbitant profits, and patriotic generippers were already working to crack the code of the calorie companies' products, fighting to keep the Kingdom fed as Burma and the Vietnamese and the Khmers all fell. AgriGen and its ilk were threatening embargo over intellectual property infringement, but the Thai Kingdom was still alive. Against all odds, they were alive. As others were crushed under the calorie companies' heels, the Kingdom stood strong.

Embargo! Chaiyanuchit had laughed. *Embargo is precisely what we want! We do not wish to interact with their outside world at all.*

And so the walls had gone up – those that the oil collapse had not already created, those that had not been raised against civil war and starving refugees – a final set of barriers to protect the Kingdom from the onslaughts of the outside world.

As a young inductee Jaidee had been astounded at the hive of activity that was the Environment Ministry. White shirts rushing from office to street as they tried to maintain tabs on thousands of hazards. In no other ministry was the sense of urgency so acute. Plagues waited for no one. A single genehack weevil found in an outlying district meant a response time counted in hours, white shirts on a kink-spring train rushing across the countryside to the epicenter.

And at every turn the Ministry's purview was expanding. The plagues were but the latest insult to the Kingdom's survival. First came the rising sea levels, the need to construct the dikes and levees. And then came the oversight of power contracts and trading in pollution credits and climate infractions. The white shirts took over the licensing of methane capture and production. Then there was the monitoring of fishery health and toxin accumulations in the Kingdom's final bastion of calorie support (a blessing that the *farang* calorie companies thought as land-locked people and had only desultorily attacked fishing stocks). And there was the tracking of human health and viruses and bacteria: H7V9; cibiscoscosis111.b, c, d; *fa' gan* fringe; bitter water mussels, and their viral mutations that jumped so easily from saltwater to dry land; blister rust ... There was no end to the duties of the Ministry.

Jaidee passes a woman selling bananas. He can't resist hopping off his bike to buy one. It's a new varietal from the Ministry's rapid prototyping unit. Fast growing, resistant to *makmak* mites with their tiny black eggs that sicken banana flowers before they can hope to grow. He peels the banana and eats it greedily as he pushes his bike along, wishing he could take the time to have a real snack. He discards the peel beside the bulk of a rain tree.

All life produces waste. The act of living produces costs, hazards and disposal questions, and so the Ministry has found itself in the center of all life, mitigating, guiding and policing the detritus of the average person along with investigating the infractions of the greedy and short-sighted, the ones who wish to make quick profits and trade on others' lives for it.

The symbol for the Environment Ministry is the eye of a tortoise, for the long view – the understanding that nothing comes cheap or quickly without a hidden cost. And if others call them the Turtle Ministry, and if the Chaozhou Chinese now curse white shirts as turtle's eggs because they are not allowed to manufacture as many kink-spring scooters as they would like, so be it. If the *farang* make fun of the tortoise for its slow pace, so be it. The Environment Ministry has ensured that the Kingdom endures, and Jaidee can only stand in awe of its past glories.

And yet, when Jaidee climbs off his bicycle outside the Ministry gate, a man glares at him and a woman turns away. Even just outside their own compound – or perhaps particularly there – the people he protects turn away from him.

Jaidee grimaces and wheels his cycle past the guards.

The compound is still a hive of activity, and yet it is so different from when he first joined. There is mold on the walls and chunks of the edifice are cracking under the pressure of vines. An old *bo* tree leans against a wall, rotting, underlining their failures. It has lain so for ten years, rotting. Unremarked amongst the other things that have also died. There is an air of wreckage to the place, of jungle attempting to reclaim what was carved from it. If the vines were not cleared from the paths, the Ministry would disappear entirely. In a different time, when the the Ministry was a hero of the people, it was different. Then, people genuflected before Ministry officers, three times *khrabbed* to the ground as though they were monks themselves, their white uniforms inspiring respect and adoration. Now Jaidee watches civilians flinch as he walks past. Flinch and run.

He is a bully, he thinks sourly. Nothing but a bully walking amongst water buffalo, and though he tries to herd them with kindness, again and again, he finds himself using the whip of fear. The whole Ministry is the same – at least, those who still understand the dangers that they face, who still believe in the bright white line of protection that must be maintained.

I am a bully.

He sighs and parks the cycle in front of the administrative offices, which are desperately in need of a whitewashing that the shrinking budget cannot finance. Jaidee eyes the building, wondering if the Ministry has come to crisis thanks to overreaching, or because of its phenomenal success. People have lost their fear of the outside world. Environment's budget shrinks yearly while that of Trade increases.

Jaidee finds a seat outside the general's office. White shirt officers walk past, carefully ignoring him. That he is waiting in front of Pracha's office should fill him with some satisfaction. It isn't often that he is called before a man of rank. He's done something right, for once. A young man approaches hesitantly. *Wais.*

'*Khun* Jaidee?'

At Jaidee's nod, the young man breaks into a grin. His hair is cropped close and his eyebrows are only slight shadows; he has just come out of the monastery.

'*Khun*, I hoped it was you.' He hesitates, then holds out a small card. It is painted in the old Sukhothai-style and depicts a young man in combat, blood on his face, driving an opponent down into the ring. His features are stylized, but Jaidee can't help smiling at the sight of it.

'Where did you get this?'

'I was at the fight, *Khun*. In the village. I was only this big—' he holds his hand up to his waist '—only like this, perhaps. Maybe smaller.' He laughs self-consciously. 'You made me want to be a fighter. When Dithakar knocked you down and your blood was everywhere, I thought you were finished. I didn't think you were big enough to take him. He had muscles . . .' he trails off.

'I remember. It was a good fight.'

The youth grins. 'Yes, *Khun*. Fabulous. I thought I wanted to be a fighter, too.'

'And now look at you.'

The boy runs his hand over his close-cropped hair. 'Ah. Well. Fighting is harder than I thought . . . but . . .' He pauses. 'Would you sign it? The card? Please. I would like to give it to my father. He still speaks highly of your fights.'

Jaidee smiles and signs. 'Dithakar was not the most clever fighter I ever faced, but he was strong. I wish all my fights were so clear-cut.'

'Captain Jaidee,' a voice interrupts. 'If you are quite finished with your fans.'

The young man *wais* and flees. Jaidee watches him run and thinks that perhaps not all of the younger generation is a waste. Perhaps . . . Jaidee turns to face the general. 'He is just a boy.'

Pracha glowers at Jaidee. Jaidee grins. 'And it's hardly my fault that I was a good fighter. The Ministry was my sponsor for those years. I think you won quite a lot of money and recruits because of me, *Khun* General, sir.'

'Don't give me your 'General' nonsense. We've known each other too long for that. Get in here.'

'Yes, sir.'

Pracha grimaces and waves Jaidee into the office. 'In!'

Pracha closes the door and goes to sit behind the expanse of his mahogany desk. Overhead, a crank fan beats desultorily at the air. The room is large, with shuttered windows open to allow light but little direct sun. The slits of the windows look out onto the Ministry's ragged grounds. On one wall are various paintings and photographs, including one with Pracha's graduating class of ministry cadets along with another of Chaiyanuchit, founder of their modern ministry. Another of Her Royal Majesty the Child Queen, looking tiny and terrifyingly vulnerable seated on her throne, and in a corner, a small shrine to Buddha, Phra Pikanet and Seub Nakhasathien. Incense and marigolds drape the shrine.

Jaidee *wais* the shrine then finds himself a seat in a rattan chair across from Pracha. 'Where did you get that class photo?'

'What?' Pracha looks back. 'Ah. We were young, then, weren't we? I found it in my mother's belongings. She had it all these years, tucked away in a closet. Who would have guessed the old lady was so sentimental?'

'It's a nice thing to see.'

'You overstepped yourself at the anchor pads.'

Jaidee returns his attention to Pracha. Whisper sheets lie scattered on the desk, rustling under the breeze of the crank fan: *Thai Rath. Kom Chad Luek. Phuchatkan Rai Wan.* Many of them with photos of Jaidee on the cover. 'The newspapers don't think so.'

Pracha scowls. He shoves the papers into a bin for composting.

'The papers love a hero. It sells copies. Don't believe these people who call you a tiger for fighting the *farang*. The *farang* are the key to our future.'

Jaidee nods at the portrait of his mentor Chaiyanuchit hanging below the Queen's image. 'I am not certain that he would agree.'

'Times change, old friend. People are hunting for your head.'

'And you'll give it to them?'

Pracha sighs. 'Jaidee, I've known you too long for this. I know you're a fighter. And I know you have a hot heart.' He holds up a hand as Jaidee stirs to protest. 'Yes, a good heart, also, just like your name, but still, *jai rawn*. Not a bit of *jai yen* in you. You relish the conflict.' He purses his lips. 'So I know that if I rein you in, you will fight. And if I punish you, you will fight.'

'Then let me go about my business. The Ministry benefits from a loose cannon like me.'

'People were offended by your action. And not just stupid *farang*. Not everyone who ships air cargo is *farang*, these days. Our interests reach far and wide. Thai interests.'

Jaidee studies the general's desk. 'I wasn't aware that the Environment Ministry only inspected cargo at others' convenience.'

'I am trying to reason with you. My hands are full with tigers: blister rust, weevil, the coal war, Trade Ministry infiltrators, yellow cards, greenhouse quotas, *fa' gan* outbreaks . . . And yet you choose to add another.'

Jaidee looks up. 'Who is it?'

'What do you mean?'

'Who is so angry that you're pissing your pants this way? Coming to ask me not to fight? It's Trade, yes? Someone in the Trade Ministry has you by the balls.'

Pracha doesn't say anything for a moment. 'I don't know who it is. Better that you don't know, either. What you do not know, you cannot fight.' He slides a card across the desk. 'This arrived today, under my door.' His eyes lock on Jaidee so that Jaidee cannot look away. 'Right here in the office. Inside the compound, you understand? We are completely infiltrated.'

Jaidee turns over the card.

Niwat and Surat are good boys. Four and Six. Young men. Fighters already. Niwat once came home with a bloody nose and bright eyes and told Jaidee that he had fought honorably and been horribly beaten, but that he was going to train and he would take the *heeya* next time.

Chaya despairs over this. She accuses Jaidee of filling their heads with impossible ideas. Surat follows Niwat and encourages him, tells Niwat he can't be beat. Tells him he is a tiger. The best of the best. That he will reign in Krung Thep, and bring honor to them all. Surat calls himself trainer and tells Niwat to hit harder next time. Niwat is not afraid of beatings. He is not afraid of anything. He is four.

It is at times like these that Jaidee's heart breaks. Only once when he was in the *muay thai* ring was he afraid. But many times when he has worked, he has been terrified. Fear is part of him. Fear is part of the Ministry. What else but fear could close borders, burn towns, slaughter fifty thousand chickens and inter them wholesale under clean dirt and a thick powdering of lye? When the Thonburi virus hit, he and his men wore little rice paper masks that were no protection and they shoveled avian corpses into mass graves, while their fears swirled around them like *phii*. Could the virus really have come so far in such little time? Would it spread further? Would it continue to accelerate? Was this the virus that would finally finish them? He and his men were quarantined for thirty days while they waited to die, and fear was their only companion. Jaidee works for a ministry that cannot hold against all the threats it faces; he is afraid all the time.

It is not fighting that he fears; it is not death; it is the waiting and uncertainty, and it breaks Jaidee's heart that Niwat knows nothing of the waiting terrors, and that the waiting terrors are all around them now. So many things can only be fought by waiting. Jaidee is a man of action. He fought in the ring. He wore his Seub luck amulets blessed by Ajahn Nopadon himself in the White Temple, and went forth. He carried only his black baton and quelled the *nam* riots of Katchanaburi single-handed by striding into the crowd.

And yet the only battles that matter are the waiting battles: when his father and mother succumbed to cibiscosis and coughed the meat of their lungs out between their teeth; when his sister and Chaya's sister both saw their hands thicken and crack with the cauliflower growths of *fa' gan* before the ministry stole the genetic map from the Chinese and manufactured a partial cure. They prayed every day to Buddha and practiced non-attachment and hoped that their two sisters would find a better rebirth than this one that turned their fingers to clubs and chewed away at their joints. They prayed. And waited.

It breaks Jaidee's heart that Niwat knows no fear, and that Surat trains him so. It breaks his heart that he cannot make himself intervene, and he curses himself for it. Why must he destroy childhood illusions of invincibility? Why him? He resents this role.

Instead, he lets his children tackle him and roars, 'Ahh, you are a tiger's sons! Too fierce! Too fierce by half!' And they are pleased and laugh and tackle him again, and he lets them win, and shows them tricks that he has learned since the ring, the tricks a fighter in the streets must know, where no combat is ritualized and where even a champion has things to learn. He teaches them how to fight, because it is all he knows. And the other thing – the waiting thing – is something he could never prepare them for, anyway.

These are his thoughts as he turns over Pracha's card, as his own heart closes in on itself, like a block of stone falling inward, as though the center of himself is plunging down a well, dragging all his innards with him, leaving him hollow.

Chaya.

Curled against a wall, blindfolded, hands behind her back, ankles tied before her. On the wall, 'All Respect to the Environment Ministry' is scrawled in brown letters that must be blood. There is a bruise on Chaya's cheek. She wears the same blue *pha sin* that she had on when she made him a breakfast of *gaeng kiew wan* and sent him on his way this morning with a laugh.

He stares dumbly at the photo.

His sons are fighters, but they do not know this warfare. He himself does not know how to skirmish like this. A faceless foe who reaches out to touch him on the throat, who strokes a demon claw along his jaw and whispers *I can hurt you* without ever showing its face, without ever presenting itself as an opponent at all.

At first, Jaidee's voice doesn't work. Finally, he manages to croak, 'Is she alive?'

Pracha sighs. 'We don't know.'

'Who did this?'

'I don't know.'

'You must!'

'If we knew, we would already have her safe in hand!' Pracha rubs his face angrily, then glares at Jaidee. 'We've received so many complaints about you, from so many quarters, that we just don't know! It could be anyone.'

A new terror seizes Jaidee. 'What about my sons?' He leaps to his feet. 'I have to—'

'Sit down!' Pracha lunges across the desk and grabs him. 'We've sent men to their school. Your own men. Loyal to you only. The only ones we could trust. They're fine. They're being brought to the Ministry. You need to have a cool heart and consider your position.

You want to keep this quiet. We don't want anyone to make sudden decisions. We want Chaya to come back to us whole and alive. Too much noise and someone will lose face and then her body will surely arrive in bloody pieces.'

Jaidee stares at the photograph still lying on the desk. He stands and starts to pace. 'It has to be Trade.' He thinks back to the night at the anchor pads, the man, watching him and his white shirts from across the landing fields. Casual. Contemptuous. Spitting a stream of betel like blood and slipping into the darkness. 'It was Trade.'

'It could have been *farang*, or the Dung Lord – he never liked that you wouldn't fix fights. It could have been some other godfather, some *jao por* who lost money on a smuggling operation.'

'None of them would stoop so low. It was Trade. There is a man—'

'Stop!' Pracha slams his hand on his desk. 'Everyone would like to stoop so low! You've made a lot of enemies very quickly. I've even had a *chaopraya* peer from the palace complaining. It could be anyone.'

'You blame me for this?'

Pracha sighs. 'There's no point in assigning blame. It's done now. You made enemies; I allowed you.' He puts his head in his hands. 'We need you to make a public apology. Something to appease them.'

'I won't.'

'Won't?' Pracha laughs bitterly. 'Put away that foolish pride of yours.' He fingers the picture of Chaya. 'What do you think their next move will be? We haven't had *heeya* like this since the last Expansion. Money at any cost. Wealth at any price.' He makes a face. 'Right now, we may still be able to get her back. But if you continue?' He shakes his head. 'They will surely slaughter her. They are animals.

'You will make a public apology for your actions at the anchor pads and you will be demoted. You will be transferred, probably to the south to process yellow cards and handle internments down there.' He sighs and studies the picture again. 'And if we are very very careful, and very lucky, perhaps you will get Chaya back.

'Don't look at me that way, Jaidee. If you were still in the *muay thai* ring, I would place every baht I own on you. But this is a different sort of fight.' Pracha leans forward, nearly begging. 'Please. Do what I say. Bow before these winds.'

12

How was Hock Seng to know that the *gaiside* anchor pads would be shut down? How was he to know that all his bribes would be wasted by the Tiger of Bangkok?

Hock Seng grimaces at the memory of his meeting with Mr. Lake. Of crouching before that pale monster as though he were some sort of god, kowtowing obeisance while the creature shouted and swore and rained newspapers down on his head, all of them with Jaidee Rojjanasukchai on their front pages. The Tiger of Bangkok, a curse in his own right, as bad as one of the Thais' demons.

'*Khun*—' Hock Seng tried to protest, but Mr. Lake cut him off.

'You told me you had everything arranged!' he shouted. 'Give me one good reason why I shouldn't fire you!'

Hock Seng huddled under the assault, forcing himself not to fight back. Tried to be reasonable. '*Khun*, everyone lost material. This is the doing of Carlyle & Sons. Mr. Carlyle is too close to Trade Minister Akkarat. He is always goading the white shirts. Always insulting them—'

'Don't change the subject! The algae tanks should have cleared Customs last week. You told me you paid the bribes. And now I find out you were keeping money back. This wasn't Carlyle, this was you. Your fault.'

'*Khun,* it was the Tiger of Bangkok. He is a natural disaster. An earthquake, a tsunami. You cannot blame me for not knowing—'

'I'm tired of being lied to. You think because I'm *farang* that I'm stupid? That I don't see how you work the books? How you manipulate and lie and sneak—'

'I do not lie—'

'I don't care about your explanations and excuses! Your words are shit! I don't care what you say. I don't care what you think, what you feel, what you say. All I care about is results. Bring the line up to forty percent reliability within the month, or go back to the yellow card towers. That's your choice. You have a month before I fire your ass and find another manager.'

'*Khun*—'

'Do you understand?'

Hock Seng stared bitterly at the floor, glad the creature couldn't see his expression. 'Of course Lake *Xiansheng,* I understand. It will be as you say.'

Before he had even finished speaking, the foreign devil was stalking out of the office, leaving Hock Seng behind. It was enough of an insult that Hock Seng considered pouring acid on the great safe and simply stealing the factory plans. In his white-hot rage, he got as far as the supply cabinets before good sense reined him in.

If harm befell the factory, or the safe were robbed, suspicion would fall to him first. And if he ever hopes to forge a life in this new country, he cannot have any more blackness attached to his name. The white shirts need few excuses to revoke a yellow card. To kick a beggar Chinese back across the border and into the hands of fundamentalists. He must be patient. He must survive in this *gaiside* factory for another day.

So instead, Hock Seng lashes the employees forward, approves repairs that bleed more money, uses even his own carefully embezzled stores of cash to grease the skids so that Mr. Lake's demands will not escalate, so that the *gaiside* foreign devil will not destroy him. They run tests on the line, rip up old drive links, canvass the city for teak that can be repurposed as a spindle.

He has Laughing Chan offering a bounty to every yellow card in the city for rumors of old Expansion properties that may have crumbled and revealed structural items worth harvesting. Anything that will allow them to bring the line back to full production before the monsoons finally pour down and make river transport of a new teak spindle practicable.

Hock Seng grinds his teeth with frustration. Everything is so close to fruition. And yet now his survival depends on a line that never worked and on people who have never been successful. It's almost enough for Hock Seng to attempt a little arm twisting of his own. To tell the *gaiside* devil that he knows something of Mr. Lake's extracurricular life, thanks to the reports of Lao Gu. That he knows every place Mr. Lake has visited, of his trips to libraries and old family homes in Bangkok. Of his fascination with seeds.

And now this strangest, most astonishing thing. The news that sent Lao Gu scurrying to Hock Seng as soon as it occurred. A windup girl. An illegal piece of genetic trash. A girl that Mr. Lake pursues as if he is drunk on the transgression. Lao Gu whispers that Mr. Lake brings the creature to his bed. Does so repeatedly. Pines for it.

Astonishing. Disgusting.

Useful.

But a weapon to be used as a last resort, if Mr. Lake attempts to truly eject him from the factory. Better to have Lao Gu watching and listening and gathering more information than revealed and fired. When Hock Seng first arranged Lao Gu's employment, it was for just this sort of possibility. He must not waste this one bit of leverage just because he is angry. And so instead, even as his face feels as if it has been thrown on the floor, Hock Seng jumps like a monkey to make the foreign devil happy.

Hock Seng grimaces as he crosses the factory floor, following Kit to another point of complaint. Problems. Always more problems.

All around them, the activity of repair echoes. Half the power train has been torn out of the floor and reset. Nine Buddhist monks chant steadily at the far side of the building, stretching the Thais' sacred thread that they call *saisin* everywhere and imploring the spirits that infest the place – half of them likely Contraction *phii* who are angered that the Thais are working for *farang* at all – begging them to allow the factory to work correctly. Hock Seng grimaces at the sight of monks and the expenses he is incurring.

'What's this new problem?' Hock Seng asks as they squeeze past the cutting presses and duck under the line.

'It's here, *Khun*. I'll show you,' Kit says.

The salty warm stink of algae thickens, a humid reek that hangs heavy in the air. Kit points to the algae tanks where they stand in damp ranks, three dozen open surface breeding vats. Their waters are coated with the rich green skim of algae breeding. A worker is dragging her net across the surface of the tanks, drawing off the skim. She smears it across a man-sized screen before hoisting it up on hemp ropes to hang overhead with the hundreds of similar screens.

'It's the tanks.' Kit says. 'They are contaminated.'

'Yes?' Hock Seng eyes the tanks, hiding his distaste. 'What is the difficulty?'

With the healthiest vats, the skim is more than six inches thick, a pillowy vibrant chlorophyll green. The voluptuous scent of sea-water and life emanates from them. Water trickles down the sides of the translucent tanks, thin lines that damp the floor and leave salty white blooms as they evaporate. Streamers of still-living algae trail down drain channels to rusty iron grates and disappear into darkness.

Pig DNA and something else . . . flax, Hock Seng thinks. It was flax that Mr. Yates always believed had been the key to this algae. That made it produce such useful skim. But Hock Seng always liked the pig proteins. Pigs are lucky. This algae should be, also. And yet it has caused nothing but trouble, despite its potential.

Kit smiles nervously as he shows Hock Seng how several of the tanks have lowered levels of algae production, an off-color skim, and a fishy reek, something more akin to shrimp paste than the verdant salty smells of the more active tanks.

'Banyat said they should not be used. That we should wait until the replacement supplies came.'

Hock Seng laughs harshly and shakes his head. 'We won't have any replacements. Not with the Tiger of Bangkok burning everything that comes off the anchor pads. You'll have to make do with what we have.'

'But it's contaminated. There are potential vectors. The problem could spread into the other tanks.'

'You're certain of that?'

'Banyat said—'

'Banyat walked under a megodont. And if we don't have this line running soon, the *farang* will be sending us all out to starve.'

'But—'

'You think another fifty Thais wouldn't like your job? A thousand yellow cards?'

Kit closes his mouth. Hock Seng nods grimly. 'Make this line work.'

'If the white shirts inspect us, they will see that the baths are impure.' Kit runs his finger through a gray froth coating the rim of one of the tanks. 'We shouldn't be seeing this. The algae should be much brighter. None of this bubbling.'

Hock Seng studies the tanks sourly. 'If we don't get the line running we all starve.' He's about to say more, but the girl Mai runs into the room.

'*Khun*. A man has come looking for you.'

Hock Seng gives her an impatient look. 'Is it someone with information on a new spindle? A teak log ripped from some temple *bot*, maybe?' Mai's mouth opens and closes, stunned at his blasphemy, but Hock Seng doesn't care. 'If this man doesn't have a winding spindle, I don't have time for him.' He turns back to Kit. 'Can you drain and scrub the tanks perhaps?'

Kit shrugs noncommittally. 'It can be tried, *Khun*, but Banyat said that if we don't have new nutrient cultures, we can't start completely fresh. We will be forced to reuse the cultures that come from these same tanks. The problem will likely return.'

'We can't sieve it? Filter somehow?'

'The tanks and cultures cannot be fully cleaned. Eventually it will be a vector. And the rest of the tanks will be contaminated.'

'Eventually? Is that all? Eventually?' Hock Seng scowls at him. 'I don't care about "eventually." I care about this month. If this factory fails to produce, we won't have a chance to worry about this "eventually" you speak of. You'll be back in Thonburi, picking through chicken guts and hoping you aren't hit with flu, and I'll be back in a yellow card tower. Don't worry about tomorrow. Worry about whether Mr. Lake throws us all out on the street today. Use your imagination. Find a way to make this *gaiside* algae breed.'

Not for the first time, he curses that he works with Thais. They simply lack the spirit of entrepreneurship that a Chinese would throw into the work.

'*Khun?*'

It's Mai, still lingering. She flinches at his glare.

'The man says that this is your last chance.'

'My last chance? Show me this *heeya*.' Hock Seng storms toward the main floor, shoving aside the curtains of the fining rooms. Out in the main hall, where the megodonts lean against spindle cranks burning money that they simply don't have, Hock Seng stops short, wiping algae fines from his hands, feeling like a terrified fool.

Dog Fucker stands in the middle of the factory like cibiscosis in the middle of Spring Festival, watching the whir and clatter of the QA line as it runs through tests. Old Bones and Horseface Ma and Dog Fucker. All of them standing so confidently. Dog Fucker, with his *fa' gan* fringe and his missing nose, and his thug cronies, hard-edged *nak leng* who have no pity for yellow cards and no fear of police.

It's only dumb luck that Mr. Lake is upstairs going over the books, only dumb luck that little Mai came to him and not to the foreign devil. Mai scampers ahead, leading him toward his future.

Hock Seng motions for Dog Fucker to join him out of sight of the observation windows above, but Dog Fucker, maddeningly, sets his feet and continues to study the rumbling line and the shamble of the megodonts.

'Very impressive,' he says. 'Is this where you make your fabulous kink-springs?'

Hock Seng glares and motions for him to move out of the factory. 'We should not be having this conversation here.'

Dog Fucker ignores him. His eyes are on the offices and the observation windows. He stares up at them intently. 'And is that where you do your work? Up there?'

'Not for long, if a certain *farang* catches sight of you.' Hock Seng forces himself to make a polite smile. 'Please. It would be better if we went outside. Your presence arouses questions.'

For a long moment, Dog Fucker doesn't move, still staring up at the offices. Hock Seng has the unnerving feeling that the man sees through the walls, that he sees the huge iron safe sitting up there, holding its valuable secrets tight.

'Please,' Hock Seng mutters. 'The workers will speak enough about this as it is.'

Abruptly the gangster turns away, nodding to his men to follow. Hock Seng stifles a rush of relief as he hurries after them. 'Someone wants to see you,' Dog Fucker says, gesturing toward the outer gates.

The Dung Lord. Now, of all times. Hock Seng glances up at the observation window. Mr. Lake will be angry if he leaves.

'Yes. Of course.' Hock Seng motions back toward the office. 'I will just tidy my papers.'

'Now,' Dog Fucker says. 'No one keeps him waiting.' He motions for Hock Seng to follow. 'Now or never.'

Hock Seng hesitates, torn, then waves for Mai. She dashes up as Dog Fucker leads them toward the gates. Hock Seng leans low and whispers. 'Tell *Khun* Anderson that I will not be returning . . . that I have an idea of where to locate a new winding spindle.' He nods sharply. 'Yes. Tell him that. A winding spindle.'

Mai nods and starts to turn away, but Hock Seng pulls her back, pulls her close. 'Remember to speak slowly, and in simple words. I don't want the *farang* to misunderstand and put me out on the street. If I go, so do you. Remember that.'

Mai grins. '*Mai pen rai.* I will make him very happy that you are working so hard.' She dashes back into the factory.

Dog Fucker smiles over his shoulder. 'And I thought you were only the king of yellow cards. Here you have a pretty Thai girl doing your bidding, too. Not bad for a Yellow Card King.'

Hock Seng makes a face. 'The king of yellow cards is not a title to aspire to.'

'Nor the Lord of Dung,' he says. 'Names hide much.' He surveys the compound. 'I've never been in a *farang* factory,' he says. 'It's very impressive. A lot of money here.'

Hock Seng forces a smile. 'The *farang* are crazy with how much they spend.' His neck prickles at the workers' eyes watching him. He wonders how many of them know of Dog Fucker. For once he is grateful that more yellow card Chinese don't work at the factory. They would recognize in an instant who he treats with. Hock Seng forces down the irritation and fear he feels at the exposure. Of course Dog Fucker would like to see him off-balance. It is part of the bargaining process.

You are Tan Hock Seng, head of the New Tri-Clipper. Do not let petty tactics unsettle you.

This mantra of self-assurance lasts until they reach the outer gates. Hock Seng stops short.

Dog Fucker laughs as he opens the door for Hock Seng. 'What's the matter? You've never seen a car before?'

Hock Seng stifles an urge to slap the man for his arrogance and stupidity. 'You're a fool,' he mutters. 'Do you know how this exposes me? How people will speak of an extravagance like this, parked in front of this factory?'

He ducks inside. Dog Fucker climbs in after him, still grinning. The rest of his men crowd in after. Old Bones calls forward to the driver. The machine's engine rumbles to life. They start to roll.

'Is it coal diesel?' Hock Seng asks. He can't help whispering.

Dog Fucker grins. 'The boss does so much for the carbon load . . .' He shrugs. 'This is a small extravagance.'

'But the cost . . .' Hock Seng trails off. The exorbitant cost of turning this steel behemoth into acceleration. An extraordinary waste. A testament to the Dung Lord's monopolies. Even in his wealthiest days in Malaya, Hock Seng would never have considered such an extravagance.

Despite the heat in the car, he shivers. There is an ancient solidity to the thing, so heavy and massive – it might as well be a tank. It's as if he's locked inside one of SpringLife's safes, isolated from the world beyond. Claustrophobia swallows him.

Dog Fucker smiles as Hock Seng tries to master his emotions. 'I hope you aren't wasting his time,' he says.

Hock Seng makes himself meet Dog Fucker's gaze. 'I think you would like it better if I failed.'

'You're right.' Dog Fucker shrugs. 'If it were up to me, we would have let your kind die on the other side of the border.'

The car accelerates, pressing Hock Seng into the leather seat.

Outside the windows, Krung Thep slides past, utterly removed from him: crowds of sun-drenched skin and dusty draft animals and bicycles like schools of fish. Eyes turn toward the car as it forges past. Mouths open wide and silent as people shout and point at his passage.

The speed of the machine is appalling.

Yellow cards crowd around the tower entrances, Malayan Chinese men and women trying to look hopeful as they wait for labor opportunities that have already faded in the heat of the afternoon. And yet still they try to look vital, try to show that their bony limbs have calories to spare, if only someone will allow them to burn.

Everyone stares as the Dung Lord's car arrives. When the door opens, they kneel in a wave, all of them performing *khrabs* of abasement, triple bows to the patron who keeps them housed, the one man in Krung Thep who willingly shoulders the burden of them, who provides a measure of safety from the red machetes of the Malays and the black batons of the white shirts.

Hock Seng's eyes slide over yellow card backs, wondering if he knows any of them, momentarily surprised that he is not among them performing his own *khrab* of obeisance.

Dog Fucker leads him into the tower darkness. The skitter of rats and the smell of close-packed sweating bodies convects down from the floors above. At a pair of gaping elevator shafts he flips open a tarnished brass speaking tube and shouts with brisk authority. They wait, eyes on one another: Dog Fucker bored; Hock Seng carefully hiding anxiety. A rattling comes from above, gears clicking, the scrape of iron on stone. A lift sinks into view.

Dog Fucker drags open the gate and steps in. The woman at the elevator controls disengages the brake and shouts into the speaking tube before yanking the gate closed again. Dog Fucker smiles through the gate. 'Wait here, yellow card.' And then he is whisked up into darkness.

A minute later, ballast men slide into view in the secondary shaft. They squeeze out of the lift and dash for the stairwell in a herd. One of them catches sight of Hock Seng. Mistakes his look. 'There aren't any more places. He has enough of us already.'

Hock Seng shakes his head. 'No. Of course not,' he mutters, but the men are already disappearing back up the stairs, sandals slapping as they scramble for the sky to make the ballast drop again.

From where he stands inside the building, the glare of the tropics is a distant rectangle, clotted with refugees, all watching the street with nothing to do and nowhere to go. A few yellow cards shuffle the halls. Babies cry, their small voices echoing against hot concrete. From somewhere above, the grunt of sex comes. People screwing in halls like animals, out in the open because they have given up on privacy. It is all so familiar. Extraordinary that he once lived in this same building, sweltered in this same pen.

Minutes tick by. Perhaps the Dung Lord has changed his mind. Dog Fucker should have returned by now. Movement catches the corner of Hock Seng's eye and he flinches, but there is nothing but shadow.

Sometimes he dreams that the Green Headbands have become cheshires, that they can molt and appear where he least expects them – while he pours water over his head as he makes his bath, or as he eats a bowl of rice, or squats over the latrine ... they simply shimmer into existence and grab him and gut him and stack his head on the streets as a warning. Just like Jade Blossom and First Wife's elder sister. Just like his sons . . .

The lift rattles. A moment later Dog Fucker descends. The elevator woman is gone, Dog Fucker's own hand runs the brake system.

'Good. You didn't run away.'

'I'm not afraid of this place.'

Dog Fucker gives him an appraising look. 'No. Of course not. You came from it, didn't you?' He steps out and motions toward the tower dimness. Guards materialize where Hock Seng thought only shadows existed. He forces himself not to yelp, but Dog Fucker still catches his twitch. Smiles at it. 'Search him.'

Hands pat Hock Seng's ribs, run down his legs, prod at his genitals. When the guards are finished, Dog Fucker gestures Hock Seng into the lift. He guesses the heft of them and shouts up the speaking tube.

From high above, the rattle of men climbing into the ballast cage filters down. And then they are rising, climbing up through the layers of hell. The heat thickens. Deep in the heart of the building, exposed as it is to the full force of the tropic sun, it is an oven.

Hock Seng remembers sleeping in the stairwells here, struggling to breathe as the bodies of his fellow refugees stank and rolled about him. Remembers how his belly pressed against his spine. And then, all in a rush he remembers blood on his hands, hot and alive. A fellow yellow card, reaching out to him, begging for aid, even as he drove the knife edge of his whiskey bottle into the man's throat.

Hock Seng closes his eyes, forcing away memory.

You were starving. There was no other way.

But he has a hard time convincing himself.

They continue to rise. A breeze caresses him. The air cools. Scents of hibiscus and citrus.

An open hall flashes by – a promenade, exposed to the city air, careful gardens, lime trees bordering the edges of wide balconies. Hock Seng wonders at the amount of water men must carry to this height. Wonders at the calories that must be spent and the man who has access to such power. It's both thrilling and terrifying. He is close. So very close.

They reach the top of the building. The sun-drenched expanse of the city spreads before them. The gold spires of the Grand Palace where the Child Queen holds court and the Somdet Chaopraya pulls the strings, the *chedi* of Mongkut's temple on its hill, the only thing that will survive if the levees fail. The broken and tumbling spires of the old Expansion. And all around, the sea.

'It's a good view, isn't it, yellow card?'

Across the wide roof, a white pavilion has been erected. It rustles gently in salt breezes. Under its shade, in a rattan chair, the Dung Lord sprawls. The man is fat. Fatter than anyone Hock Seng has seen since Pearl Koh in Malaya cornered the market on blister rust-resistant durian. Perhaps not as fat as Ah Deng who ran a sweet stand in Penang, but still, the man is astonishingly fat, given the privations of the calorie economy.

Hock Seng approaches slowly, *wais*, lowering his head until his chin touches his chest and his pressed palms are nearly above his head with the respect he shows the man.

The fat man regards Hock Seng. 'You wish to treat with me?'

Hock Seng's throat catches. He nods. The man waits, patient. A servant brings cold sweet coffee and offers it to the Dung Lord. He takes a sip. 'Are you thirsty?' he asks.

Hock Seng has the presence of mind to shake his head. The Dung Lord shrugs. Sips again. Says nothing. Four servants in white suits shuffle over, carrying a linen draped table. They set the table before him. The Dung Lord nods to Hock Seng.

'Come now, don't worry about being polite. Eat. Drink.'

A chair is produced for him. The Dung Lord offers Hock Seng wide fried U-Tex noodles, a crab and green papaya salad, along with *laab mu, gaeng gai,* and steamed U-Tex. Along with it all, he offers a plate of sliced papaya. 'Don't be afraid. The chicken is latest generip and the papaya are just picked, from my eastern plantation. Not a trace of blister rust in the last two seasons.'

'How – ?'

'We burn any trees that show the disease and those around them as well. Also, we have widened our buffer perimeter to five kilometers. With UV sterilization, it seems to be enough.'

'Ah.'

The Dung Lord nods at the small kink-spring, sitting on the table. 'A gigajoule?'

Hock Seng nods.

'And you have them to sell?'

Hock Seng shakes his head. 'The way of making them.'

'What makes you think I am a buyer?'

Hock Seng shrugs, forcing himself to hide his nervousness. There was a time when this sort of bargaining was easy for him. Second nature. But he wasn't desperate then. 'If you are not, then there are others.'

The Dung Lord nods. Finishes his coffee. A servant pours more. 'And why do you come to me?'

'Because you are rich.'

The Dung Lord laughs at that. He nearly spits out his coffee. His belly rolls and his body shakes. The servants freeze, watchful. When the Dung Lord finally controls his laughter, he wipes his mouth and shakes his head. 'A fair answer, that.' His smile disappears. 'But I am also dangerous.'

Hock Seng buries his nervousness and speaks directly. 'When the rest of the Kingdom would have rejected our kind, you took us in. Not even our own people, the Thai-Chinese, were so generous.

Her Royal Majesty the Queen showed mercy, allowing us to come across the border, but it was you who provided safe haven.'

The Dung Lord shrugs. 'No one uses these towers anyway.'

'And yet you are the only one who showed compassion. An entire country full of good Buddhist people, and only you gave shelter, instead of forcing us back across the border. I would be dead by now if not for you.'

The Dung Lord studies Hock Seng a moment longer. 'My advisors thought it was foolish. That it would put me in opposition with the white shirts. Set me at odds with General Pracha. Maybe even threaten my methane deals.'

Hock Seng nods. 'Only you had enough influence to risk it.'

'And what do you want for this wondrous bit of technology?'

Hock Seng readies himself. 'A ship.'

The Dung Lord looks up, surprised. 'Not money? Not jade? Not opium?'

Hock Seng shakes his head. 'A ship. A fast clipper. Mishimoto-designed. Registered and approved to transport cargo to the Kingdom and throughout the South China Sea. Under the protection of her Majesty the Queen . . .' He waits a beat. 'And your patronage.'

'Ah. Clever yellow card.' The Dung Lord smiles. 'And I thought you were truly grateful.'

Hock Seng shrugs. 'You are the only person who has the influence to provide such permits and guarantees.'

'The only one who can make a yellow card truly legitimate, you mean. The only one who could convince white shirts to allow a yellow card shipping king to develop.'

Hock Seng doesn't blink. 'Your union lights the city. Your influence is unparalleled.'

Unexpectedly, the Dung Lord forces himself out of his seat, stands. 'Yes. Well. So it is.' He turns and shambles across the patio to the edge of his terrace, hands behind his back, surveying the city below. 'Yes. I suppose I still have strings I can pull. Ministers I can influence.' He turns back. 'You're asking for a lot.'

'I give even more.'

'And if you're selling this to more than one?'

Hock Seng shakes his head. 'I do not need a fleet. I need one ship.'

'Tan Hock Seng, seeking to restore his shipping empire here in the Thai Kingdom.' The Dung Lord turns abruptly. 'Maybe you've already sold it to others.'

'I can only swear that it is not so.'

'Would you swear on your ancestors? On your family's ghosts all walking hungry in Malaya?'

Hock Seng shifts uneasily. 'I would.'

'I want to see this technology you claim.'

Hock Seng looks up surprised. 'You haven't already started to wind it?'

'Why don't you demonstrate now?'

Hock Seng grins. 'You're afraid it is a booby trap of some sort? A blade bomb maybe?' He laughs. 'I do not play games. I come for business only.' He looks around. 'You have a winding man? Let us both see how many joules he can put into it. Wind it and see. But do be careful with it. It is not as resilient as a standard spring, because of the torque it operates under. It cannot be dropped.' He points at a servant. 'You there, put this spring on your winding spindle, see how many joules you can shove into it.'

The servant looks uncertain. The Dung Lord nods agreement. A sea breeze rustles across the high garden as the young man sets the kink-spring on its spindle and settles on the winding cycle.

Hock Seng is suddenly seized by new worry. He confirmed with Banyat that he was taking one of the good springs, that it had passed QA, unlike the ones that always failed and cracked as soon as they started their winding. Banyat assured him that he should take one from a certain stack. But now, as the servant prepares to lean on his pedals, doubt flares. If he chose wrong, if Banyat was wrong ... and now Banyat is dead under the feet of a crazed megodont. Hock Seng couldn't confirm one last time. He was sure ... and yet ...

The servant leans against the pedals. Hock Seng holds his breath. Sweat appears on the servant's brow and he looks over at Hock Seng and the Dung Lord, surprised at the resistance. He changes gears. The pedals turn, slowly at first, then faster. He begins cycling up through the gears as his momentum increases, jamming more and more energy into the kink-spring.

The Dung Lord watches thoughtfully. 'I knew a man who worked at your kink-spring company. A few years ago. He didn't spread his wealth around as you do. Didn't curry favor with so many of his fellow yellow cards.' He pauses. 'I understand that the white shirts killed him for his watch. Beat him bloody, robbed him blind, right in the street, because he was out after curfew.'

Hock Seng shrugs, forcing down memories of a man lying on cobbles, a ruined mess, broken already, begging for help ...

The Dung Lord's eyes are thoughtful. 'And now you work for this company as well. It seems like an unlikely coincidence.'

Hock Seng doesn't say anything.

The Dung Lord says, 'Dog Fucker should have paid more attention. You're a dangerous one.'

Hock Seng shakes his head emphatically. 'I only wish to reestablish myself.'

The servant continues to pedal, cranking more joules into the spring, forcing more energy into the tiny box. The Dung Lord watches, trying to hide his astonishment as the process continues, but still, his eyes have widened. Already the servant has pushed more energy into the box than any spring its size should accept.

The cycle whines as the servant pedals. Hock Seng says, 'It will take all night for a man like this to wind it. You should take it to a megodont.'

'How does it work?'

Hock Seng shrugs. 'There is a new lubricating solution, it allows the springs to be tightened to significantly higher tensions, without breaking or locking.'

The man continues to pour power into the spring. Servants and bodyguards begin to gather around, all of them watching with a certain awe as he cranks away at the box.

'Astonishing,' the Dung Lord mutters.

'If you chain it to a more efficient animal – a megodont or a mulie – the calorie-to-joule transfer is nearly lossless,' Hock Seng says.

The Dung Lord watches the spring as the man continues to wind. He is smiling. 'We'll test your spring, Hock Seng. If it performs as well as it winds, you'll have your ship. Bring the specifications and blueprints. Your kind I can do business with.' He motions to a servant and orders liquor. 'A toast. To a new business partner.'

Relief floods through Hock Seng. For the first time since blood washed his hands in an alley long ago, since a man begged for mercy and found none, liquor flows in Hock Seng's veins, and he is content.

13

Jaidee remembers when he first met Chaya. He had just finished one of his early *muay thai* bouts; he can't even remember who he competed against but he remembers coming out of the ring, people congratulating him, everyone saying that he moved better even than Nai Khanom Tom. He drank *laolao* that night, and then stumbled out into the streets with his friends, all of them laughing, trying to kick a *takraw* ball, drunk, absurd, and all of them flushed with victory and with life.

And there Chaya was, closing her parents' shop, propping up the wooden panels that secured the storefront where they sold marigolds and newly reengineered jasmine flowers for temple offerings. When he smiled at her, she gave him and his drunk friends a look of disgust. But Jaidee felt a shock of recognition – as if they had known one another in a past life, and were at last meeting again, fated lovers.

He had stared at her, stunned, and his friends had caught the look – Suttipong and Jaiporn and all the rest, all of them lost when the violet comb epidemic hit and they went into the breach to burn the villages where it had struck, all of them gone – but he remembers them all catching him staring, suddenly stupid with infatuation, and how they teased him. Chaya looked at him with a studied contempt and sent him stumbling away.

For Jaidee, it had always been easy to attract a girlfriend, some girl either pleased by his *muay thai* or his white uniform. But Chaya had simply looked through him and turned her back.

It took him a month to get up the nerve to return. That first time, he dressed well, shopped for temple offerings, took his change, and slipped out silently. Over the course of weeks he dropped by, talking with her more, establishing a connection. At first, he thought that she knew him for the drunken fool trying to make amends, but over time it became apparent that she had not made the connection, that the arrogant drunk on the streets that night had been completely forgotten.

Jaidee never told her how they first met, not even after they were married. It was too humiliating to admit to what she had seen in him that night on the street. To tell her that the man she loved was that other fool as well.

And now he prepares to do something worse. He puts on his white dress uniform while Niwat and Surat watch. They are solemn as he prepares to bring himself low in their eyes. He kneels before them.

'Whatever you see today, do not let it shame you.'

They nod solemnly, but he knows they do not understand. They are too young to understand pressures and necessity. He pulls them close, and then he goes out into blinding sunlight.

Kanya awaits him in a cycle rickshaw, compassion in her eyes, even if she is too polite to speak what is in her heart.

They ride silently through the streets. The Ministry appears ahead and they ride through the gates. Servants and rickshaw men and carriages clog the outer gates, waiting for their patrons to return. The witnesses have already been arriving, then.

Their own rickshaw makes its way to the temple. Wat Phra Seub was erected inside the Ministry in honor of the biodiversity martyr. It is the place where white shirts make their vows and are formally ordained as protectors of the Kingdom, before they are given their first ranks. It is here that they receive their ordination, and it is here—

Jaidee starts, and nearly jumps to his feet in anger. *Farang* are milling all around the temple's steps. Foreigners inside the Ministry compound. Traders and factory owners and Japanese, sunburned sweating stinking creatures, invading the Ministry's most sacred place.

'*Jai yen yen,*' Kanya mutters. 'It's Akkarat's doing. Part of the bargain.'

Jaidee can't hide his disgust. Worse yet, Akkarat is standing beside the Somdet Chaopraya, saying something to him, telling a joke, perhaps. The two of them have become too close by far. Jaidee looks away and sees General Pracha watching from the top of the temple steps, his face expressionless. Around him, the brothers and sisters that Jaidee has worked with and warred with are all streaming into the temple. Bhirombhakdi is there, smiling widely, pleased to have his revenge for his lost revenue.

People catch sight of Jaidee's arrival. A hush overtakes the crowd.

'*Jai yen yen,*' Kanya murmurs again, and then they are climbing down and he is being escorted inside.

Golden statues of Buddha and Phra Seub gaze down on the assembling people, serene. The screens on the temple walls portray scenes of the fall of Old Thailand: The *farang* releasing their plagues on the earth, animals and plants collapsing as their food webs unravelled; his Royal Majesty King Rama XII mustering his final pitiful human forces, flanked by Hanuman and his monkey warriors. Images of Krut and Kirimukha and an army of half-human *kala* fighting back the rising seas and plagues. Jaidee's eyes sweep over the panels, remembering how proud he had been at his own ordination.

No cameras are allowed anywhere inside the Ministry, but the whisper sheet scribblers are there with their pencils. Jaidee removes his shoes and enters, followed by the jackals who slaver after this rendering down of their greatest enemy. The Somdet Chaopraya kneels beside Akkarat.

Jaidee eyes the designated protector of the Queen, wondering how someone as divine as the last king could have been fooled into making the Somdet Chaopraya the protector of Her Royal Majesty the Child Queen. The man has so little that is good. Jaidee shivers at the thought of the Queen so close to someone so well-known for his darkness—

Jaidee sucks in his breath. The man from the anchor pads is kneeling beside Akkarat. A long rat-face, watchful and arrogant.

'Cool heart,' Kanya mutters again as she leads him forward. 'It's for Chaya.'

Jaidee forces down his rage, the shock of seeing the man. He leans close to Kanya. 'That's the one who took her. The one from the airfields. Right there! Beside Akkarat.'

Kanya scans the faces. 'Even if it is true, we must do this. It's the only way.'

'Do you truly believe that?'

Kanya has the grace to duck her head. 'I am sorry, Jaidee. I wish—'

'Don't worry, Kanya.' He nods toward the man and Akkarat. 'Just remember those two. Remember that they will stop at nothing for power.' He looks at her. 'Will you remember that?'

'I will.'

'You swear on Phra Seub?'

She has the grace to look embarrassed, but she nods. 'If I could perform the triple bow before you, I would.'

He thinks he sees tears in her eyes as she backs away. The crowd hushes as the Somdet Chaopraya stands and steps forward to witness the proceedings. Four monks begin to chant. On happier occasions, they would be seven or nine in number, and consecrating a wedding, or blessing the laying of a new building's cornerstone. Instead they are here to oversee a humiliation.

Minister Akkarat and General Pracha go to stand before the assembled people. Incense fills the room along with the monk's chanting, a drone in Pali as they remind everyone that all is transient, that even Phra Seub in his despair recognized transience, even as his compassion for the natural world overwhelmed him.

The chanting of the monks dies. The Somdet Chaopraya motions for both Akkarat and Pracha to come before him. To *khrab* and make obeisance. The Somdet Chaopraya watches without emotion as the two ancient enemies pay their respects to the only thing that binds them together: their respect for royalty and the palace.

The Somdet Chaopraya is a tall man, well fed, and he towers over them. His face is hard. Rumors circle around him, about his tastes, about his darkness, but still, he is the one designated to protect Her Majesty the Child Queen until her ascension. He is not royalty, could never be so, and it terrifies Jaidee that she lives within his circle of influence. If it weren't for the fact that the man's own fate is tied so tightly to hers, he would probably ... Jaidee stifles the nearly blasphemous thought as Pracha and Akkarat approach.

Jaidee kneels. Around him, whisper sheet pencils scratch frantically as he performs a *khrab* before Akkarat. Akkarat smiles with satisfaction and Jaidee stifles an urge to lunge at the man. *I will pay you back in my own time.* He stands carefully.

Akkarat leans close. 'Well done, Captain. I almost believe you really are sorry.'

Jaidee keeps his features impassive, turns to address the people, the scribblers – his heart closes as he sees that his sons are present, brought to witness the humiliation of their father.

'I have overstepped my authority.' His eyes go to General Pracha, watching coldly from the edge of the dais, 'I have dishonored my patron, General Pracha, and I have dishonored the Environment Ministry.

'All my life, the Ministry has been my home. I am ashamed that I have selfishly used its powers for my own benefit. That I have misled my fellow officers, and my patrons. That I have been bankrupt morally.' He hesitates. Niwat and Surat are watching, held by their grandmother, Chaya's mother, all of them watching as he humiliates himself. 'I beg forgiveness. I beg an opportunity to rectify my wrongs.'

General Pracha strides toward him. Jaidee drops again to his knees and makes a *khrab* of submission before him. General Pracha ignores him, walks past his bowing face, his feet within inches of Jaidee's head. Speaks to the assembly.

'An independent investigating tribunal has determined that Captain Jaidee is guilty of accepting bribes, of corruption and the abuse of his powers.' He glances down at Jaidee. 'It has further been determined that he is no longer fit for service with the Ministry. He will become a monk, and perform a penance of nine years. His possessions will be disposed of. His sons will be adopted into the care of the Ministry, but their family name will be erased.'

He looks down at Jaidee. 'If the Buddha is merciful, you will eventually come to understand that your pride and avarice has brought this upon you. We hope that if you do not attain understanding in this life, that your next one will provide you with hope of improvement.' He turns away, leaving Jaidee still in his bow.

Akkarat speaks, 'We accept the apologies of the Environment Ministry and the failures of General Pracha. We look forward to an improved working relationship in the future. Now that this snake has had its fangs pulled.'

The Somdet Chaopraya motions to the two great powers of the government that they should show one another respect. Jaidee remains crouched. A sigh runs through the crowd. And then people are streaming out, to tell of what they have seen.

Only once the Somdet Chaopraya is gone is Jaidee invited to stand by a pair of monks. Their aspect is serious, their heads shaven, their saffron robes aged and faded. They indicate to him where they will take him next. He is theirs now. Nine years of penance, for doing the right thing.

Akkarat steps before him. 'Well, *Khun* Jaidee. It seems that you have at last discovered limits. It's a pity you didn't listen to warnings. All of this was so unnecessary.'

Jaidee forces himself to *wai*. 'You have what you wanted,' he mutters. 'Now let Chaya go.'

'So sorry. I don't know what you're talking about.'

Jaidee searches the man's eyes, hunting for the lie, but he can't tell.

Are you my enemy? Or is it another? Is she dead already? Is she still alive, trapped in one of your friends' prison cells, an unnamed prisoner? Alive or dead?

He forces down his worries. 'Bring her back, or I'll hunt you down and kill you like a mongoose killing a cobra.'

Akkarat doesn't flinch. 'Careful with the threats, Jaidee. I'd hate to see you lose anything else.' His eyes stray toward Niwat and Surat.

A chill runs through Jaidee. 'Stay away from my children.'

'Your children?' Akkarat laughs. 'You have no children now. You have nothing at all. You're lucky that General Pracha is your friend. If I were him, I would have turned those two boys of yours out into the street to beg for blister rust scraps. That would have been a true lesson.'

14

Crushing the Tiger of Bangkok should be more satisfying. But frankly, without a cue card of the various names involved, the ceremony looks like any number of impenetrable Thai religious and social events. In fact, the man's actual demotion is surprisingly quick.

Within twenty minutes of being ushered into the Environment Ministry's temple, Anderson finds himself watching silently as the vaunted Jaidee Rojjanasukchai makes *khrabs* of humility to Trade Minister Akkarat. The golden statues of the Buddha and Seub Nakhasathien gleam dully, overseeing the solemn moment. None of the participants show any expression at all. Not even a smile of triumph from Akkarat. And then a few minutes later, the chanting monks end their droning, and everyone is standing to leave.

That's it.

And so now Anderson finds himself cooling his heels outside the Phra Seub Temple *bot*, waiting to be escorted out of the compound. After enduring the astonishing series of security checks and body searches to get into the Environment Ministry campus, he had begun to fantasize that he might glean some useful bit of intelligence about the place, perhaps get some better sense of where their lovely seedbank might be tucked away. It was foolish, and he knew it, but after the fourth patdown he was almost convinced that he was about to run into Gibbons himself, perhaps cradling a newly engineered *ngaw* like a proud father.

Instead, he encountered grim cordons of white shirts and was whisked by cycle rickshaw directly to the temple steps where he was required to remove his shoes and stand in bare feet under tight supervision before being led inside with all the other witnesses.

Around the temple, a thicket of rain trees prevents much view of the place at all. AgriGen-arranged 'accidental' dirigible over-flights have given him more information about the compound than he's got right now, standing dead in the heart of the thing.

'I see you got your shoes back.'

Carlyle, sauntering over, grinning.

'The way they inspected,' Anderson says, 'I thought they were going to lock them in quarantine.'

'They just don't like your *farang* smell.' Carlyle pulls out a cigarette and offers Anderson one as well. Under the close gaze of their white shirt guards, they light up. 'Enjoy the ceremony?' Carlyle asks.

'I thought there might be more pomp and circumstance.'

'They don't need it. Everyone knows what this means. General Pracha has lost his face.' Carlyle shakes his head. 'For a second I was sure we were going to look up and see their Phra Seub statue crack in half with the shame. You can feel the Kingdom changing. It's in the air.'

Anderson thinks of the few buildings he glimpsed as he was escorted to the temple. They were all dilapidated. Water stained and covered with vines. If the Tiger's fall isn't proof enough, the fallen trees and unkempt grounds are fine indicators. 'You must be very proud of what you've accomplished.'

Carlyle draws on his cigarette and exhales slowly. 'Let's just say it's a satisfying step.'

'You've impressed them.' Anderson nods toward the *Farang*

Phalanx, who seem to be already drunk on their reparation money. Lucy is trying to convince Otto to sing the Pacific Anthem under the stern gazes of the armed white shirts. The trader catches sight of Carlyle and lurches over. His breath stinks with *laolao*.

'Are you drunk?' Carlyle asks.

'Completely.' Otto smiles dreamily. 'I had to finish everything at the gate. Bastards wouldn't let me bring the celebration bottles inside. Took Lucy's opium, too.'

He drapes an arm over Carlyle's shoulder. 'You were right, you bastard. Right as rain. Look at all these damn white shirts' expressions. They've been eating bitter melon all day!' He gropes for Carlyle's hand, tries to shake it. 'God damn it's good to see them taken down a notch. Them and their thieving 'gifts of goodwill.' You're a good man, Carlyle. Good man.'

His grins blearily. 'I'm going to be rich because of you. Rich!' He laughs and paws for Carlyle's hand again. 'Good man,' he says as he gets a grip. 'Good man.'

Lucy shouts for him to get back in line. 'Rickshaw's here, you drunk bastard!'

Otto stumbles away and with Lucy's help tries to crawl into the rickshaw. The white shirts watch coldly. A woman in an officer's uniform studies them all from the top of the temple steps, her face expressionless.

Anderson watches her. 'What do you think she's thinking?' he asks, nodding up at the woman officer. 'All these drunk *farang* crawling through her compound? What does she see?'

Carlyle draws on his cigarette and lets out smoke in a slow stream. 'The dawn of a new era.'

'Back to the future,' Anderson murmurs.

'Sorry?'

'Nothing.' Anderson shakes his head. 'Something Yates used to say. We're in the sweet spot, now. The world's shrinking.'

Lucy and Otto finally manage to climb into the rickshaw. They roll out with Otto shouting blessings on all the honorable white shirts who have made him so rich with their reparation money. Carlyle quirks an eyebrow at Anderson, the question unspoken. Anderson draws on his cigarette, considering the branches of possibility that underlie Carlyle's question.

'I want to talk to Akkarat directly.'

Carlyle snorts. 'Children want all sorts of things.'

'Children don't play this game.'

'You think you can twist him around your finger? Turn him into a good little administrator, like in India?'

Anderson favors him with a cold eye. 'More like Burma.' He smiles at Carlyle's stricken expression. 'Don't worry. We're not in the nation-breaking business anymore. All we're interested in is a free market. I'm sure we can work toward that common goal, at least. But I want the meet.'

'So cautious.' Carlyle drops his cigarette on the ground, grinds it out with his foot. 'I would have thought you'd have a more adventurous spirit.'

Anderson laughs. 'I'm not here for the adventure. That's for all of those drunks over there . . .' He trails off, stunned.

Emiko is in the crowd, standing with the Japanese delegation. He catches a glimpse of her movement in the knot of business people and political officers as they cluster around Akkarat, talking and smiling.

'My god.' Carlyle sucks in his breath. 'Is that a windup? In the compound?'

Anderson tries to say something, but can't make his throat work.

No, he's wrong. It's not Emiko. The movement is the same, but the girl is not. This one is richly dressed, with gold glimmering around her throat. A slightly different face. She lifts her hand, stutter-stop motion, tucks black silk hair behind an ear. Similar, but not the same.

Anderson's heart starts beating again.

The windup girl smiles graciously at whatever story Akkarat is telling. She turns to make introductions for a man Anderson recognizes from intelligence photos as a general manager of Mishimoto. Her patron says something to her and she ducks her head to him, then hurries away to the rickshaws, odd and graceful.

She's so much like Emiko. So stylized, so deliberate. Everything about the windup before him reminds him of that other, so much more desperate girl. He swallows, remembering Emiko in his bed, small and alone. Starving for information about windup villages. *What are they like? Who lives within them? Do they really live without patrons?* So desperate for hope. So different from this glittering windup that threads gracefully between white shirts and officials.

'I don't think she was allowed in the temple,' Anderson finally says. 'They couldn't have gone that far. The white shirts must have made her wait outside.'

'Still, they must be seething.' Carlyle cocks his head, watching the Japanese delegation. 'You know, Raleigh has one of those, too. Uses it for a freak show in the back of his place.'

Anderson swallows. 'Oh? I hadn't heard.'

'Sure. It'll fuck anything. You should see it. Truly bizarre.' Carlyle laughs low. 'Look, she's catching attention. I think the Queen's Protector is actually smitten.'

The Somdet Chaopraya is staring at the windup, wide-eyed like a cow struck on the side of the head before slaughter.

Anderson frowns, shocked despite himself. 'He wouldn't risk his status. Not with a windup.'

'Who knows? The man doesn't exactly have a clean reputation. Positively debauched, from what I've heard. He was better when the old king was alive. Kept himself under control. But now ...'

Carlyle trails off. He nods at the windup girl. 'I wouldn't be surprised if the Japanese end up making a gift of goodwill in the near future. No one refuses the Somdet Chaopraya.'

'More bribes.'

'Always. But the Somdet Chaopraya would be worth it. From everything I've heard, he's taken over most of the palace functions. Accumulated a lot of power. And that would give you a lot of insurance when the next coup happens.' Carlyle observes. 'Everyone looks calm, but below the surface things are boiling. Pracha and Akkarat can't go on like this. They've been circling each other ever since the December 12 coup.' He pauses. 'With the right pressure, we help decide who comes out on top.'

'Sounds expensive.'

'Not to your people. A bit of gold and jade. Some opium.' He lowers his voice. 'Might even be cheap, by your standards.'

'Stop selling me. Am I going to meet Akkarat or not?'

Carlyle claps Anderson on the back and laughs. 'God, I love working with *farang*. At least you're direct. Don't worry. It's already arranged.' And then he's striding back toward the Japanese delegation and hailing Akkarat. And Akkarat is looking at Anderson with bright appraising eyes. Anderson *wais* a greeting. Akkarat, as befits his high rank, favors Anderson with the barest nod of acknowledgement.

Outside the gates of the Environment Ministry, as Anderson hails Lao Gu for a ride back to the factory, a pair of Thais sweep up on either side.

'This way, *Khun*.'

They take Anderson by the elbows and guide him down the street. For a moment, Anderson thinks he's being grabbed by the white shirts, but then he sees a coal-diesel limo. He fights down paranoia as he's guided inside.

If they wanted to kill you, they could wait for any number of better times.

The door slams closed. Trade Minister Akkarat sits across from him.

'*Khun* Anderson.' Akkarat smiles. 'Thank you for joining me.'

Anderson scans the vehicle, wondering if he can break out or if the locks are controlled up front. The worst part of any job is the moment of exposure, when too many people suddenly know too many things. Finland went that way: Peters and Lei, with nooses around their necks and their feet kicking air as they were raised above the crowds.

'*Khun* Richard tells me that you have a proposal,' Akkarat prompts.

Anderson hesitates. 'I understand we have mutual interests.'

'No.' Akkarat shakes his head. 'Your people have tried to destroy mine for the last five hundred years. We have nothing in common.'

Anderson smiles tentatively. 'Of course, we see some things differently.'

The car starts to roll. Akkarat says, 'This is not a question of perspective. Ever since your first missionaries landed on our shores, you have always sought to destroy us. During the old Expansion your kind tried to take every part of us. Chopping off the arms and legs of our country. It was only through our Kings' wisdom and leadership that we avoided your worst. And yet still you weren't done with us. With the Contraction, your worshipped global economy left us starving and over-specialized.' He looks pointedly at Anderson. 'And then your calorie plagues came. You very nearly took rice from us entirely.'

'I didn't know the Minister of Trade was a conspiracy theorist.'

'Which are you?' Akkarat studies him. 'AgriGen? PurCal? Total Nutrient Holdings?'

Anderson spreads his hands. 'I understand that you would like help in arranging a more stable government. I have resources to offer, provided that we can come to an agreement.'

'What is it you want?'

Anderson looks him in the eye, serious. 'Access to your seed-bank.'

Akkarat jerks back. 'Impossible.' The car turns and begins to accelerate down Thanon Rama XII. Bangkok streams by in a blur of images as Akkarat's retinue clears the avenue ahead of them.

'Not to own.' Anderson puts out a calming hand. 'Only to sample from.'

'The seedbank has kept us independent of your kind. When blister rust and genehack weevil swept the globe, it was only the seedbank that allowed us to stave off the worst of the plagues, and even so, our people died in droves. When India and Burma and Vietnam all fell to you, we stood strong. And now you come asking for our finest weapon.' Akkarat laughs. 'I may want to see General Pracha with his hair and eyebrows shaved off, living in a forest monastery and despised by all, but on this, at least, he and I agree. No *farang* should ever touch the heart of us. You may take an arm or a leg from our country, but not the head, and certainly not the heart.'

'We need new genetic material,' Anderson says. 'We've exhausted many of our options and the plagues keep mutating. We don't have a problem sharing our research results. Profits, even.'

'I'm sure you offered the same to the Finns.'

Anderson leans forward. 'Finland was a tragedy, and not just for us. If the world is going to keep eating, we need to stay ahead of cibiscosis and blister rust and Nippon genehack weevil. It's the only way.'

'You're saying that you yoked the world to your patented grains and seeds, happily enslaved us all – and now you finally realize that you are dragging us all to hell.'

'That's what the Grahamites like to say.' Anderson shrugs. 'The reality is that weevils and blister rust don't wait. And we're the only ones with the scientific resources to hack our way out of this mess. We're hoping that somewhere in your seedbank we'll find a key.'

'And if you don't?'

'Then it won't really matter who runs the Kingdom; we'll all be coughing blood from the next mutation of cibiscosis.'

'It's impossible. The Environment Ministry controls the seed stock.'

'I was under the impression that we were discussing a change in administration.'

Akkarat frowns. 'You want samples, this is all? You're offering weapons, equipment, payoffs, and this is all you want?'

Anderson nods. 'And one other thing. A man. Gibbons.' He watches Akkarat for a reaction.

'Gibbons?' Akkarat shrugs. 'I have never heard of him.'

'A *farang*. One of ours. We'd like him back. He's been infringing on our intellectual property.'

'And that bothers you a great deal, I'm sure.' Akkarat laughs. 'It's very interesting to actually meet one of your kind. Of course we all talk about the calorie men crouching on Koh Angrit, like demons or *phii krasue,* plotting to swallow the Kingdom, but you . . .' He studies Anderson. 'I could have you executed by megodont if I chose, ripped apart and left for kites and crows. And no one would raise a finger. In the past, if even a whisper of a calorie man amongst us touched the streets it was enough to trigger protests and riots. And yet here you sit. So confident.'

'Times have changed.'

'Not as much as you suggest. Are you brave, or simply foolish?'

'I could ask the same question,' Anderson says. 'Not many people poke the white shirts in the eye and expect to get away with it.'

Akkarat smiles. 'If you had come to me last week with your offers of money and equipment, I would have been very grateful.' He shrugs. 'This week, in light of present circumstances and recent successes, I will take your offer under advisement.' He taps on the window for the driver to pull over.

'You're lucky I'm in a good mood. On another day, I would have seen a calorie man torn into blood pieces and called it a very good day.' He indicates that Anderson should get out. 'I'll consider your offer.'

15

There is a place for New People.

The hope of it runs through Emiko's head every day, every minute, every second. The memory of the *gaijin* Anderson, and his conviction that the place truly exists. His hands on her in the darkness, eyes solemn as he nodded and confirmed.

So now she stares at Raleigh every night, wondering what the man knows, and if she dares to ask him about what he has seen in the north. About the route to safety. Three times she has approached him and each time her voice has failed her, leaving the question unasked. Each night she returns home, exhausted from the abuse that Kannika metes out, and falls into dreams of a place where New People dwell in safety, without patrons or masters.

Emiko remembers Mizumi-sensei at the *kaizen* studio where she taught all the young New People as they knelt in kimonos and took their lessons.

'*What are you?*'

'*New People.*'

'*What is your honor?*'

'*It is my honor to serve.*'

'*Who do you honor?*'

'*I honor my patron.*'

Mizumi-sensei was swift with a switch, one hundred years old and terrifying. An early New Person, her skin was nearly unaged. Who knew how many young ones she had shepherded through her studio? Mizumi-sensei, always there, always advising. Brutal in her anger, and yet fair in her punishments. And always the instruction, the faith that if they served their patron well, that they had attained their highest state.

Mizumi-sensei introduced them all to Mizuko Jizo Bodhisattva, who has compassion even for New People, and who would hide them in his sleeves after their deaths and smuggle them out of the hell world of genetically engineered toys and into the true cycle of life. Their duty was to serve, their honor was to serve, and their reward would come in the next life, when they became fully human. Service would yield the greatest rewards.

How Emiko had hated Mizumi-sensei when Gendo-sama abandoned her.

But now her heart beats again at the thought of a new patron: a wise man, a guide into a different world, one who can provide what Gendo-sama would not.

Another who lies to you? Who will betray you?

She squashes the thought. It is the other Emiko who thinks this. Not her highest self at all, as if she is nothing but a cheshire, bent on glutting herself, unconcerned with what her niche may be, overrunning everything. Not a thought appropriate to New People at all.

Mizumi-sensei taught that there are two parts to a New Person's nature. The evil half, ruled by the animal hungers of their genes, by the many splicings and additions that changed them into what they were. And balanced against this, the civilized self, the side that knows the difference between niche and animal urge. That comprehends its place in the hierarchies of their country and people, and appreciates the gift their patrons provide by giving them life.

Dark and light. *In-Yo*. Two sides of a coin, two sides of the soul. Mizumi-sensei helped them own their souls. Prepared them for the honor of service.

To be honest, it is only Gendo-sama's poor treatment of her that makes Emiko think so badly of him. He was a weak man. Or, perhaps, if she is honest, she was not all she could have been. She did not serve to her utmost. That is the sad truth. A bit of shame that she must accept, even as she strives to live without the loving hand of a patron. But perhaps this strange *gaijin* . . . perhaps . . . She will not let the cynical animal into her mind tonight; she will let herself dream.

Emiko spills out of her tower slum into Bangkok's cooling evening. A carnival feel informs the green-tinged streets, woks burning their nighttime noodles, offering simple dishes to the farmers of the market before they return to distant fields for the night. Emiko wanders through the night market, one eye out for white shirts, one on dinner.

She finds a vendor of grilled squid and takes one dipped in chile sauce. In the candlelight and shadows, she has cover of sorts. Her *pha sin* hides the movement of her legs. It is only her arms she must concern herself with, and if she is slow, careful, and keeps them close to her side, her movements can be mistaken for daintiness.

From a woman and her daughter, Emiko buys a folded banana leaf plate, cupping a nest of fried U-Tex *padh seeu*. The woman fries the noodles over blue methane, illegal, but not impossible to obtain. Emiko sits at a makeshift counter to shovel them in, her mouth burning at the spice. Others look at her strangely, a few make faces of distaste, but they do nothing. Some of them are even familiar with her. The rest have enough troubles without tangling themselves in the business of windups and white shirts. It is a strange advantage, she supposes. The white shirts are so despised that people don't draw their attention unless absolutely necessary. She shovels the noodles into her mouth and again thinks of the *gaijin's* words.

There is a place for New People.

She tries to imagine it. A village full of people with stuttering telltale motions and smooth smooth skin. She craves it.

But there is an opposing feeling, also. Not fear. Something she never expected.

Revulsion?

No, too strong a word. More a shiver of distaste that so many of her kind have shamefully fled their duties. All of them living among one another, and not a single one as fine as Gendo-sama. A whole village of New People who have no one to serve.

Emiko shakes her head forcefully. And what has service gotten her? People like Raleigh. And Kannika.

And yet . . . a whole tribe of New People, huddled in the jungle? What would it be like to hold an eight-foot laborer in her arms? Would that be her lover? Or one of the tentacle monsters of Gendo-sama's factories, ten arms like a Hindu god and a drooling mouth that demands nothing but food and a place to put its hands? How can such a creature make its way north? Why are they there, in the jungle?

She forces back her revulsion. It is surely no worse than Kannika. She has been enslaved to think against New People, even when she herself is one of them. If she thinks logically, she knows that no New Person can be any worse than the client last night, who fucked her and then spat on her before he left. Surely, to lie with a smooth-skinned New Person could not be worse.

But what kind of life could it be in the village? Eating cockroaches and ants and whatever leaves haven't succumbed to ivory beetle?

Raleigh is a survivor. Are you?

She stirs her noodles with her four-inch RedStar bamboo chopsticks. What would it be like, to serve no one? Would she dare? It makes her dizzy, almost giddy to think of it. What would she do without a patron? Would she then become a farmer? Perhaps grow opium in the hills? Smoke a silver pipe and blacken her teeth as she has heard some of those strange hilltribe ladies do? She laughs to herself. Can she imagine it?

Lost in her thoughts, she nearly misses it. Only luck – the chance movement of a man at the table across from her, his startled glance and then the duck of his head as he buries his attention in his food – saves her. She freezes.

The night market has fallen silent.

And then, like hungry ghosts, the men in white appear behind her, talking in their quick song-song to the woman at the wok. The woman bustles to serve, obsequious. Emiko trembles before them, noodles halfway between mouth and lips, her slender arm suddenly shaking under the strain. She wants to put the chopsticks down, but there is nothing to do. No way to hide herself if she moves, and so she sits frozen while the men speak behind her, looming over her as they wait.

'... finally overstepped himself. I heard Bhirombhakdi was screaming up and down the offices saying he was going to get his head. 'Jaidee's head on a platter, he's gone too far!"

'He gave 5000 baht to his men, every one of them, for the raid.'

'A lot of good it does them now that he's been stripped.'

'Still, 5000, no wonder Bhirombhakdi was spitting blood. It must have been half a million that he lost.'

'And Jaidee just charged in like a megodont. The old man probably thought Jaidee was Torapee the bull, measuring his father's footprint. Looking to take him down.'

'Not anymore.'

Emiko trembles as they jostle her. This is the end. She will drop the chopsticks and they will see the windup girl, as they haven't seen her yet though they cluster around her, though they bump against her with a self-confident maleness, though one white shirt's hand is touching her neck as though accidentally pressed there by the jostle of others. Suddenly she will no longer be invisible. She will appear before them, fully formed, a New Person with nothing but expired papers and import licenses and then she will be mulched, recycled as quickly as they compost dung and cellulose, thanks to the telltale twitching movements that mark her as clearly as if she were painted in the excreta of glowworms.

'I never thought I'd see him *khrab* before Akkarat, though. That was a bad thing. We all lose face with that.'

There is a pause. Then one of them says, 'Auntie. It looks like your methane is the wrong color.'

The woman grins uncomfortably. Her daughter's smile mirrors the uncertainty. 'We made a gift to the Ministry last week,' she says.

The man who has his hand on Emiko's neck speaks, caressing her idly. She tries not to shiver under his touch. 'Then perhaps we were told wrong.'

The woman's smile falters. 'Perhaps my memory is bad.'

'Well, I'm happy to check the state of your accounts.'

She keeps the smile on her face. 'No need to trouble yourself. I'll send my daughter, now. In the meantime, why not just take these two fish for yourselves? You don't get paid enough to eat well.' She pulls two large tilapia off her grill and offers them to the men.

'That's very kind of you, auntie. I am hungry.' With the banana-leaf wrapped *plaa* tucked in their hands, the white shirts turn away and continue their journey through the night market, seemingly unaware of the terror they spread before them.

The woman's smile fades as soon as they're gone. She turns to her daughter and pushes baht into her hands. 'Go down to the police box and make sure that Sergeant Siriporn is the one you give the money to. I don't want those two coming back.'

The touch of the white shirt burns on the back of Emiko's neck. Too close. Too close by far. Strange how she sometimes forgets that she is hunted. Sometimes fools herself and thinks she is almost human. Emiko shovels the last of her noodles into her mouth. She cannot delay anymore. She must face Raleigh.

'I wish to leave this place.'

Raleigh turns on his barstool, expression bemused. 'Really, Emiko?' He smiles. 'You have a new patron, do you?'

Around them, the other girls are arriving, chattering and laughing with one another, making *wais* to the spirit house, a few of them making little offerings in hopes of encouraging a kind customer or rich patron.

Emiko shakes her head. 'Not a new patron. I wish to go north. To the villages where New People live.'

'Who told you about that?'

'It exists, yes?' From his expression she knows that it does. Her heart starts to pound. It's not just a rumor. 'It exists,' she says more firmly.

He gives her an appraising look. 'It might.' He signals Daeng the bartender for another drink. 'But I should warn you, it's a hard life out there in the jungle. You eat bugs to survive if your crops fail. Not much to hunt, not after blister rust and Nippon genehack weevil killed so much fodder.' He shrugs. 'A few birds.' He looks at her again. 'You should stay closer to the water. You'll overheat out there. Take it from me. It's damn hard living. You should look for a new patron, if you really want to get out of here.'

'The white shirts almost caught me today. I will die here, if I stay.'

'I pay them not to catch you.'

'No. I was at a night market—'

'What the hell were you doing at a night market? You want something to eat, you come here.' Raleigh scowls.

'I am so sorry. I must go. Raleigh-san, you have influence. People you can influence to help me get travel permits. To allow me to pass the checkpoints.'

Raleigh's drink arrives. He takes a sip. The old man is like a crow, all death and putrescence sitting on his barstool, watching his whores arrive for their night's work. He looks her over with barely masked disgust, as if she is a piece of dog shit stuck to his shoe. He takes another drink. 'It's a hard road north. Damn expensive.'

'I can earn my passage.'

Raleigh doesn't respond. The bartender finishes polishing the bar. He and an assistant set out a chest of ice from the luxury manufacturer *Jai Yen, Nam Yen*. Cool Heart, Cool Water.

Raleigh holds out his glass and Daeng drops a pair of cubes in with a tinkling report. Out of the insulated chest, they start to melt in the heat. Emiko watches the ice cubes sag into liquid. Daeng pours water over the cubes. She is burning up, herself. The club's open windows do nothing to catch the breeze and at this early hour the swelter inside the building is still overwhelming. None of the yellow card fan men have arrived yet, either. The club radiates heat from walls and floor, encasing them. Raleigh takes a swallow of his cool water.

Emiko watches, burning, wishing she could sweat. '*Khun* Raleigh. Please. So sorry. Please,' she hesitates, 'a cold drink.'

Raleigh sips his water and watches as more of his girls filter in. 'Keeping a windup is damn expensive.'

Emiko smiles embarrassment, hoping to assuage him. Finally, Raleigh makes a face of irritation. 'Fine.' He nods to Daeng. A glass of ice water is passed across. Emiko tries not to lunge for it. She holds it to her face and neck, almost gasping with relief. She drinks and presses the glass against herself again, clutching it like a talisman. 'Thank you.'

'Why should I help you get out of the city?'

'I will die if I stay here.'

'It's not good business. Wasn't good business to hire you. And it's definitely not good business to bribe you all the way north.'

'Please. Anything. I will pay it. I will do it. You may use me.'

He laughs. 'I've got real girls.' His smile disappears. 'The problem, Emiko, is that you've got nothing to give. You drink the money you earn every night. Your bribes cost money, your ice costs money. If I weren't so nice, I'd just throw you out in the street for the white shirts to mulch. You're not a good business proposition.'

'Please.'

'Don't piss me off. Go get ready for work. I want you out of your street clothes when the customers arrive.'

His words have the finality of true authority. Reflexively, Emiko starts to bow, acquiescing to his wishes. She stops short. *You are not a dog*, she reminds herself. *You are not a servant. Service has gotten you abandoned amongst demons in a city of divine beings. If you act like a servant, you will die like a dog.*

She straightens. 'So sorry, I must go north, Raleigh-san. Soon. How much would it cost? I will earn it.'

'You're like a goddamn cheshire.' Raleigh stands suddenly. 'You just keep coming back to pick over the dead.'

Emiko flinches. Even though he is old, Raleigh is still *gaijin*, born and fed before the Contraction. He stands tall. She takes another step back, unnerved by his sudden loom. Raleigh smiles grimly. 'That's right, don't forget your place. You'll go north, all right. But you'll do it when I'm good and ready. And not until you've earned every baht for the white shirt bribes.'

'How much?'

His face reddens. 'More than you've made 'til now!'

She jumps back but Raleigh grabs her. He yanks her close. His voice is a low whiskey growl. 'You were useful to someone, once, so I see how a windup like you might forget herself. But let's not fool ourselves. I own you.'

His bony hand fumbles at her breast, seizes a nipple and twists. She whimpers in pain and wilts under his hand. His pale blue water eyes watch her like a snake's.

'I own every part of you,' he murmurs. 'If I want you mulched tomorrow, you're gone. No one will care. People in Japan might value a windup. Here, you're just trash.' He squeezes again. She takes a shuddering breath, trying to keep her feet. He smiles. 'I own you. Remember that.'

He releases her abruptly. Emiko stumbles back and catches the bar's edge.

Raleigh returns to his drink. 'I'll let you know when you've earned enough to go north,' he says. 'But you'll work for it, and work for it good. No more of your picky ways. If a man wants you, you go with him and make him happy enough that he wants to come back and try the novelty again. I've got plenty of natural girls offering natural sex. If you're going to go north, you'd better start offering something more.'

He upends his drink, gulping it, and slaps the glass down on the bar for Daeng to refill.

'Now quit sulking and start earning.'

16

Hock Seng scowls at the safe where it squats across from him. It's early morning in the SpringLife office, and he should be busy forging a ledger before Mr. Lake arrives, but the safe is all he can focus on. It mocks him, sitting there, enveloped in the smoke of offerings which have done nothing to open it.

Ever since the anchor pad incident the safe is always locked, and now the devil Lake is always looking over his shoulder, asking about the state of accounts, always prying and asking questions. And still the Dung Lord waits. Hock Seng has seen him twice more. Each time the man has been patient, and yet Hock Seng senses a growing irritation, a willingness perhaps to take matters into his own hands. The window of opportunity is closing.

Hock Seng scratches numbers into the ledger, reconciling the money he skimmed from the purchase of a temporary spindle. Should he simply rob the safe? Take the risk of suspicion falling on himself? There are industrial supplies in the factory that would burn through the iron in mere hours. Is this better than making the Dung Lord wait, risking that the godfather of all godfathers will do the deed himself? Hock Seng ponders his options. All his choices come loaded with risks that make his skin crawl. If the safe is damaged, his face will soon be plastered on lamp-posts and it is a very bad time to be an enemy of the foreign devils. With Akkarat in ascendancy, the *farang* are also on the rise. Every day brings more news of white shirt humiliation. The Tiger of Bangkok is now a shaven-headed monk without family or property.

What if Mr. Lake were removed entirely? An anonymous knife in the gut as he walks down the street perhaps? It would be easy. Cheap, even. For fifteen baht Laughing Chan would do it willingly, and the foreign devil would trouble Hock Seng no more.

A knock at the door startles him. Hock Seng straightens and shoves the newly forged ledger under the desk. 'Yes?'

It's Mai, the skinny girl from the production line, standing at the threshold. Hock Seng relaxes slightly as she *wais*. '*Khun*. There is a difficulty.'

He uses a cloth to wipe the ink from his hands. 'Yes? What is it?'

Her eyes flick around the room. 'It would be better if you came. Yourself.'

She positively reeks of fear. The hairs on the back of Hock Seng's neck prickle. She's little more than a child. He has done her decent favors. She has even earned bonuses crawling down the tight passages of the drive trains, inspecting the links as they brought the factory back into working order ... and yet, something in her demeanor reminds him of when the Malays turned on his people. When his workers, always so loyal and appreciative, suddenly could not look him in the eye. If he had been clever, he would have seen the turn of the tide. Seen that the days of the Malayan Chinese were numbered. That even a man of his stature – who gave freely to charities, who helped his employees' children as if they were his own – that even his head was slated to be stacked in a gutter.

And now here is Mai, looking shifty. Is this the way they will come for him? Furtive? Sending a harmless-looking girl as bait? Is this the end of the yellow cards? Is it the Dung Lord, moving against him? Hock Seng feigns nonchalance and reclines slightly in his chair even as he watches her. 'If you have something to say,' he murmurs, 'then say it now. Here.'

She hesitates. Her fear is obvious. 'Is the *farang* near?'

Hock Seng glances at the clock on the wall. Six o'clock. 'He shouldn't be here for another hour or two. He is seldom early.'

'Please, if you could just come.'

So this is the way it will be. He nods shortly. 'Yes, of course.'

He stands and crosses to her. Such a pretty girl. Of course they would send a pretty one. She looks so harmless. He scratches at his back, lifting the loose hem of his shirt and slips the knife out, holds it behind his back as he approaches. Waits until the last moment—

He grabs her hair and yanks her close. Presses the knife against her throat.

'Who sent you? The Dung Lord? White shirts? Who?'

She gasps, unable to free herself without cutting her throat. 'No one!'

'Do you think I'm a fool?' He presses the knife home, breaking skin. 'Who is it?'

'No one! I swear!' She is shaking with fear but Hock Seng doesn't release her.

'Is there something you wish to say? Some secret you must keep? Tell it now.'

She gasps at the pressure of his blade on her neck. 'No! *Khun*! I swear! No secret! But ... But ...'

'Yes?'

She sags against him. 'The white shirts,' she whispers. 'If the white shirts find out ...'

'I'm no white shirt.'

'It's Kit. Kit is ill. And Srimuang. Both of them. Please. I don't know what to do. I don't want to lose the job. I don't know what to do. Please don't tell the *farang*. Everyone knows the *farang* might close the factory. Please. My family needs . . .Please. Please.' She is sobbing now, sagging against him, begging him as if he might be her savior, mindless of the knife.

Hock Seng grimaces and pulls the knife away, suddenly feeling old. This is what it is to live in fear. To suspect thirteen-year-old girls, to think that daughter mouths intend your death. He feels sick. He can't meet her eyes. 'You should have said so,' he mutters gruffly. 'Stupid girl. These are not matters to be coy about.' He lifts his shirt and slides the knife back into its sheathe. 'Show me your friends.'

She carefully wipes her tears away. She is not resentful. She is adaptable as young people often are. With the crisis past, she obediently leads him out of the office.

Down on the factory floor, workers are beginning to arrive. The great doors rattle wide and sun pours into the huge hall. Dung and dust motes swirl in the light. Mai leads him through the fining room, kicking through pale dust residue and on into the cutting rooms.

Overhead, the screens of algae fill the room with the sea reek of their drying. She leads him past the cutting presses, and ducks under the line. On the other side, the algae tanks sit in silent ranks, full of salt and life. More than half of the tanks show signs of reduced production. Algae barely covers their surfaces, even though the skim should be more than four inches thick after a night without harvesting.

'There,' Mai whispers, pointing. Kit and Srimuang both lie against a wall. The two men look up at Hock Seng with dull eyes. Hock Seng kneels close, but doesn't touch.

'Have they eaten together?'

'I don't think so. They are not friends.'

'It couldn't be cibiscosis? Blister rust? No.' He shakes his head. 'I'm a stupid old man. It is neither. There is no blood on their lips.'

Kit moans, tries to sit up. Hock Seng flinches away, fighting an urge to wipe his hands on his shirt. The other man, Srimuang, looks even worse.

'What was this one's responsibility?'

Mai hesitates. 'I think he fed the tanks. Poured the sacks of fish meal for the algae.'

Hock Seng's skin crawls. Two bodies. Lying beside the tanks that Hock Seng himself brought back to full production for the benefit of Mr. Anderson, rushing to please him. Is it coincidence? He shivers, eyeing the room from a new perspective. Overflow from the vats dampens the floor and pools near the rusting drains. Blooms of algae decorate the damp surface, feeding on left-over nutrients. Vectors everywhere, if there is something wrong with the tanks.

Hock Seng instinctively starts to wipe his hands, then stops short, skin crawling anew. The gray powders of the fining room cling to his palms, marking where he pushed the curtains aside as he passed through. He's surrounded by potential vectors. Overhead, the drying screens hang suspended, their racks filling the warehouse dimness, bank after bank, smeared with blackening skim. A drop of water falls from a screen. Spatters the floor beside his foot. And with it comes awareness of a new sound. He never heard it when the factory was full of people. But now, in this early morning quiet, it is all around: the gentle patter of rain from the screens above.

Hock Seng stands abruptly, fighting rising panic.

Don't be a fool. You don't know it is the algae. Death comes in many forms. It could be any sort of disease.

Kit's breathing is strangely ragged in the stillness, a panting bellows as his chest rises and falls.

'Do you think it is pandemic?' Mai asks.

Hock Seng glares at her. 'Don't say those words! Do you wish to bring demons down on us? White shirts? If news gets out, they'll shut down the factory. We'll be starving like yellow cards.'

'But—'

Outside, in the main hall, voices echo.

'Hush, child.' Hock Seng motions her to silence, thinking furiously. A white shirt investigation would be disastrous. Just the excuse the foreign devil Mr. Lake would need to shut the place down, to fire Hock Seng. To send him back to the towers to starve. To die after coming so far, after coming so close.

More morning greetings echo from the rest of the factory. A megodont groans. Doors rattle wide. The main flywheels rumble to life as someone runs a line test.

'What should we do?' Mai asks.

Hock Seng glances around at the vats and machinery. The still empty rooms. 'You're the only one who knows they are sick?'

Mai nods. 'I found them when I came in.'

'You're sure? You didn't mention it to anyone else as you came to find me? No one else has been in here? No one was here with you and perhaps thought they would take the day off when they saw these two?'

Mai shakes her head. 'No. I came alone. I catch a ride with a farmer near the edge of the city. He brings me on his long-tail, up the *khlongs*. I always get here early.'

Hock Seng, looks down at the two sick men, then at the girl. Four of them in the room. Four. He winces at the thought. Such an unlucky number, four. *Sz.* Four. *Sz.* Death. A better number is three, or two . . .

Or one.

One is the ideal number for a secret. Unconsciously, Hock Seng's hand strays to his knife, considering the girl. Messy. But still, less messy than the number four.

The girl's long black hair is tied up in a careful bun at the top of her head to keep it free of running line equipment. Her neck is exposed. Her eyes are trusting. Hock Seng looks away, evaluating the bodies again, calculating against inauspicious numbers. Four, four, four. Death. One is better. One is best. He takes a breath and makes a decision. He reaches for her. 'Come here.'

She hesitates. He scowls at her, waves her closer. 'You want to keep your job, yes?'

She nods slowly.

'Then come. These two need to go to a hospital, yes? We cannot help them here. And two sick men lying beside the algae baths will do none of us any good. Not if we want to keep on eating. Gather them and meet me at the side door. Not through the main room. The side one. Go under the line with them, through the service access. The side, you understand?'

She nods uncertainly. He claps his hands together, spurring her to action. 'Quickly now! Quickly! Drag them if you must!' He motions to the bodies. 'People will be arriving. One person is already too many to keep a secret, and here we stand, four. Let us make this a secret of two, at least. Anything is better than four.' *Death.*

She takes a frightened breath, then her eyes narrow with determination. She crouches to wrestle with Kit's body. Hock Seng watches to make sure she is underway, then ducks out.

In the main hall, people are still stowing their lunches and laughing. No one in a rush. The Thai are lazy. If they were Chinese yellow cards they would already be working and all would be lost. For once, Hock Seng is glad he works with Thais. He still has a little time. He ducks out the side door.

Outside, the alley is empty. High factory walls pin the narrow way. Hock Seng jogs toward Phosri Street and its jumble of break-fast stalls, steaming noodles and ragged children. A cycle rickshaw flashes across the gap.

'*Wei!*' He calls out. '*Samloh! Samloh!* Wait!' But he is too far away.

He limps to the intersection favoring his bad knee, catches sight of another rickshaw. He flags the driver. The man glances behind to see if he is threatened by competition, then angles toward Hock Seng with a lackadaisical pedal, allowing the slight slope of the street to let him coast.

'Faster!' Hock Seng shouts. '*Kuai yidian,* you dog fucker!'

The man ignores the abuse, lets his cycle coast to a stop. 'You called me, *Khun?*'

Hock Seng climbs in and waves down the alley. 'I have passengers for you, if you'll hurry up.'

The man grunts and steers down the narrow way. The cycle's chain clicks sedately. Hock Seng grits his teeth. 'Double pay. Quickly, quickly!' He motions the man onward.

The man leans on his pedals marginally more aggressively, but still he shambles like a megodont. Ahead, Mai appears. For a moment Hock Seng is afraid that she will be stupid and bring out the bodies before the rickshaw arrives, but Kit is nowhere in sight. It is only when the rickshaw comes close that she slips back inside and drags the first incoherent worker into view.

The rickshaw man shies at the body, but Hock Seng leans over his shoulder and hisses, 'Triple pay.' He grabs Kit and wrestles him into the rickshaw's seat before the man can protest. Mai disappears back inside.

The cycle-rickshaw man eyes Kit. 'What's wrong with him?'

'He's a drunk,' Hock Seng says. 'He and his friend. If the boss catches them, they're fired.'

'He doesn't look drunk.'

'You're mistaken.'

'No. That one looks like—'

Hock Seng stares at the man. 'The white shirts will cast their net over you as surely as they will me. He is on your seat, in your breathing presence.'

The rickshaw man's eyes widen. He draws back. Hock Seng nods confirmation, holding the man's gaze. 'There's no point in making a complaint now. I say they are drunk. Triple pay to you, when you return.'

Mai reappears with the second worker and Hock Seng helps lever him into the seat. He ushers Mai into the rickshaw with the men. 'Hospitals,' he says. And then he leans close. 'But different hospitals, yes?'

Mai nods sharply.

'Good. Clever girl.' Hock Seng steps back. 'Go on then! Go! Beat it!'

The rickshaw man sets off, pedalling much faster than before. Hock Seng watches them ride away, the heads of the three passengers and the rickshaw man, rattling and bouncing as the bike's wheels chatter over cobbles. He grimaces. Four again. A bad number for certain. He pushes paranoia away, wondering if he is even capable of strategizing these days. An old man who jumps at shadows.

Would he be better off if Mai and Kit and Srimuang were feeding red-fin *plaa* in the murky waters of the Chao Phraya River? If they were just a collection of anonymous parts bobbing amongst the roiling bodies of hungry carp, would he not be safer?

Four. *Sz*. Death.

His skin crawls at the proximity of sickness. He rubs his hands unconsciously against his trousers. He'll have to bathe. Rub down with a chlorine bleach scrub and hope it does the job. The rickshaw man turns out of sight, carrying his diseased cargo. Hock Seng heads back inside, to the factory floor where the lines rattle with test runs and voices call out to one another in morning greeting.

Please let it be coincidence, he prays. *Please don't let it be the line.*

17

How many nights has he gone without sleep? One night? Ten nights? Ten thousand? Jaidee cannot remember anymore. Moons have passed awake and suns have passed in dream and everything is counting, numbers spinning out in a steady accumulation of days and hopes dashed. Propitiations and offerings unanswered. Fortune tellers with their predictions. Generals with their assurances. Tomorrow. Three days, for certain. There are indications of a softening, whispers of a woman's whereabouts.

Patience.

Jai yen.

Cool heart.

Nothing.

Apologies and humiliations in the newspapers. A personal criticism, by his own hand. More false admissions of greed and corruption. Two hundred thousand baht that he cannot repay. Editorials and condemnations in the whisper sheets. Stories spread by his enemies that he spent stolen money on whores, on a private stock of U-Tex rice against famines, that he squirrelled it away for personal benefit. The Tiger was nothing more than another corrupt white shirt.

Fines are meted out. The last of his property confiscated. The family home burned, a funeral pyre, while his mother-in-law wails and his sons, already stripped of his name, watch somnolent.

It has been decided that he will not serve his penance in a nearby monastery. Instead he will be banished to the forests of Phra Kritipong where ivory beetle has turned the land into waste and where blister rust rewrites waft across the border from Burma. Banished to the wastelands to contemplate the *damma*. His eyebrows are shaved, his head is a simple pate. If he happens to return from his penance alive, he looks forward to a lifetime of guarding yellow cards in their internments down in the south: the lowest work, for the lowest white shirt.

And yet still no word of Chaya.

Is she alive? Is she dead? Was it Trade? Was it another? A *jao por,* incensed at Jaidee's audacity? Was it someone within the Environment Ministry? Bhirom-bhakdi, irritated at Jaidee's disregard for protocol? Was it meant as a kidnapping, or murder? Did she die fighting to get free? Is she still in that concrete room of the photograph, somewhere in the city, sweating in an abandoned tower, waiting for him to rescue her? Does her corpse feed cheshires in an alley? Does she float in the Chao Phraya, food now for the Boddhi Carp rev 2.3 that the Ministry has bred with such success? He has nothing but questions. He shouts into the well, but no echo returns.

And so now he sits in a barren monk's *kuti* on the temple grounds of Wat Bowonniwet, waiting to hear whether Phra Kritipong's monastery will actually accept the task of reforming him. He wears the white of a novice. He will not wear orange. Not ever. He is not a monk. He does a special penance. His eyes follow rusty water stains on the wall, the blooms of mold and rot.

On one wall, a *bo* tree is painted, the Buddha sitting beneath it as he seeks enlightenment.

Suffering. All is suffering. Jaidee stares at the *bo* tree. Just another relic of history. The Ministry has artificially preserved a few, ones that didn't burst to kindling under the internal pressure of the ivory beetles breeding, the beetles burrowing and hatching in the tangled trunks of the *bo* until they burst forth, flying, and spreading to their next victim and their next and their next . . .

All is transient. Even *bo* trees cannot last.

Jaidee touches his eyebrows, fingering the pale half-moons above his eyes where hair once stood. He still hasn't gotten used to his shaven state. Everything changes. He stares up at the *bo* tree and the Buddha.

I was asleep. All along, I was asleep and never understood.

But now, as he stares at the relic *bo* tree, something shifts.

Nothing lasts forever. A *kuti* is a cell. This cell is a prison. He sits in a prison, while the ones who took Chaya live and drink and whore and laugh. Nothing is permanent. This is the central teaching of the Buddha. Not a career, not an institution, not a wife, not a tree . . . All is change; change is the only truth.

He stretches a hand toward the painting and traces the flaking paint, wondering if the man who painted it used a real living *bo* tree as model, if he was lucky enough to live when they lived, or if he modeled it from a photo. Copied from a copy.

In a thousand years will they even know that *bo* trees existed? Will Niwat and Surat's great-grandchildren know that there were other fig trees, also all gone? Will they know that there were many many trees and that they were of many types? Not just a Gates teak, and a generipped PurCal banana, but many, many others as well?

Will they understand that we were not fast enough or smart enough to save them all? That we had to make choices?

The Grahamites who preach on the streets of Bangkok all talk of their Holy Bible and its stories of salvation. Their stories of Noah Bodhisattva, who saved all the animals and trees and flowers on his great bamboo raft and helped them cross the waters, all the broken pieces of the world piled atop his raft while he hunted

for land. But there is no Noah Bodhisattva now. There is only Phra
Seub who feels the pain of loss but can do little to stop it, and the
little mud Buddhas of the Environment Ministry, who hold back
rising waters by barest luck.

The *bo* tree blurs. Jaidee's cheeks are wet with tears. Still he
stares up at it and the Buddha in his pose of meditation. Who
would have thought the calorie companies would attack figs? Who
would have thought the *bo* trees would die as well? The *farang* have
no respect for anything but money. He wipes the water off his face.
It is stupid to think that anything lasts forever. Perhaps even
Buddhism is transient.

He stands and gathers his white novice robes around him. He
wais to the flaking paint of the Buddha under his disappeared tree.

Outside, the moon shines bright. A few green methane lamps
glow, barely lighting the paths through the reengineered teak trees
to the monastery gates. It is foolish to grasp for things that cannot
be regained. All things die. Chaya is already lost to him. Such is
change.

No one guards the gates. It is assumed that he is obedient. That
he will scrape and beg for any hope of Chaya's return. That he will
allow himself to be broken. He's not even sure if anyone cares now
about his final fate. He has served his purpose. Dealt a blow to
General Pracha, lost face for the entire Environment Ministry. If
he stays or leaves, what of it?

He walks out onto the night streets of the City of Divine Beings
and heads south, toward the river, toward the Grand Palace and
the glittering lights of the city, down through streets half-popu-
lated. Toward the levees that keep the city from drowning under
the curse of the *farang*.

The City Pillar Shrine rises ahead of him, its roofs gleaming,
Buddha images alight with offerings, sweet incense pouring from
them. It was here that Rama XII declared that the city of Krung

Thep would not be abandoned. Would not fall to the likes of the *farang* the way that Ayutthaya fell to the Burmese so many centuries before.

Over the chanting of nine hundred ninety-nine monks dressed in saffron robes, the King declared that the city would be saved, and from that moment he charged the Ministry of the Environment with its defense. Charged them with the building of the great levees and the tide pools that would buffer the city against the wash of monsoon flood and the surge of typhoon waves. Krung Thep would stand.

Jaidee walks on, listening to the steady chant of monks who pray every minute of the day, summoning the power of the spirit worlds to Bangkok's aid. There were times when he himself knelt on the cool marble of the shrine, prostrate before the city's central pillar, begging for the help of the King and the spirits and whatever life force the city was imbued with as he went forth to do his work. The city pillar was talismanic. It gave him faith.

Now he walks past in his white robes and doesn't look twice.

All things are transient.

He continues through the streets, makes his way into the crowded quarters along the back of Charoen Khlong. The waters lap quietly. No one poles its dark surface this late at night. But ahead, on one of the screened porches a candle flickers. He steals closer.

'Kanya!'

His old lieutenant turns, surprised. She composes her features, but not before Jaidee has a chance to read her shock at what stands before her: this forgotten man without a hair on his head, without even his eyebrows, grinning madly at her from the foot of her steps. He removes his sandals and climbs in white like a ghost up the stairs. Jaidee is aware of the appearance he presents, can't help but enjoy the humor as he opens the screens and slips within.

'I thought you had already gone to the forests,' Kanya says.

Jaidee settles beside her, arranging his robes around him. He stares out at the stinking waters of the *khlong*. A mango tree's branches reflect against the moonlight liquid silver. 'It takes a long time to find a monastery willing to soil itself with my sort. Even Phra Kritipong seems to have second thoughts when it comes to enemies of Trade.'

Kanya makes a face. 'Everyone talks about how they are in ascendancy. Akkarat speaks openly of allowing windup imports.'

Jaidee startles. 'I hadn't heard of such. A few *farang*, but . . .'

Kanya makes a face. ''All respect to the Queen, but windups do not riot." She forces her thumb into the hard peel of a mangosteen. Its purple skin, nearly black in the darkness, peels away. 'Torapee measuring his father's footprints.'

Jaidee shrugs. 'All things change.'

Kanya grimaces. 'How can one fight their money? Money is their power. Who remembers their patrons? Who remembers their obligations when money comes surging in as strong and deep as the ocean against the seawalls?' She grimaces. 'We are not fighting the rising waters. We are fighting money.'

'Money is attractive.'

Kanya makes a bitter face. 'Not to you. You were a monk even before they sent you to a *kuti*.'

'Perhaps that's why I make such a poor novice.'

'Shouldn't you be in your *kuti* now?'

Jaidee grins. 'It was cramping my style.'

Kanya stills, looks hard at Jaidee. 'You're not ordaining?'

'I'm a fighter, not a monk.' He shrugs. 'Sitting in a *kuti* and meditating will do no good. I let myself become confused about that. Losing Chaya confused me. '

'She will return. I'm sure of it.'

Jaidee smiles sadly at his protégé, so full of hope and faith. It's surprising that a woman who smiles so little and sees so much melancholy in the world can believe that in this case – this one exceptional case – that the world will turn in a positive direction.

'No. She will not.'

'She will!'

Jaidee shakes his head. 'I always thought you were the skeptical one.'

Kanya's face is anguished. 'You've done everything to signal capitulation. You have no face left! They must let her go!'

'They will not. I think that she was dead within a day. I only clung to hope because I was mad for her.'

'You don't know she's dead. They could still be holding her.'

'As you pointed out, I have no face left. If this were a lesson, she would have returned by now. It was a different sort of message than we thought.' Jaidee contemplates the still waters of the *khlong*. 'I need a favor from you.'

'Anything.'

'Loan me a spring gun.'

Kanya's eyes widen. '*Khun* ...'

'Don't worry. I'll bring it back. I don't need you to come with me. I just need a good weapon.'

'I ...'

Jaidee grins. 'Don't worry. I'll be fine. And there's no reason to destroy two careers.'

'You're going after Trade.'

'Akkarat needs to understand that the Tiger still has teeth.'

'You don't even know if it was Trade who took her.'

'Who else, really?' Jaidee shrugs. 'I have made many enemies, but in the end, there is really only one.' He smiles. 'There is Trade and there is me. I was foolish to let people convince me otherwise.'

'I'll come with you.'

'No. You will stay here. You will keep an eye on Niwat and Surat. That is all I ask of you, Lieutenant.'

'Please don't do this. I will beg Pracha, I will go to—'

Jaidee cuts her off, before she speaks of ugliness. There was a time when he would have let her lose face before him, would have allowed her apologies to spill forth like a waterfall during the monsoon, but not anymore.

'I don't wish for anything else,' he says. 'I am content. I will go to Trade and I will make them pay. All of this is *kamma*. I was not meant to keep Chaya forever, or she to keep me. But I think there are still things we can do if we hold tight to our *damma*. We all have our duties, Kanya. To our patrons, to our men.' He shrugs. 'I've had many different lives. I was a boy, and a *muay thai* champion, and a father, and a white shirt.' He glances down at the folds of his novice's clothes. 'A monk, even.' He grins. 'Don't worry about me. I have a few more stages yet to traverse before I give up on this life and go to meet Chaya.' He lets his voice harden. 'I still have unfinished business, and I won't stop until it is done.'

Kanya watches him, eyes anguished. 'You can't go alone.'

'No. I will take Somchai.'

Trade: the ministry that functions with impunity, that scoffs at him so easily, that steals his wife and leaves a hole in him the size of a durian.

Chaya.

Jaidee studies the building. In the face of all those blazing lights, he feels like a savage in the wilderness, like a hilltribe spirit doctor staring at the advance of a megodont army. For a moment, his sense of mission falters.

I should see the boys, he tells himself. *I could go home.*

And yet here he is in the darkness, watching the lights of the Ministry of Trade, where they burn their coal allocation as though the Contraction never happened, as though there are no seawalls needed to keep back the ocean.

Somewhere in there a man squats and plans. The man who watched him at the anchor pads so long ago. Who spat betel and sauntered away as if Jaidee were nothing more than a cockroach to be crushed. Who sat beside Akkarat and observed silently as Jaidee was thrown down. That man will lead to Chaya's resting place. That man is the key. Somewhere inside those glowing windows.

Jaidee ducks back into the darkness. He and Somchai wear dark street clothes, stripped of all identifiers, the better to blend with the night. Somchai is a fast one. One of the best. Dangerous close in, and quiet. He knows his way around a lock, and, like Jaidee, he is motivated.

Somchai's face is serious as he studies the building. Almost as serious as Kanya, when Jaidee considers it. The demeanor seems to creep up on all of them, eventually. Seems to come with the work. Jaidee wonders if the Thai ever really smiled as he has heard in legends. Every time he hears his boys laugh, it is as if some beautiful orchid has blossomed in the forest.

'They sell themselves cheaply,' Somchai murmurs.

Jaidee nods shortly. 'I remember when Trade was just a bit portfolio under Agriculture, and now look at it.'

'You're showing your age. Trade was always a big ministry.'

'No. Just a tiny department. A joke.' Jaidee waves at the new complex with its high-tech convection vents, with its awnings and porticos. 'It's a new world, once again.'

As if to taunt him, a pair of cheshires jump up on a balustrade to preen and wash. They molt in and out of view, careless of discovery. Jaidee pulls out his spring gun and takes aim. 'That's what Trade has given us. Cheshires should be on their badge.'

'Please don't.'

He looks at Somchai. 'It carries no karmic cost. They have no soul.'

'They bleed like any other animal.'

'You could say the same of ivory beetles.'

Somchai ducks his head, but doesn't say anything more. Jaidee scowls and puts his spring gun back in its holster. It would be a waste of ammunition anyway. There are always more.

'I used to be on the poison details for cheshires,' Somchai says finally.

'Now it's you who shows your age.'

Somchai shrugs. 'I had a family then.'

'I didn't know.'

'Cibiscosis.118.Aa. It was quick.'

'I remember. My father died with that one as well. A bad iteration.'

Somchai nods. 'I miss them. I hope they reincarnated well.'

'I'm sure they did.'

He shrugs. 'One can hope. I became a monk for them. Ordained for a full year. I prayed. Did many offerings.' He says again, 'One can hope.'

The cheshires yowl again as Somchai watches. 'I've killed thousands of them. Thousands. I've killed six men in my life and never regretted any of them, but I've killed thousands of cheshires and have never felt at ease.' He pauses, scratches behind his ear at a bloom of arrested *fa' gan* fringe. 'I sometimes wonder if my family's cibiscosis was karmic retribution for all those cheshires.'

'It couldn't be. They're not natural.'

Somchai shrugs. 'They breed. They eat. They live. They breathe.' He smiles slightly. 'If you pet them, they will purr.'

Jaidee makes a face of disgust.

'It's true. I have touched them. They are real. As much as you or I.'

'They're just empty vessels. No soul fills them.'

Somchai shrugs. 'Maybe even the worst monstrosities of the Japanese live in some way. I worry that Noi and Chart and Malee and Prem have been reborn in windup bodies. Not all of us are good enough to become Contraction *phii*. Maybe some of us become windups, in Japanese factories, working working working, you know? We're so few in comparison to the past, where did all the souls go? Maybe to the Japanese? Maybe into windups?'

Jaidee masks his uneasiness at the direction of Somchai's words. 'It's impossible.'

Somchai shrugs again. 'Still. I could not bear to hunt a cheshire again.'

'Then let's hunt men.'

Across the street, a door is opening and a Ministry worker steps outside. Jaidee is already crossing the street, sprinting to catch the man. Their target strides to a rack of bicycles and bends down to unlock a wheel. Jaidee's club slides free. The man looks up and gasps and then Jaidee is on top of him, baton swinging. The man has time to raise an arm. Jaidee swats it aside and then he is inside the man's reach and clubs him across the head.

Somchai catches up. 'You're fast for an old man.'

Jaidee smiles. 'Take his feet.'

They lug the body back across the street, slipping into the puddled blackness between the methane lamps. Jaidee goes through his pockets. Keys jingle. He grins and raises them to show the prize. He ties the man quickly, blindfolds and gags him. A cheshire drifts close, watching, a molting of calico and shadow and stone.

'Will the cheshires eat him?' Somchai wonders.

'If you cared, you would have let me kill them.'

Somchai ponders this, but doesn't say anything. Jaidee finishes binding the man. 'Come on.' They jog back across the street, slip to the door. The key enters easily, and they are inside.

In the glare of electricity, Jaidee stifles the urge to locate light switches and plunge the Ministry into darkness. 'Stupid to have people working so late. Burning all this carbon.'

Somchai shrugs. 'Our man may be here in the building, even now.'

'Not if he's lucky.' But Jaidee has the same thought. He wonders if he will be able to restrain himself if he catches Chaya's killer. Wonders why he should.

They slip through more lighted halls. A few people are still present, but no one gives them a second glance as they stride by. Both of them walk with authority, have the air of men others must defer to. Jaidee acknowledges others with a quick inclination of his head as he walks past. Eventually he finds the records offices he requires. Somchai and Jaidee pause in front of glass doors. Jaidee hefts his baton.

'Glass.' Somchai notes.

'You want to try?'

Somchai examines the lock, pulls out a set of tools, sets to work probing the aperture, massaging its tumblers. Jaidee stands beside him, waiting impatiently. The corridor blazes with light.

Somchai fiddles with the locks.

'Eh. Never mind.' Jaidee hefts his baton. 'Move aside.'

The shattering is quick; the sound echoes and fades. They wait for footsteps but there are none. They both slip inside and proceed to rifle through the cabinets. Eventually Jaidee finds the personnel files, and then there is a long period of examining poor photographs, of setting aside ones that seem familiar, sifting, sorting.

'He knew me.' Jaidee mutters. 'He looked right at me.'

'Everyone knows you,' Somchai observes. 'You are famous.'

Jaidee grimaces. 'You think he was at the anchor pads to collect something? Or just there for the inspections themselves?'

'Or perhaps they wanted whatever was in Carlyle's holds. Or some other dirigible that aborted arrival and dropped in Occupied Lanna, instead. There are a thousand possibilities, no?'

'Here!' Jaidee points. 'This is the one.'

'You're sure? His face was narrower, I thought.'

'I'm sure of it.'

Somchai frowns as he scans the file over Jaidee's shoulder. 'A low-level man. Not important at all. No one with influence.'

Jaidee shakes his head. 'No. He has power. I saw the way he looked at me. He was at the ceremony when I was demoted.' He frowns. 'There is no address information from him. Just Krung Thep.'

The sound of scuffling comes from outside. A pair of men stand in the broken doorway with their spring guns drawn. 'Hold!'

Jaidee grimaces. Clasps the file behind his back. 'Yes? There is a difficulty?' The guards step through the door, survey the office.

'Who are you?'

Jaidee looks at Somchai. 'I thought you said I was famous.'

Somchai shrugs. 'Not everyone loves *muay thai*.'

'But still, everyone gambles. They should have at least placed bets on my fights.'

The guards come closer. They order Jaidee and Somchai onto their knees. As the guards come around to secure them, Jaidee lashes out with an elbow. Catches one guard in the gut. Whirls with a knee that slams the man in the head. The other guard fires a stream of blades before Somchai hits him in the throat. The man falls, dropping his pistol, gurgling through a broken windpipe.

Jaidee grabs the surviving guard, drags him close. 'Do you know this man?' He holds up the picture of his target. The guard's eyes widen and he shakes his head, tries to crawl away towards his pistol. Jaidee kicks it out of reach, then kicks the man in his ribs. 'Tell me everything about him! He's yours. Akkarat's.'

The guard shakes his head. 'No!'

Jaidee kicks him in the face, drawing blood. Gets down beside the mewling man. 'Tell me, or you follow your friend.'

Both their eyes travel to the gurgling man, strangling on his own crushed airway.

'Tell me,' Jaidee says.

'No need for that.'

At the door, the object of Jaidee's hunger stands.

Men pour in through the door ahead of him. Jaidee draws his pistol, but they fire and blades slash into his gun arm. He drops the pistol. Blood pours. He turns to run for the office's windows, but men tackle him, skidding on the wet marble. Everyone goes down in a tangle of limbs. Somewhere far away, Jaidee hears Somchai bellowing. His arms are yanked behind him. Zip straps bind his wrists in rattan bonds.

'Tourniquet that!' the man orders. 'I don't want him bleeding to death.'

Jaidee looks down. Blood is welling out of his arm. His captors staunch the flow. He's not sure if he's lightheaded from blood loss or the sudden lust he has for his enemy's death. They yank him upright. Somchai joins him, his nose pouring blood, his eye closed. Teeth red. Behind him on the floor, two men lie still.

The man studies the two of them. Jaidee returns the gaze, refusing to look away.

'Captain Jaidee. You were supposed to have entered the monkhood.'

Jaidee tries to shrug. 'My *kuti* didn't have enough light. I thought I'd do my penance here, instead.'

The man smiles slightly. 'We can arrange that.' He nods to his men. 'Take them upstairs.'

The men yank him and Somchai out of the room, drag them down the corridor. They reach an elevator. A real electric elevator, with dials that glow and designs of the Ramakin on the walls. Each button a small demon's mouth, and busty women playing *saw duang* and *jakae* around the edges. The doors close.

'What is your name?' Jaidee asks the man.

The man shrugs. 'It's not important.'

'You're Akkarat's creature.'

The man doesn't answer.

The doors open. They come out on the roof. Fifteen stories into the air. The men shove him and Somchai toward the lip of the building.

'Go on,' says the man. 'You wait up here. Over by the edge, where we can see you.'

They point their spring guns and order him forward until he and Somchai stand at the lip, looking down on the faint glows of the methane lamps. Jaidee studies the plunge.

So this is what it is to face death. He stares down into the depths. The street far below. The air waiting for him.

'What did you do with Chaya?' he calls back to the man.

The man smiles. 'Is that why you are here? Because we didn't return her to you soon enough?'

Jaidee feels a thrill of hope. Could he have been wrong? 'You can do what you want with me. But let her go.'

The man seems to falter. Is it guilt that makes him hesitate? Jaidee cannot tell. He is too far away. Is Chaya dead then, for certain? 'Just let her go. Do what you want with me.'

The man doesn't say anything.

Jaidee wonders if there is anything he should have done differently. It was brash of him to come here. But she was lost already. And the man has made no promises, no taunts to suggest she is alive. Was he foolish?

'Is she alive or not?' he asks.

The man smiles slightly. 'I suppose it hurts not to know.'

'Let her go.'

'It wasn't personal, Jaidee. If there had been another way ...' The man shrugs.

She is dead. Jaidee is sure of it. All part of some plan. He shouldn't have let Pracha convince him otherwise. He should have attacked immediately with the full power of his men, taught Trade a lesson in retribution. He turns to Somchai. 'I'm sorry about this.'

Somchai shrugs. 'You were always a tiger. It's in your nature. I knew that when I came with you.'

'Still, Somchai, if we die here . . .'

Somchai smiles. 'Then you will come back as a cheshire.'

Jaidee can't help a bark of surprised laughter. It feels good, this bubbling noise. He finds he can't stop. The laughter fills him up, lifting him. Even the guards snicker. Jaidee catches another glimpse of Somchai's widening smile, and his mirth redoubles.

Behind them, footsteps. A voice. 'Such a humorous party. So much laughter for a pair of thieves.'

Jaidee can barely master himself. He gasps for breath. 'There must be a mistake. We just work here.'

'I think not. Turn around.'

Jaidee turns. The Trade Minister stands before him. Akkarat in the flesh. And beside him . . . Jaidee's hilarity leaves him like hydrogen gusting from a dirigible. Akkarat is flanked by bodyguards. Black Panthers. Royal Elites, a sign of the palace's esteem to have them on his leash. Jaidee's heart goes cold. No one in the Environment Ministry is so protected. Not even General Pracha himself.

Akkarat smiles slightly at Jaidee's shock. He surveys Jaidee and Somchai as though examining tilapia in the market but Jaidee does not care. His eyes are on the nameless man behind him. The unassuming one. The one . . . Puzzle pieces click into place. 'You're not Trade at all.' He murmurs. 'You're with the palace.'

The man shrugs.

Akkarat speaks. 'You're not so bold now, are you Captain Jaidee?'

'There, I told you you were famous,' Somchai murmurs.

Jaidee almost laughs again, though the implications of this new understanding are deeply troubling. 'You truly have the palace's backing?'

Akkarat shrugs. 'Trade is in ascendancy. The Somdet Chaopraya favors an open policy.'

Jaidee measures the distance between them. Too far. 'I'm surprised a *heeya* like you would dare come so close to your dirty work.'

Akkarat smiles. 'I wouldn't miss this. You've been an expensive thorn.'

'Do you intend to push us yourself, then?' Jaidee taunts. 'Will you stain your own *kamma* with my death, *heeya*?' He nods at the men around them. 'Or will you try to put the stain on your men? See them come back as cockroaches in their next life to be squashed ten thousand times before a decent rebirth? Blood on their hands for killing in cold blood. For the sake of profit?'

The men shift nervously and glance at one another. Akkarat scowls. 'You're the one who will come back as a cockroach.'

Jaidee grins. 'Come then. Prove your manhood. Push the defenseless man to his death.'

Akkarat hesitates.

'Are you a paper tiger?' Jaidee goads. 'Come on then. Hurry up! I'm getting dizzy, waiting so close to the edge.'

Akkarat studies him. 'You've gone too far, white shirt. This time, you've gone too far.' He strides forward.

Jaidee whirls. His knee rises, slams into the Trade Minister's ribs. The men are all shouting. Jaidee leaps again, moving as smoothly as he ever did in the stadiums. It's almost as though he never left Lumphini. Never left the crowds and the roar of gamblers. His knee crushes the Trade Minister's leg.

Fire crackles in Jaidee's joints, unused to these contortions, but even with his hands tied behind his back, his knees still fly with the efficiency of a champion's. He kicks again. The Trade Minister grunts and stumbles to the building's edge.

Jaidee raises his foot to drive Akkarat over the precipice but pain blossoms in his back. He stumbles. Blood mists in the air. Spring gun disks rip through him. Jaidee loses his rhythm. The building's edge surges toward him. He glimpses Black Panthers grabbing their patron, yanking him away.

Jaidee kicks again, trying for a lucky strike, but he hears the whine of more blades in the air, the whir of pistol springs unwinding as they spit disks into his flesh. The blooms of pain are hot and deep. He slams against the edge of the building. Falls to his knees. He tries to rise again, but now the spring gun whine is steady – many men firing; the high-pitched squeal of releasing energy fills his ears. He can't get his legs under him. Akkarat is wiping blood off his face. Somchai is struggling with another pair of Panthers.

Jaidee doesn't even feel the shove that sends him over the edge. The fall is shorter than he expected.

18

The rumor travels like fire in the dead timber of Isaan. The Tiger is dead. Trade is in ascendancy for certain. Hock Seng's neck prickles as tension blossoms in the city. The man who sells a newspaper to him does not smile. A pair of white shirts on patrol scowls at every pedestrian. The people who sell vegetables seem suddenly furtive, as if they are dealing contraband.

The Tiger is dead, shamed somehow, though no one seems to know the specifics. Was he truly unmanned? Was his head truly mounted in front of the Environment Ministry as a warning to the white shirts?

It makes Hock Seng want to gather his money and flee, but the blueprints in the safe keep him bound to his desk. He hasn't felt undercurrents like this since the Incident.

He stands and goes to the office shutters. Peers out to the street. Goes back to his treadle computer. A minute later, he moves to the factory's observation window to study the Thais working on the lines. It's as if the air is charged with lightning. A storm is coming, full of water spouts and tidal waves.

Hazards outside the factory, and hazards within. Halfway into the shift, Mai came again, shoulders slumped. Another sick worker, sent off to a third hospital, Sukhumvit this time. And down below, at the heart of the manufacturing system, something foul reaches for them all.

Hock Seng's skin crawls at the thought of disease brewing in those vats. Three is too many for coincidence. If there are three, then there will be more, unless he reports the problem. But if he reports anything, the white shirts will burn the factory to the ground and Mr. Lake's kink-spring plans will go back across the seas, and everything will be lost.

A knock comes on the door.

'*Lai.*'

Mai slips into the room, looking frightened and miserable. Her black hair is disarrayed. Her dark eyes scan the room, looking for signs of the *farang*.

'He's gone to his lunch.' Hock Seng supplies. 'Did you deliver Viyada?'

Mai nods. 'No one saw me drop her.'

'Good. That's something.'

Mai gives him a miserable *wai* of acknowledgment.

'Yes? What is it?'

She hesitates. 'There are white shirts about. Many of them. I saw them at the intersections, all the way to the hospital.'

'Did they stop you? Question you?'

'No. But there are a lot of them. More than usual. And they seem angry.'

'It is the Tiger, and Trade. That is all. It can't be us. They don't know about us.'

She nods doubtfully, but does not leave. 'It is difficult for me to work here,' she says. 'It's too dangerous now. The sickness.' She stumbles on her words, finally says, 'I'm very sorry. If I'm dead ...' she trails off. 'I'm very sorry.'

Hock Seng nods sympathetically. 'Yes. Of course. You do no good for yourself if you are sick.' Privately, though, he wonders what safety she can really find. Nightmares of the yellow card slum towers still wake him at night, shaking and grateful for what he has. The towers have their own diseases, poverty is its own killer. He grimaces, wondering how he himself would balance the terrors of some unknown sickness against the certainty of work.

No, this work is not a certainty. This is the same thinking that caused him to leave Malaya too late. His unwillingness to accept that a clipper ship was sinking and to abandon it when his head was still above the waves. Mai is wise where he is dull. He nods sharply. 'Yes. Of course. You should go. You have youth. You are Thai. Something will come to you.' He forces a smile. 'Something good.'

She hesitates.

'Yes?' he asks.

'I hoped I could have my last pay.'

'Of course.' Hock Seng goes to the petty cash safe, swings it open, reaches in and pulls out a handful of red paper. In a fit of reckless generosity that he doesn't quite understand himself, he hands the entire wad over to her. 'Here. Take this.'

She gasps at the amount. '*Khun*. Thank you.' She *wais*. 'Thank you.'

'It's nothing. Save it. Be careful with it—'

A shout rises from the factory floor, then more shouts. Hock Seng feels a surge of panic. The manufacturing line stalls. The stop bell rings belatedly.

Hock Seng rushes to the door, looks down at the lines. Ploi is waving her hand toward the gates. Others are abandoning their posts, running to the doors. Hock Seng cranes his neck, seeking the cause.

'What is it?' Mai asks.

'I can't tell.' He turns and runs to the shutters, yanks them open. White shirts fill the avenue, marching in ordered ranks. He sucks in his breath. 'White shirts.'

'Are they coming here?'

Hock Seng doesn't answer. He looks over his shoulder at the safe. *With a little time*... No. He's being a fool. He waited too long in Malaya; he won't make the same mistake twice. He goes to the petty cash safe and begins pulling out all the remaining cash. Stuffing it into a sack.

'Are they coming because of the sick?' Mai asks.

Hock Seng shakes his head. 'It doesn't matter. Come here.' He goes to another window and opens the shutters, revealing the blaze of the factory rooftop.

Mai peers out over hot tiles. 'What's this?'

'An escape route. Yellow cards always prepare for the worst.' He smiles as he hoists her up. 'We are paranoid, you know.'

19

'You emphasized to Akkarat that this was a time-sensitive offer?' Anderson asks.

'What are you complaining about?' Carlyle toasts Anderson over a warm glass of rice beer. 'He hasn't had you ripped apart by megodonts.'

'I can put resources in his hands. And we aren't asking for much in return. Not by historical standards.'

'Things are going his way. He might not think he needs you. Not with the white shirts bowing and scraping. He hasn't had this much influence since before the December 12 debacle.'

Anderson makes a face of irritation. He reaches for his drink then sets it back. He doesn't want more warm booze. Between the swelter of the day and the Sato, his mind is already dumb and clouded. He's starting to suspect that Sir Francis is trying to drive *farang* away, slowly whittling them down with empty promises and warm whiskey – *no ice today, so sorry.* Around the open bar, the few other patrons all look as heat-stunned as he is.

'You should have joined up when I first offered,' Carlyle observes. 'You wouldn't be stewing now.'

'When you first offered, you were a blowhard who'd just lost an entire dirigible.'

Carlyle laughs. 'Missed the big picture on that one, didn't you?'

Anderson doesn't respond to the man's needling. It's annoying to have Akkarat dismiss the offer of support so easily, but the truth is, Anderson can barely focus on his job. Emiko fills his thoughts, and his time. Every night he seeks her out at Ploenchit, monopolizes her, rains baht on her. Even with Raleigh's greed, the windup's company is cheap. In a few more hours, the sun will sink, and she will once again totter up on stage. The first time he saw her perform, she caught him watching and her eyes had clutched at him, begging to be saved from what was about to occur.

'My body is not mine,' she told him, her voice flat when he asked about the performances. 'The men who designed me, they make me do things I cannot control. As if their hands are inside me. Like a puppet, yes?' Her fists clenched, opening and closing unconsciously, but her voice remained subdued. 'They made me obedient, in all ways.'

And then she had smiled prettily and flowed into his arms, as if she had made no complaint at all.

She is an animal. Servile as a dog. And yet if he is careful to make no demands, to leave the air between them open, another version of the windup girl emerges. As precious and rare as a living *bo* tree. Her soul, emerging from within the strangling strands of her engineered DNA.

He wonders if she were a real person if he would feel more incensed at the abuse she suffers. It's an odd thing, being with a manufactured creature, built and trained to serve. She herself admits that her soul wars with itself. That she does not rightly know which parts of her are hers alone and which have been inbuilt genetically. Does her eagerness to serve come from some portion of canine DNA that makes her always assume that natural people outrank her for pack loyalty? Or is it simply the training that she has spoken of?

The sound of marching boots intrudes on Anderson's thoughts.

Carlyle straightens from his slump, craning for a view of the commotion. Anderson turns, and nearly knocks over his beer.

White uniforms fill the street. Pedestrians and bicycles and food carts are scattering aside, frantically piling against the walls of rubble and factories, making way for the Environment Ministry's troops. Anderson cranes his neck. Spring rifles and black batons and gleaming white uniforms as far as he can see. A streaming dragon of determination marching past. The resolute face of a nation that has never been conquered.

'Jesus and Noah,' Carlyle mutters.

Anderson watches carefully. 'That's a lot of white shirts.'

At some unknown signal, two of the white shirts peel away from the main group and enter Sir Francis'. They survey the *farang* lying stupid in the heat with barely masked disgust.

Sir Francis, normally so absent and unconcerned, bustles out and *wais* deeply to the men.

Anderson jerks his head toward the door. 'Time to go, you think?'

Carlyle gives a grim nod. 'Let's not be too obvious, though.'

'A little late for that. You think they're looking for you?'

Carlyle's face is tight. 'I was actually hoping it was you they were after.'

Sir Francis finishes speaking with the white shirts. He turns and calls out to his patrons. 'So sorry. We are closed now. Everything is closed. You must leave immediately.'

Anderson and Carlyle both sway to their feet. 'I shouldn't have drunk so much.' Carlyle mutters.

They stumble outside with the other bar patrons. Everyone stands under the blazing sun, blinking stupidly as more white shirts stream by. The thud of bootfalls fills the air. Echoes from the walls. Thrums with the promise of violence.

Anderson leans close to Carlyle's ear. 'This isn't another of

Akkarat's manipulations, I don't suppose? Not like your lost dirigible or anything?'

Carlyle doesn't answer but the grim expression on his face tells
Anderson everything he needs to know. Hundreds of white shirts
fill the street, and more keep coming. The uniformed river is
unending.

'They have to be pulling troops in from the countryside. There's
no way this many white shirts work in the city.'

'They're the Ministry's front line, for the burnings,' Carlyle says.
'For when cibiscosis or poultry flu gets out of hand.' He starts to
point then drops his hand, not wanting to draw attention to them.
Nods instead. 'See the badge? The tiger and the torch? They're
practically a suicide division. That's where the Tiger of Bangkok
got his start.'

Anderson nods grimly. It's one thing to complain about the
white shirts, to joke about their stupidity and hunger for bribes. It's
another to watch them march by in shining ranks. The ground
shakes with tramping feet. Dust rises. The street reverberates with
their increasing number. Anderson has an almost uncontrollable
urge to flee. They are predators. He is prey. He wonders if Peters
and Lei had even this much warning before Finland went wrong.

'You have a gun?' he asks Carlyle.

Carlyle shakes his head. 'More trouble than they're worth.'

Anderson scans the street for Lao Gu. 'My rickshaw man's gone
missing.'

'Goddamn yellow cards.' Carlyle laughs quietly. 'Always got their
fingers to the wind. I'll bet there's not a yellow card in the city
who's not in hiding right now.'

Anderson grips Carlyle's elbow. 'Come on. Try not to draw
attention to yourself.'

'Where we going?'

'To put our own fingers to the wind. See what's happening.'

Anderson leads him down a side street, aiming for the main freight *khlong,* the canal that leads to the sea. Almost immediately, they run into a cordon of white shirts. The guards lift their spring rifles and wave Anderson and Carlyle away.

'I think they're securing the whole district,' Anderson says. 'The locks. The factories. '

'Quarantine?'

'They'd have masks if they were here to burn.'

'A coup then? Another December 12?'

Anderson glances at Carlyle. 'A bit ahead of schedule for that, aren't you?'

Carlyle eyes the white shirts. 'Maybe General Pracha has gotten the jump on us.'

Anderson tugs him in the opposite direction. 'Come on. We'll go to my factory. Maybe Hock Seng knows something.'

All along the street, white shirts are busily rousting people from their shops, encouraging them to close their doors. The last of the shop keepers are shoving wooden panels into sockets and sealing their storefronts. Another company of white shirts marches by.

Anderson and Carlyle arrive at the SpringLife factory in time to see megodonts streaming out of the main gates. Anderson snags one of the megodont men. The *mahout* switches his beast to halt and regards Anderson as the megodont snorts and shuffles its feet impatiently. Line workers stream around their obstruction.

'Where's Hock Seng?' Anderson asks. 'Yellow Card Boss. Where?'

The man shakes his head. More workers are hurrying out.

'Did the white shirts come here?' he asks.

The man says something too fast for Anderson to pick up. Carlyle translates. 'He says the white shirts are coming for revenge. Coming to get back their face.'

The man motions emphatically and Anderson steps out of the way.

Across the street, the Chaozhou factory is also evacuating its workers. None of the street's storefronts are open now. Food carts have all been dragged indoors or wheeled away in fright. Every door on the street is shut. A few Thais peer out from high windows but the street itself contains only disbursing workers and marching white shirts. The last of the SpringLife workers hurry past, none of them looking at Carlyle or Lake as they flee.

'Worse by the minute,' Carlyle mutters. His face has gone pale under his tropical tan.

A new wave of white shirts rounds the corner, six wide, a snake extending down the length of the street.

Anderson's skin prickles at the sight of the closed shop fronts. It's as if everyone is preparing for a typhoon. 'Let's make like the natives and get inside.' He grabs one of the heavy iron gates and hauls against it. 'Help me.'

It takes them both to drag the gates closed and set the crossbars. Anderson slaps locks into place and leans against hot iron, panting. Carlyle studies the bars. 'Does this mean we're safe? Or trapped?'

'We're not in Khlong Prem Prison yet. So let's assume we're winning.'

But inwardly, Anderson wonders. There are too many variables in play, and it makes him nervous. He remembers a time in Missouri when the Grahamites rioted. There had been tension, some small speeches, and then it had simply erupted in field burning. No one had seen the violence coming. Not a single intelligence officer had anticipated the cauldron boiling beneath the surface.

Anderson had ended up perched atop a grain silo, choking on the smoke of HiGro fields going up in sheets of flame, firing steadily at rioters on the ground with a spring rifle he'd salvaged from a slow-moving security guard, and all the while he had wondered how everyone had missed the signs. They lost the facility because of that blindness. And now it is the same. A sudden eruption, and the surprise of realizing that the world he understands is not the one he actually inhabits.

Is this Pracha, making a play for absolute power? Or Akkarat, causing more trouble? Or is it simply a new plague? It could be anything. As Anderson watches white shirts stream past, he can almost smell the smoke of burning silos and HiGro.

He waves Carlyle into the factory. 'Let's find Hock Seng. If anyone knows anything, it will be him.'

Upstairs, the administrative offices are empty. Hock Seng's incense burns steadily, sending up gray silk streamers. Papers lie abandoned on his desk, rustling under the gentle breeze of the crank fans.

Carlyle laughs, low and cynical. 'Lost an assistant?'

'Looks that way.'

The petty cash safe is unlocked. Anderson peers at the shelves. At least 30,000 baht gone missing. 'Goddamn. The bastard robbed me.'

Carlyle pushes open a shutter, revealing roof tiles stretching down the length of the factory. 'Take a look at this.'

Anderson frowns. 'He was always messing with the latches on that one. I thought he wanted to keep people out.'

'I think he's ducked out of it, instead.' Carlyle laughs. 'You should have fired him when you had a chance.'

The tramp of more boots on cobbles echoes up to them, the only sound now in the street.

'Well, give him points for foresight.'

'You know what the Thais say: 'When a yellow card runs, watch out for the megodont behind him.''

Anderson surveys the offices one last time, then leans out the window. 'Come on. Let's see where my assistant went.'

'You serious?'

'If he didn't want to meet the white shirts, then we don't either. And he obviously had a plan.' Anderson hoists himself up and climbs out into the sun. His hands burn on the tiles. He straightens, shaking them. It's like standing on a skillet. He studies the roof, breathing shallowly in the blast furnace heat. Down the length of the roof, the Chaozhou factory beckons. Anderson goes a few paces then turns and calls back. 'Yeah. I think he went this way.'

Carlyle climbs out onto the roof. Sweat gleams on his face and soaks his shirt. They make their way over reddish tiles as the air boils around them. At the far end of the roof, their route terminates at an alley, shielded from Thanon Phosri by a winding of the lane. Across the gap, a ladder dangles to the ground.

'I'll be damned.'

They both stare down into the alley three stories below. 'Your old Chinaman jumped that?' Carlyle asks.

'Looks like it. And then went down the ladder.' Anderson peers over the edge. 'Long way down.' He can't help smiling darkly at Hock Seng's resourcefulness. 'Sly bastard.'

'It's a long jump.'

'Not too bad. And if Hock Seng—'

Anderson doesn't get a chance to finish his sentence. Carlyle flies past him, hurtling across the gap. The man lands hard and hits the roof rolling. A second later he's up, grinning and waving for Anderson to follow.

Anderson scowls and makes his own run at the gap. The landing rattles his teeth. By the time he straightens, Carlyle is already disappearing over the edge, climbing down the ladder. Anderson follows, favoring a bruised knee. Carlyle is surveying the alley when Anderson drops down beside him.

'That way goes back to Thanon Phosri and our friends,' Carlyle says. 'We don't want that.'

'Hock Seng is paranoid,' Anderson says. 'He'll have a path worked out. And it won't be on main streets.' He heads in the opposite direction. Almost immediately, a slot between two factory walls appears.

Carlyle shakes his head in admiration. 'Not bad.' They squeeze into the narrow way, scraping along for more than a hundred meters until they reach a door of rusted tin. As they push aside the crude gate, a grandmother looks up from a bundle of washing. They're in a courtyard of sorts. Laundry hangs everywhere, sun pouring a rainbow through damp fabrics. The old woman waves at them to proceed past her.

A moment later, they're out in a tiny *soi*, which in turn gives way to a series of maze-like alleys that twist through a makeshift slum for the coolie laborers who work the levee locks, transporting goods from the factories to the sea. More micro alleys, laborers crouched over noodles and fried fish. WeatherAll shacks. Sweat and the dimness of overhanging roofs. Burning chile smoke that makes them cough and cover their mouths as they forge through the swelter.

'Where the hell are we?' Carlyle murmurs. 'I'm completely turned around.'

'Does it matter?'

They thread past dogs lying dazed in the heat and cheshires perched atop refuse piles. Sweat runs down Anderson's face. The buzz of afternoon alcohol is long gone. More shadowy alleys, more tight walking spaces, twists and turns, squeezing around bicycles and scavenged piles of metal and coconut plastics.

A gap opens. They spill out into diamond sunlight. Anderson sucks at the relatively fresh air, grateful to be out of the claustrophobia of the alleys. It is not a large road, but still, there is traffic on it. Carlyle says, 'I think I recognize this. There's a coffee guy somewhere around here that one of my clerks likes.'

'No white shirts, at least.'

'I need to find a way back to the Victory.' Carlyle says. 'I've got money in their safe.'

'How much is your head worth?'

Carlyle grimaces. 'Eh. Maybe you're right. I need to get in touch with Akkarat, at least. Find out what's going on. Decide on our next move.'

'Hock Seng and Lao Gu both disappeared.' Anderson says. 'For now, let's make like the yellow cards and lie low. We can take a rickshaw to Sukhumvit *khlong*, and then take a boat to near my place. That will keep us far away from any of the factory and trade areas. And far away from all those damn white shirts.'

He flags down a rickshaw man, not bothering to bargain as he and Carlyle climb aboard.

Away from the white shirts, Anderson can feel himself relaxing. Almost feels foolish for his earlier fear. For all he knows, they could have just walked down the street and never been bothered. No need to go running across rooftops at all. Perhaps . . . He shakes his head, frustrated. There's too little information.

Hock Seng didn't wait. Just gathered up the money and ran. Anderson thinks back on the carefully planned escape route again. The jump . . . He can't help laughing.

'What's so funny?'

'Just Hock Seng. He had it all worked out. Everything set. As soon as there was trouble – Shooo! Out the window he goes.'

Carlyle grins. 'I never knew you were keeping a geriatric ninja.'

'I thought—' Anderson breaks off. The traffic is slowing. Up ahead, he catches a glimpse of white and stands for a better view. 'Hell.' The starched whites of the Environment Ministry are in the road, blocking traffic.

Carlyle pops up beside him. 'Checkpoint?'

'Looks like this isn't just the factories.' Anderson glances behind, hunting for a way out, but more people and cyclists are piling up, jamming the way.

'Should we make a run for it?' Carlyle asks.

Anderson scans the crowd. Beside him, another rickshaw driver stands on his pedals, studying the scene, then settles back on his seat and jangles his passing bell irritably. Their own rickshaw man joins the bell ringing.

'No one seems worried.'

Along the road, Thais barter over piled reeking durian, baskets of lemon grass and bubbling buckets of fish. They, too, seem unconcerned.

'You want just to bluff through?' Carlyle asks.

'Hell if I know. Is this some kind of power play of Pracha's?'

'I keep telling you, Pracha's had his teeth pulled.'

'Doesn't look like it.'

Anderson cranes his neck, trying to glimpse what's happening at the road block. From what he can make out, someone is arguing with the white shirts, gesturing as he speaks. A Thai man, deep mahogany skin and a flash of gold thumb rings on his hands. Anderson strains to hear, but the words are drowned out as more cyclists pile into the jam and join in the impatient ringing of their bells.

The Thais seem to believe this is nothing but an irritating traffic jam. No one is frightened, just impatient. More bicycle bells tinkle and chime, surrounding him in music.

'Oh ... Shit,' Carlyle murmurs.

The white shirts yank the arguing man off his bicycle. His arms flail as he goes over. His thumb rings flash in the sunlight and then he disappears under a knot of white uniforms. Ebony clubs rise and fall. Blood whips from the clubs, glistening.

A doglike yelping fills the street.

The cyclists all stop ringing their bells. The street noise fades as everyone turns and cranes their necks to see. In the silence, the man's ragged pleading carries easily. Around them, hundreds of bodies shift and breathe. People glance left and right, suddenly nervous, like an ungulate herd that has suddenly found a predator in its midst.

The dull slap of the clubs continues.

Finally, the man's sobbing breaks off. The white shirts straighten. One of them turns and motions traffic forward. It is an impatient gesture, businesslike, as though the people have stopped to gawk at flowers or a carnival. Hesitantly, cyclists push forward. Traffic begins to roll. Anderson sits down in his seat. 'Christ.'

Their rickshaw man stands on his own pedals and they start forward. Carlyle's expression has gone tight with anxiety. His eyes flick from left to right. 'Last chance to run for it.'

Anderson can't take his gaze from the approaching white shirts. 'We'll be obvious if we bolt.'

'We're fucking *farang*. We're already obvious.'

Pedestrians and cyclists inch forward, merging through the chokepoint, shuffling past the carnage.

A half-dozen white shirts stand around the body. Blood pools from the man's head. Flies already buzz in the red rivulets, sticky winged, drowning in the surfeit of calories. A cheshire shadow crouches eagerly at the periphery, blocked from the congealing pool by a white picket barrier of uniformed trouser legs. All the officers' cuffs are spattered red, dew kisses of kinetic energy absorbed.

Anderson stares at the carnage. Carlyle clears his throat nervously.

A white shirt glances up at the noise and their eyes lock. Anderson isn't sure how long they stare at one another, but the hate in the officer's eyes is unmistakable. The white shirt raises an eyebrow, challenging. He slaps his club against his leg, leaving a bloody smear.

Another slap of the club and the officer jerks his head sideways, indicating that Anderson should look away.

20

Death is a stage. A transience. A passage to a later life. If Kanya meditates on this idea long enough, she imagines that she will be able to assimilate it, but the truth is that Jaidee is dead and they will never meet again and whatever Jaidee earned for his next life, whatever incense and prayers Kanya offers, Jaidee will never be Jaidee, his wife will never be returned, and his two fighting sons can only see that loss and suffering are everywhere.

Suffering. Pain is the only truth. But it is better for young ones to laugh a while and feel the softness, and if this desire to coddle a child ties a parent to the wheel of existence so be it. A child should be indulged. This is what Kanya thinks as she rides her bicycle across the city toward the Ministry and the housing that Jaidee's descendants have been placed in: a child should be indulged.

The streets are patrolled by white shirts. Thousands of her colleagues out on the street, locking down Trade's crown jewels, barely controlling the rage that all in the Ministry feel.

The fall of the Tiger. The slaughter of their father. The living saint, fallen.

It's as painful as if they had lost Seub Nakhasathien again. The Environment Ministry mourns and the city will mourn with them. And if all proceeds according to General Pracha's plan, Trade and Akkarat will mourn as well. Trade has finally overstepped itself. Even Bhirombhakdi says that someone must pay for the insult.

At the Ministry gates, she shows her passes and makes her way into the compound. She cycles down bricked paths between teak and banana trees to the housing quarters. Jaidee's family always kept a modest house. Modest, as Jaidee was modest. But now the last whittlings of his family live in something infinitely smaller. A bitter end for a great man. He deserved better than these mildewed concrete barracks.

Kanya's own home is much larger than Jaidee's ever was, and she lives alone. Kanya leans her bicycle against a wall and stares up at the barracks. It is one of several the Ministry has abandoned. In front of the place, there is a patch of weeds and a broken swing. Not far away is a weedy *takraw* court for the use of Ministry men. At this time of day, no one is playing, and the net hangs limp in the heat.

Kanya stands outside the dilapidated building, watching children play. None of them are Jaidee's. Surat and Niwat are apparently within. Probably already preparing for his funeral urn, calling the monks to chant and help ensure his successful trip into his next incarnation. She takes a breath. An unpleasant task, truly.

Why me? she wonders. *Why me? Why was I forced to work for a bodhisattva? Why was I the one?*

She always suspected that Jaidee knew of the extra take she got for herself and the men. But there was always Jaidee: pure Jaidee, clear Jaidee. Jaidee did the work because he believed. Not like Kanya. Cynical Kanya. Angry Kanya. Not like the others who did the job because it had the potential to pay well and a pretty girl might pay attention to a man in dress whites, a man who also had the authority to shut down her *pad thai* cart.

Jaidee fought like a tiger, and died like a thief. Dismembered, disemboweled, tossed to dogs and cheshires and crows so that there was little left of him. Jaidee, with his cock in his mouth and blood on his face, a package delivered to the Ministry grounds. An invitation to war – if only the Ministry could be sure of its enemy. Everyone whispers Trade, but only Kanya knows for certain. She has kept Jaidee's last mission to herself.

Kanya burns at the shame of it. She starts up the stairs. Her heart thuds in her chest as she climbs. Why couldn't that damn honorable Jaidee keep his nose out of Trade? Take the warning? And now she must visit herself on the sons. Must tell the warrior boys that their father was a good fighter, and had a pure heart. *And now I must have his equipment. Thank you so much. It is, after all, the Ministry's.*

Kanya raps on the door. Goes back down the steps to give the family time to arrange itself. One of the boys, Surat she thinks, opens the door, *wais* deeply to her, calls back inside. 'It's Elder Sister Kanya.' Soon Jaidee's mother-in-law is at the door. Kanya *wais* and the old woman *wais* even more in return and lets her in.

'I'm sorry to bother you.'

'No bother.' Her eyes are red. The two boys regard her solemnly. Everyone stands uncertainly together. The old woman finally says, 'You'll want to collect his things.'

Kanya is almost too embarrassed to answer, but she manages to nod. The mother-in-law guides her inside to a sleeping room. It is a sign of the old woman's grief that nothing is in order. The boys watch. The old woman points to a small desk jammed into a corner, a box of his belongings. Files that Jaidee was reading. 'That's everything?' Kanya asks.

The old woman shrugs dully. 'It's what he kept with him after the house was burned. I haven't touched it. He brought it here before he went to the *wat.*'

Kanya smiles her embarrassment. '*Kha*. Yes. Sorry. Of course.'

'Why did they do this to him? Hadn't they done enough?'

Kanya shrugs helplessly. 'I don't know.'

'Will you find them? Will you get revenge on them?'

She hesitates. Niwat and Surat watch her solemnly. Their playfulness is entirely gone. They have nothing. Kanya ducks her head, *wais*. 'I will find them. I swear it. If it takes me all my life.'

'Do you have to take his things?'

Kanya smiles uncertainly. 'It's protocol. I should have come before. But ...' She trails off helplessly. 'We hoped that the tides would turn. That he would be back on the job. If there are private effects or mementos, I will return them. But I need his equipment.'

'Of course. It's valuable.'

Kanya nods. She kneels beside the WeatherAll box of files and gear. It is a careless mangle of files and papers and envelopes and Ministry gear. A spare clip of blades for a spring gun. A baton. His zip cuffs. Files. All piled together.

Kanya imagines Jaidee filling this box, Chaya already lost to him, everything else soon to be lost. No wonder he didn't bother being careful with any of it. She sifts through the stuff. Finds a photograph of Jaidee during his cadet days, standing next to Pracha, both of them looking young and confident. She takes it out, thoughtful, and sets it on the desk.

She looks up. The old woman has left the room but Niwat and Surat are still there, watching her like a pair of crows. She holds out the photo. Finally, Niwat reaches out and takes it, shows it to his brother.

Kanya goes through the rest of the box quickly. Everything else seems to be the Ministry's. She's obscurely relieved; she won't have to return, then. A small teak box catches her attention. She opens it. Medals from Jaidee's *muay thai* championships gleam. Kanya hands them over to the silent boys. They cluster around the evidence of their father's triumphs as Kanya finishes going through the papers.

'There's something in here,' Niwat says. He holds up an envelope. 'Is this for us, as well?'

'It was with the medals?' Kanya shrugs, continuing to go through the box. 'What's in it?'

'Pictures.'

Kanya looks up, puzzled. 'Let me see.'

Niwat passes them across. Kanya shuffles through them. They seem to be a record of suspicious people that Jaidee was interested in. Akkarat figures in many. *Farang*. Many photos of *farang*. Smiling photos of men and women around the Minister like ghosts, hungry to suck at his blood. Akkarat, unaware, smiling with them, happy to be standing with them. Kanya shuffles more photos. Men she doesn't recognize. Trader *farang*, presumably. Here a fat one, glutted on calories from abroad, some PurCal or AgriGen representative visiting from Koh Angrit perhaps, looking to curry favor in the newly opening kingdom where Trade is in ascendancy. There another, the Carlyle man who lost his dirigible. Kanya smiles slightly. How that one must have hurt. She flips past the photo and sucks in her breath, stunned.

'What is it?' Niwat asks. 'What's wrong?'

'Nothing,' Kanya forces herself to say. 'It's nothing.'

The photo is of herself, drinking with Akkarat on his pleasure barge. A long lens, a bad image, but herself, clearly.

Jaidee knew.

Kanya stares at the photo for a long time, forcing herself to breathe. Staring at the photo. Meditating on *kamma* and duty, while Jaidee's sons watch her, solemn. Meditating on her patron who never spoke of this photo. Meditating on what a man of Jaidee's stature knows, and what he does not reveal, and what secrets can cost a person. She studies the photo, debating. Finally she pulls it and puts it in her pocket. The rest she shoves back into the envelope.

'Was it a clue?'

Kanya nods solemnly. The boys nod back. They do not ask for more. They are good boys.

She goes over the rest of the room carefully, looking for other evidence that she might have missed, but finds nothing. Finally she bends down to pick up the box of equipment and files. It's heavy but none of it weighs as heavily as the photo that now sits in her breast pocket like a coiled cobra.

Outside, in the open air, she forces herself to breathe deeply. The stink of shame is strong in her nostrils. She can't make herself look back at the boys in the doorway. The orphans who pay the price for their father's unbending bravery. They suffer because their father chose an opponent worthy of him. Instead of shaking down noodle carts and night markets, he chose a true enemy, an implacable and relentless one. Kanya closes her eyes.

I tried to tell you. You shouldn't have gone. I tried.

She straps the box of belongings to her cycle's cargo rack and pedals across the compound. By the time she arrives at the main administrative building, she has recovered.

General Pracha stands under the shade of a banana tree, smoking a Gold Leaf cigarette. She is surprised that she can meet the man's eyes. She approaches and *wais.*

The general nods, accepting Kanya's greeting. 'You have his belongings?'

Kanya nods.

'And you've seen his sons?'

She nods again.

He scowls. 'They piss in our house. On our own doorstep they leave his body. It should not be possible, and yet here, within our own Ministry, they throw down their challenge.' He grinds out the cigarette.

'You're in charge now, Captain Kanya. Jaidee's men are yours. It's time that we fought as Jaidee always wished. Make the Trade Ministry bleed, Captain. Get our face back.'

21

On the crumbling tower's precipice, Emiko stares north.

She has done it every day since Raleigh confirmed the windup land. Ever since Anderson-sama hinted that it was possible. She cannot help herself. Even when she lies in Anderson-sama's arms, even when he sometimes invites her to stay with him, paying her bar fines for days at a time, she cannot help dreaming of that place without patrons.

North.

She breathes deep, taking in the scents of sea and burning dung and the bloom of orchid creepers. Down below, the wide delta of the Chao Phraya laps at Bangkok's levees and dikes. On the far side, Thonburi floats as best it can on bamboo rafts and stilt houses. The Temple of the Dawn's *prang* rise from the water, surrounded by the rubble of the drowned city.

North.

Shouts come from below, breaking her reverie. It takes a moment for her brain to translate the noise filtering up, but then her mind shifts from Japanese to Thai and the sounds become words. The words become screams.

'*Be quiet!*

'*Mai ao! No! No nonono!*'

'*Down! Map lohng dieow nee! On your face!*'

'*Please pleaseplease!*'

'*Get down!*'

She cocks her head, listening to the altercation. She has good hearing, another thing the scientists gave her along with her smooth skin and her doglike urge to obey. She listens. More screams. The thud of footsteps and something breaking. Her nape prickles. She wears nothing but slim pants and a string halter. Her other clothing lies below, awaiting her change into street clothes.

More shouts filter up. The scream of someone in pain. Primal, animal pain.

White shirts. A raid. Adrenaline surges through her. She has to get off the roof before they arrive. Emiko turns and runs for the stairs but stops short at the stairwell. The tramp of feet echoes up.

'*Squad Three. Clear!*'

'*Wing Clear?*'

'*Secure!*'

She shoves the door closed and presses her back to it, trapped. Already they clog the stairwells. She casts about the rooftop, looking for another escape route.

'*Check the roof!*'

Emiko sprints for the edge of the tower. Thirty feet below, the first of the tower's balconies extends. A penthouse balcony from a time when the tower must have been luxurious. She stares down at the tiny balcony, dizzy. Below it, there is nothing but the plunge to the street and the people who fill it like black spider mites.

Wind gusts, tugging her toward the edge. Emiko sways and barely catches her balance. It's as if the spirits of the air are trying to kill her. She stares down at the balcony. No. It's impossible.

She turns and runs back to the door, searching for something to wedge it shut. Chips of brick and tile litter the rooftop along with the clothing draped on drying lines, but nothing – she spies a piece of an old broom. Scrambles for it and jams it against the door frame.

The door's hinges are so rusted that it sags with the pressure she applies. She shoves the broom handle tighter against it, grimacing. The WeatherAll of the broom is stronger than the metal of the door.

Emiko casts about for another solution. She's already boiling from running back and forth like a frantic rat. The sun is a thick red ball, sinking for the horizon. Long shadows stretch across the broken surface of the building's roof. She turns in a panicked circle. Her eyes fall on the clothing and the lines. Perhaps she can use the rope to climb down. She runs to the clotheslines and tries to yank one off but it's tough and well-tied. It won't come free. She yanks again.

Behind her, the door shudders. A voice on the other side curses. 'Open up!' The door jumps in its frame as someone slams against it, trying to force past her improvised brace.

Inexplicably, she hears Gendo-sama in her head, telling her she is perfect. Optimal. Delightful. She grimaces at the old bastard's voice as she yanks again on the line, hating him, hating the old snake who loved her and discarded her. The line cuts into her hands but refuses to give way. Gendo-sama. Such a traitor. She will die because she is optimal, but not optimal enough for a return ticket.

I'm burning up.

Optimal.

Another thud from behind her. The door cracks. She gives up on the line. Turns in another circle, searching desperately for a solution. There is nothing except rubble and the open air all around. She might as well be a thousand miles high. Optimally high.

A hinge shatters, throwing bits of metal. The door sags. With a final glance at the door, Emiko sprints again for the edge of the building, still hoping for a solution. A way to climb down.

She stops, windmilling at the edge. The precipice yawns. The wind gusts. There is nothing. No handholds. No way to climb. She looks back at the clotheslines. If only—

The door breaks from its hinges. A pair of white shirts spill through, stumbling, waving spring guns. They catch sight of her and charge across the roof. 'You! Come here!'

She peers over the edge. The people are dots far below; the balcony is as small as a postage envelope.

'*Stop! Yoot dieow nee! Halt!*'

The white shirts are running for her – running full bore – and yet somehow, strangely, they suddenly seem slow. Slow as honey on a cold day.

Emiko watches them, puzzled. They are halfway across the roof, but they are so very very slow. They seem to be running through rice porridge. Their every motion drags. So slow. As slow as the man who chased her in the alleys and tried to knife her. So slow . . .

Emiko smiles. Optimal. She steps up onto the roof ledge.

The white shirts' mouths open to shout again. Their spring guns rise, seeking her. Emiko watches their slit barrels zero in on her. Wonders absently if perhaps she is actually the slow one. If gravity itself will be too slow.

The wind gusts around her, beckoning. The spirits of the air tug at her, blow the black net of her hair across her eyes. She pushes it aside. Smiles calmly at the white shirts – still running, still pointing their spring guns – and steps backward into open air. The white shirts' eyes widen. Their guns glint red. Disks spit toward her. One, two, three . . . she counts them as they fly . . . four, five –

Gravity yanks her down. The men and their projectiles disappear. She smashes into the balcony. Her knees slam into her chin. Her ankle twists as metal shrieks. She rolls, crashing into the balcony's railing. It shatters and peels away and she plunges into open air. Emiko grabs for a broken copper balustrade as she goes over. Yanks to a stop, dangling above an abyss.

Empty air yawns all around, beckoning free-fall. Hot wind gusts. Tugs at her. Emiko pulls herself up to the listing balcony, gasping. Her whole body is shaking, feels bruised, and yet all her limbs still work. She has not broken a single bone in the fall. *Optimal.* She swings a leg up onto the balcony, and hauls herself to safety. Metal grinds. The balcony sags under her weight, its ancient bolts loosening. She's burning up. She wants to collapse. To let herself slide from her precarious ledge and pour into the open air . . .

Shouts from above.

Emiko looks up. White shirts peer over the edge, aiming their spring guns at her. Disks pour down like silver rain. They ricochet, slash her skin, spark on metal. Fear gives her strength. She lunges for the safety of the balcony's glass doors. *Optimal.* The doors shatter. Glass slices her palms. Sparkling shards envelope her and then she's through the glass and in the apartment and she's running fast, blurringly fast. People are staring at her, shocked, impossibly slow—

Frozen.

Emiko smashes through another door and out into the hall. White shirts surround her. She plunges through them. Their surprised shouts are leaden as she streaks past. Down the stairwells. Down, down, down the stairs, leaving the white shirts far behind. Shouts from high above.

Her blood is on fire. The stairwells burn. She stumbles. Leans against a wall. Even the heat of the concrete is better than her skin. She's becoming dizzy, but still she stumbles on. Men shout from above, chasing after her. Their boots thump on the stairs.

Around and around and down she goes. She shoves through

obstructing knots of people, jams herself between dwellers rousted by the raid. She is delirious with the furnace inside her.

Tiny beads of sweat speckle her skin, forcing their way out through her absurdly designed pores, but in the heat and humidity, it does nothing to cool her. She has never felt moisture on her skin before. Always she is dry—

She brushes against a man. He recoils in surprise from her blazing skin. She's burning up. She cannot blend amongst these people. Her limbs move like the flash-frame pages of a child's animation book, fast, fast, fast, but choppy. Everyone is staring.

She turns from the stairwell and jams through a door, stumbles down a hall, leans against a wall, panting. She can hardly keep her eyes open with the fire that burns within.

I jumped, she thinks.

I jumped.

Adrenaline and shock. Cocktail terror, giddy amphetamine high. She's shaking. A windup's jitters. She's boiling. Faint with heat. She presses herself against the wall, trying to absorb its cool.

I need water. Ice.

Emiko tries to control her breathing, to listen, to know where the exterminators come from, but her mind is dizzy and clouded. How far down is she? How many flights?

Keep moving. Keep going.

Instead, she collapses.

The floor is cool. Her breath saws in and out of her lungs. Her halter is torn. There is blood on her arms and hands where she went through the glass. She stretches out, fingers wide, palms pressed to tile, trying to absorb the coolness of the floor. Her eyes close.

Get up!

But she can't. She tries to control her beating heart and listen for her pursuers, but she can barely breathe. She's so hot, and the floor is so cool.

Hands seize her. Voices exclaim and drop her. Grab her again. Then the white shirts are all around, dragging her down the stairs, and she's grateful, thankful that they're at least dragging her down and out into the blessed evening air, even as they scream at her and slap her.

Their words wash over her. She can't understand any of it. It's all just sounds, dark and dizzy heat. They do not speak Japanese, they are not even civilized. None of them are optimal—

Water splashes over her. She gags and chokes. Another deluge, in her mouth, her nose, drowning her.

People are shaking her. They yell into her face. Slap her. Ask questions. Demand answers.

They grab her hair and jam her face down into a bucket of water, trying to drown her, to punish her, to kill her and all she can think is *thank you thank you thank you thank you* because some scientist made her optimal, and in another minute this slip of a windup girl that they shout at and slap will be cool.

22

The white shirts are everywhere: inspecting passes, stalking through food markets, confiscating methane. It's taken hours for Hock Seng to cross the city. Rumors say that all the Malayan Chinese have been interned in the yellow card towers. That they're about to be shipped south, back across the border to the mercy of the Green Headbands. Hock Seng listens to every whisper as he scuttles through alleys on his way back to his cash and gems, sending native Mai ahead of him, using her local's accent to scout.

By the time night falls, they are still far from his destination. SpringLife's stolen money weighs heavy on him. At times he fears that Mai will suddenly turn on him and report him to the white shirts in return for a share of the cash he carries. At other times, he mistakes her for a daughter mouth, and wishes he could protect her from everything that is coming.

I'm going mad, he thinks. *To mistake some silly Thai girl for my own.*

And yet still he trusts the slight girl, the child of fish farmers, who previously proved so obedient when he still had a scrap of managerial authority, and who he prays will not turn on him now that he is a target.

Darkness falls completely.

'Why are you so frightened?' Mai asks.

Hock Seng shrugs. She does not – cannot – understand the complexities swirling around them. For her it is a game. Frightening, to be sure, but still a game.

'When the brown people turned on the yellow people in Malaya, it was like this. All at once, everything was different. The religious fanatics came with their green headbands and their machetes ...' He shrugs. 'The more careful we are, the better.'

He peers out into the street from their hiding place and ducks back. A white shirt is pasting up another image of the Tiger of Bangkok, edged in black. Jaidee Rojjanasukchai. How quickly he falls from grace, and then rises like a bird to sainthood. Hock Seng grimaces. A lesson of politics.

The white shirt moves on. Hock Seng scans the street again. People are starting to come out, encouraged by the relative cool of the evening. They walk through the humid darkness, coming out to do their shopping, to find a meal, to locate a favorite *som tam* cart. White shirts glow green under approved-burn methane. They move in teams, hunting like jackals for wounded meat. Small shrines to Jaidee have appeared before store fronts and homes. His image surrounded by flickering candles and draped with marigolds, displaying solidarity and begging for protection against white shirt rage.

Accusations fill the airwaves on National Radio. General Pracha speaks of the need to protect the Kingdom from those – carefully unnamed – who would topple it. His voice crackles over the people, tinny from hand-cranked radios. Vendors and housewives. Beggars and children. The green of the methane lamps turns skin shimmery, a carnival. But amongst the rustle of sarongs and *pha sin* and the clank of red and gold megodont handlers, there are always the white shirts, hard eyes looking for an excuse to vent their rage.

'Go on.' Hock Seng prods Mai forward. 'See if it is safe.'

A minute later Mai is back, motioning for him, and they are off again, threading through the crowds. Knots of silence warn them when new white shirts are near, fear sending laughing lovers silent, and children running. Heads duck low as the white shirts pass. Hock Seng and Mai work their way past a night market. His eyes rove over candles, frying noodles, cheshire shimmers.

A shout rises ahead of them. Mai darts forward, scouting. She's back a moment later, tugging at his hand. '*Khun*. Come quickly. They're distracted.' And then they're slipping past a clot of white shirts and the object of their abuse.

An old woman lies beside her cart, her daughter at her side, clutching a shattered knee. A crowd has gathered as the daughter struggles to drag her mother upright.

All around, the glass cases that held their ingredients are shattered. Shards glitter in chile sauce, amongst bean sprouts, on lime, like diamonds under the green light of methane. The white shirts stir through the woman's ingredients with their batons.

'Come Auntie, there must be some more money here. You thought you could bribe white shirts, but you haven't done nearly enough to burn untaxed fuel.'

'Why are you doing this?' the daughter cries. 'What have we done to you?'

The white shirt studies her coldly. 'You took us for granted.' His baton crashes down on her mother's knee again. The woman shrieks and the daughter cowers.

The white shirt calls to his men. 'Put their methane tank in with the rest. We have three more streets to go.' He turns to the watching silent crowd. Hock Seng freezes as the officer's eyes travel across him.

Don't run. Don't panic. You can pass, as long as you don't speak.

The white shirt smiles at the watching people. 'Tell your friends what you see here. We are not dogs you feed with scraps. We are tigers. Fear us.' And then he raises his baton and the crowd scatters, Hock Seng and Mai with them.

A block later, Hock Seng leans against a wall, panting with the effort of their flight. The city has grown monstrous. Every street holds hazard now.

Down the alley, a hand-cranked radio crackles with more news. The docks and factories have been shut down. Access to the waterfront is restricted to those with permits.

Hock Seng suppresses a shiver. It's happening again. The walls are going up and he is stuck inside the city, a rat in a trap. He fights down panic. He planned for this. There are contingencies. But first he has to make it home.

Bangkok is not Malacca. This time you are prepared.

Eventually the familiar shacks and smells of the Yaowarat slums surround them. They slip through tight squeezeways. Past the people who do not know him. He forces down another rush of fear. If the white shirts have influenced the slum's godfathers, he could be in danger. He forces the thought away, drags open the door to his hovel, guides Mai inside.

'You did well.' He digs in his bag and hands her a bundle of the stolen money. 'If you want more, come back to me tomorrow.'

She stares at the wealth that he has so casually handed her.

If he were smart, he would strangle her and reduce the chances that she will turn on him for the rest of his savings. He forces down the thought. She has been loyal. He must trust someone. And she is Thai, which is useful when yellow cards are suddenly as disposable as cheshires.

She takes the money and stuffs it into a pocket.

'You can find your way from here?' he asks.

She grins. 'I'm not a yellow card. I don't have anything to fear.'

Hock Seng makes himself smile in return, thinking that she does not know how little anyone cares to separate wheat from chaff, when all anyone wants to do is burn a field.

23

'Goddamn General Pracha and goddamn white shirts!'

Carlyle pounds the railing of the apartment. He's unshaven and unbathed. He hasn't been back to the Victory in a week, thanks to the lockdown of the *farang* district. His clothing is beginning to show the wear of the tropics.

'They've got the anchor pads locked down, they've got the locks closed. Banned access to the piers.' He turns and comes back inside. Pours himself a drink. 'Fucking white shirts.'

Anderson can't help smiling at Carlyle's irritation. 'I warned you about poking cobras.'

Carlyle scowls. 'It wasn't me. Someone in Trade had a bright idea and went too far. Fucking Jaidee,' he fumes. 'They should have known better.'

'Was it Akkarat?'

'He's not that stupid.'

'It doesn't matter, I suppose.' Anderson toasts him with warm scotch. 'A week of lockdown, and it looks like the white shirts are just getting started.'

Carlyle glowers. 'Don't look so satisfied. I know you're hurting, too.'

Anderson sips. 'Honestly, I can't say that I care. The factory was useful. Now it's not.' He leans forward. 'Now I want to know if

Akkarat has really done as much groundwork as you claimed.' He nods toward the city. 'Because it's looking like he's overstretched.'

'And you think that's funny?'

'I think that if he's isolated, he needs friends. I want you to reach out to him again. Offer him our sincere support in this crisis.'

'You've got a better offer than the one that had him threatening to have you trampled?'

'The price is the same. The gift is the same.' Anderson sips again. 'But maybe Akkarat is willing to listen to reason now.'

Carlyle stares out at the green glow of methane lamps. Grimaces. 'I'm losing money every day.'

'I thought you had leverage with your pumps.'

'Stop smirking.' Carlyle scowls. 'You can't even threaten these bastards. They won't take messengers.'

Anderson smiles slightly. 'Well, I don't feel like waiting until the monsoons for the white shirts to come to their senses. Set up a meeting with Akkarat. We can offer him all the help he needs.'

'You think you'll just swim out to Koh Angrit and lead a revolution back in? With what? A couple clerks and shipping captains? Maybe some junior trade rep who sits out there drinking all day and hoping the Kingdom will have a famine and drop its embargoes? Pretty threatening.'

Anderson smiles. 'If we come, we'll come from Burma. And no one will notice until its too late.' He holds Carlyle's eyes until the man looks away.

'Same terms?' Carlyle asks. 'You're not changing anything?'

'Access to the Thai seedbank, and a man named Gibbons. That's all.'

'And you'll give what?'

'What does Akkarat need? Money for bribes? Gold? Diamonds? Jade?' He pauses. 'Shock troops.'

'Christ. You're serious about the Burma thing.'

Anderson waves his glass toward the night beyond. 'My cover here is blown. I accept that and move forward or I pack up and head back to Des Moines with my tail between my legs. Let's be honest. AgriGen has always played for keeps. Ever since Vincent Hu and Chitra D'Allessa started the company. We're not afraid of a little mess.'

'Like Finland.'

Anderson smiles. 'I'm hoping for a better return on investment, this time.'

Carlyle grimaces. 'Christ. All right. I'll set up the meeting. But you better remember me when this is over.'

'AgriGen always remembers its friends.'

He ushers Carlyle out the door and closes it behind him, thoughtful. It's interesting to see what crisis brings out in a man. Carlyle, always so cocky and confident, now harried by the realization that he stands out as if he were painted blue. That the white shirts could begin interning *farang* or executing them at any time, and no one would mourn. Suddenly Carlyle's confidence is stripped away like a used filter mask.

Anderson goes to the balcony and stares out at the darkness, to the waters far beyond, to the island of Koh Angrit and the powers that wait so patiently at the Kingdom's edge.

Almost time.

24

Amid the wreckage of white shirt reprisals, Kanya sits, sipping coffee. In the far corner of the noodle shop, a few patrons squat sullenly, listening to a *muay thai* match on a hand-cranked radio. Kanya, monopolizing the customer bench, ignores them. No one dares to sit beside her.

Before, they might have hazarded the companionship, but now the white shirts have shown their teeth and she sits alone. Her men have already proceeded ahead of her, ravening like jackals, cleaning out old history and bad alliances, starting fresh.

Sweat trickles off the owner's chin as he leans over steaming bowls of rice noodles. Water beads on his face, glinting blue with the flare of illegal methane. He doesn't look at Kanya, probably rues the day he decided to buy fuel on the black market.

The radio's tinny crackle and the faint shout of the Lumphini crowds competes with the burn of the wok as he boils *sen mi* for soup. None of the listeners look at her.

Kanya sips her coffee and smiles grimly. Violence, they understand. A soft Environment Ministry they ignored or scoffed at. But this Ministry – one with its batons swinging and spring guns ready to cut a body down – elicits a different response.

How many illegal burn stands has she already trashed? Ones just

like this one? Ones where some poor coffee or noodle man could-
n't afford the Kingdom's taxed and sanctioned methane? Hundreds,
she supposes. Methane is expensive. Bribes are cheaper. And if black
market fuel lacked the additives that turned the methane a safe
shade of green, well, that was a risk they all took willingly.

We were so easy to bribe.

Kanya pulls out a cigarette and lights it on the damning blue
flame under the man's wok. He doesn't stop her, acts as though she
doesn't exist – a comfortable fiction for both of them. She is not
a white shirt sitting at his illegal burn stand; he is not a yellow card
that she could throw into the towers to sweat and die with his
countrymen.

She draws on her cigarette, thoughtful. Even if he doesn't show
his fear, she knows his feelings. Remembers when the white shirts
came to her own village. They filled her aunt's fish ponds with lye
and salt and burned her poultry in slaughter piles.

*You're lucky, yellow card. When the white shirts came for us, they
didn't care about preserving anything at all. They came with their
torches and they burned and burned. You'll get better treatment than
we did.*

The memory of those sooty pale men, demon-eyed behind bio-
hazard masks makes her want to cower even now. They came at
night. There was no warning. Her neighbors and cousins fled
naked and screaming ahead of the torches. Behind them, their stilt
houses erupted in flames, bamboo and palm roaring orange and
alive in the blackness. Ash swirled around them, scalding skin,
sending everyone coughing and retching. She still carries scars
from that burning, pale pocks where flakes of burning palm
landed hot and permanent on her thin childish arms. How she
hated the white shirts. She and her cousins had huddled together,
watching in awe and terror as the Environment Ministry razed
their village, and she had hated them with all her heart.

And now she marshals her own troops to do the same. Jaidee
would appreciate the irony.

In the distance, shouts of fear rise up like smoke, as black and
oily as farmers' hovels burning. Kanya sniffs. It's nostalgic, in a way.
The smoke is the same. She draws again on her cigarette, exhales.
Wonders if her men have gotten ahead of themselves. A fire in
these WeatherAll slums would be problematic. The oils that keep
the wood from rotting ignite easily in the heat. She takes another
puff of her cigarette. Nothing she can do about it now. Perhaps it
is only an officer torching illegally scavenged scrap. She reaches out
to sip her coffee and eyes the bruise on the cheek of the man who
serves her.

If the Environment Ministry had anything to say about it, all
these yellow card refugees would be on the other side of the
border. A Malayan problem. The problem of another sovereign
country. Not a problem for the Kingdom at all. But Her Royal
Majesty the Child Queen is merciful, compassionate in a way
Kanya is not.

Kanya snuffs her cigarette. It's a good tobacco, Gold Leaf, local
engineering, better than anything else in the Kingdom. She pulls
another cigarette from its switchgrass-cellophane box, lights it on
the blue flame.

The yellow card keeps his expression polite as Kanya motions
for him to pour more sweet coffee. The radio crackles with the stadium's cheers and the men huddling around it all cheer as well,
momentarily forgetting the white shirt nearby.

The footsteps are almost silent, timed with the sound of pleasure, but the yellow card's expression gives the arrival away. Kanya
doesn't look up. She motions for the man standing behind to join
her.

'Either kill me or sit down,' she says.

A low chuckle. The man sits.

Narong wears a loose black high-collar shirt and gray trousers. Tidy clothes. He could work as a clerk perhaps. Except for his eyes: his eyes are too alert. And his body is too relaxed. There is an easy confidence to him. An arrogance that has difficulty fitting into his clothes. Some people are simply too powerful to pretend a lower status. It made him stand out at the anchor pads as well. She bottles her anger, waits without speaking.

'You like the silk?' He touches his shirt. 'It's Japanese. They still have silk worms.'

She shrugs. 'I don't like anything about you, Narong.'

He smiles at that. 'Come now, Kanya. Here you are, promoted to captain and not a single smile in you.'

He motions to the yellow card for coffee. They watch the rich brown liquid splash into a glass. The yellow card sets a bowl of soup down before Kanya, fish balls and lemongrass and chicken stock. She starts fishing out U-Tex noodles.

Narong sits quietly, patiently. 'You asked for this meeting,' he says finally.

'Did you kill Chaya?'

Narong straightens. 'You always lacked social grace. Even after all these years in the city and all the money we've given to you, you might as well be a Mekong fish farmer.'

Kanya looks at him coldly. If she's honest with herself, he frightens her, but she won't let that show. Behind her, another cheer from the radio. 'You're the same as Pracha. You're all disgusting,' she says.

'You didn't think so when we came to you, a very small and vulnerable girl, and invited you to Bangkok. You didn't think so when we supported your aunt through the rest of her years. You didn't think so when we offered you an opportunity to strike at General Pracha and the white shirts.'

'There are limits. Chaya did nothing.'

Narong is as still as a spider, regarding her. Finally he says, 'Jaidee overstepped himself. You even warned him. Be careful that you don't dive down the cobra's throat yourself.'

Kanya starts to speak, then closes her mouth. Starts again, keeping her voice under control. 'Will you do the same to me as you did to Jaidee?'

'Kanya, how long have I known you?' Narong smiles. 'How long have I cared for your family? You are our valued daughter.' He slides a thick envelope across to her. 'I would never hurt you,' he says. 'We are not like Pracha.' Narong pauses. 'How is the loss of the Tiger affecting the department?'

'Look around you.' Kanya jerks her head toward the sounds of conflict. 'The general is enraged. Jaidee was almost a brother to him.'

'I hear he wants to come after Trade directly. Maybe even burn the Ministry to the ground.'

'Of course he wants to go after Trade. Without Trade, our problems would be halved.'

Narong shrugs. The envelope sits between them. It might as well be Jaidee's heart lying on the counter. The return on her long-ago investment in revenge.

I'm sorry, Jaidee. I tried to warn you.

She takes the envelope, empties the money and stuffs it into a belt pouch as Narong looks on. Even the man's smiles are sharp with cutting edges. His hair is slicked back on his head, sleek. He is both entirely still and entirely terrifying.

And this is the sort you consort with, mutters a voice inside her head.

Kanya jerks at the voice. It sounds like Jaidee. It has the telltales of Jaidee, of his humor and his relentlessness. The hint of laughter along with judgment. Jaidee never lost his sense of *sanuk*.

I'm not your kind, Kanya thinks.

Again the grin and the chuckle. *I knew that.*

Why didn't you simply kill me if you knew?

The voice is silent. The sound of the *muay thai* match continues to crackle behind them. Charoen and Sakda. A good match. But either Charoen has radically improved, or Sakda has been paid to fail. Kanya's bet will be a losing one. The match reeks of interference. Perhaps the Dung Lord has taken an interest in the fight. Kanya makes a face of irritation.

'Bad match?' Narong asks.

'I always bet on the wrong man.'

Narong laughs. 'That's why it's so helpful to have information ahead of time.' He hands her a scrap of paper.

Kanya looks through the names on the list. 'These are Pracha's friends. Generals, some of them. They're protected by him as the cobra sheltered the Buddha.'

Narong grins. 'That's why they will be so surprised when he suddenly turns on them. Hit them. Make them hurt. Let them know that the Environment Ministry is not to be trifled with. That the Ministry views *all* infractions equally. No more favoritism. No more friendships and easy deals. Show them that this new Environment Ministry is unbending.'

'You're trying to drive a wedge between Pracha and his allies? Make them angry at him?'

Narong shrugs. Doesn't say anything. Kanya finishes her noodles. When no other instructions seem to be forthcoming, she stands. 'I must go. I can't have my men see me with you.'

Narong nods, dismissing her. Kanya stalks out of the coffee shop, followed by new groans of disappointment from the radio listeners as Sakda is cowed by Charoen's newfound ferocity.

On the street corner, under the green glow of methane, Kanya straightens her uniform. There is a blotchy stain on her jacket, residue of the destruction she has wreaked tonight. She frowns with distaste. Brushes at it. Again opens the list that Narong gave her, memorizing the names.

The men and women are General Pracha's closest friends. And they will now be enforced against as vigorously as the yellow cards in their towers. As vigorously as General Pracha once enforced against a small village in the northeast, leaving starving families and burning homes behind him.

Difficult. But, for once, fair.

Kanya crumples the list in her hand. *This is the shape of our world,* she thinks. *Tit for tat until we're all dead and cheshires lap at our blood.*

She wonders if it was really better in the past, if there really was a golden age fueled by petroleum and technology. A time when every solution to a problem didn't engender another. She wants to curse those *farang* who came before. The calorie men with their active labs and their carefully cultured crop strains that would feed the world. Their modified animals that would work so much more efficiently on fewer calories. The AgriGens and PurCals who claimed that they were happy to feed the world, to export their patented grains, and then always found a way to delay.

Ah, Jaidee, she thinks. *I am sorry. So sorry. For everything I have done to you and yours. I did not set out to hurt you. If I had known how much it would cost to balance against Pracha's greed, I would have never come to Krung Thep.*

Instead of going after her men, she makes her way to a temple. It is small, a neighborhood shrine more than anything, with only a few monks in attendance. A young boy kneels before the glittering Buddha image with his grandmother, but otherwise, the place is empty. Kanya buys some incense from the vendor at the gate and goes inside. She lights the incense and kneels, holds the burning sticks to her forehead, raises them three times in the Triple Gem: *buddha, damma, sanga.* She prays.

How many evils has she committed? How much bad *kamma* must she atone for? Was it more important to honor Akkarat and his promises of a balancing of the scales? Or was it more important to honor her adoptive father, Jaidee?

A man comes to your village with a promise of food for your belly, a life in the city, and money for your aunt's cough and your uncle's whiskey. And he doesn't even want to buy your body. What else can one wish for? What else could buy loyalty? Everyone needs a patron.

May you have much better friends in your next life, loyal fighter. Ah, Jaidee, I am sorry.

May I wander as a ghost for a million years to make atonement. May you be reborn in a better place than this.

She stands and makes a final *wai* to the Buddha and goes out of the temple. On the steps, she looks up at the stars. She wonders how it is that her *kamma* has so destroyed her. She closes her eyes, fighting back tears.

In the distance, a building explodes in flame. She has over a hundred men working this district, letting everyone feel the pain of real enforcement. Laws are a fine thing on paper, but painful when no bribery can ease their bind. People have forgotten this. Suddenly she feels tired. She turns away from the carnage. She has enough blood and soot on her hands for one night. Her men know their work. Home is not far.

'Captain Kanya?'

Kanya opens her eyes to dawn light filtering into her home. For a moment, she is too groggy to remember anything about the days, about her position ...

'Captain?' The voice is calling in through her screened window.

Kanya pulls herself out of bed and goes to her door. 'Yes?' she calls through. 'What is it?'

'You're wanted at the Ministry.'

Kanya opens the door and takes an envelope from the man, unbinds the seal. 'This is from the Quarantine Department,' she says, surprised.

He nods. 'It was a volunteer duty that Captain Jaidee had . . .' he trails off. 'With everyone working, General Pracha asked . . .' he hesitates.

Kanya nods. 'Yes. Of course.'

Her skin crawls, remembering Jaidee's stories of the wars against early strains of cibiscosis. How he worked with his heart in his throat alongside his men, all of them wondering who would die before the week was done. All of them in a terror of sickness and a sweat of work as they burned whole villages: homes and *wats* and Buddha images all going up in smoke while monks chanted and called spirits to their aid and people all around them lay on the ground and died, gagging on fluids as their lungs ruptured. The Quarantine Department. She reads the message. Nods sharply to the boy. 'Yes. I see.'

'Any return?'

'No.' She sets the envelope on a side table, a scorpion crouched. 'This is all I need.'

The messenger salutes and runs down the steps to his bicycle. Kanya closes the door, thoughtful. The envelope hints at horrors. Perhaps this is her *kamma*. Retribution.

In a short time she is on her way to the Ministry, cycling through leafy streets, crossing canals, coasting down city boulevards built for five lanes of petroleum-burning cars that now carry herds of megodonts.

At the Quarantine Department, she endures a second security check before she is allowed to enter the complex.

Computer and climate fans hum relentlessly. The whole building seems to vibrate with the energy burning within. More than three-quarters of the Ministry's carbon allocation goes to this single building, the brain of the Quarantine Department that evaluates and predicts the shifts in genetic architecture that necessitate a Ministry response.

Behind glass walls, LEDs on servers wink red and green, burning energy, drowning Krung Thep even as they save it. She walks down the halls, past a series of rooms where scientists sit before giant computer screens and study genetic models on the brightly glowing displays. Kanya imagines that she can feel the air combusting with all the energy being burned, all the coal being consumed to keep this single building running.

There are stories of the raids that were necessary to create the Quarantine Department. Of the strange marriages that gave them footholds in these technologies. *Farang* brought across at great expense, foreign experts used to transfer the viruses of their knowledge, the invasive concepts of their generip criminality to the Kingdom, the knowledge needed to preserve the Thai and keep them safe in the face of the plagues.

Some of these people are famous now, as important in folklore as Ajahn Chanh and Chart Korbjitti and Seub Nakhasathien. Some of them have become *boddhis* in their own right, merciful spirits, dedicated to the salvation of an entire kingdom.

She passes through a courtyard. In the corner, a small spirit house sits, housing miniature statues of Teacher Lalji, looking like a small wizened *saddhu,* and the AgriGen Saint Sarah. The twinned *boddhis*. Male and Female, the calorie bandit and the generipper. The thief and the builder. There are only a few incense sticks burning, the usual plate of breakfast and garlands of marigolds that are always strung. When the plagues are bad, the place seethes with prayers as scientists struggle to find a solution.

Even our prayers are to *farang,* Kanya thinks. A *farang* antidote for a *farang* plague.

Take any tool you can find. Make it your own, Jaidee said in times past, explaining why they consorted with the worst. Why they bribed and stole and encouraged monsters like Gi Bu Sen.

A machete doesn't care who wields it, or who made it. Take the knife and it will cut. Take the farang *if they will be a tool in your hand. And if it turns on you, melt it down. You will have at least the raw materials.*

Take any tool. He was always practical.

But it hurts. They hunt and beg for scraps of knowledge from abroad, scavenge like cheshires for survival. So much knowledge sits inside the Midwest Compact. When a promising genetic thinker arises somewhere in the world, they are cowed and bullied and bribed to work with the other best and brightest in Des Moines or Changsha. It takes a strong researcher to resist a PurCal or AgriGen or RedStar. And even if they do stand up to the calorie companies, what does the Kingdom offer them? Even their best computers are generations behind those of the calorie companies.

Kanya shakes off the thought. *We are alive. We are alive when whole kingdoms and countries are gone. When Malaya is a morass of killing. When Kowloon is underwater. When China is split and the Vietnamese are broken and Burma is nothing but starvation. The Empire of America is no more. The Union of the Europeans splintered and factionalized. And yet we endure, even expand. The Kingdom survives. Thank the Buddha that he extends a compassionate hand and that our Queen has enough merit to attract these terrifying* farang *tools without which we would be completely defenseless.*

She reaches a final checkpoint. Endures another inspection of her papers. Doors slide aside and then she is invited into an electric elevator. She feels the air sucked in with her, negative pressure, and then the doors close.

Kanya plunges into the earth, as though she is falling into hell. She thinks of the hungry ghosts that populate this awful facility.

The spirits of the dead who sacrificed themselves to leash the demons of the world. Her skin prickles.

Down.

Down.

The elevator's doors open. A white hall and an airlock. Out of her clothes. Into a shower heavy with chlorine. Out on the other side.

A boy offers her lab clothes and reconfirms her identification from a list. He informs her she won't need secondary containment procedures and then leads Kanya down more halls.

The scientists here carry the haunted looks of people who know they are under siege. They know that beyond a few doors, all manner of apocalyptic terrors wait to swallow them. If Kanya thinks about it, her bowels go watery. That was Jaidee's strength. He had faith in his past lives and future ones. Kanya, though? She will be reborn to die of cibiscosis a dozen times before she is allowed to progress once more. *Kamma.*

'You should have considered that before you gave me up to them,' Jaidee says.

Kanya stumbles at his voice. Jaidee is trailing a few paces behind her. Kanya gasps and presses her back against a wall. Jaidee cocks his head, studying her. Kanya can't breathe. Will he simply strangle her here, to pay her back for her betrayals?

Her guide stops. 'Are you sick?' he asks.

Jaidee is gone.

Kanya's heart is pounding. She's sweating. If she were any further into containment, she would have to ask to be quarantined, beg not to be let out, to accept that some bacteria or virus had made the jump and that she was going to die.

'I'm—' she gags, remembering the blood on the steps of General Pracha's administrative building. Jaidee's dismembered body, a careful brutal package. Ragged death.

'Do you need a doctor?'

Kanya tries to control her breathing. Jaidee is haunting her. His *phii* following her. She tries to control her fear. 'I'm fine.' She nods to the guide. 'Let's go. Finish this now.'

A minute later the guide indicates a door and nods that Kanya should step through. As Kanya opens the door, Ratana looks up from her files. Smiles slightly in the glow of her monitor.

The computers down here all have large screens. Some of them are models that haven't existed in fifty years and burn more energy than five new ones, but they do their work and in return are meticulously maintained. Still, the amount of power burning through them makes Kanya weak in the knees. She can almost see the ocean rising in response. It's a horrifying thing to stand beside.

'Thank you for coming,' Ratana says.

'Of course I came.'

No mention of earlier trysts. No mention of shared history, gone awry. That Kanya could not play *tom* and *dee* with one she would inevitably betray. That was too much hypocrisy, even for Kanya. And yet Ratana is still beautiful. Kanya remembers laughing with her, taking a skiff out across the Chao Phraya and watching paper boats glowing all around them during Loi Kratong. Remembers the feel of Ratana curled against her as the waves lapped and as thousands of little candles burned, the city's wishes and prayers blanketing the waters.

Ratana motions her over. Shows her a set of photos on her screen. She catches sight of Kanya's captain's tags on her white collar. 'I'm sorry about Jaidee. He was ... good.'

Kanya grimaces, trying to shake off the memory of his *phii* in the halls outside. 'He was better than that.' She studies the bodies that glow in front of her. 'What am I seeing?'

'Two men. From two different hospitals.'

'Yes?'

'They had something in them. Something worrisome. It seems to be a variant of blister rust.'

'Yes? And? They ate something tainted. They died. So?'

Ratana shakes her head. 'It was hosted in them. Propagating. I've never seen it host itself in a mammal.'

Kanya looks over the hospital records. 'Who are they?'

'We don't know.'

'No family visited them? No one saw them arrive? They didn't say?'

'One was incoherent when he was admitted. The other was already deep into blister rust collapse.'

'You're sure they didn't just eat tainted fruit?'

Ratana shrugs. Her skin is smooth and pale from a life underground. Not like Kanya whose skin has darkened like a peasant's in the harsh sun of active patrol. And yet Kanya would always choose to work above ground, not down here, in the darkness. Ratana is the brave one. Kanya is sure of it. She wonders what personal demons have driven Ratana to work in this hellish place. When they were together, Ratana never talked about her past. About her losses. But they are there. They have to be, like rocks under the waves and froth of a coastline. There are always rocks.

'No, of course I'm not sure. Not one hundred percent.'

'Fifty percent?'

She shrugs again, uncomfortable, goes back to her papers. 'You know I can't make assertions like that. But the virus is different, the protein alterations in their samples are variants. The breakdown of the tissue doesn't match the standard fingerprint of blister rust. In testing, it conforms to blister rusts we've seen before. AgriGen and TotalNutrient variations, AG134.s and TN249.x.d. Both of them offer strong similarities.' She pauses.

'Yes?'

'But it was in the lungs.'

'Cibiscosis, then.'

'No. It was blister rust.' Ratana looks at Kanya. 'You see the problem?'

'And we know nothing about their history, their travel? Were they abroad maybe? On a clipper ship? Crossing into Burma. Over into South China? They're not from the same village, perhaps?'

Ratana shrugs. 'We have no history for either of them. Just the sickness to link them. We used to have a population database with DNA records, family history, work and housing data, but they were taken offline to provide more processing power for pre-emptive research.' She shrugs. 'In any case, so few people were bothering to register, it didn't make any sense.'

'So we have nothing. Any other cases?'

'No.'

'You mean not so far.'

'This is beyond me here. We only noticed it because of the crackdowns. The hospitals are reporting everything, far more than they normally do, just to show that they're compliant. It was an accident that they reported and another that I noticed it in all the other reports that are coming in. We need Gi Bu Sen's help.'

Kanya's skin crawls. 'Jaidee's dead. Gi Bu Sen won't help us now.'

'Sometimes he takes an interest. Not just in his own research. With this, it's possible.' She looks up at Kanya, hopeful. 'You went with Jaidee before. You saw him convince the man. Perhaps he will take an interest in you, too?'

'It's doubtful.'

'Look at this.' Ratana shuffles through the medical charts. 'It has the markings of an engineered virus. DNA shifts don't look like ones that would reproduce in the wild. Blister rust has no reason to jump the animal kingdom barrier. Nothing is encouraging it, it is not easily transferred. The differences are marked. It's as though we're looking into its future. At what it will be like after being reborn 10,000 times. It's a true puzzle. And truly worrisome.'

'If you're right, we're all dead. General Pracha will have to be briefed. The palace told.'

'Quietly,' Ratana begs. She reaches out, grasps Kanya's sleeve, her face anguished. 'I could still be wrong.'

'You aren't.'

'I don't know that it can jump, or how readily. I want you to go to Gi Bu Sen. He will know.'

Kanya makes a face. 'All right. I'll try. In the meantime, put out word to the hospitals and street clinics to look out for more symptoms. Draw up a list. With everyone already worried about crackdowns, it won't even look suspicious for us to demand more information from them. They'll think we're just trying to keep them on their toes. That will tell us something, at least.'

'There will be riots if I'm right.'

'There will be worse than that.' Kanya turns for the door, feeling sick. 'When your tests are done and your data is ready for him to examine, I'll meet your devil.' She makes a face of distaste. 'You'll have your confirmations.'

'Kanya?'

She turns.

'I'm truly sorry about Jaidee,' Ratana says. 'I know you were close.'

Kanya grimaces. 'He was a tiger.' She pulls open the door, leaving Ratana to her demon's lair. An entire facility dedicated to the Kingdom's survival, kilowatts of power burning all day and all night, and none of it of any real use.

25

Anderson-sama appears without warning, sitting down on a bar stool beside her, ordering water with ice for her and a whiskey for himself. He doesn't smile at her, hardly acknowledges her at all but still Emiko feels a rush of gratitude.

For the last several days she has hidden in the bar, waiting for the moment when the white shirts will decide to mulch her. She exists on sufferance and astronomical bribes and now she knows as Raleigh looks at her that it is unlikely he will let her go. He has too much invested in her now to allow her departure.

And then Anderson-sama appears, and for a moment, she feels safe, feels as though she is back in the arms of Gendo-sama. She knows it is her training that does this and yet she cannot help it. She smiles when she sees him sitting beside her, under the phosphorescent light of glow worms, his *gaijin* features so strange amongst the sea of Thais and the few Japanese men who know of her existence.

As is proper, he does not acknowledge her existence, but he stands and goes over to Raleigh and she knows that as soon as her performance is done, that she will sleep safe tonight. For once since the crackdown, she will not live in fear of the white shirts.

She is surprised when Raleigh comes over immediately. 'Looks like you're doing something right. The *farang* wants to fine you out early.'

'No show tonight?'

Raleigh shrugs. 'He paid.'

Emiko feels a rush of relief. She hurries to ready herself and then she's slipping down the stairs. Raleigh has arranged that the white shirts will only come and raid at specific times, and so she has assurance that within the confines of Ploenchit she can do as she likes. Nevertheless she is cautious. There were three raids early on, before the new patterns were settled. A number of owners spat blood before a new *detente* was agreed upon. Not Raleigh though. Raleigh seems to have a supernatural understanding of the workings of enforcement and bureaucracy.

Outside Ploenchit, Anderson is waiting in his rickshaw, smelling of whiskey and tobacco, his face rough with evening stubble. She leans against him. 'I hoped you would come.'

'I'm sorry it took so long. Things are a bit unsettled for me.'

'I missed you.' She is surprised to find that it is true.

They ease through the night traffic, past shambling shadow megodonts and cheshire flickers, past burning candles and sleeping families. They pass white shirt uniforms patrolling, but the officers are busy checking a vegetable stall. The green illumination of the gas lights flickers over them.

'Are you all right?' He nods at the white shirts. 'Is the Ministry raiding?'

'It was bad at first. But now it is better.'

There was panic during the first raids, as the white shirts stormed up the stairwells rousting mama-sans, shutting off pirate methane taps, swinging their batons. Ladyboys screaming, owners rushing to find more cash and then falling under the clubs when they failed to bribe their way free. Emiko had huddled amongst the other girls, still as a statue as the white shirts stalked the bar, pointing out problems, threatening to beat them all until they couldn't earn. Not a trace of good humor in them, only anger at the loss of their Tiger, only an urge to teach lessons to everyone who had ever laughed at white shirt rules.

Terror. Nearly pissing herself as she held still amongst the girls, sure that Kannika would shove her out and reveal her, that she would choose this moment to effect Emiko's demise.

Raleigh, performing careful obeisances to all of them, a farce for some of the regular takers of his bribes, some of them even looking directly at her – Suttipong and Addilek and Thanachai – all of them fully aware of her and her role in the place, having gone so far as to sample her even, and all of them staring at her, trying to decide if they would 'discover' her. Everyone playing their roles, and Emiko waiting for Kannika to break the charade, to force everyone to look at the windup girl that had been so lucrative a source for bribes.

Emiko shivers at the memory. 'It is better now,' she says again.

Anderson-sama nods.

Their rickshaw stops in front of his building. He climbs down first, checks to ensure that no white shirts are about, then ushers her inside. The paired security guards scrupulously ignore her existence. When she leaves, she will tip them to make sure that they forget entirely. She may disgust them, but they will play along if she is respectful, and if she pays. With the white shirts on edge, she will have to pay more. But it can be done.

She and Anderson-sama enter the elevator, and the elevator woman calls out the estimated weight, her face carefully expressionless.

Safely inside his flat, they come together. Emiko is surprised at how happy she is that he delights in her, that he runs his hands over her skin, that he wishes to touch her. She has forgotten what it is to look almost human, to be nearly respected. In Japan, there was no such compunction about looking upon her. But here she feels as if she is an animal every day.

It is a relief to be loved, even if it is only for her physicality.

His hands run over her breasts, down across her stomach, slip between her legs, burrow deeper. She is relieved that it is easy, that he will know her pleasure. Emiko presses herself to him, and their mouths find one another, and for a time she forgets entirely that people call her windup and *heechy-keechy*. For a moment she feels entirely human, and she loses herself in the touching. In Anderson-sama's skin. In the security of pleasure and duty.

But after their union, her depression returns.

Anderson-sama brings her cool water, solicitous of her exertion. He lies down beside her, naked, careful not to touch, not to add to the heat she has built up. 'What's the matter?' he asks.

Emiko shrugs, tries to make herself into a smiling New Person. 'It is nothing. Nothing that can be changed.' It's almost impossible to speak her needs. It goes against all her nature. Mizumi-sensei would strike her for it.

Anderson-sama watches her, his eyes surprisingly tender for a man with scars that crisscross his body. She can catalogue those scars. Each one a mystery of violence on his pale skin. Perhaps the puckered scars on his chest came from spring gun attacks. Perhaps the one on his shoulder came from a machete. The ones on his back look like whip marks, almost certainly. The only one she's certain about is the neck scar, from his factory.

He reaches out to touch her gently. 'What's wrong?'

Emiko rolls away from him. She can barely speak through her embarrassment. 'The white shirts . . . they will never let me out of the city. And now Raleigh-san has paid more bribes to keep me. He will never let me go, I think.'

Anderson-sama doesn't respond. She can hear his breathing, slow and steady, but nothing else. Her shame is all encompassing.

Stupid greedy windup girl. You should be grateful for what he is willing to provide.

The silence stretches. Finally, Anderson-sama asks, 'You're sure Raleigh can't be convinced? He's a businessman.'

Emiko listens to the sound of his breathing. Is he offering to buy her free? If he were Japanese, it would be an offer, carefully couched. But with Anderson-sama, it is hard to tell.

'I do not know. Raleigh-san likes money. But I think also that he likes to see me suffer.'

She waits, straining for a clue as to what he is thinking. Anderson-sama doesn't ask for more information. Leaves her hint dangling. She can feel his body though, close to her, the heat of his skin. Is he listening still? If he were civilized, she would take this lack of response as a definitive slap. But *gaijin* are not subtle.

Emiko steels herself. Presses again, almost gagging with humiliation as she overcomes her training and genetic imperatives. Fighting to keep herself from cowering like a dog, she tries again.

'I am living in the bar, now. Raleigh-san pays the bribes to keep the white shirts away, triple bribes now, some to the other bars, and some to the white shirts, to allow me to be there. I do not know how much longer I can last. My niche is vanishing, I think.'

'Do you . . .' Anderson-sama breaks off, hesitating. Then says, 'You could stay here.'

Emiko's heart skips. 'Raleigh-san would follow, I think.'

'There are ways to handle people like Raleigh.'

'You can free me from him?'

'I doubt I have the funds to buy you out.'

Emiko's heart crashes as Anderson-sama continues, 'With tension so high, I can't provoke him by just taking you away. Not when he could just send the white shirts hunting here. It would be too risky. But I think I can arrange for you to sleep here at least. Raleigh might even appreciate the lessened exposure.'

'But would this not create problems for you? The white shirts do not like *farang*, either. You are very precarious now.' *Help me fly from this place. Help me find the New People villages. Help me, please.* 'If I were to pay Raleigh-san's fines . . . I could go north.'

Anderson-sama tugs her shoulder gently. Emiko lets herself be pulled back to him. 'You hope for too little,' he says. His hand traces across her stomach. Idle. Thoughtful. 'A lot of things may be changing soon. Maybe even for windups.' He favors her with a small secretive smile. 'The white shirts and their rules won't be here forever.'

She is begging for survival, and he speaks of fantasy.

Emiko tries to keep her disappointment hidden. *You should be content, greedy girl. Grateful for what you have.* But she can't keep the bitterness from her voice. 'I am a windup. Nothing will change. We will always be despised.'

He laughs at that, pulls her close. 'Don't be so sure.' His lips brush her ear, whispering. Conspiratorial. 'If you pray to that *bak-eneko* cheshire god of yours, I might be able to give you something better than a village in the jungle. With a little luck, you might end up with a whole city.'

Emiko pushes away, looks at him sadly. 'I understand if you cannot change my lot. But you should not tease me.'

Anderson-sama only laughs again.

26

Hock Seng crouches in an alley just outside the *farang* manufacturing district. It's night, but still there are white shirts everywhere. Everywhere he goes, he finds cordons of uniforms. On the quays, clipper ships sit isolated, waiting for permission to unload cargo. In the factory district, Ministry officers stand on every corner, preventing access for workers and owners and shopkeepers alike. Only a few people are allowed in and out, ones who show residence cards. Locals.

With only a yellow card for identification, it took Hock Seng half the evening to traverse the city, avoiding checkpoints. He misses Mai. Those young eyes and ears made him feel safe. Now he crouches with cheshires and the stink of urine, watching white shirts check another man's identification and cursing that he is cut off from the SpringLife factory. He should have been brave. Should have simply robbed the safe when he had the chance. Should have risked everything. And now it's too late. Now the white shirts own every inch of the city, and their favorite target is yellow cards. They like to test their batons on yellow card skulls, like to teach them lessons. If the Dung Lord didn't have so much influence, Hock Seng is sure that the ones in the towers would already be slaughtered. The Environment Ministry sees yellow cards the same way it sees the other invasive species and plagues it manages. Given a choice, the white shirts would slaughter every yellow card Chinese and then make a *khrab* of apology for their over-enthusiasm to the Child Queen. But only after the fact.

A young woman shows her pass and clears the cordon. She disappears down the street, deeper into the manufacturing district. Everything is so tantalizingly close, and yet so impossibly out of reach.

Looked at objectively, it is probably best that the factory is closed. Safer for everyone. If he weren't so dependent on the contents of the safe, he would just report the line's infections and be done with the *gaiside* thing entirely. And yet, in the midst of all that illness, ensconced above the miasma of the algae baths, the blueprints and specifications still beckon.

Hock Seng wants to tear out the last of his hair with frustration.

He glares at the checkpoint, willing the white shirts to go away, to look somewhere else. Wishing, praying to the goddess Kuan Yin, begging to fat gold Budai for a little luck. With those manufacturing plans and the support of the Dung Lord, so much would be possible. So much future. So much life. Offerings for his ancestors again. Perhaps a wife. Perhaps a son to carry on his name. Perhaps . . .

A patrol stalks past. Hock Seng eases deeper into shadow. The enforcers remind him of when the Green Headbands began patrolling at night. They started out looking for couples holding hands in the evening, displaying immorality.

At the time, he told his children to watch themselves, to understand that the tides of conservatism came and went and if they could not live as freely and openly as their parents had, well then, what of it? Didn't they have food in their bellies and family and friends whose company they enjoyed? And within their high-walled compounds, it was irrelevant what the Green Headbands thought.

Another patrol. Hock Seng turns and slips back down the alley. There is no way to sneak into the manufacturing district. The white shirts are determined to shut down Trade and hurt the *farang*. He grimaces and begins the long circuitous route back through the *sois* toward his hovel.

Others in the Ministry were corrupt, but not Jaidee. Not if anyone is honest about the man. Even *Sawatdee Krung Thep!*, the whisper sheet which loved him most, and then denigrated him so completely during his disgrace, has printed pages and pages in praise of the hero of the country. Captain Jaidee was too well-loved to be cut into pieces, to be treated like offal that is dumped in methane composters. Someone must be punished.

And if Trade is to blame, then trade must be punished. So the factories are closed along with anchor pads and roads and docks, and Hock Seng cannot squeeze out. He cannot book passage on a clipper, cannot ride upriver to the ruined Ayutthaya, cannot flee on a dirigible to Kolkata or Japan.

He makes his way past the docks and, sure enough, the white shirts are still there, along with small knots of workers, squatting on the ground, idled by the blockade. A beautiful clipper ship lies anchored a hundred meters offshore, rocking gently in the water. As beautiful a clipper as he ever owned. Latest generation, switch hulls and hydrofoils, palm oil polymer, wind wings. Fast. Capable of hauling plenty of cargo. It sits out there, gleaming. And he stands on the dock, staring at it. It might as well be docked in India.

He spies a food cart, a vendor frying generipped tilapia in a deep wok. Hock Seng steels himself. He has to ask, even if he reveals himself as a yellow card. He is blind without information. With the white shirts at the other end of the dock, if the man calls out, he should still have time to flee.

Hock Seng eases close. 'Is there any way of passengers crossing?' he murmurs. He tilts his head toward the clipper. 'Over there?'

'No transit for anyone,' the vendor mutters.

'Not even a single man?'

The man scowls, nods at the others in the shadows, squatting and smoking cigarettes, playing at cards. Huddled around the hand-crank radio of a shop keeper. 'Those ones have been there for the last week. You'll have to wait, yellow card. Just like everyone else.'

Hock Seng fights the urge to flinch at being identified. Forces himself to pretend as if they are all equals in this, to create a hopeful fiction that the man will see him as a person, and not as some unwelcome cheshire. 'You haven't heard of small boats, further down the coast? Away from the city? For money?'

The fish vendor shakes his head. 'No one's going either way. They've caught two different groups of passengers trying to make their way ashore from the ships, too. The white shirts won't even allow a resupply boat to go out. We're betting on whether the captain will weigh anchor or the white shirts will open up first.'

'What are the odds?' Hock Seng asks.

'I'll give you eleven to one that the clipper leaves first.'

Hock Seng makes a face. 'I don't think I'll risk it.'

'Twenty to one, then.'

A few others seem to have been listening to the exchange. They laugh quietly. 'Don't bet unless he gives you fifty to one,' one of them says. 'The white shirts aren't going to bend. Not this time. Not with the Tiger dead.'

Hock Seng makes himself laugh with them. He pulls out a cigarette and lights it, offers more to the people around him. A small gift of good will for these Thais, for this moment of shared brotherhood. If he were not a yellow card with a yellow card accent, he might even try a gift of goodwill for the white shirts, but on a night like tonight it will earn him nothing but a baton on the skull. He has no interest in seeing his head splintered against paving stones. He smokes and studies the blockade.

Time is passing.

The idea of a sealed city makes his hands shake. *This isn't about yellow cards,* he tells himself. *We are not the reason for this.* But he has a hard time believing a noose isn't tightening. It might be about Trade right now, but there are too many yellow cards in the city and if trade is cut off for long, even these friendly people will begin to notice the lack of work, and then they will drink, and then they will think of the yellow cards in the towers.

The Tiger is dead. His face is on every gaslight pole. Pasted to every building. Three images of Jaidee in a fighting pose stare out from a warehouse wall even now. Hock Seng smokes his cigarette and scowls at that face. The hero of the people. The man who could not be bought, who faced down ministers and *farang* companies and petty businessmen. The man who was willing to fight even his own ministry. Sent to a desk job when he became too troublesome, and then put back on the street when he became even more so. The man who laughed at death threats, and survived three assassinations before the fourth felled him.

Hock Seng grimaces. The number four is everywhere in his mind these days. The Tiger of Bangkok only got four chances. How many has he himself used up? Hock Seng studies the docks and the clustered people, all unable to make their ships. With the sharpened senses of a refugee, he smells hazard in the wind, sharper than the sea air that sweeps across a clipper and presages typhoon.

The Tiger is dead. Captain Jaidee's painted eyes stare out at Hock Seng, and Hock Seng has the sudden, horrified feeling that the Tiger is not dead. That in fact, he is hunting.

Hock Seng shies away from the poster as if it is a blister-rusted durian. He knows in his bones, knows as surely as his clan is all dead and buried in Malaya, that it's time to run. Time to hide from tigers that hunt through the night. Time to plunge into leech-infested jungles and eat cockroaches and slither through the mud of the rainy season as it gushes in torrents. It doesn't matter where he goes. All that matters is that it's time to flee. Hock Seng stares out at the anchored clipper ship. Time to make hard decisions. Time, in truth, to give up on the SpringLife factory and its blue-prints. Delays will only make it worse. Money must be spent. Survival secured.

This raft is sinking.

27

Carlyle is already waiting anxiously in the rickshaw when Anderson comes out of his building. The man's eyes flick from right to left, cataloguing the darkness around him in a nervous rotation. The man has the trembling cautiousness of a rabbit.

'You look jumpy,' Anderson notes as he climbs in.

Carlyle grimaces. 'The white shirts just took the Victory. Confiscated everything.'

Anderson glances up at his own apartment, glad that poor old Yates chose to locate far from the rest of the *farang*. 'You lose much?'

'Cash in the safe. Some customer lists that I was keeping away from our offices.' Carlyle calls forward to the rickshaw driver, giving directions in Thai. 'You'd better have something to offer these people.'

'Akkarat knows what I'm offering.'

They begin rolling through the humid night. Cheshires scatter. Carlyle glances behind them, scanning for followers. 'No one's officially going after *farang*, but you know we're next on the list. I'm not sure how much longer we'll be able to keep a toehold in the country.'

'Look on the bright side. If they go after *farang*, Akkarat won't be far behind.'

They spin across the darkened city. Ahead of them, a checkpoint materializes. Carlyle mops his forehead. He's sweating like a pig. The white shirts hail their rickshaw and they slow.

Anderson feels a prickle of tension. 'You're sure this will work?'

Carlyle wipes his brow again. 'We'll know soon enough.' The rickshaw coasts to a stop and the white shirts surround them. Carlyle speaks rapidly. Hands across a piece of paper. The white shirts confer for a moment, and then they're giving obsequious *wais* and motioning the *farang* forward.

'I'll be damned.'

Carlyle laughs, relief obvious in his voice. 'The right stamps on a piece of paper do wonders.'

'I'm amazed that Akkarat still has any influence.'

Carlyle shakes his head. 'Akkarat couldn't do this.'

The buildings turn to slums as they near the seawall. The rickshaw swerves around pieces of concrete that have fallen from the heights of an old Expansion hotel. Anderson supposes that it must have been lovely in the past. The terraced levels rise above them, silhouetted in moonlight. But now slum shacks lap all around it, and the last bits of its plate glass windows glimmer like teeth. The rickshaw slows to a halt at the foot of the seawall's embankment. Paired guardian *naga* flank the stairs to the top of the seawall. They watch as Carlyle pays the rickshaw man.

'Come on.' Carlyle leads Anderson up the steps, his hand trailing along the scales of the naga. From the top of the levee, they have a clear view of the city. The Grand Palace shines in the distance. High walls obscure the inner courts that house the Child Queen and her entourage, but its gold-spiked *chedi* rise above, gleaming softly in the moonlight. Carlyle tugs Anderson's sleeve. 'Don't dawdle.'

Anderson hesitates, searching the darkness of the shoreline below. 'Where are the white shirts? They should be all over this place.'

'Don't worry. They don't have authority here.' He laughs at some secret joke and ducks under the *saisin* that strings along the levee's top. 'Come on.' He scrambles down the rubbled embankment, picking his way toward the lap of the waves. Anderson hesitates, still scanning the open area, then follows.

As they reach the shoreline, a kink-spring skiff materializes out of the darkness, hurtling toward them. Anderson almost bolts, thinking it's a white shirt patrol, but Carlyle whispers, 'It's ours.' They wade out into the shallows and clamber aboard. The boat pivots sharply and they cut away from shore. Moonlight glints on the waves, a blanket of silver. The only sounds in the boat come from the slap of waves on the hull and the tick of kink-springs unwinding. Ahead of them, a barge looms, dark except for a few LED running lights.

Their skiff bumps up against the side. A moment later, a rope ladder lofts over the side, and they clamber up into the darkness. Crewmen *wai* respectfully as they come aboard. Carlyle makes a motion for Anderson to keep quiet as they are led below decks. At the end of corridor, guards flank a door. They call through, announcing the arriving *farang*, and the door opens, revealing a group of men at a large dining table, all laughing and drinking.

One of the men is Akkarat. Another Anderson recognizes as an admiral who harries the calorie ships going to Koh Angrit. Another he thinks is perhaps a southern general. In one corner, a sleek man wearing a black military uniform stands watching, eyes attentive. Another . . .

Anderson sucks in his breath.

Carlyle whispers, 'Get down and show some respect.' He's already falling to his knees and making a *khrab*. Anderson drops as quickly as he can.

The Somdet Chaopraya watches expressionless as they pay obeisance.

Akkarat laughs at their bowing and scraping. He comes around the table and brings them to their feet. 'No need for so much formality here,' he says, smiling. 'Come. Join us. We're all friends here.'

'Indeed.' The Somdet Chaopraya smiles and raises a glass. 'Come and drink.'

Anderson *wais* again, as deeply as he is able. Hock Seng claims that the Somdet Chaopraya has killed more people than the Environment Ministry has slaughtered chickens. Before he was appointed protector of the Child Queen, he was a general, and his campaigns in the east are the brutal stuff of legend. If it weren't for the accident of his common birth line, it is speculated that he might even think to supplant royalty. Instead, he looms behind the throne, and all *khrab* before him.

Anderson's heart is pounding. With the Somdet Chaopraya backing a change of government, anything is possible. After years of searching and the failure in Finland, a seedbank is close. And with it, the answer to nightshades and *ngaw* and a thousand other genetic puzzles. This hard-eyed man who toasts him with a smile that could be friendly or feral holds the keys to everything.

A servant offers wine to Anderson and Carlyle. They join the assembled men at the table. 'We were just talking about the coal war,' Akkarat supplies. 'The Vietnamese have given up on Phnom Penh for the moment.'

'Good news, then.'

The conversation continues, but Anderson only half listens. Instead, he furtively observes the Somdet Chaopraya. The last time he saw the man was outside the Environment Ministry's temple to Phra Seub, as they both gawked at the Japanese delegation's windup girl. In person, the man appears much older than in the pictures that adorn the city and depict him as a loyal defender of the Child Queen. His face is mottled with drink, and his eyes are sunken with the debauch he is rumored to like so well. Hock Seng claims that his brutal reputation on the battlefield is matched in his private life, and though the Thais may *khrab* before his image, he is not loved as the Child Queen is. And now, as the Somdet Chaopraya looks up and catches Anderson's gaze, Anderson thinks he sees why.

He's met calorie executives like this. Men intoxicated on their power and influence, their ability to bring nations to heel with the threat of a SoyPRO embargo. A hard, brutal man. Anderson wonders if the Child Queen will actually reach the fullness of her power with this man standing so close. It seems unlikely.

Conversation around the table continues to carefully avoid the reason for their midnight rendezvous. They speak of harvests in the north, and discuss the problem of the Mekong now that the Chinese have placed more dams at its source. They talk about new clipper ship designs that Mishimoto is preparing for production.

'Forty knots with favorable winds!' Carlyle pounds the table gleefully. 'A hydrofoil package and fifteen hundred tons of cargo. I'm going to buy a fleet of them!'

Akkarat laughs. 'I thought air freight was the future. Heavy-lift dirigibles.'

'With those clippers? I'm willing to hedge my bets. During the old Expansion there was a mix of transit options. Air and sea. I don't see why it won't be the same this time.'

'The new Expansion is on everyone's minds these days.' Akkarat's smile fades. He glances at the Somdet Chaopraya, who gives a barely discernable nod. The Trade Minister goes on, speaking directly to Anderson. 'Some elements in the Kingdom oppose this progress. Benighted elements, to be sure, but inconveniently tenacious as well.'

'If you're asking for assistance,' Anderson says, 'we remain happy to provide it.'

Another pause. Akkarat's eyes stray again to the Somdet

Chaopraya. He clears his throat. 'There are concerns, still, about the nature of your assistance. The history of your sort doesn't invite confidence.'

'A bit like climbing into bed with a nest of scorpions,' the Somdet Chaopraya supplies.

Anderson smiles slightly. 'It seems you are already surrounded by a number of nests. With your permission, some of them could be removed. To mutual benefit.'

'The price you're asking is too high,' Akkarat says.

Anderson keeps his voice neutral. 'We are asking for nothing other than access.'

'And this man, this Gibbons.'

'You know of him, then?' Anderson leans forward. 'You know where he is?'

The table falls silent. Akkarat glances again at the Somdet Chaopraya. The man shrugs, but it's enough of an answer for Anderson. Gibbons is here. Somewhere in the country. Probably in the city. No doubt designing a follow-up triumph to the *ngaw*.

'We're not asking for the country,' Anderson says. 'The Thai Kingdom is nothing like Burma or India. It has its own history, one of independence. We respect that absolutely.'

The assembled men's faces turn stony.

Anderson curses himself. *Fool. You're speaking to their terrors.* He changes tacks. 'There are significant opportunities here. Cooperation benefits both parties. My people are prepared to offer significant assistance to the Kingdom if we can come to agreement. Help with your border disputes, calorie security that hasn't been enjoyed since the Expansion, all of this can be yours. This is an opportunity for all of us.'

Anderson trails off. The general is nodding. The admiral is frowning. Akkarat and the Somdet Chaopraya are blanks. He can't read them at all.

'Please excuse us,' Akkarat says.

It is not a request. The guards indicate that Anderson and Carlyle should leave. A moment later they are out in the passageway with four guards surrounding them.

Carlyle stares at the floor. 'They don't seem convinced. Can you think of any reason why they wouldn't trust you?'

'I've got weapons and the money for bribes ready to be landed. If they can open communication with Pracha's generals, I can buy and equip them. Where is the risk for them?' Anderson shakes his head, irritated. 'They should be jumping at the opportunity. It's the most equitable deal we've ever offered.'

'It's not the offer. It's you. You, and AgriGen, and every bit of your damn history. If they trust you, it happens. If not . . .' Carlyle shrugs.

The door opens and they're invited back in. Akkarat says, 'Thank you so much for your time. I'm sure that we will take your offer under advisement.'

Carlyle slumps, deflated by the polite refusal. The Somdet Chaopraya smiles slightly as the news is delivered. Pleased, perhaps, to slap the *farang* down. More polite words are passed around the cabin, but Anderson hardly hears them. Rejection. He's so close he can almost taste the *ngaw*, and still they throw up barriers. There has to be a way to reopen discussion. He stares at the Somdet Chaopraya. He needs a lever. Something to break this impasse—

Anderson almost laughs out loud. Pieces click into place. Carlyle is still mumbling disappointment, but Anderson just smiles and *wais*, hunting for a way in. A way to keep the conversation going a bit longer. 'I completely understand your concerns. We have not earned sufficient trust. Perhaps we could discuss something different. A project of friendship, say. Something less high stakes.'

The admiral grimaces. 'We want nothing from your hand.'

'Please, don't be hasty. We offer in good faith. And regarding that other project, if you change your mind about our assistance, whether it happens in a week, or a year, or ten years, you will always find us supportive.'

'A very fine speech.' Akkarat says. He's smiling, even as he shoots the admiral a sharp look. 'I'm sure there are no hard feelings, here. Please, at least have one last drink. We've troubled you to come so far, there's no reason we shouldn't part as friends.'

Still in the game then. Anderson feels a rush of relief. 'Our sentiments exactly.'

Soon the drink is flowing, and Carlyle is promising that he would happily ship an order of saffron from India as soon as the current embargo is lifted, and Akkarat is telling a story about a white shirt trying to take three bribes from three different food stalls who keeps losing his count, and all the while, Anderson watches the Somdet Chaopraya, waiting for an opening.

When the man goes to a window to look out at the water, Anderson moves to join him.

'It's a pity that your proposal wasn't accepted,' the man says.

Anderson shrugs. 'I'm happy to be walking out alive. A few years ago, I would have been trampled by megodonts for simply trying to meet with you.'

The Somdet Chaopraya laughs. 'You're confident we'll let you walk out?'

'Confident enough, anyway. It's not a bad gamble,' Anderson says. 'You and Akkarat are honorable, even if we don't agree on every particular. I don't consider it a particularly risky bet.'

'No? Half the people in this room suggested that feeding you to the river carp tonight was the wisest course.' He pauses, hard sunken eyes staring at Anderson. 'It was a very close thing.'

Anderson makes himself smile. 'I gather you weren't in agreement with your admiral?'

'Not tonight.'

Anderson *wais*. 'Then I'm grateful.'

'Don't thank me yet. I may yet decide to have you killed. Your kind have a very poor reputation.'

'Would you at least give me a chance to bargain for my life?' Anderson asks wryly.

The Somdet Chaopraya shrugs. 'It wouldn't do you any good. Your life is the most interesting thing I could take.'

'Then I would have to offer something unique.'

The man's hollow eyes flick back to Anderson. 'Impossible.'

'Not at all,' Anderson says. 'I can give you something you've never seen before. Could do it tonight even. Something exquisite. It's not for the squeamish, but it is astonishing and unique. Would that keep you from feeding me to the river carp?'

The Somdet Chaopraya gives him a look of annoyance. 'There is nothing you can show me that I have not already seen.'

'Would you care to wager?'

'Still gambling, *farang*?' The Somdet Chaopraya laughs. 'Haven't you risked enough for one night?'

'Not at all. I'm just trying to make sure my limbs stay attached. It hardly seems like a risk, given how much I might lose otherwise.' He meets the Somdet Chaopraya's eye. 'But I am willing to bet. Are you?'

The Somdet Chaopraya gives him a hard look, calls to his men. 'Our calorie man is a gambler! He says he can show me something I haven't seen before. What do you all think of that?'

His men all laugh. 'The odds are very much against you,' the Somdet Chaopraya observes.

'Still, I think the bet is a good one. And I'm willing to place good money on it.'

'Money?' The Somdet Chaopraya makes a face. 'I thought we were talking about your life.'

'What about the plans for my kink-spring factory, then?'

'I could simply take that, if I wanted.' The Somdet Chaopraya snaps his fingers, irritated. 'Just like that, and they're mine.'

'All right.' Anderson grimaces. *All or nothing.* 'What if I offered you and your Kingdom my company's next iteration of U-Tex rice? Would that be a worthwhile bet? And not just the rice, but the grain before it is rendered sterile. Your people can plant it and replant it for as long as it's viable against blister rust. My life can't be worth more than that.'

The room falls quiet. The Somdet Chaopraya studies him. 'And to balance that risk? What is it you want if you win?'

'I want to go forward with the political project we discussed earlier. Under the same terms as we already proposed. Terms which we both know are entirely favorable to you and your Kingdom.'

The Somdet Chaopraya's eyes narrow. 'You're a tenacious one, aren't you? And what's to keep you from simply withholding the U-Tex you're offering, if you lose?'

Anderson smiles and waves a hand toward Carlyle. 'I assume that you would have myself and Mr. Carlyle here torn apart by megodonts if we fail to make good. Would that be satisfactory?'

Carlyle laughs, his voice tinged with hysteria. 'What kind of bet is that?'

Anderson doesn't take his eyes away from the Somdet Chaopraya. 'The only one that matters. I trust absolutely that his Excellency will be honest if I manage to surprise him. And we will place ourselves in his hands as a token of that trust. It's a perfectly reasonable bet. We're both honorable men.'

The Somdet Chaopraya smiles. 'I accept your bet.' He laughs and claps Anderson on the back. 'Surprise me *farang*. And good luck to you. To see you trampled would be a pleasure.'

They make a strange party as they move across the city. The Somdet Chaopraya's retinue guarantees them access through checkpoints, and the surprised shouts of white shirts echo in the darkness as they realize who they are trying to halt.

Carlyle wipes his forehead with a handkerchief. 'Christ, you're a crazy bastard. I should have never agreed to introduce you.'

Now that the bet is made and the risk defined, Anderson is inclined to agree. The U-Tex rice offering is a real risk. Even if his handlers back the play, the finance people will fight. One lost calorie man is infinitely more replaceable than primary seedstock. If the Thais start exporting the rice, it will undercut profits for years. 'It's fine,' he mutters. 'Trust me.'

'Trust you?' Carlyle's hands are shaking. 'Trust you to put me under a megodont?' He glances around. 'I should just run for it.'

'Don't bother. The Somdet Chaopraya gave his guards instructions. If we have second thoughts now . . .' He jerks his head back toward the men riding in the rickshaw behind. 'They'll kill you as soon as you try to run.'

A few minutes later, familiar towers rise into view.

'Ploenchit?' Carlyle asks. 'Jesus and Noah, you're seriously taking the Somdet Chaopraya here?'

'Calm down. You're the one who gave me the idea.'

Anderson gets down from his rickshaw. The Somdet Chaopraya and his retinue all mill before the entrance. The Somdet Chaopraya gives him a pitying look. 'This is the best you can do? Girls? Sex?' He shakes his head.

'Don't be too quick to judge.' Anderson indicates that they should come inside. 'Please. I'm sorry that we'll have to climb the stairs. The accommodations do not befit your rank, but I assure you that the experience is worth it.'

The Somdet Chaopraya shrugs and lets Anderson lead. His guards crowd close, nervous in the dark confines. The junkies and whores in the stairwells all catch sight of the Somdet Chaopraya and collapse into panicked *khrabs*. Word of their arrival rushes up the stairwells. The Chaopraya's guards run ahead, searching the darkness.

The doors of Soil open. Girls drop to their knees. The Somdet Chaopraya looks around himself with distaste. 'This is a place you *farang* frequent?'

'As I said, not the finest. I am very sorry for that.' Anderson beckons him. 'It's this way.' He strides across the room and pulls aside the curtain, revealing the inner theater.

Emiko lies on stage with Kannika kneeling over her. Men crowd around as Kannika draws out the telltale movements of the windup girl's design. Her body twitches and jerks in the light of glow-worms. The Somdet Chaopraya stops short and stares.

'I thought only the Japanese had them,' he murmurs.

28

'We found another.'

Kanya starts. It's Pai, standing at her doorway. Kanya rubs her face. She was sitting at her desk, trying to write another report, waiting for word from Ratana. And now drool soaks the back of her hand and her pen leaks everywhere. Asleep. And dreaming of Jaidee who simply sits and pokes fun at all her justifications.

'Were you sleeping?' Pai asks.

Kanya rubs her face. 'What time is it?'

'Second hour in the morning. The sun's been up for a while.' Pai waits patiently for her to gather her wits, a pockmarked man who should be her senior, but who Kanya has overtaken. He is of the old guard. One who worshipped Jaidee and his ways, and who remembers the Environment Ministry when it was not ridiculed, but feted. A good man. A man whose bribes are all known to Kanya. Pai may be corrupt, but she knows who owns which parts, and so she trusts him.

'We found another,' he repeats.

Kanya straightens. 'Who else knows?'

Pai shakes his head.

'You took it to Ratana?'

He nods. 'It wasn't tagged as a suspicious death. It took some effort to find. This is like looking for a silver minnow in the rice paddies.'

'Not even tagged?' Kanya sucks in her breath, lets it out in an irritated hiss. 'They're all incompetent. No one remembers how it always comes. They forget so quickly.'

Pai nods easily, listening to his mistress rant. The pits and holes of his face stare back at her. Another worming disease. Kanya can't remember if it was a genehack weevil that did it, or a variation on *phii* bacteria. All Pai says is, 'This makes two, then?'

'Three.' Kanya pauses. 'A name? Did the man have a name?'

Pai shakes his head. 'They were careful.'

Kanya nods sourly. 'I want you to go around to the districts and see if anyone has reported any missing relatives. Three people missing. Get photos taken.'

Pai shrugs.

'You have a better idea?'

'Perhaps forensics will find something to link them,' he suggests.

'Yes, fine. Do that as well. Where is Ratana?'

'She has sent the body to the pits. She asks for you to meet her.'

Kanya grimaces. 'Of course.' She tidies her papers and leaves Pai to his futile searches.

As she leaves the administrative building, she wonders what Jaidee would do in this situation. For him, inspiration came easily. Jaidee would stop in the middle of the road, struck suddenly by enlightenment, and then they would be off, running through the city, hunting for the source of contamination, and invariably, the man would be *right*. It sickens Kanya to think that the Kingdom must rely on her instead.

I am bought, she thinks. *I am paid for. I am bought.*

When she first arrived at the Environment Ministry as Akkarat's mole, it was a surprise to discover that the little privileges of the Environment Ministry were always enough. The weekly take from street stalls to burn something other than expensive approved-source methane. The pleasure of a night patrol spent sleeping well. It was an easy existence. Even under Jaidee, it was easy. And now by ill-luck she must work, and the work is important, and she has had two masters for so long that she cannot remember which one should be ascendant.

Someone else should have replaced you, Jaidee. Someone worthy. The Kingdom falls because we are not strong. We are not virtuous, we do not follow the eightfold path and now the sicknesses come again.

And she is the one who must stand against them, like Phra Seub – but without the strength or moral compass.

Kanya strides across the quads, nodding at other officers, scowling. *Jaidee, what is it in your* kamma *that placed me second to you? That placed your life's work in my fickle hands? What joker did this? Was this Phii Oun, the cheshire trickster spirit, happy to see more carrion and offal in the world? Happy to see our corpses piled high?*

Ahead, men wearing filter masks jump to attention as they spy her pushing open the gates to the crematory grounds. She has a mask issued, but leaves it dangling around her neck. It does no good for an officer to show fear, and she knows the mask will not save her. She places more faith in a Phra Seub amulet.

The open dirt expanse of the pits lies before her, massive holes cut into the red earth, lined to keep out the seep of the water table that lies close below. Wet land, and yet the surface bakes in the heat. The dry season never ends. Will the monsoon even come this year? Will it save them or drown them? There are gamblers who bet on nothing else, changing the odds on the monsoon daily. But with the climate so much altered, even the Environment Ministry's own modelling computers are unsure of the monsoon from year to year.

Ratana stands at the edge of a pit. Oily smoke roils up from the burning bodies below. Overhead a few ravens and vultures circle.

A dog has gotten into the compound and skulks along the walls, looking for scraps.

'How did that get in?' Kanya asks.

Ratana looks up and spies the dog. 'Nature finds a way,' she observes dully. 'If we leave food, it will reach for it.'

'You found another body?'

'Same symptoms.' Ratana's body is slumped, her shoulders bowed inward. Below them, the fires crackle. A vulture sweeps low. A uniformed officer fires a cannon and the explosion sends the vulture screeching skyward again. It circles. Ratana closes her eyes briefly. Tears threaten at the corners of her eyes. She shakes her head, seeming to steel herself. Kanya watches sadly, wondering if either of them will be alive at the end of this newest plague.

'We should warn everyone,' Ratana says. 'Inform General Pracha. The palace as well.'

'You're sure now?'

Ratana sighs. 'It was in a different hospital. Across the city. A street clinic. They assumed it was *yaba* stick overdose. Pai found them by accident. A casual conversation on his way to Bangkok Mercy to look for evidence.'

'By accident.' Kanya shakes her head. 'He didn't tell me that. How many could there be out there? Hundreds already? Thousands?'

'I don't know. The only good thing is that we haven't seen any sign that they themselves are contagious.'

'Yet.'

'You must go ask Gi Bu Sen for advice. He is the only one who knows what sort of monster we face. These are his children, coming to torment us. He will recognize them. I'm having the new samples prepared. Between the three, he will know. '

'There's no other way?'

'Our only other choice is to begin quarantining the city, and then the riots will begin and there will be nothing left to save.'

Rice paddies sprawl in all directions, emerald green, bright and neon in the tropic sun. Kanya has been inside the sinkhole of Krung Thep for so long that it's a relief to see this growing world. It makes her imagine that there is hope. That the rice grasses will not wilt red under some new variant of blister rust. That some engineered spore will not float over from Burma and take root. Flooded fields still grow, the dikes still hold, and His Royal Majesty King Rama XII's pumps still move water.

Tattooed farmers make *wais* of respect as Kanya cycles past. By the stamps on their arms, most of them have already done corvée labor for the year. A few others are marked for the start of the rainy season when they will be required to come to the city and shore up its dikes for the deluge. Kanya has her own tattoos from her time in the countryside, before Akkarat's agents tasked her with this burrowing into the very heart of the Environment Ministry.

After an hour of steady pedalling down raised causeways, the compound materializes. First the wires. Then the men with their dogs. Then the walls topped with glass and razor wire and high bamboo stakes. Kanya keeps to the road, avoiding trip patches. Technically, it is simply the home of a wealthy man, perched atop an artificial hill of concrete and Expansion tower rubble.

Given the loss of life over the last century it is an impressive focusing of human labor for something so silly – when dikes need repairs and fields need sowing and wars need fighting – that a man was able to channel labor into the building of a hill. A rich man's retreat. It was originally Rama XII's, and officially it is still the property of the palace. From the vantage of a dirigible passing overhead, it is nothing. Just another compound. An extravagance for some branch of royalty. And yet, a wall is a wall, a tiger pit is a tiger pit, and men with dogs look both ways.

Kanya shows the guards her papers as mastiffs growl and lunge against their chains. The beasts are larger than any natural dog. Windups. Hungry and deadly and well-built for their work. They weigh twice what she does, all muscle and teeth. The horror of Gi Bu Sen's imagination, brought to life.

The guards unpattern encryptions with their hand-cranked code breakers. They wear the black livery of the Queen's own, and are frightening in their seriousness and efficiency. Finally they wave her past their dogs' straining teeth. Kanya cycles toward the gate, her neck prickling with the knowledge that she can never ride as fast as those dogs can run.

At the gates, another set of guards reconfirm her passes before guiding her inside to a tiled terrace, and a blue jewel swimming pool.

A trio of ladyboys titter and smile from where they lounge in the shade of a banana tree. Kanya smiles in return. They are pretty. And if they love a *farang*, then they are only foolish.

'I am Kip,' one of them says. 'The doctor is having his massage.' She nods at the blue water. 'You can wait for him by the pool.'

The scent of the ocean is strong. Kanya walks to the edge of the terrace. Below her, waves lap and curl, scrubbing white across beach sands. A breeze pours over her, clean and fresh and astonishingly optimistic after the claustrophobic stink of Bangkok behind its seawalls.

She takes a deep breath, enjoying the salt and wind. A butterfly flutters past and alights on the terrace railing. Closes its jewel wings. Opens them gently. Folding itself over and over again, bright and cobalt and gold and black.

Kanya studies it, stricken by its beauty, the gaudy evidence of a world beyond her own. She wonders what hungers have driven it to fly to this alien mansion with its strange *farang* prisoner. Of all the things of beauty, here is one that cannot be denied. Nature has worked itself into a frenzy.

Kanya leans close, studying it as it clings to the rail. An unwary hand might brush it and grind it into dust without ever realizing the destruction.

She reaches out with a careful finger. The butterfly startles, then allows her to gather it in, to walk it into her cupped palm. It has come a long distance. It must be tired. As tired as she feels. It has travelled continents. Crossed high steppes and emerald jungles to land here, amongst hibiscus and paving stones, so that Kanya can now hold it in her hand and appreciate its beauty. Such a long way to travel.

Kanya makes a fist on its fluttering. Opens her hand and lets its dust drop to the tiles. Wing fragments and pulped body. A manufactured pollinator, wafted from some PurCal laboratory most likely.

Windups have no souls. But they are beautiful.

A splash comes from behind her. Kip is wearing a bathing suit now. She flickers under water, rises, pushing her long black hair back and smiling, before turning and beginning another lap. Kanya watches her swim, the graceful crawl of blue suit and brown limbs. A pretty girl. A pleasant creature to watch.

Eventually, the demon wheels out to the pool edge. He is much worse than when she last saw him. *Fa' gan* scars mark his throat and curl to his ear. An opportunistic infection that he fought off despite the doctor's prognosis. He is in a wheelchair, pushed by an attendant. A thin blanket covers his stick legs.

So his disease truly is progressing. For a long time, she thought it was only a myth, but now she can see. The man is ugly. Horrifying in his disease and his burning intensity. Kanya shivers. She'll be glad when the demon finally goes on to his next life. Becomes a corpse they can burn in quarantine. Until then, she hopes the drugs will continue to suppress his contagion. He is a crabbed hairy man with brushy eyebrows, a fat nose, and wide rubbery lips that break into a hyena grin when he sees Kanya.

'Ah. My jailer.'

'Hardly.'

Gibbons glances at Kip where she swims. 'Just because you give me pretty girls with pretty mouths doesn't mean I am not jailed.' He looks up. 'So, Kanya, I haven't seen you in a while. Where is your upright lord and master? My most favorite keeper? Where is our fighting Captain Jaidee? I don't deal with subordinates—' He breaks off, studying Kanya's collar ranks. His eyes narrow. 'Ah. I see.' He leans back, regarding Kanya. 'It was just a matter of time before someone disposed of him. Congratulations on your promotion, Captain.'

Kanya forces herself to remain impassive. On her previous visits it was Jaidee who always treated with the devil. They went away into interior offices, leaving Kanya to wait beside the pool with whatever creature the doctor had chosen for his pleasure. When Jaidee returned, it was always with a purse-lipped silence.

On one occasion, as they left the compound, Jaidee had nearly spoken, had nearly said whatever was churning in his head. He opened his mouth and said, 'But—' a protest that remained half-formed, dead as soon as it passed his lips.

Kanya had the impression that Jaidee was still carrying on a conversation, a verbal battle that pinged back and forth, like a *takraw* game. A war of words, flying and ricocheting, with Jaidee's skull as the playing court. On another occasion, Jaidee had simply left the compound with a scowl and the words, 'He is too dangerous to keep.'

Kanya had responded, confused. 'But he does not work for AgriGen any longer,' and Jaidee had looked at her surprised, only then realizing that he had spoken aloud.

The doctor was legendary. A demon to frighten children with. When Kanya first met him, she expected the man to be bound in chains, not sitting complacently and scooping out the guts of a *Koh Angrit* papaya, happy and grinning with juice running down his chin.

Kanya was never sure if it was guilt or some other strange driving force that had sent the doctor to the Kingdom. If the lure of ladyboys and his imminent death had caused it. If a falling out with his colleagues had driven him. The doctor seemed to have no regrets. No concerns over the damage he had inflicted in the world. Spoke jokingly of foiling Ravaita and Domingo. Of wrecking ten years' labor for Doctor Michael Ping.

A cheshire steals across the patio, breaking Kanya's thoughts. It leaps into the doctor's lap. Kanya steps back, disgusted, as the man scratches behind the cheshire's ears. It molts, legs and body changing hue, taking on the colors of the old man's quilt.

The doctor smiles. 'Don't cling too tightly to what is natural, Captain. Here, look,' he bends forward, makes cooing noises. The shimmer of the cheshire cranes toward his face, mewling. Its tortoiseshell fur glimmers. It licks tentatively at his chin. 'A hungry little beast,' he says. 'A good thing, that. If it's hungry enough, it will succeed us entirely, unless we design a better predator. Something that hungers for it, in turn.'

'We've run the analysis of that,' Kanya says. 'The food web only unravels more completely. Another super-predator won't solve the damage already done.'

Gibbons snorts. 'The ecosystem unravelled when man first went a-seafaring. When we first lit fires on the broad savannas of Africa. We have only accelerated the phenomenon. The food web you talk about is nostalgia, nothing more. Nature.' He makes a disgusted face. '*We* are nature. Our every tinkering is nature, our every biological striving. We are what we are, and the world is ours. We are its gods. Your only difficulty is your unwillingness to unleash your potential fully upon it.'

'Like AgriGen? Like U Texas? Like RedStar HiGro?' Kanya shakes her head. 'How many of us are dead because of *their* potential unleashed? Your calorie masters showed us what happens. People die.'

'Everyone dies.' The doctor waves a dismissal. 'But you die now because you cling to the past. We should all be windups by now. It's easier to build a person impervious to blister rust than to protect an earlier version of the human creature. A generation from now, we could be well-suited for our new environment. Your children could be the beneficiaries. Yet you people refuse to adapt. You cling to some idea of a humanity that evolved in concert with your environment over millennia, and which you now, perversely, refuse to remain in lockstep with.

'Blister rust is our environment. Cibiscosis. Genehack weevil. Cheshires. They have adapted. Quibble as you like about whether they evolved naturally or not. Our environment has changed. If we wish to remain at the top of our food chain, we will evolve. Or we will refuse, and go the way of the dinosaurs and *Felis domesticus*. Evolve or die. It has always been nature's guiding principle, and yet you white shirts seek to stand in the way of inevitable change.' He leans forward. 'I want to shake you sometimes. If you would just let me, I could be your god and shape you to the Eden that beckons us.'

'I'm Buddhist.'

'And we all know windups have no souls.' Gibbons grins. 'No rebirth for them. They will have to find their own gods to protect them. Their own gods to pray for their dead.' His grin widens. 'Perhaps I will be that one, and your windup children will pray to me for salvation.' His eyes twinkle. 'I would like a few more worshippers, I must admit. Jaidee was like you. Always such a doubter.

Not as bad as Grahamites, but still, not particularly satisfactory for a god.'

Kanya makes a face. 'When you die, we will burn you to ash and bury you in chlorine and lye and no one will remember you.'

The doctor shrugs, unconcerned. 'All gods must suffer.' He leans back in his chair, smiling slyly. 'So, would you like to burn me at the stake now? Or would you like to prostrate yourself before me, and worship my intelligence once again?'

Kanya hides her disgust at the man. Pulls out the bundle of papers and hands them across. The doctor takes them, but doesn't do anything else. Doesn't open them. Barely glances at them.

'Yes?'

'It's all in there,' she says.

'You haven't knelt yet. You give more respect to your father, I'm sure. To the city pillar, for certain.'

'My father is dead.'

'And Bangkok will drown. It doesn't mean you shouldn't show respect.'

Kanya fights the urge to take out her baton and club him.

Gibbons smiles at her resistance. 'Shall we chat awhile then, first?' he asks. 'Jaidee always liked to talk. No? I can see from your expression you despise me. You think I'm some murderer, perhaps? Some killer of children? You won't break bread with one such as me?'

'You *are* a killer.'

'Your killer. Your tool entirely. What does that make you?' He watches her, amused. It feels to Kanya as if the man is using his eyes to carefully cut open her innards, lifting and examining each organ in turn: lungs, stomach, liver, heart . . .

Gibbons smiles slightly. 'You want me dead.' His pale mottled face splits into a wider grin, his eyes mad and intense. 'You should shoot me if you hate me so.' When Kanya doesn't respond, he throws up his hands in disgust. 'Fuck me, you're all so shy! Kip's the only one of you who's worth a damn.' His eyes turn to the girl where she swims, watches her, mesmerized for a moment. 'Go ahead and kill me. I'd be happy to die. I'm only alive because you keep me this way.'

'Not for much longer.'

The doctor looks down at his paralyzed legs, laughs. 'No. Not for long. And then what will you do when AgriGen and its ilk launch another assault? When spores float to you from Burma? When they wash up on the beach from India. Will you starve the way the Indians did? Will your flesh rot off you as it did for the Burmese? Your country only stays one step ahead of the plagues because of me, and my rotting mind.' He waves at his legs. 'Will you rot with me?' He pulls aside his blankets, shows the sores and scabs on his pale fishy legs, pasty with the loss of blood and weals of suppurating flesh. 'Will you die like this?' He grins mirthlessly.

Kanya looks away. 'You deserve it. It's your *kamma*. Your death will be painful.'

'Karma? Did you say karma?' The doctor leans closer, brown eyes rolling, tongue lolling. 'And what sort of karma is it that ties your entire country to me, to my rotting broken body? What sort of karma is it that behooves you to keep me, of all people, alive?' He grins. 'I think a great deal about your karma. Perhaps it's your pride, your hubris that is being repaid, that forces you to lap seed-stock from my hand. Or perhaps you're the vehicle of my enlightenment and salvation. Who knows? Perhaps I'll be reborn at the right hand of Buddha thanks to the kindnesses I do for you.'

'That's not the way it works.'

The doctor shrugs. 'I don't care. Just give me another like Kip to fuck. Throw me another of your sickened lost souls. Throw me a windup. I don't care. I'll take what flesh you throw me. Just don't bother me. I'm beyond worrying about your rotting country now.'

He tosses the papers into the pool. They scatter across the water. Kanya gasps, horrified, and nearly lunges after them before steeling herself and forcing herself to draw back. She will not allow Gibbons to bait her. This is the way of the calorie man. Always manipulating. Always testing. She forces herself to look away from the parchment slowly soaking in the pool and turn her eyes to him.

Gibbons smiles slightly. 'Well? Are you going to swim for them or not?' He nods at Kip. 'My little nymph will help you. I'd enjoy seeing you two little nymphs frolicking together.'

Kanya shakes her head. 'Get them out yourself.'

'I always like it when an upright person such as yourself comes before me. A woman with pure convictions.' He leans forward, eyes narrowed. 'Someone with real qualifications to judge my work.'

'You were a killer.'

'I advanced my field. It wasn't my business what they did with my research. You have a spring gun. It's not the manufacturer's fault that you are likely unreliable. That you may at any time kill the wrong person. I built the tools of life. If people use them for their own ends, then that is their karma, not mine.'

'AgriGen paid you well to think so.'

'AgriGen paid me well to make them rich. My thoughts are my own.' He studies Kanya. 'I suppose you have a clean conscience. One of those upright Ministry officers. As pure as your uniform. As clean as sterilizer can make you.' He leans forward. 'Tell me, do you take bribes?'

Kanya opens her mouth to retort, but words fail her. She can almost feel Jaidee drifting close. Listening. Her skin prickles. She forces himself not to look over her shoulder.

Gibbons smiles. 'Of course you do. All of your kind are the same. Corrupt from top to bottom.'

Kanya's hand slides toward her pistol. The doctor watches,

smiling. 'What? Are you threatening to shoot me? Do you want a bribe from me as well? Would you like me to suck your cunt? To offer you my not-quite girl?' He stares at Kanya, hard-eyed. 'You've taken my money already. My life is already shortened and full of pain. What else do you want? Why not take my girl?'

Kip looks up expectantly from the pool, treading water. Her body shimmers under the clear ripples of the waves. Kanya looks away. The doctor laughs. 'Sorry, Kip. We don't have the bribes this one likes.' He drums his fingers on his chair. 'What about a young boy, then? There's a lovely twelve-year-old who works my kitchen. He would be happy to perform. The pleasure of a white shirt is always paramount.'

Kanya glares at him. 'I could break your bones.'

'Do it then. But hurry up. I want a reason not to help you.'

'Why did you help AgriGen for so long?'

The doctor's eyes narrow. 'The same reason you run like a dog for *your* masters. They paid me in the coin I wanted most.'

Her slap rings across the water. The guards start forward, but Kanya is already drawing back, shaking off the sting in her hand, waving away the guards. 'We're fine. Nothing is wrong.'

The guards pause, unsure of their duty and loyalties. The doctor touches his broken lip, examines the blood thoughtfully. Looks up. 'A sore spot, there … How much of yourself have you already sold?' He smiles showing teeth rimed bloody from Kanya's strike. 'Are you AgriGen's then? Complicit?' He looks into Kanya's eyes. 'Are you here to kill me? To end my thorn in their side?' He watches closely, eyes peering into her soul, observant, curious. 'It is only a matter of time. They must know that I am here. That I am yours. The Kingdom couldn't have fared so well for so long without me. Couldn't have released nightshades and *ngaw* without my help. We all know they are hunting. Are *you* my hunter, then? Are you my destiny?'

Kanya scowls. 'Hardly. We're not done with you yet.'

Gibbons slumps. 'Ah, of course not. But then, you never will be. That is the nature of our beasts and plagues. They are not dumb machines to be driven about. They have their own needs and hungers. Their own evolutionary demands. They must mutate and adapt, and so you will never be done with me, and when I am gone, what will you do then? We have released demons upon the world, and your walls are only as good as my intellect. Nature has become something new. It is ours now, truly. And if our creation devours us, how poetic will that be?'

'*Kamma*,' she murmurs.

'Precisely.' Gibbons leans back, smiling. 'Kip. Get the pages. Let us see what can be deciphered from this puzzle.' He drums his fingers on his ruined legs, thoughtful. Smirks at Kanya. 'Let us see how close to death your precious Kingdom lies.'

Kip swims to collect the pages, rippling through the water as she gathers them to her, pulling them dripping and limp from the pool. A smile flickers across Gibbons' lips as he watches her swim. 'You're lucky I like Kip. If I didn't, I would have let you all succumb years ago.'

He nods to his guards. 'The captain will have samples on her bicycle. Get them. We'll take them down into the lab.'

Kip finally emerges from the pool and sets the sopping stack of papers on the doctor's lap. He motions and she begins pushing him toward the door of his villa. The doctor waves for Kanya to follow.

'Come on, then. This won't take long.'

The doctor squints over one of the slides. 'I'm surprised you think this is an inert mutation.'

'Three cases, only.'

The doctor looks up. 'For now.' He smiles. 'Life is exponential.

Two becomes four, becomes ten thousand, becomes a plague. Maybe it's everywhere in the population already and we never noticed. Maybe this is end-stage. Terminal without symptoms, like poor Kip.'

Kanya glances at the ladyboy. Kip gives a gentle return smile. Nothing shows on her skin. Nothing shows on her body. It is not the doctor's disease she dies of. And yet ... Kanya steps away, involuntarily.

The doctor grins. 'Don't look so worried. You have the same sickness. Life is, after all, inevitably fatal.' He looks into the microscope. 'Not an indie genehack. Something else. Not a blister rust. Nothing of AgriGen's markings.' Abruptly, he makes a face of disgust. 'This is nothing interesting for me. Just a stupid mistake by some fool. Hardly worth my intellect at all.'

'That's good, then?'

'An accidental plague kills just as surely.'

'Is there a way to stop it?'

The doctor picks up a crust of bread. A greenish mold covers it. He eyes the stuff. 'So many growing things are beneficial to us. And so many are deadly.' He offers the piece of bread to Kanya. 'Try it.'

Kanya recoils. Gibbons grins and takes a bite. Offers it again. 'Trust me.'

Kanya shakes her head, forcing herself not to mouth superstitious prayers to Phra Seub for luck and cleanliness. She envisions the revered man sitting in a lotus, forces herself not to respond to the doctor's taunts, touches her amulets.

The doctor takes another bite. Grins as crumbs cascade down his chin. 'If you take a bite, I'll guarantee you an answer.'

'I wouldn't take anything from your hand.'

The doctor laughs. 'You already have. Every injection you took as a child. Every inoculation. Every booster since.' He offers the bread. 'This is just more direct. You'll be glad you did.'

Kanya nods at the microscope. 'What is that thing? Do you need to test it more?'

Gibbons shakes his head. 'That? It's nothing. A stupid mutation. A standard outcome. We used to see them in our labs. Junk.'

'Then why haven't we ever seen it before?'

Gibbons makes a face of impatience. 'You don't culture death the way we do. You don't tinker with the building blocks of nature.' Interest and passion flicker briefly in the old man's eyes. Mischief and predatory interests. 'You have no idea what things we succeeded in creating in our labs. This stuff is hardly worth my time. I hoped you were bringing me a challenge. Something from Drs. Ping and Raymond. Or perhaps Mahmoud Sonthalia. Those are challenges.' For a moment, his eyes lose their cynicism. He becomes entranced. 'Ah. Now those are worthy opponents.'

We are in the hands of a gamesman.

In a flash of insight, Kanya understands the doctor entirely. A fierce intellect. A man who reached the pinnacle of his field. A jealous and competitive man. A man who found his competition too lacking, and so switched sides and joined the Thai Kingdom for the stimulation it might provide. An intellectual exercise for him. As if Jaidee had decided to fight a *muay thai* match with his hands tied behind his back to see if he could win with kicks alone.

We rest in the hands of a fickle god. He plays on our behalf only for entertainment, and he will close his eyes and sleep if we fail to engage his intellect.

A horrifying thought. The man exists only for competition, the chess match of evolution, fought on a global scale. An exercise in ego, a single giant fending off the attacks of dozens of others, a giant swatting them from the sky and laughing. But all giants must fall, and then what must the Kingdom look forward to? It makes Kanya sweat, thinking about it.

Gibbons is watching her. 'You have more questions for me?'

Kanya shakes off her terror. 'You're sure about this? You know what we need to do, already? You can tell just by looking?'

The doctor shrugs. 'If you don't believe me, then go back and follow your standard methods. Textbook your way to your deaths. Or you can simply burn your factory district to the ground and root out the problem.' He grins. 'Now there's a blunt-instrument solution for you white shirts. The Environment Ministry was always fond of those.' He waves a hand. 'This garbage isn't particularly viable, yet. It mutates quickly, certainly, but it is fragile, and the human host is not ideal. It needs to be rubbed on the mucus membranes: in the nostrils, in the eyes, in the anus, somewhere close to blood and life. Somewhere it can breed.'

'Then we're safe. It's no worse than a hepatitis or *fa' gan*.'

'But *much* more inclined to mutate.' He looks at Kanya again. 'One other thing you should know. The manufacturer you want will have chemical baths. Someplace where they can culture biological products. A HiGro factory. An AgriGen facility. A windup manufactory. Something like that.'

Kanya glances at the mastiffs. 'Would windups carry it?'

He reaches down and pats one of the guard dogs, goading her. 'If it's avian or mammalian, it could. A bath facility is where I would look first. If this were Japan, a windup crèche would be my first guess, but anyone involved in biological products could be the index source.'

'What kind of windups?'

Gibbons blows out an exasperated breath. 'It's not a *kind*. It's a matter of *exposure*. If they were cultured in tainted baths, they may be carriers. Then again, if you leave that garbage to mutate, it will be in people soon enough. And the question of its index will be moot.'

'How long do we have?'

Gibbons shrugs. 'This isn't the decay of uranium or the velocity of a clipper ship. This is not predictable. Feed the beasts well, and they will learn to gorge. Culture them in a humid city of dense-packed people and they will thrive. Decide for yourself how worried you should be.'

Kanya turns, disgusted, and heads out the door.

Gibbons calls after her, 'Good luck! I'll be interested to see which of your many enemies kills you first.'

Kanya ignores the taunt and bolts into clean open air.

Kip approaches her, towelling her hair. 'Was the doctor helpful?'

'He gave me enough.'

Kip laughs, a soft twittering. 'I used to think so. But I've learned that he never tells everything the first time. He leaves things out. Vital things. He likes company.' She touches Kanya's arm and Kanya has to force herself not to recoil. Kip sees the movement but only smiles gently. 'He likes you. He'll want you to return.'

Kanya shivers. 'He'll be disappointed then.'

Kip watches her with wide liquid eyes. 'I hope you don't die too soon. I also like you.'

As Kanya leaves the compound, she catches sight of Jaidee, standing at the edge of the ocean, watching the surf. As if sensing her gaze, he turns and smiles, before shimmering into nothingness. Another spirit with no place to go. She wonders if Jaidee will ever manage to reincarnate, or if he will continue to haunt her. If the doctor is right, perhaps he is waiting to come back as something that will not fear the plagues, some creature that has not yet been conceived. Maybe Jaidee's only hope for reincarnation is to find new life in the husk of a windup body.

Kanya squashes the thought. It's an evil idea. She hopes instead that Jaidee will reincarnate into some heaven where windups and blister rust can never be, that even if he never achieves *nibbana*, never finishes his time as a monk, never makes his way into buddha-hood, that at least he will be saved from the anguish of watching the world he so dutifully defended stripped of its flesh by the slavering mass of nature's new successes, these windup creatures that seethe all around.

Jaidee died. But perhaps that is the best that anyone can hope for. Perhaps if she put a spring gun in her mouth and pulled the trigger, she would be happier. Perhaps if she had no large house and no *kamma* of betrayal ...

Kanya shakes her head. If anything is certain, she must do her duty here. Her own soul will certainly be sent back to this world again, at best as a human being, at worst as something else, some dog or cockroach. Whatever mess she leaves behind, she will undoubtedly face it again and again and again. Her betrayals guarantee it. She must fight this battle until her kamma is finally cleansed. To flee it now in suicide would be to face it in an uglier form in the future. There is no escape for such as she.

29

Despite the curfews and the white shirts, Anderson-sama seems almost reckless with his attentions. It's almost as if he is making up for something. But when Emiko repeats her concerns about Raleigh, Anderson-sama only smiles a secret smile and tells her she needn't worry. All things are in flux. 'My people are coming,' he says. 'Very soon, everything will be different. No more white shirts.'

'It sounds very beautiful.'

'It will be,' he says. 'I'll be gone for a few days, making arrangements. When I get back, everything will be different.'

And then he disappears, leaving her with the admonishment that she should not change her patterns, and should not tell Raleigh anything. He gives her a key to his flat.

And so it is that Emiko wakes on clean sheets in a cool room in the evening, with a crank fan beating slowly overhead. She can barely remember the last time she slept without pain or fear, and she is groggy with it. The rooms are dim, lit only by the glow of the street's gaslights flickering alive like fireflies.

She is hungry. Ravenous. She finds Anderson-sama's kitchen and roots through sealed bins for snacks, for crackers, for snaps, for cakes, anything. Anderson-sama has no fresh vegetables, but he has rice and there is soy and fish sauce and she heats water on a burner, marvelling at the methane jug that he keeps unsecured. It is difficult for her to remember that she ever took such things for granted. That Gendo-sama kept her in accommodations twice as luxurious, on the top floor of a Kyoto apartment with a view of Toji Temple and the slow movement of old men tending the shrine in their black robes.

That long-ago time is like a dream to her. The autumn sky with its clear breathless blue. She remembers the pleasure of watching New People children from their crèche feeding the ducks or learning a tea ceremony with attention both total and without redemption.

She remembers her own training . . .

With a chill, she sees that she was trained to excellence, to the eternal service of a master. She remembers how Gendo-sama took her and showered her with affection and then discarded her like a tamarind hull. It was always her destiny. It was no accident.

Her eyes narrow as she stares at the pan and its boiling water, at the rice she has so perfectly measured by sight alone, without a measure cup but simply scooped with a bowl, knowing precisely how much she needed, and then unconsciously settling that rice into a perfect layer as if it were a gravel garden, as if she were preparing to perform *zazen* meditation on its grains, as if she would rake and rake and rake for her life with a little bowl of rice.

She lashes out. The rice bowl shatters, shards spinning in different directions, the pot of water flying, scalding jewels gleaming.

Emiko stands amidst the whirlwind, watching droplets fly, rice grains suspended, all of it stopped in motion, as if grain and water are windups, stuttering in flight as she herself is forced to stumble herky-jerky through the world, strange and surreal in the eyes of the naturals. In the eyes of the people she so desperately desires to serve.

Look what service has brought you.

The pot hits the wall. Rice grains skitter across marble. Water soaks everything. Tonight she will learn the location of this New People village. The place where her own kind live and have no masters. Where New People serve only themselves. Anderson-sama may say that his people are coming, but in the end, he will always be natural, and she will always be New People, and she will always serve.

She stifles the urge to clean up the rice, to make things neat for Anderson-sama when he returns. Instead, she makes herself stare at the mess and recognize that she is no longer a slave. If he wishes rice cleaned off the floor there are others to do his dirty work. She is something else. Something different. Optimal in her own way. And if she was once a falcon tethered, Gendo-sama has done one thing she can be grateful for. He has cut her jesses. She can fly free.

It is almost too easy to slip through the darkness. Emiko bobs amid the crowds, new color bright on her lips, her eyes darkened, glinting silver hoops at her lobes.

She is New People, and she moves through the crowds so smoothly that they do not know she is there. She laughs at them. Laughs and slips between them. There is something suicidal ticking in her windup nature. She hides in the open. She does not scuttle. Fate has cupped her in its protective hands.

She slips through the crowds, people jerking away startled from the windup in their midst, from the bit of transgressive manufactuary that has the effrontery to stain their sidewalks, as if their land were half as pristine as the islands that have ejected her. She wrinkles her nose. Even Nippon's effluent is too good for this raucous stinking place. They simply do not recognize how she graces them. She laughs to herself, and realizes when others look at her that she has laughed out loud.

White shirts ahead. Flashes of them between the trundle of megodonts and handcarts. Emiko stops at the rail of a *khlong* bridge, looking down into the waters, waiting for the threat to pass. She sees herself in the canal's reflection with the green glow of the lamps all around, backlighting her. She feels perhaps she could become one with the water, if she simply stares at the glow long enough. Become a water lady. Already is she not part of the floating world? Does she not deserve to float and slowly sink? She stifles the thought. That is the old Emiko. The one who could never teach her to fly.

A man approaches and leans against the rail. She doesn't look up, watches his reflection in the water.

'I like to watch when the children race their boats through the canals,' he says.

She nods slightly, not trusting herself to speak.

'Is there something you see in the water? That you look so long?'

She shakes her head. His white uniform is tinged green. He is so close he can reach out and touch her. She wonders what his kind eyes would look like if his hands touched the furnace of her skin.

'You don't have to be afraid of me,' he says. 'It's just a uniform. You haven't done anything wrong.'

'No.' she whispers. 'I am not afraid.'

'That's good. A pretty girl like you shouldn't be.' He pauses. 'Your accent is odd. When I first saw you, I thought you might be Chaozhou . . .'

She shakes her head, slightly. A jerk. 'So sorry. Japanese.'

'With the factories?'

She shrugs. His eyes bore into her. She makes her head turn – slowly, slowly, smoothly, smoothly, not a single stutter, not a single jerk – and meet his eyes, return his steady gaze. Older than she first thought. Middle-aged, she thinks. Or not. Perhaps he is young and only worn down by the evils of his job. She stifles the urge to extend pity to him, fights her genetic need to serve him even if he would sooner see her dismembered. Slowly, slowly, she turns her eyes back to the water.

'What is your name?'

She hesitates. 'Emiko.'

'A nice name. Does it mean something?'

She shakes her head. 'Nothing important.'

'So modest, for a woman so beautiful.'

She shakes her head, 'No. Not so. I am ugly—' she breaks off, sees him staring, realizes that she has forgotten herself. Her movements have betrayed her. His eyes are wide, surprised. She backs away from him, all pretense of humanity forgotten.

His eyes harden. '*Heechy-keechy*,' he breathes.

She smiles tightly. 'It was an honest mistake.'

'Show me your import permits.'

She smiles. 'Of course. I'm sure they are here. Of course.' She backs away, flashbulb movements broadcasting every kink in her DNA. He reaches for her, but she pulls her arm from his grasp, a quick twist, and then she is turning away, breaking into flight, blurring into traffic as he shouts after her.

'Stop her! Stop! Ministry business! Stop that windup!'

Her whole essence cries to stop and give herself up, to bend to his command. It is all she can do to keep running, to push herself against the lashings of Mizumi-sensei when she dared disobey, the disapproving sting of Mizumi's tongue when she dared to object to another's desires.

Emiko burns with shame as his commands echo behind her, but then the crowds have swallowed her and the surge of megodont traffic is all around, and he is far too slow to discover which alley hides her as she recovers.

It takes extra time to avoid the white shirts, but at the same time, it is a game. Emiko can play this game now. If she is quick and careful, and allows time between her sudden surges she evades them easily. At speed, she marvels at the movements of her body, how startlingly fluid she becomes, as if she is finally being true to her nature. As if all the training and lashes from Mizumi-sensei were designed to keep this knowledge buried.

Eventually she makes Ploenchit and climbs the tower. Raleigh is waiting by the bar, as he always is, impatient. He glances up. 'You're late. I'm fining you for that.'

Emiko forces herself not to feel guilt, even as she apologizes. 'So sorry, Raleigh-san.'

'Hurry up and get changed. You have VIP guests tonight. They're important, and they'll be here soon.'

'I want to ask you about the village.'

'What village?'

She keeps her face pleasant. Did he lie about it? Was it always a lie? 'The place for New People.'

'Still worrying about that?' He shakes his head. ' I told you. Earn up and I'll make sure you get there, if that's what you want.' He waves her toward the dressing rooms. 'Now go get changed.'

Emiko starts to press again, then simply nods. Afterward. When he is drunk. When he is pliable, she will pry the information from him.

In the dressing room, Kannika is already pulling on her performance clothes. She makes a face at Emiko but doesn't say anything as Emiko changes and then goes out to get her first glass of ice for the evening. She drinks carefully, savoring the coolness and sense of well-being that overcomes her even in the swelter of the tower. Out beyond the roped-off windows, the city glows. From a height it is beautiful. Without natural people in it, she thinks that she could even enjoy it here. She drinks more water.

A rustle of warning and surprise. Women drop to their knees and press their foreheads to the ground in a *khrab*. Emiko joins them. The man is back, again. The hard man. The one who came with Anderson-sama before. She searches for signs of Anderson-sama, hoping that he will be there too, but there is no sign of him. The Somdet Chaopraya and his friends are already flushed and drunk as they come through the doors.

Raleigh rushes to them and ushers them into his VIP room.

Kannika slips up behind her. 'Finish your water, *heechy-keechy*. You've got work to do.'

Emiko stifles the urge to snap at the girl. It would be insane to do so. But she looks at Kannika and prays that when she knows the village's location that she will have an opportunity to pay the woman back for all the abuse she has delivered.

The VIP room is crowded with men. There are windows to the outside, but with the door closed, there is little circulation. And the act is worse than when Emiko is on the stage. Normally there are patterns to Kannika's abuse. Here though, Kannika leads her around, introducing her to the men, encouraging them to touch her and feel the heat of her skin, saying things like, 'You like her? You think she's a nasty dog? Watch. You'll see a nasty one tonight.' The powerful one and his bodyguards and his friends are all laughing and making jokes at the sight of her, at the feel of her as they pinch her ass and tug at her breasts, run their fingers up between her thighs, all of them a little nervous at this novelty of entertainment.

Kannika points to the table. 'Up.'

Emiko climbs awkwardly onto the gleaming black surface. Kannika snaps at her, making her walk, making her bow. Makes her totter back and forth in her strange windup way while liquor flows and more girls come in and sit with the men and laugh and make jokes and all the while Emiko is shown off, and then, as it must be, Kannika takes her.

She forces Emiko down on the table. The men gather round

as Kannika begins her abuse. Slowly, it builds, first playing at her nipples, then sliding the jadeite cock between her legs, encouraging the reactions that have been designed into her and which she cannot control, no matter how much her soul fights against it.

The men cheer at Emiko's degradation, encouraging escalation, and Kannika, flushed with excitement, begins to devise new tortures. She squats over Emiko. Parts the cheeks of her ass and encourages Emiko to plumb her depths. The men laugh as Emiko obeys and Kannika narrates:

'Ah yes, I feel her tongue now.'

Then: 'Do you like it with your tongue there, dirty windup?'

To the men: 'She likes it. All these dirty windups like it.'

More laughter.

'More, nasty girl. More.'

And then she is pressing down, smothering her, encouraging Emiko to redouble her efforts as her humiliation mounts, encouraging her to work harder to please. Kannika's hand joins Emiko's tongue, playing, taking pleasure from Emiko's subservience.

Emiko hears Kannika speaking again. 'You want to see her? Go ahead.'

Hands on Emiko's thighs, pushing them apart so that she is completely exposed. Fingers play at her folds, penetrate her. Kannika laughs. 'You want to fuck her? Fuck the windup girl? Here. Give me her legs.' Her hands close on Emiko's ankles, pull them up, exposing her completely.

'No.' Emiko whispers, but Kannika is implacable. She pries Emiko's legs wide. 'Be a good little *heechy-keechy*.' Kannika settles herself again over Emiko, narrating her degradation to the assembled men. 'She'll eat anything you put in her mouth,' she says, and the men are laughing. And then Kannika is pressing down hard on Emiko's face and Emiko can't see anymore, can only hear as

Kannika calls her a slut and a dog and a nasty windup toy. Calls her no better than a dildo ...

And then there is silence.

Emiko tries to move, but Kannika keeps her pinned, muffled from the world. 'Stay there,' Kannika says.

Then: 'No. Use this.'

Emiko feels men taking her arms, pinning her down. Fingers prod her, invade her, slide in.

'Oil it,' Kannika whispers, excitement in her voice. Her hands tighten on Emiko's ankles.

Wetness at her anus, slick, and then a pressure, cold pressure.

Emiko moans a protest. The pressure lets up for a moment, but then Kannika says, 'You call yourselves men? Fuck her! Look how she jerks. Look at her arms and legs when you push! Make her do her *heechy-keechy* dance.'

And then the pressure comes back and the men are holding her down more tightly, and she can't get up and the cold thing presses again against her ass, penetrates her, spreads her wide, splits her open, fills her and she is crying out.

Kannika laughs. 'That's right windup; earn your keep. You can get up when you make me come.'

And then Emiko is licking again, slobbering and lapping like a dog, desperate, as the champagne bottle penetrates her again, as it withdraws and shoves deep into her, burning.

The men all laugh. 'Look at how she moves!'

Tears jewel in her eyes. Kannika encourages her to greater effort and the falcon if there is any falcon in Emiko at all, if it ever existed, is a dead thing, dangling. Not meant to live or fly or escape. Meant to do nothing but submit. Emiko learns her place once again.

All night long, Kannika teaches the merits of obedience and Emiko begs to obey and stop the pain and violation, begs to serve, to do anything at all, anything at all to let the windup live just a little longer and Kannika laughs and laughs.

By the time Kannika is done with her, it is late. Emiko sits against a wall, exhausted and broken. Her mascara has run. Inside, she is dead. Better to be dead than a windup, she thinks. She watches dully as a man starts to mop the club. At the other end of the bar, Raleigh drinks his whiskey and laughs.

The man with the mop slowly approaches. Emiko wonders if he will try to mop her away with the rest of the filth. If he will take her out and throw her into one of the trash piles, leave her for the Dung Lord's collection. She can simply lie there, and let them mulch her . . . thrown away as Gendo-sama should have discarded her. She is trash. Emiko understands this now. The man pushes his rag mop around her.

'Why don't you throw me away?' she croaks. The man looks at her uncertainly, then turns his eyes to his work. Keeps mopping. She says it again. 'Answer me!' she shouts. 'Why don't you throw me away?' Her words echo in the open room.

Raleigh glances up and frowns. She realizes that she has been speaking in Japanese. She says it again in Thai. 'Throw me away, why not? I'm trash, too. Throw me away!' The mopping man flinches and draws back, smiling uncertainly.

Raleigh approaches. Kneels down beside her. 'Emiko. Get up. You're frightening my cleaning guy.'

Emiko makes a face. 'I don't care.'

'Sure you do.' He nods toward the door, to the private room where the men are still reclining, drinking and talking after their abuse of her. 'I've got a bonus for you. Those guys tip well.'

Emiko looks up at him. 'They tip Kannika, too?'

Raleigh studies her. 'It's not your business.'

'They tip her triple? Give me 50 baht?'

His eyes narrow. 'Don't.'

'Or what? Or you throw Emiko into a methane composter? Dump me with the white shirts?'

'Don't push me. You don't want to piss me off.' He stands up. 'Come get your money when you're done feeling sorry for yourself.'

Emiko watches dully as he stalks back to his barstool, gets himself a drink. He glances back at her, makes a comment to Daeng, who smiles dutifully and pours water with ice. Raleigh waves the water at her. Sets it on top of a purple sheaf of baht. He goes back to his drinking, seeming to ignore her staring.

What happens to windup girls who are broken? She never knew a windup girl who died. Sometimes an old patron did. But the windup girl lived. Her girlfriends lived. They lasted longer. Something she never asked Mizumi-sensei. Emiko hobbles to the bar, stumbles. Leans against it. Drinks the ice. Raleigh shoves the money over.

She finishes the ice water. Swallows the cubes. Feels their cold seeping into her core. 'Have you asked, yet?'

'About what?' He's playing solitaire on the bar.

'Going north.'

He glances up at her, then flips another set of cards. He's quiet for a second. 'That's tough work. Not something you set up in a day.'

'Have you asked?'

He glances at her. 'Yeah. I asked. And no one's going anywhere while the white shirts are pissed off about the Jaidee massacre. I'll let you know when the situation changes.'

'I want to go north.'

'You already told me. Earn up, and it will happen.'

'I earn plenty. I want to go now.'

Raleigh's slap comes fast, but she sees it coming. It is fast for him, but not for her. She watches his hand proceed toward her face with the sort of servile gratitude that she used to feel when Gendo-sama took her to dinner at a fancy restaurant. Her cheek stings and then floods with puffy numbness. She touches it with her fingers, savoring the wound.

Raleigh looks at her coldly. 'You'll go when it's damn well convenient.'

Emiko bows her head slightly, allowing the well-deserved lesson to filter into her core. 'You aren't going to help me, are you?'

Raleigh shrugs, goes back to his cards.

'Does it even exist?' she asks.

Raleigh glances over at her. 'Sure. If it makes you happy. It's there. If you keep hassling me about it, it doesn't. Now get out of my face.'

The falcon dangles dead. She is dead. Mulch for composters. Meat for the city, rot for gaslights. Emiko stares at Raleigh. The falcon lies dead.

And then she thinks that some things are worse than dying. Some things can never be borne.

Her fist is very fast. Raleigh-san's throat is soft.

The old man topples, hands flying to his throat, eyes wide with shock. It is all slow-motion: Daeng turning at the sound of the stool clattering to the floor; Raleigh sprawling, his mouth working, trying to suck air; the cleaning man dropping his mop; Noi and Saeng at the other side of the bar with their men waiting to escort them home, all of them turning toward the sound, and every one of them is slow.

By the time Raleigh hits the floor, Emiko is already bolting across the room, toward the VIP door and the man who hurt her most. The man who sits and laughs with his friends and thinks nothing of the pain he inflicts.

She slams into the door. Men look up with surprise. Heads turn, mouths open to cry out. The bodyguards are reaching for their spring guns, but all of them are moving too too slow.

None of them are New People.

30

Pai crawls up beside Kanya, stares down at the shadow village below. 'That's it?'

Kanya nods and glances back at the rest of her squad, who have spread out to cover the other approaches to the shrimp farms where they breed bitter water-resistant prawns for the Krung Thep fish markets.

The houses are all on bamboo rafts currently grounded, but when the floods come, the houses will float, rising, as water and silt rushes across their paddy and ponds. Her own family on the Mekong used something similar long years ago, before General Pracha came.

'It was a good lead,' she murmurs.

Ratana had been almost ecstatic. A link, a clue: fish mites between the third body's toes.

And if fish mites, then shrimp farms, and if shrimp farms then the only ones that would have sent a worker into Bangkok. And that meant shrimp farms that had experienced a die-off. Which led her to this Thonburi half-floating settlement with all of her men at the edge of the embankment, ready to raid in the darkness.

Down below, a few candles flicker inside the bamboo houses. A dog barks. They're all wearing their containment suits. Ratana insisted that the likelihood of a jump was slender, and yet still a worry. A mosquito whines in Kanya's ear. She slaps it away and draws her containment suit's hood tight. Starts to sweat in earnest.

The sound of laughter carries across the fish ponds. A family, all together in the warmth of their hut. Even now, with all their hardship, people still can laugh. Not Kanya, though. Something in her is broken, it seems.

Jaidee always insisted that the Kingdom was a happy country, that old story about the Land of Smiles. But Kanya cannot think of a time when she has seen smiles as wide as those in museum photos from before the Contraction. She sometimes wonders if those people in the photos were acting, if perhaps the National Gallery is intended to depress her, or if it is really true that at one point people smiled so totally, so fearlessly.

Kanya pulls her mask over her face. 'Send them in.'

Pai signals the men, and then her troops are all up and over the edges, coming down on the village, surrounding it as they always do before the burning begins.

When they came to her own village, the white shirts appeared between two huts in the space of a minute, flares hissing and sparking in their hands. This is different. No blaring megaphones. No officers splashing through ankle-deep waters, dragging screaming people away from their houses as bamboo and WeatherAll burst orange and alive with flame.

General Pracha wants it quiet. As he signed the quarantine waivers he said, 'Jaidee would have turned this into an emergency, but we don't have the resources to stir the cobra nest with Trade and also handle this. It could even be used against us. Deal with this quietly.'

'Of course. Quietly.'

The dog starts barking madly. It's joined by others as they approach. A few villagers come out on their porches, peer out into the darkness. Catch the gleam of white in the night. They shout warnings to their families as Kanya's white shirts break into a run.

Jaidee kneels beside her, watching the action. 'Pracha talks about me as if I were some sort of a megodont, trampling rice shoots,' he says.

Kanya ignores him but Jaidee doesn't shut up. 'You should have seen him when we were both cadets,' he says. 'He would piss his pants when we went out into the field.'

Kanya glances over at Jaidee. 'Stop. Just because you are dead doesn't mean that you should heap disrespect upon him.'

Her men's shakelight LEDs blaze alive, illuminating the village in a bitter glare. Families are dashing about like chickens, trying to hide food and animals. Someone tries to dash past the cordon, splashing through the water, diving into a pond and flailing for the other side . . . where more of Kanya's net appears. The man treads water in the center of the muddy shrimp hole, trapped.

Jaidee asks, 'How can you call him your leader when we both know where your true loyalties lie?'

'Shut up.'

'Is it hard being a horse ridden by two men at once? Both of them riding you like—'

'Shut up!'

Pai startles. 'What is it?'

'Sorry.' Kanya shakes her head. 'My fault. I was thinking.'

Pai nods down at the villagers. 'It looks like they're ready for you.'

Kanya gets to her feet and she and Pai and Jaidee – uninvited but smiling and pleased with himself – all descend. She has a photo of the dead man, a black and white thing developed in the lab with fumbling dark fingers. She shows it to the farmers under the beam of her shakelight's LEDs, shining it from the photo to their eyes, trying to catch them in a flinch of recognition.

With some people, a white uniform opens doors, but with fish farmers it is always a problem. She knows them well, reads the calluses on their hands, smells the stink of their successes and failures in the reek of the ponds. She sees herself through their eyes, and knows she might as well be an enforcer from a calorie company, hunting for signs of a genehack. Still the charade continues, all of them shaking their heads, Kanya shining her light into each one's eyes. One by one, they look away.

Finally she finds a man and waves the picture in front of him. 'Do you know him? Won't his relatives be looking for him?'

The man looks at the picture and then at Kanya's uniform. 'He doesn't have any relatives.'

Kanya jerks with surprise. 'You know him? Who was he?'

'He's dead then?'

'Doesn't he look dead?'

They both study the bloodless photo, the ravaged face. 'I told him there were better things than factory jobs. He didn't listen.'

'You say he worked in the city.'

'That's right.'

'Do you know where?'

He shakes his head.

'Where did he live?'

The man points toward a black shadow stilt-house. Kanya waves at her men. 'Quarantine that hut.'

She tightens her mask and enters, sweeping her light around the space. It's gloomy. Broken and strange and empty. Dust gleams in her beam. Knowing that the owner is already dead gives her a sense of foreboding. The man's spirit might be here. His hungry ghost lurking and angry that he is still in this world, that he has been sickened. That he may have been murdered. She fingers the man's few effects and wanders around the place. Nothing. She steps back outside. Off in the distance, the city rises, haloed in green, the place the dead man ran to when fish farming proved untenable. She goes back to the man. 'You're sure you don't know anything about where he worked?'

The man shakes his head.

'Nothing? Not a name? Anything.' She tries not to let her desperation show. He shakes his head again. She turns in frustration and surveys the village blackness. Crickets chirp. Ivory beetles creak steadily. They're in the right place. She's so close. Where is this factory? Gi Bu Sen was right. She should just burn the entire factory district. In the old days, when the white shirts were strong, it would have been easy.

'You want to burn now?' Jaidee snickers beside her. 'Now you see my side?'

She ignores his jab. Not far away, a young girl is watching her intently. When Kanya catches her staring, she looks away. Kanya touches Pai on the shoulder. 'That one.'

'The girl?' He's surprised. Kanya is already walking, closing on her. The girl looks as if she will bolt. Kanya kneels, still a good distance away. Beckons her over. 'You. What's your name?'

The girl is obviously torn. She wants to flee, but Kanya has an authority that cannot be denied. 'Come over here. Tell me your name.' She beckons again and this time the girl allows herself to be reeled close.

'Mai,' the girl whispers.

Kanya holds up the photo. 'You know where this man worked, don't you?'

Mai shakes her head, but Kanya knows the girl is lying. Children are terrible liars. Kanya had been a terrible liar. When the white shirts questioned where her family was hiding their carp breeding stock, she had told them south and they had gone north, with knowing adult smiles.

She offers the photo to the girl. 'You understand how dangerous this is, yes?'

The girl hesitates. 'Will you burn the village?'

Kanya tries to keep the flood of reaction off her face. 'Of course not.' She smiles again, speaks soothingly. 'Don't worry, Mai. I know what it is to fear. I grew up in a village like this. I know how hard it is. But you must help me find the source of this sickness, or more will die.'

'I was told not to tell.'

'And it is good for us to respect our patrons,' Kanya pauses. 'But we all owe loyalty to Her Royal Majesty the Queen, and she wishes that we all be safe. The Queen would want you to help us.'

Mai hesitates, then says, 'Three others worked at the factory.'

Kanya leans forward, trying to hide her eagerness. 'Which one?'

Mai hesitates. Kanya leans close. 'How many *phii* will blame you if you allow them to die before their *kamma* allots their passing?'

Still Mai hesitates.

Pai says, 'If we break her fingers, she will tell us.'

The girl looks frightened. But Kanya holds out a soothing hand. 'Don't worry. He won't do anything. He is a tiger, but I have his leash. Please. Just help us save the city. You can help us save Krung Thep.'

The girl looks away, toward the crumbling glow of Bangkok across the waters. 'The factory is closed now. Closed by you.'

'That's very good then. But we must make sure the disease doesn't go any further. What is the name of the factory?'

The answer comes unwillingly. 'SpringLife.'

Kanya frowns, trying to remember the name. 'A kink-spring company? One of the Chaozhou?'

Mai shakes her head. '*Farang*. Very rich *farang*.'

Kanya settles beside her. 'Tell me more.'

31

Anderson finds Emiko huddled outside his door, and all at once a good night becomes an uncertain one.

For the last several days he has worked frantically to prepare the invasion, all of it crippled by the fact that he never expected to be cut off from his own factory. His own piss-poor planning forced him to waste extra days scouting a safe route back into the SpringLife facility without being caught by the plethora of white shirt patrols that cordoned the manufacturing district. If it hadn't been for the discovery of Hock Seng's escape route, he might still have been lurking around the back alleys, wishing for an access method.

As it was, Anderson slipped in through the shutters of the SpringLife offices with a blackened face and grapple slung over his shoulder while giving thanks to a crazy old man who just days before had robbed the company's entire payroll.

The factory had reeked. The algae baths had all gone to rot but not a thing moved in the gloom, and for that he was grateful. If the white shirts had posted guards within ... Anderson held a hand over his mouth as he slipped down to the main hall and then down along the manufacturing lines. The stink of rot and megodont dung thickened.

Under the shadow of algae racks and the loom of the cutting

presses, he examined the floor. This close to the algae tanks, the stink was horrific, as if a cow had died and rotted. The end-stage reek of Yates' optimistic plan for a new energy future.

Anderson knelt and pushed away desiccated algae strands from around one of the drains. He felt along the edges, seeking purchase. Lifted. The iron grate came up with a squeal. As quietly as he could, Anderson rolled the heavy grate away and set it with a clank on concrete. He lay down on the floor, prayed he wouldn't surprise a snake or scorpion, and plunged his arm down the hole. His fingers scrabbled in the darkness, questing. Straining deeper into moist blackness.

For a moment he feared it had slipped loose, had floated down the drain and on through the sewers to King Rama's groundwater pumps, but then his fingers touched oilskin. He peeled it from the drain wall, drew it out, smiling. A code book. For contingencies that he never seriously believed would come to pass.

In the blackness of the offices, he dialed numbers and brought operators alert in Burma and India. Sent secretaries scurrying for code strings unused since Finland.

Two days later, he stood on the floating island of Koh Angrit, arranging the last details with strike team leaders in the AgriGen compound. The weaponry would arrive within days, the invasion teams were assembling. And the money had already been shipped across, the gold and jade that would help generals change their loyalties and turn on their old friend General Pracha.

But now, with all the preparations completed, he returns to the city to find Emiko huddled at his door, miserable, and covered with blood. As soon as she sees him, she lunges into his arms, sobbing.

'What are you doing here?' he whispers. Cradling her against him he unlocks the door and urges her inside. Her skin burns. The blood is everywhere. Slashes mark her face and scar her arms. He shuts the door quickly. 'What happened to you?' He pries her off him, tries to inspect her. She's a furnace of blood, but the wounds on her face and arms don't account for the sticky spattering that coats her. 'Whose blood is this?'

She shakes her head. Begins sobbing again.

'Let's get you cleaned up.'

He leads her into the bath, turns on cool water spray, puts her under it. She's shivering now, her eyes fever bright and panicked as she looks around. She looks half-mad. He tries to peel off her half-jacket, to get rid of the bloody clothing, but her face twists, enraged.

'No!' She slashes at him with her hand and he jerks back, touching his cheek.

'What the hell?!' He stares at her, shocked. Christ she was fast. He's hurting. His hand comes away bloody. 'What the hell's wrong with you?'

The panicked animal flicker leaves her eyes. She stares at him blankly, and then seems to recover herself, becomes human. 'I am sorry,' she whispers. 'So sorry.' She collapses, curls into a ball under the water. 'So sorry. So sorry.' She lapses into Japanese.

Anderson squats down beside her, his own clothing becoming soaked in the spray. 'Don't worry about it.' He speaks gently. 'Why don't you get out of those clothes? We'll get you something else. Okay? Can you do that?'

She nods dully. Peels off her jacket. Unwraps her *pha sin*. Huddles nude in the cool water. He leaves her in the spray. Takes her bloody clothes and bundles them into a sheet and carries them down the stair, out into the darkness. People are all around. He ignores them, walking quickly into the shadows, carrying the clothes until he reaches a *khlong*. Tosses the bloody garments into the water, where snakehead fish and boddhi carp will consume them with an obsessive determination. The water roils, splashing as they tear at the blood food scent.

By the time he's back in his apartment, Emiko is out of the shower, her black hair clinging to her face, a small frightened creature. He goes to his medicine supplies. Pours alcohol on the cuts, rubs antivirals in after. She doesn't cry out. Her nails are broken and ravaged. Bruises are blooming all across her body. But for all the blood she arrived with, she seems miraculously little damaged.

'What happened?' he asks gently.

She huddles against him. 'I'm alone,' she whispers. 'There is no place for New People.' Her shaking increases.

He pulls her to him, feeling the burning heat through her skin. 'It's all right. Everything will change soon. It will be different.'

She shakes her head. 'No. I do not think so.'

A moment later, she is asleep, breathing steadily, her body finally releasing its tension into unconsciousness.

Anderson wakes with a start. The crank fan has stopped, run out of joules. He's covered with sweat. Beside him Emiko moans and thrashes, a furnace. He rolls away and sits up.

A slight breeze from the sea runs through the apartment, a relief. He stares out through mosquito nets to the blackness of the city. All the methane has been shut off for the night. Off in the distance, he can see a few glimmers in the floating sea communities of Thonburi where they farm fish and float from one genehack to the next in a perpetual seeking of survival.

Someone pounds on his door. Hammering insistently.

Emiko's eyes snap open. She sits up. 'What is it?'

'Someone's at the door.' He starts to climb out of bed but she grabs him, ragged nails digging into his arm.

'Don't open it!' she whispers. Her skin is pale in the moonlight, her eyes wide and frightened. 'Please.' The banging on his door increases. Thudding, insistent.

'Why not?'

'I—' she pauses. 'It will be white shirts.'

'What?' Anderson's heart skips over. 'They followed you here? Why? What happened to you?'

She shakes her head miserably. He stares at her, wondering what sort of animal has invaded his life. 'What happened tonight, really?'

She doesn't answer. Her eyes remain locked on the door as the thumping continues. Anderson climbs out of bed and hurries to the door. Shouts, 'Just a second! I'm getting dressed!'

'Anderson!' The voice from the far side of door is Carlyle's. 'Open up! It's important!'

Anderson turns and looks pointedly at Emiko. 'It's not white shirts. Now hide.'

'No?' For a moment relief floods Emiko's features. But it disappears almost as quickly. She shakes her head. 'You are mistaken.'

Anderson glares at her. 'Was it white shirts that you tangled with? Is that where you got those cuts?'

She shakes her head miserably, but says nothing, just huddles in a small defensive ball.

'Jesus and Noah.' Anderson goes and pulls clothes out of his closet, tosses them at her, gifts that he bought her as tokens of his intoxication. 'You might be ready to go public, but I'm not ready to be ruined. Get dressed. Hide in my closet.'

She shakes her head again. Anderson tries to control his voice, to speak reasonably. It's as though he's talking to a block of wood. He kneels and takes her chin in his hands, turns her face to him.

'It's one of my business associates. It's not about you. But I still need you to hide until he goes away. Do you understand? You just need to hide for a little while. I want you to hide until he's gone. I don't want him to see us together. It might give him leverage.'

Slowly, her eyes focus. The look of hypnotized fatalism fades. Carlyle bangs on the door again. Her eyes flick to the door, then back to Anderson. 'It is white shirts,' she whispers. 'There are many of them out there. I can hear them.' She suddenly seems to collect herself. 'It will be white shirts. Hiding will do no good.'

Anderson fights the urge to scream at her. 'It's not white shirts.'

The banging continues on his door. 'Open the fuck up, Anderson!'

He calls back, 'Just a second!' He pulls on a pair of pants, glaring at her. 'It's not the damn white shirts. Carlyle would slit his throat before he'd get into bed with white shirts.'

Carlyle's voice again echoes through the door. 'Hurry up, goddamnit!'

'Coming!' He turns to her, orders her. 'Hide. *Now.*' Not a request anymore, but an order, driving at her genetic heritage and her training.

Her body goes still, then suddenly she becomes animated. Nodding. 'Yes. I will do as you say.'

Already she is dressing. Her stutter motion is fast, almost a blur. Her skin gleams as she pulls on a blouse and a pair of loose trousers. Suddenly she's shockingly fast. Fluid in her movements, strangely and suddenly graceful.

'Hiding will do no good,' she says. She turns and runs for the balcony.

'What are you doing?'

She turns back and smiles at him, seems about to say something, but instead she plunges over the balcony's edge and disappears into the blackness.

'Emiko!' Anderson runs to the balcony.

Below, there is nothing. No person, no scream, no thud, no complaints from the street as she spatters across the ground.

Nothing. Only emptiness. As though the night has swallowed her completely. The banging on the door comes again.

Anderson's heart thuds in his chest. Where is she? How did she do that? It is unnatural. She was so fast, so determined at the end. One minute on the balcony, the next gone, over the edge. Anderson peers into the blackness. It's impossible that she jumped to another balcony, and yet . . . Did she fall? Is she dead?

The door crashes open. Anderson whirls. Carlyle spills into the apartment room, stumbling.

'What the— ?'

Black Panthers pour in after Carlyle, slamming him aside. Combat armor gleams in the dimness, military shadows. One of the soldiers grabs Anderson, whirls him about and slams him into the wall. Hands search his body. When he struggles they jam his face against the wall. More men pour in. Doors are being kicked open, splintering. Boots thud around him. An avalanche of men. Glass breaks. Dishes in his kitchen shatter.

Anderson cranes his neck to see what is happening. A hand grabs him by the hair and slams his face back against the wall. Blood and pain flood his mouth. He's bitten his tongue. 'What the hell are you doing? Do you know who I am?'

He chokes off as Carlyle is dumped on the floor beside him. He can see now that the man is tied. Bruises pepper his face. One eye is swollen shut, black blood scabs on the orbital bone. His brown hair is clotted with blood.

'Christ.'

The soldiers wrench Anderson's hands behind his back and bind them. They grab his hair and jerk him around. A soldier shouts at him, speaking so fast he can't understand. Wide eyes and spittle in his face as the man rages. Finally Anderson catches words: *Heechy-keechy.*

'*Where is the windup? Where is it? Where? Where?*'

The Panthers tear through his apartment. Rifle butts to smash open locks and doors. Huge black windup mastiffs scramble inside, barking and slavering, snuffling everywhere, howling as they catch their target's scent. A man shouts at him again, some kind of captain.

'What's going on?' Anderson demands again. 'I have friends—'

'Not many.'

Akkarat strides through the door.

'Akkarat!' Anderson tries to turn but the Panthers slam him back against the wall. 'What's going on?'

'We have the same question for you.'

Akkarat shouts orders in Thai to the men tossing Anderson's apartment. Anderson closes his eyes, desperately thankful that the windup girl didn't hide in the closet as he suggested. To be found with her, caught out . . .

One of the Panthers returns, carrying Anderson's spring gun.

Akkarat makes a face of distaste. 'Do you have a permit to be armed?'

'We're starting a revolution and you're asking about permits?'

Akkarat nods to his men. Anderson slams back against the wall. Pain explodes in his skull. The room dims and his knees buckle. He staggers, barely keeps his feet. 'What the hell's going on?'

Akkarat motions for the pistol. Takes it. Pumps it idly, the heavy dull thing massive in his fist. 'Where is the windup girl?'

Anderson spits blood. 'Why do you care? You're not a white shirt or a Grahamite.'

The Panthers slam Anderson against the wall again. Colored dots swim in Anderson's vision.

'Where did the windup come from?' Akkarat asks.

'She's Japanese! From Kyoto I think!'

Akkarat puts the pistol to Anderson's head. 'How did you get her into the country?'

'*What?*'

Akkarat strikes him with the butt of the pistol. The world darkens.

– water gushes into his face. Anderson gasps and splutters. He's sitting on the floor. Akkarat presses the spring gun to Anderson's throat, pushing him to climb up to his feet again, then to teeter onto his toes. Anderson gags at the pressure.

'How did you get the windup into the country?' Akkarat repeats.

Sweat and blood sting Anderson's eyes. He blinks and shakes his head. 'I didn't get her in.' He spits blood again. 'She was a Japanese discard. How would I get my hands on a windup?'

Akkarat smiles, says something to his men. 'A military windup is a Japanese discard?' He shakes his head. 'I think not.' He slams the pistol butt into Anderson's ribs. Once. Twice. Each side, cracking. Anderson yowls and doubles over, coughing and cringing away. Akkarat drags him upright. 'Why would a military windup be in our City of Divine Beings?'

'She's not military,' Anderson protests. 'She's just a secretary . . . was just a—'

Akkarat's expression doesn't change. He spins Anderson around and forces his face against the wall, grinding bones. Anderson thinks his jaw is broken. He feels Akkarat's hands, prying his fingers apart. Anderson tries to make a fist, whimpering, knowing what is coming, but Akkarat's hands are strong, prying them open. Anderson experiences a moment of tingling helplessness.

His finger twists in Akkarat's grip. Snaps.

Anderson howls into the wall as Akkarat supports him.

When he's done whimpering and shaking, Akkarat grabs him by the hair and pulls his head back so that they can look into one another's eyes. Akkarat's voice is steady.

'She is military, she is a killer, and you are the one who introduced her to the Somdet Chaopraya. Where is she now?'

'A killer?' Anderson shakes his head, trying to think straight. 'But she's nothing! A Mishimoto discard. Japanese trash—'

'The Environment Ministry is right about one thing. You AgriGen animals can't be trusted. You call the windup a simple pleasure toy, and so conveniently introduce your assassin to the Queen's protector.' He leans close, eyes full of rage. 'You might as well have killed royalty.'

'But that's impossible!' Anderson doesn't even try to keep the hysteria from his voice. His broken finger throbs, blood fills his mouth again. 'She's just a piece of trash. She couldn't do something like that. You have to believe me.'

'She killed three men and their bodyguards. Eight trained men. The proof is unassailable.'

Unbidden, he remembers Emiko huddled on his doorstep, soaked in blood. *Eight men?* Remembers her disappearing over the balcony, plunging into darkness like some kind of spirit creature. *What if they're right?*

'There's got to be another explanation. She's just a goddamn windup. All they do is obey.'

Emiko in bed, huddled. Sobbing. Her body torn and scratched.

Anderson takes a breath, tries to control his voice. 'Please. You have to believe me. We would never jeopardize so much. AgriGen doesn't benefit from the Somdet Chaopraya's death. Nobody does. This plays right into the Environment Ministry's hands. We have too much to gain from a good relationship.'

'And yet you introduced the killer to him.'

'But it's insane. How would anyone get a military windup here and keep it under wraps? That windup has been around for years and years. Ask around. You'll see. She bribed her way with the white shirts, her papa-san had that show running for ages . . .'

He's babbling, but he can see Akkarat listening now. The cold rage is gone from the man's eyes. Now there is consideration. Anderson spits blood and looks Akkarat in the eye. 'Yes. I introduced that creature. But it was only because she was a novelty. Everyone knows his reputation.' He flinches as a new surge of anger twists Akkarat's face. 'Please listen to me. Investigate this. If you investigate, you'll find out it wasn't us. There has to be another explanation. We had no idea . . .' He breaks off, tiredly. 'Just investigate.'

'We cannot. The Environment Ministry has the case.'

'*What?*' Anderson can't hide his surprise. 'By what authority?'

'The windup makes it a case for their Ministry. She is an invasive.'

'And you think I'm the one behind it? When those bastards are controlling the investigation?'

Anderson works through the implications, hunting for reasons, excuses, anything to buy time. 'You can't trust them. Pracha and his people . . .' He pauses. 'Pracha would set us up. He'd do it in a second. Maybe he's caught wind of our plans, he could be moving against us right now. Using this as cover. If he knew the Somdet Chaopraya was against him—'

'Our plans were secret,' Akkarat says.

'Nothing's secret. Not on the scale we're working. One of the generals could have leaked to their old friend. And now he's just assassinated three of ours, and we're pointing fingers at each other.'

Akkarat considers. Anderson waits, breath held.

Finally Akkarat shakes his head. 'No. Pracha would never attack royalty. He is garbage, but still, he is Thai.'

'But it wasn't me, either!' He looks down at Carlyle. 'It wasn't us! There has to be another explanation.' He starts to cough with panic, a cough that becomes an uncontrolled spasm. At last it stops. His ribs ache. He spits blood, and wonders if his lung is punctured from the beating.

He looks up at Akkarat, trying to control his words. To make them count. To sound reasonable. 'There must be some way to find out what really happened to the Somdet Chaopraya. Some connection. Something.'

A Panther leans forward and whispers in Akkarat's ear. Anderson thinks he recognizes him from the party on the barge. One of the Somdet Chaopraya's men. The hard one with the feral face and the still eyes. He whispers more words. Akkarat nods sharply. '*Khap.*' Motions his men to push Anderson and Carlyle into the next room.

'All right, *Khun* Anderson. We will see what we can learn.' They shove him down on the floor beside Carlyle. 'Make yourself comfortable,' Akkarat says. 'I've given my man twelve hours to investigate. You had better pray to whatever Grahamite god you worship that your story is confirmed.'

Anderson feels a surge of hope. 'Find out everything you can. You'll see it wasn't us. You'll see.' He sucks on his split lip. 'That windup isn't anything other than a Japanese toy. Someone else is responsible for this. The white shirts are just trying to get us to go after each other. Ten to one says it's the white shirts, moving on us all.'

'We will see.'

Anderson lets his head loll back against the wall, adrenaline and nervous energy firing under his skin. His hand throbs. The broken finger dangles useless. Time. He's bought time. Now it's just a matter of waiting. Of trying to find the next fingerhold to survival. He coughs again, wincing at the pain in his ribs.

Beside him, Carlyle groans, but doesn't wake up. Anderson coughs again and stares at the wall, collecting himself for the next round of conflict with Akkarat. But even as he considers the many angles, trying to understand what has caused this rapid change in circumstance, another image keeps intruding. The sight of the windup girl running for the balcony and plunging into darkness, faster than anything he has ever seen, a wraith of movement and feral grace. Fast and smooth. And at speed, terrifyingly beautiful.

32

Smoke billows around Kanya. Four more bodies discovered, in addition to the ones they'd already found in the hospitals. The plague is mutating more quickly than she expected. Gi Bu Sen hinted that it might, but the counting of bodies fills her with foreboding.

Pai moves along the edges of a fish pond. They've thrown lye and chlorine into the pond, huge sacks. Clouds of acrid scent waft across everyone, making them cough. The stench of fear.

She remembers other ponds filled, other people huddled while the white shirts ranged through the village, burning burning burning. She closes her eyes. How she had hated the white shirts then. And so when the local *jao por* found her intelligent and driven, he sent her to the capital with instructions: to volunteer with the white shirts, to work for them, to ingratiate herself. A country godfather, working in concert with the enemies of the white shirts. Seeking revenge for the usurpation of his power.

Dozens of other children went south to beg on the Ministry's doors, and all of them with the same instructions. Of the ones she arrived with, she is the only one who rose so high, but there are others, she knows, others like her, seeded throughout. Other embittered loyal children.

'I forgive you,' Jaidee murmurs.

Kanya shakes her head and ignores him. Waves to Pai that the ponds are ready to be buried. If they are lucky, the village will cease to exist entirely. Her men work quickly, eager to be gone. They all have masks and suits, but in the relentless heat these shields are more torture than protection.

More clouds of acrid smoke. The villagers are crying. The girl Mai stares at Kanya, her expression flat. A formative moment for the child. This memory will lodge like a fish bone in the throat; she will never be free of it.

Kanya's heart goes out to her. *If only you could understand.* But it is impossible for one so small to comprehend the gray brutalities of life.

If only I could have understood.

'Captain Kanya!'

She turns. A man is coming across the dikes, stumbling in the mud of the paddies, stumbling through jewel-green rice shoots. Pai looks up with interest, but Kanya waves him away. The messenger arrives breathless. 'Buddha smiles on you, and the Ministry.' He waits expectantly.

'Now?' Kanya stares at him. Looks back at the burning village. 'You want me now?'

The young boy looks around nervously, surprised at her response. Kanya waves impatiently. 'Tell me again. Now?'

'Buddha smiles on you. And the Ministry. All roads start at the heart of Krung Thep. All roads.'

Kanya grimaces and calls to her lieutenant. 'Pai! I must go.'

'Now?' He masters his surprise as he comes over to her.

Kanya nods. 'It's unavoidable.' She waves at the flaming bamboo houses. 'Finish up here.'

'What about the villagers?'

'Keep them roped here. Send food. If no one else sickens this week, we are likely finished.'

'You think we could be so lucky?'

Kanya makes herself smile, thinking how unnatural it is to reassure someone with Pai's experience. 'We can hope.' She waves at the boy. 'Take me, then.' She glances at Pai. 'Meet me at the Ministry when you have finished here. We have one more place left to burn.'

'The *farang* factory?'

Kanya almost smiles at his eagerness. 'We cannot let the source go uncleansed. Is that not our job?'

'You are a new Tiger!' Pai exclaims. He claps her on the back before he remembers his station and *wais* apology for his forwardness and then hurries back to the destruction of the village.

'A new Tiger,' Jaidee mutters beside her. 'Very nice for you.'

'It's your own fault. You trained them to need a radical.'

'And so they choose you?'

Kanya sighs. 'If you carry a burning torch, apparently it is enough.'

Jaidee laughs at that.

A kink-spring scooter is waiting for her on the far side of the dikes. The boy climbs on and waits for her to perch behind and then they are off through the city streets, weaving around megodonts and bicycles. Their little air horn blares. The city blurs past. Fish sellers, cloth merchants, amulet men with their Phra Seubs which Jaidee used to make so much fun of and which Kanya secretly keeps herself, close to her heart on a small chain.

'Currying favor with too many gods,' Jaidee observed when she touched it before leaving the village. But she ignored his mockery and still whispered prayers to Phra Seub, hoping for protection that she knew she didn't deserve.

The scooter slews to a stop and she hops down. The gold filigree of the City Pillar Shrine gleams in the dawn. All around, women sell marigolds for offerings. The chanting of monks carries over the whitewashed walls along with the music of *khon* dances. The boy is gone before she has a chance to thank him. Just another of the many who owe favors to Akkarat. Likely the scooter is a gift from the man, and loyalty the price of it.

'And what do you get, dear Kanya?' Jaidee asks.

'You know,' Kanya mutters. 'I get what I swore I would get.'

'And do you still desire it?'

She doesn't answer him, steps over the barrier door to the shrine's interior. Even at dawn, the shrine is crowded with worshippers, people crouched before the Buddha statues and the shrine of Phra Seub, second only to the one at the Ministry. The grounds bustle with people making offerings of flowers and fruit, shaking out their fortunes with divining sticks – and over it all, the monks chant, guarding the city with their prayers and amulets and the *saisin* that stretches from the shrine to the dikes and pumps. The sacred thread wavers in the gray light, held aloft on poles where it crosses thoroughfares, stretching miles from this blessed hub to the pumps and then circling the seawalls. The monks' chanting is a steady drone, keeping the City of Divine Beings safe from the swallowing waves.

Kanya buys her own incense and food offering, takes it into the cool confines of the pillar shrine, down the marble steps. She kneels before the old city pillar of sacked Ayutthaya, and the larger one of Bangkok. The place where all miles are marked from. The heart of Krung Thep, and the home of the spirits that protect it. If she stands in the shrine's doorway and looks out toward the dikes, she can see the rise of the levees. It is obvious that they are in the depths of a bathtub. They are exposed on all sides. This shrine ... she lights her incense and pays her respects.

'Don't you feel like a hypocrite, coming here, of all places, at Trade's whim?'

'Shut up, Jaidee.'

Jaidee kneels beside her. 'Well, at least you're giving some good fruit.'

'Shut up.'

She wants to pray, but with Jaidee bothering her, it's useless. After another minute, she gives up and goes back outside to the increasing morning light and heat. Narong is there, leaning against a post, watching the *khon* dances. The drums beat and the dancers go through their stylized turns, their voices raised high and stark, competing with the drone of the ranked monks across the courtyard. Kanya joins him.

Narong holds up a hand. 'Wait until they're done.'

She masters her irritation and finds a seat, watches as the story of Rama is played out. Finally Narong nods, satisfied. 'It's good, isn't it?' He tilts his head toward the pillar shrine. 'Have you made your offerings?'

'You care?'

Other white shirts cluster in the compound, making their own offerings. Asking for promotions to better paying assignments. Asking for success in their investigations. Asking for protection from the diseases that they run up against every day. By its nature, this is a shrine for the Environment Ministry, almost as important as the temple of Phra Seub, the biodiversity martyr. It makes her nervous to speak with Narong in front of them all, but he appears entirely unconcerned.

'We all love the city,' he says. 'Not even Akkarat will fail to defend it.'

Kanya makes a face. 'What do you want from me?'

'So impatient. Let's walk.'

She scowls. Narong seems unhurried, and yet he has summoned her as if it is an emergency. She tamps her fury and mutters, 'Do you know what you've interrupted?'

'Tell me as we walk.'

'I have a village with five dead and we still haven't isolated the cause.'

He glances over, interested. 'A new cibiscosis?' He guides her out of the compound, past the marigold sellers. Walking onward.

'We don't know.' She masters her frustration. 'But you're delaying me from my work, and though it may please you to make me run like a dog when you call—'

'We have a problem,' Narong interrupts. 'And though you think your village is important, it is nothing in comparison to this. There has been a death. A very prominent one. We need your help in the investigation.'

She laughs, 'I'm not the police—'

'It's not a police matter. There was a windup involved.'

She stops short. 'A what?'

'The killer. We believe it is an invasive. A military windup. *Heechy-keechy.*'

'How is that possible?'

'It is something we also are trying to understand.' Narong looks at her seriously. 'And we cannot ask the question, because General Pracha has taken control of the investigation, claiming jurisdiction because the windup is an interdicted creature. As if it were a cheshire or a yellow card.' He laughs bitterly. 'We are blocked entirely. You will investigate on our behalf.'

'That's difficult. It is not my investigation. Pracha will not—'

'He trusts you.'

'Trusting me to do my job and allowing me to meddle are two different things.' She shrugs and turns away. 'It's impossible.'

'No!' Narong grabs her and yanks her back. 'This is vital! We must know the details!'

Kanya whirls, throws Narong's hand off her shoulder. 'Why? What is so important about this? People die all over Bangkok, every day. We find bodies faster than we can shovel them into methane composters. What's so important about this one, that you'd have me cross the general?'

Narong pulls her close. 'It's the Somdet Chaopraya. We have lost Her Royal Majesty's protector.'

Kanya's knees buckle. Narong drags her upright, keeps talking, fiercely insistent. 'Politics has become uglier since I started in this game.' He has a smile on his face, but now Kanya sees the rage banked below. 'You're a good girl, Kanya. We have always held our part of the bargain. But this is why you are here. I know this is difficult. You have loyalty to your superiors in the Environment Ministry as well. You pray to Phra Seub. This is good. It is right for you. But we require your help. Even if you have no taste for Akkarat anymore, the palace requires it.'

'What do you want?'

'We need to know if this was Pracha's doing. He has been quick to take over the investigation. We *must* know if it was he who drove the knife. Your patron and the safety of the palace depends on this. It is possible that Pracha wishes to hide something. It could be some of his December 12 elements striking against us.'

'It's not possible—'

'It is too convenient. We have been locked out entirely because it is a windup who did the killing.' Narong's voice cracks with a sudden intensity. 'We *must* know if the windup was planted by your ministry.' He passes her a bundle of cash. Kanya stares at the amount, shocked. 'Bribe anyone who gets in your way,' he says.

She shakes off her paralysis, takes the money and stuffs it into her pockets. He touches her gently. 'I am very sorry, Kanya. You're all I have. I depend on you to find our enemies and root them out.'

The heat of a Ploenchit tower in the middle of the day is stifling. Investigators clog the dingy rooms of the club, adding to the swelter. It is a sick place to die. A place of hunger and desperation and appetites unfilled. Palace staffers crowd in the halls. Watching, conferring, preparing to collect the Somdet Chaopraya's body for placement in his funeral urn, waiting as Pracha's people investigate. Anxiety and anger hang in the air, politeness filed to an exquisite edge in this most humiliating and frightening moment. The rooms have the feeling of the monsoon just about to break, electric with energy, fraught with the unknown darkness of roiling clouds.

The first body lies on the floor outside, an old *farang*, surreal and alien. There is little physical damage to him, except the bruising where his throat was crushed, the livid torture that was done to his windpipe. He sprawls beside the bar with the mottled look of a corpse raised from the river. Some gangster bit of fish bait. The old man stares at her with wide blue eyes, two dead seas. Kanya studies the damage without speaking, then allows General Pracha's secretary to lead her to the interior rooms.

She gasps.

Blood stains everything, great swirls of it spatter the walls and drool across the floors. Bodies lie in tangled heaps. And among them lies the Somdet Chaopraya, his throat not smashed as was the old *farang*, but literally torn out, as though a tiger has fed upon him. His bodyguards lie dead, one with a spring gun blade buried in his eye socket, the other still clutching his own spring gun but peppered with blades.

'*Kot rai,*' Kanya murmurs. She hesitates, uncertain of what to do in the presence of this sordid death. Ivory beetles tangle in the bloody froth. They skitter and scatter through it all, making tracks in the coagulant.

Pracha is in the room, conferring with his subordinates. He looks up at her gasp of dismay. The others have their own looks of shock, anxiety and embarrassment flickering on their faces. The thought that Pracha could arrange such a killing fills Kanya with sickness. The Somdet Chaopraya was no friend of the Environment Ministry, but the enormity of the act makes her ill. It is one thing to plot coups and counter-coups, another to reach inside the palace. She feels like a bamboo leaf drowning in flood-water currents.

So we all go, she tells herself. *Even the richest and the most powerful are only meat for cheshires in the end. We are all nothing but walking corpses and to forget it is folly. Meditate on the nature of corpses and you will see this.*

And yet still she is unnerved, almost panicked by the sight of a near-god's mortality before her. *What have you done, General?* It is too horrifying to consider. The flood currents threaten to suck her under.

'Kanya?' Pracha waves her over. She searches her general's face for signs that he carries the guilt for this act, but Pracha seems only puzzled. 'What are you doing here?'

'I—' she has words prepared. Excuses. But they fail her with the Crown Protector and his retinue strewn about the room. Pracha's eyes follow her gaze to the Protector's body. His voice softens. He touches her gently on the arm. 'Come. This is too much.' Guides her out.

'I—'

Pracha shakes his head. 'You've heard already.' He sighs. 'By the end of the day, it will be all over the city.'

Kanya finds her voice, spills her lie, pretending to the role that Narong has given her. 'I didn't think it could be true.'

'Worse than that.' Pracha shakes his head grimly. 'It was a windup that did it.'

Kanya forces herself to show surprise. She glances back at the bloodshed. 'A windup? Just one?' Her eyes trace along a peppering of spring blades embedded in the walls. She recognizes one of the other bodies as a Trade Ministry official, the son of a secondary patriarch. Another from a Chaozhou manufacturing clan, a man making his way in the business press. All of them faces from the whisper sheets. All of them great tigers. 'It's awful.'

'It doesn't seem possible, does it? Six bodyguards. Three men additionally. And only a single windup, if we believe the witnesses.' Pracha shakes his head. 'Even cibiscosis kills more cleanly.'

His eminence the Somdet Chaopraya's neck has been ripped entirely away, breaking it, snapping and tearing so that though the spine seems attached still, it acts as a hinge rather than a support. 'It looks like a demon tore him open.'

'A wild animal, anyway. It's the sort of thing a military genehack would do. We've seen this sort of activity in the north, where the Vietnamese operate. They use Japanese windups as scouts and shock troops. We're lucky they don't have many.' He looks seriously at Kanya. 'It will go hard on us. Trade will say that we failed in this. That we allowed this animal into the country. They'll try to take advantage. Make a pretext out of it to seize more power.' His expression turns bleak. 'We have to find out why this windup was here. If Akkarat has set us up, has used the Protector as a pawn, to seize power.'

'He would never—'

Pracha makes a face of dismissal. 'Politics is ugly. Never doubt what small men will do for great power. We think Akkarat was here before. Some of the staff seem to recognize his image, seem to recall—' he shrugs. 'But of course, everyone is afraid. No one wants to admit too much. But it looks as if Akkarat and some of his *farang* trader friends brought the Somdet Chaopraya to the *heechy-keechy.*'

Is he playing me? Does he know that I work for Akkarat? Kanya stifles her fears. *If he knew, he would never have promoted me to Jaidee's position.*

Jaidee whispers in her ear. 'You never know. A snake in its nest is better than a snake slithering through the jungle. This way, he always knows exactly where you are.'

'I need you to go to the records department,' Pracha says. 'We don't want information to conveniently disappear, you understand? Trade has its own agents amongst us. Pull everything you find and bring it to me. Find out how she lived here, and survived. As soon as word gets out, there will be a cover-up. Men will lie. Permit records will disappear. Someone was allowing the windup to exist against all our laws. The Ministry is vulnerable on this. Someone took the bribes. Someone allowed the windup to live here. I want to know who, and I want to know if they are on Akkarat's payroll.'

'Why me?'

Pracha smiles sadly. 'Jaidee is the only one I would trust more.'

'He's setting you up,' Jaidee comments. 'If he wants to blame this on Trade, you're the perfect tool. The mole in the ministry.'

There is no guile in Pracha's face, but he is a clever man. *How much does he know?*

'Find the information for me,' Pracha says. 'Bring it to me. And speak to no one of this.'

'I will do it,' she says. Inside though, she wonders if the records even exist anymore. So many ways to profit. A cover-up would have already been effected. If it is truly a murder plot against the Protector, the payoffs would go to all levels. She shivers, wonders who would do such a thing. Political killings are one thing. To touch the palace in this way . . . Rage and frustration threaten to overwhelm her. She forces it down. 'What do we know of the windup, so far?'

'She claimed to be a Japanese discard. The girls here say she has been in place for years.'

Kanya makes a face of distaste. 'It's difficult to believe that anyone would soil— ,' she breaks off, finding herself on the verge of scorning the Somdet Chaopraya. Sick feelings of confusion and sadness overwhelm her. She masks her discomfort by asking another question. 'How did the Protector come to be here?'

'All we know is that he was accompanied by Akkarat's ilk.'

'Will you question Akkarat?'

'If we could find him.'

'He's missing?'

'You're surprised? Akkarat was always good at protecting himself. It's why he's managed to survive so many times.' Pracha grimaces. 'He might as well be a cheshire. Nothing ever touches him.' Pracha looks at her seriously. 'We must find who allowed this windup creature to live here so long. How it got into the city. How the assassination was arranged. We are blind in this, and when we are blind, we are vulnerable. This news will make everything unstable.'

Kanya *wais*. 'I will do everything I can.' Even if Jaidee peers over her shoulder and laughs at her. 'I may need more information than this. To track down those responsible.'

'You have enough to start. Find where this windup came from. Who took the bribes. This is what I must know.'

'And Akkarat and these *farang* who introduced the windup to the Protector?'

Pracha smiles slightly. 'I will attend to it.'

'But—'

'Kanya, it is understandable that you wish to do more. We all care for the well-being of the palace and the Kingdom. But we must secure and protect the information we have about this windup creature.'

Kanya controls her response. 'Yes. Of course. I will locate the information on the bribes.' She pauses delicately. 'Will someone be required to demonstrate their regrets as well?'

Pracha makes a face. 'A little harmless bribe income is one thing. It is not a rich year for the Ministry. But this?' He shakes his head.

'I remember when we were respected,' Kanya murmurs.

Pracha glances at her. 'Do you? I thought that had ended by the time you came to us.' He sighs. 'Don't worry. This will not be a cover-up. Atonements will be made. I will ensure it personally. Do not doubt my commitment to the Kingdom or Her Royal Majesty the Queen. The guilty will be punished.'

Kanya studies the Protector's body and the dingy room where he met his end. A windup. A whore and a windup. She tries to contain her sickness at the thought. A windup. That someone would try to . . . she shakes his head. An ugly affair. A destabilizing move. And now some young men will have to pay for it. Whoever took the bribes in Ploenchit, perhaps others.

On the street, Kanya flags down a cycle rickshaw. From the corner of her eye, she catches a glimpse of palace Panthers, formed in ranks at the door. A crowd is gathering, watching with interest. In a few more hours rumors and news will be all over the city.

'The Environment Ministry, as quickly as you can.'

She waves Akkarat's bribe money at the rickshaw man, encouraging greater effort, but even as she does, she wonders on whose behalf she waves it.

33

At noon, an army truck arrives. It's a huge thing, gouting exhaust, astonishingly loud, like something out of the old Expansion. She can hear it coming from a block away, but even with so much warning, she almost cries out when she sees the thing. So fast. So awfully loud. Once in Japan, Emiko saw a similar vehicle. Gendo-sama explained that it was powered by liquefied coal. Astonishingly dirty and terrible for carbon limits, but almost magically powerful. As if a dozen megodonts were chained within. Perfect for military applications, even if civilians could not justify either the power or the taxation.

Exhaust clouds swirl blue around it as it comes to a halt. A small fleet of kink-spring scooters sweep up behind, ridden by men wearing the black of the palace's Panthers and the green of the Army. Men begin to pour from the truck and charge for Anderson-sama's tower entrance.

Emiko crouches lower in her alley hiding place. At first she thought to flee, but before she had gone a block she realized there was no place left to run. Anderson-sama was her only raft left in the raging ocean.

And so she remains close by, watching the hive of ants that is Anderson-sama's tower. Trying to understand. She's still astounded that the people who came crashing through the door were not in fact white shirts. They should have been. In Kyoto, the police would have already hunted her down with sniffer dogs, and she would have already been compassionately put down. She has never heard of a New Person so completely failing to show obedience. Certainly not anything like her own ugly bloodletting and flight. She burns with shame and hatred at the same time. She cannot stay, and yet it is more than apparent that the *gaijin's* apartment, invaded though it is, is her last place of safety. The city around her is no friend.

More men pour from the military truck. Emiko slips deeper into the alley as they approach, expecting them to widen their search, preparing herself for a burst of heat and motion to escape. If she runs she can reach the *khlong*, and cool herself before fleeing again.

But they only post themselves along the major thoroughfares and do not seem to care to search for her.

Another flurry of motion. Panthers dragging out a pair of burlap-hooded men with pale hands. *Gaijin* for certain. One of them is Anderson-sama, she thinks. The clothes are his. They shove him forward, making him stumble. He slams into the back of the truck.

Cursing, two of the Panthers drag him aboard. They cuff him beside the other *gaijin*. More troops swarm inside, surrounding them.

A limousine sweeps up to the curb, purring with its own coal-diesel engine. It's strange and silent in comparison to the roar of the troop carrier, but the exhaust is the same. A rich man's vehicle. Almost unimaginable that someone could be so wealthy –

Emiko gasps. It's Trade Minister Akkarat, being hustled by bodyguards into the car. Onlookers pause and stare. Emiko gawks with them. Then the limousine is moving and the troop carrier as well, its massive engine roaring. The two vehicles tear down the street trailing clouds of smoke and disappear around the corner.

Silence rushes into the void, almost physical after the rumble of the truck engine. She hears people murmuring, 'Political ... Akkàrat ... *farang*? ... General Pracha ...'

But even with her excellent hearing, it makes no sense. She stares after the truck. With determination, she might follow ... She gives up the idea. It is impossible. Wherever Anderson-sama has gone, she cannot involve herself. Whatever political problem he has become entangled in will end with the ugliness of all such conflicts.

Emiko wonders if she can simply slip back inside the apartment now that everyone is gone. Near the building's entrance, a pair of men have begun handing out fliers to everyone they can reach. Another pair coast past on a cargo bike, its bin stacked with more fliers. One man jumps down and sticks a flier to a lamp post before hopping back up on the slowly moving bike.

Emiko starts toward the bike to collect a flier herself, but a prickle of paranoia stops her. Instead, she lets them rattle past, then cautiously approaches the light pole to read what they have posted. She moves carefully, all her energy focused on making her movement appear natural, trying not to draw undue attention. She pushes gently into a gathering crowd, bumping against them, craning for a view over the sea of black hair and straining bodies.

An angry murmur rises. Someone sobs. A man turns away, his eyes wide with grief and terror. He shoves past her. Emiko slips forward into the gap. The murmur grows. Emiko eases closer, careful, careful, slow, slow ... Her breath catches.

The Somdet Chaopraya. The Protector of Her Majesty the Queen. And words ... she forces her brain to work, to translate from Thai to Japanese and as she does, she becomes aware of the people all around her, the people who press in on every side, all of them reading about a windup girl who walks amongst them, a windup who slaughters the Queen's own protector, an agent of the Environment Ministry, a creature of deadly power.

People jostle around her as they try to read, shoving closer, squeezing past, all of them thinking she is one of them. All of them allowing her to live only because they do not yet see.

34

'Will you sit down? Your pacing makes me nervous.'

Hock Seng pauses in the perambulation of his hovel to glare at Laughing Chan. 'I pay for *your* calories, not the other way around.'

Laughing Chan shrugs and goes back to playing cards. They've all been huddled in the room for the last several days. Laughing Chan is a congenial companion along with Pak Eng and Peter Kuok. But even the most congenial company . . .

Hock Seng shakes his head. It doesn't matter. The storm is coming. Bloodshed and mayhem on the horizon. It's the same feeling he had before the Incident, before his sons were beheaded and his daughters raped senseless. And he sat in the middle of that brewing storm, willfully ignorant, telling anyone who would listen that the men in K.L. would never let what had happened down in Jakarta happen to the good Chinese here. After all, were they not loyal? Did they not contribute? Did he not have friends at every level of government who assured him that the Green Headbands were but a bit of political posturing?

The storm was surging all around him, and he had refused to accept it . . . but not this time. This time, he is prepared. The air is electric with what is about to occur. Ever since the white shirts closed down the factories it was apparent. And now it is about to break. And this time, he is ready. Hock Seng smiles to himself, examines his little bunker with its stores of money and gems and food.

'Is there any more word on the radio?' he asks.

The three men exchange glances. Laughing Chan nods at Pak Eng. 'It's your turn to wind it.'

Pak Eng scowls and goes over to the radio. It's an expensive device, and Hock Seng is regretting that he purchased it at all. There are other radios in the slums, but lurking beside them draws attention and so he spent money on this one, unsure if it would even carry anything other than rumor, and yet unable to deny himself another source of information.

Pak Eng kneels beside the thing and starts to wind it. Its speaker crackles to life, barely loud enough over the whine of the crank.

'You know, if you fitted this with a decent gear system, it would be a lot more efficient.'

Everyone ignores him, their attention entirely focused on the tiny speaker: Music, *saw duang*...

Hock Seng crouches by the radio, listening intently. Changes the dial. Pak Eng is starting to sweat. He winds for another thirty seconds and stops, puffing. 'There. That should last a little while.'

Hock Seng works the dial on the machine, listening to the divining winds of radio waves. Twirls across stations. Nothing but entertainments. Music.

Laughing Chan looks up. 'What time is it?'

'Four, perhaps?' Hock Seng shrugs.

'There should be *muay thai*. They should be doing the opening rituals by now.'

Everyone exchanges glances. Hock Seng moves through more stations. Music only. No news. Nothing... And then a voice. Filling all the stations, speaking as one voice and one station. They all crouch round, listing.

'Akkarat, I think.' Hock Seng pauses. 'The Somdet Chaopraya has died. Akkarat is blaming the white shirts.' He looks at them all. 'It is beginning.'

Pak Eng and Laughing Chan and Peter all look at Hock Seng with respect. 'You were right.'

Hock Seng nods impatiently. 'I learn.'

The storm is gathering. The megodonts must do battle. It is their fate. The power sharing of the last coup could never last. The beasts must clash and one will establish final dominance. Hock Seng murmurs a prayer to his ancestors that he will come out of this maelstrom alive.

Laughing Chan stands. 'I guess we'll have to earn this bodyguard money after all.'

Hock Seng nods seriously. 'It will not be pretty, not for anyone who is not prepared.'

Pak Eng begins pumping his spring gun. 'It reminds me of Penang.'

'Not this time,' Hock Seng says. 'This time, we are ready.' He waves to them. 'Come. It's time we saw to whatever else we can—'

A banging on the door makes them all straighten.

'Hock Seng! Hock Seng!' A hysterical voice, more pounding from outside.

'It's Lao Gu.' Hock Seng pulls open the door and Lao Gu stumbles in.

'They've taken Mr. Lake. The foreign devil and all his friends.'

Hock Seng stares at the rickshaw man. 'The white shirts are moving against him?'

'No. The Trade Ministry. I saw Akkarat himself do the deed.'

Hock Seng frowns. 'It makes no sense.'

Lao Gu shoves a flier into his hands. 'It's the windup. The one that he kept bringing to his flat. She's the one that killed the Somdet Chaopraya.'

Hock Seng reads quickly. Nods to himself. 'You're sure about this windup creature? Our foreign devil was working with an assassin?'

'I only know what it says on the whisper sheet, but that's the *heechy-keechy* for sure, from the way it describes her. He brought her from Ploenchit many times. Let her sleep there, even.'

'Is it a problem?' Laughing Chan asks.

'No.' Hock Seng shakes his head, allows himself a smile. He goes and digs a ring of keys out from under his mattress. 'An opportunity. A better one than I expected.' He turns to them all. 'We won't be hiding here after all.'

'No?'

Hock Seng grins. 'There's one last place we must go before we depart the city. One last thing to collect. Something from my old offices. Gather up the weapons.'

To his credit, Laughing Chan does not question. Simply nods and holsters his pistols, slings a machete across his back. The rest do the same. Together, they file out through the door. Hock Seng closes it behind him.

Hock Seng jogs down the alley after his people, the keys to the factory jingling in his hand. For the first time in a long time, fate moves in his favor. Now all he needs is a little luck and a little more time.

Up ahead, people are shouting about white shirts and the death of their Queen's protector. Angry voices, ready for a riot. The storm is brewing. The battle pieces are being aligned. A little girl hurries past, pressing whisper sheets into each of their hands before dashing on. The political parties are already at work. Soon the godfather of the slum will have his own people down in the alleys inciting violence.

Hock Seng and his men make their way out of the squeezeways

and pour out into the street. Nothing is moving. Even the freelance rickshaw men have gone to ground. A group of shopkeepers huddle around a hand-crank radio. Hock Seng waves at his men to wait, goes over to the listeners. 'What news?'

A woman looks up. 'National Radio says the Protector ...'

'Yes, I know that. What else does it say?'

'Minister Akkarat has denounced General Pracha.'

It's happening even faster than he expected. Hock Seng straightens and calls to Laughing Chan and the others. 'Come on. We're going to run out of time if we don't hurry.'

As he calls to them, a huge truck comes around the corner, engine revving. It is astonishingly noisy. Exhaust trails behind it like an illegal dung fire. Dozens of hard-faced troops stare out from the back as it roars by. Hock Seng and his men duck back into the alley, coughing. Laughing Chan peers out, following the truck's progress. 'Its running on coal diesel,' he says wonderingly. 'It's the army.'

Hock Seng wonders if it is December 12 loyalists, some component of the Northeastern generals coming to aid General Pracha and retake the National Radio Tower. Or perhaps they are Akkarat's allies, rushing to secure the sea locks or the docks or the anchor pads. Or perhaps they are simply opportunists, getting ready to take advantage of the coming chaos. Hock Seng watches as they disappear around a corner. Harbingers of the storm, regardless.

The last pedestrians are disappearing into their homes. Shop keepers are barring their storefronts from within. The clank and rattle of locks fills the street. The city knows what is going to happen.

Memories peck and swirl at Hock Seng. Alleys running thick with blood. The scent of green bamboo, smoking and burning. He reaches for the reassurance of his spring gun and machete. The city may be a jungle full of tigers, but this time he is not some little deer, running from Malaya. At last, he has learned. It is possible to prepare for chaos.

He motions to his men. 'Come. This is our time.'

35

'It was not Pracha! He's not involved in this!'

Kanya shouts into the crank phone, but she might as well be raving through the bars of a jail cell for all the impact it makes. Narong hardly seems to be listening. The line crackles with jumbled voices and the hum of machinery, and Narong, apparently, speaking to someone nearby, his words unintelligible.

Suddenly Narong's voice crackles loud, blotting out the background sounds. 'I'm sorry, we have our own information.'

Kanya scowls at the whisper sheets on her desk, the ones that Pai brought in with a grim smile. Some speak of the fallen Somdet Chaopraya, others of General Pracha. They all talk of the assassin windup girl. Fast-copies of *Sawatdee Krung Thep!* are already pouring into the city. Kanya scans the words. It's full of impassioned complaints against the white shirts who shut down harbors and anchor pads but cannot protect the Somdet Chaopraya from a single invasive.

'These whisper sheets are yours then?' she asks.

Narong's silence is answer enough.

'Why did you even ask me to investigate?' She can't keep the bitterness from her voice. 'You were already moving.'

Narong's cold voice crackles on the line. 'It's not your place to question.'

His tone brings her up short. 'Did Akkarat do it?' she whispers fearfully. 'Was he the one responsible? Pracha says that Akkarat was involved somehow. Did he do it?'

Another pause. Is it a thoughtful one? She can't tell. Finally Narong says, 'No. I swear this. We are not the ones responsible.'

'So you guess it must be Pracha then?' She shuffles through the licenses and permits on her desk. 'I'm telling you he is not the one! I have all the windup's records here. Pracha himself *wanted* me to investigate. To find every trace of her. I have her arrival papers with the Mishimoto people. I have disposal papers. I have visas. Everything.'

'Who signed the disposal papers?'

She fights her frustration. 'I can't read the signature. I need more time to cross-reference who was on duty around that time.'

'And by the time you do, they will inevitably be dead.'

'Then why did Pracha set me to the task of finding this information? It doesn't make sense! I talked to the officers who took the bribes at that bar. They were nothing but silly boys, making a little extra money.'

'He's clever then. He's covered his tracks.'

'Why do you hate Pracha so much?'

'Why do you love him? Did he not order your village razed?'

'Not from malice.'

'No? Did he not sell the fish farming permits to another village the next season? Sell them and line his pockets with the profits?'

She falls silent. Narong moderates his tone. 'I'm sorry, Kanya. There's nothing we can do. We are certain of his crime. We have authorization from the palace to resolve this.'

'With riots?' She shoves the whisper sheets off her desk. 'With a burning of the city? Please. I can stop this. It's not necessary. I can find the proof that we need. I can prove that the windup is not Pracha's. I can prove it.'

'You're too close to this. Your loyalties are divided.'

'I'm loyal to our Queen. Just give me a chance to stop this madness.'

Another pause. 'I can give you three hours. If you have nothing by sunset, I can do nothing more.'

'But you'll wait until then?'

She can almost hear the smile on the other end of the line. 'I will.' And then the line is closed. And she is alone in her office.

Jaidee settles himself on her desk. 'I'm curious. How will you prove Pracha's innocence? It's obvious that he's the one who placed her.'

'Why can't you leave me alone?' Kanya asks.

Jaidee smiles. 'Because it's *sanuk*. Very fun to watch you flail around and try to run for two masters.' He pauses, studying her. 'Why do you care what happens to General Pracha? He's not your real patron.'

Kanya looks at him with hatred. She waves at the whisper sheets strewn about her office. 'It's just like it was five years ago.'

'With Pracha and Prime Minister Surawong. With the December 12 gatherings.' Jaidee studies the whisper sheets. 'Akkarat moving against us, this time, though. So it's not entirely the same.'

Outside the window of her office, a megodont bellows. Jaidee smiles. 'You hear that? We're arming. There's no way you can keep these two old bulls from clashing. I don't know why you would even try. Pracha and Akkarat have been bellowing and snorting at each other for years. It's time we had a good fight.'

'This isn't *muay thai*, Jaidee.'

'No. You're right about that.' For a moment his smile turns sad.

Kanya stares at the whisper sheets, the collected paperwork on the windup's import. The windup is missing. But still, it came from the Japanese. Kanya studies the notes: she was brought across on a dirigible flight from Japan. An executive assistant—

'And a killer,' Jaidee interjects.

'Shut up. I'm thinking.'

A Japanese windup. An abandoned bit of the island nation. Kanya stands abruptly, grabs her spring gun and shoves it into her holster as she gathers papers.

'Where are you going?' Jaidee asks.

She favors him with a thin smile. 'If I told you, that would take away the *sanuk*.'

Jaidee's *phii* grins. 'Now you're getting into the spirit of things.'

36

The crowd around Emiko grows. People jostle her. There's nowhere to run. She's in the open, waiting to be discovered.

Her first urge is to slash her way free, to fight for survival, even though there is no hope of escaping the crowd before she overheats. *I will not die like an animal. I will fight them. They will bleed.*

She forces down that increasing panic. Tries to think. More people squeeze around her, trying to get close to the posted sheet. She is trapped among them, but no one has noticed her yet. As long as she doesn't move ...

The press of the crowd is almost an advantage. She can barely shake, let alone display the stutter-stop motions that would betray her.

Slowly. Carefully.

Emiko allows herself to lean against the people, to push slowly through them, head down, pretending to be a woman sobbing, shaking with grief at a blow against the palace. She stares at her feet, finding her way through the crowd, pressing carefully through until she reaches the outer edge. People huddle in groups, crying, sitting on the ground, staring around the street, stunned. Emiko feels a certain pity for them. Remembers watching Gendo-sama board his dirigible after he told her that he had done her a kindness, even as he abandoned her to the streets of Krung Thep.

Focus, she tells herself angrily. She needs to get away. Needs to reach the alley where people will not notice her. Wait for darkness.

Your description is everywhere: on methane posts, on the street, being trampled by the crowds. You have nowhere to go. She stifles the thought. The alley is enough. The alley, first. Then a new plan. She keeps her eyes on the ground. Clutches herself and mimes at sobbing. Shuffles for the alley. Slowly. Slowly.

'You! Get over here!'

Emiko freezes. Forces herself to look up slowly. A man beckons her, angry. She starts to speak, to protest, but someone behind her speaks instead.

'You have something to say to me, *heeya*?'

A young man pushes past her, wearing a yellow headband and carrying a fistful of leaflets.

'What's that you've got there, boy?'

Others begin to drift over to watch the argument. The two start shouting at one another, posturing as they each try to establish dominance. Others start to take sides. To shout encouragement. Emboldened, the older slaps the younger and tries to tear off his yellow headband. 'You're not for the Queen. You're a traitor!' He strips the flyers from the young man's hand and throws them onto the ground. Stamps on them. 'Get out of here! Take *heeya* Pracha's lies with you.' As leaflets blow through the crowd, Emiko catches a glimpse of Akkarat's face, drawn in caricature, smiling as he tries to eat the Grand Palace.

The younger one scrambles after his leaflets. 'They're not lies! Akkarat seeks to tear down the Queen. It's obvious!'

People in the crowd jeer at him. But others shout encouragement. The boy turns away from the man, speaks to the crowd. 'Akkarat is hungry for power. He always wants—'

The man kicks him in the ass. The boy whirls, enraged, and attacks. Emiko sucks in her breath. The boy is a fighter. *Muay thai* for certain. His elbow smashes into the man's head. The man collapses. The boy stands over him, screaming epithets, but his voice is drowned out by the crowd shouting and then others surge forward, enveloping him in a clot of fists. His screams fill the street.

Emiko turns and slips through the growing fight, no longer careful of her movements. People jostle her, rushing to aid or defend, and she shoves through as quickly as she can. In this moment, she is nothing to any of these people. She stumbles out of the riot and into the alley's shadows.

The fight is spreading down the street. Emiko hunts for garbage to cover herself. Behind her, glass shatters. Someone is screaming. She huddles beside a shattered WeatherAll crate, pulling refuse around her, durian rinds, the ripped hemp of a basket, discarded banana leaves, anything to give her cover. She freezes and hunkers low as rioters pelt down the alley, shouting. Everywhere she looks, she sees faces twisted with rage.

37

The main compounds of Mishimoto & Co. lie on the far side of the water, in Thonburi. The boat makes its way into a *khlong*, Kanya's hand careful on the tiller. Even here, outside of Bangkok proper, whisper sheets complain of Pracha and the windup killer.

'Do you think it's a good idea to come alone?' Jaidee asks.

'I've got you. It's enough company for anyone.'

'I'm not so great at *muay thai* in this state.'

'Pity.'

The company's gates and jetties rise over the waves. The late afternoon sun scalds down on them. A water merchant paddles close, but even though Kanya is hungry, she does not dare waste even a moment. Already the sun seems to be crashing out of the sky. Her boat thumps against the pier and she whips its bow rope around a cleat.

'I don't think they'll let you in,' Jaidee says. Kanya doesn't bother answering. It's odd that he has remained with her all the way across the water. The pattern of his *phii* was to take interest in her for a short time, and then to drift off to other things and other people. Perhaps he visited his children. Made apologies to Chaya's mother. But now he is with her all the time.

Jaidee says, 'They won't be impressed with that white uniform, either. They've got too much influence with the Trade Ministry and the police.'

Kanya doesn't answer, but sure enough, a Thonburi detachment of a police patrol guards the main gates of the compound. All around, the sea and *khlongs* lap. The Japanese are forward-looking, and have built themselves entirely on the water, on floating bamboo rafts that are said to lie nearly fifty feet thick, creating a compound nearly impervious to the floods and tides of the Chao Phraya River.

'I need to speak with Mr. Yashimoto.'

'He is not available.'

'It concerns property of his that was damaged during the unfortunate raids on the airfields. Paperwork for reparations.'

The guard smiles uncertainly. Ducks inside.

Jaidee snickers. 'Clever.'

Kanya makes a face at him. 'At least you have some use.'

'Even if I'm dead.'

A moment later they are being led into the halls of the compound. It is not a long walk. High walls obscure all evidence of manufacturing activity. The Megodont Union complains that no work could be accomplished without a power source, and yet the Japanese neither import their own megodonts, nor hire the union. It reeks of illegal technology. And yet the Japanese have provided a great deal of technical assistance to the Kingdom. In return for Thai seedstock advances, the Japanese provide the best of their sailing technologies. And so everyone is exquisitely careful not to ask too many questions about how a ship's hull is built and if the development process is entirely legal.

A door opens. A pretty girl smiles and bows. Kanya nearly draws her spring gun. The creature before her is a windup. The girl doesn't seem to notice Kanya's unease, though. Simply motions in her stutter-stop way for her to enter. Inside, the room is carefully decorated with tatami mats and Sumi-e paintings. A man Kanya assumes is Mr. Yashimoto kneels, painting. The windup leads Kanya to a seat.

Jaidee admires the art on the walls. 'He painted it all, you know.'

'How would you know?'

'I came to see if they really have ten-hands in their factory. Right after I died.'

'And do they?'

Jaidee shrugs. 'Go look for yourself.'

Mr. Yashimoto dips his brush, and in an exquisitely swift motion completes the painting. He rises and bows to Kanya. He begins speaking in Japanese. The windup girl's own voice follows a second later, with a translation into Thai.

'I am honored by your visit.'

He is silent for a moment and the windup girl falls silent as well. She is very pretty, Kanya supposes. In a strange porcelain way. Her cropped jacket is open at the collar, revealing the hollow of her throat, and her pale skirt molds fetchingly around her hips. She would be beautiful, if she were not so perverse.

'You know why I'm here?'

He nods shortly. 'We have heard rumors of an unfortunate incident. And have seen our country discussed in your papers and whisper sheets.' He looks at her significantly. 'Many voices are being raised against us. Most unfair and inaccurate observations.'

Kanya nods. 'We have questions—'

'I wish to assure you that we are a friend of the Thai. From times long ago when we cooperated in the great war to now, we have always been a friend of the Thai.'

'I want to know how—'

Yashimoto interrupts again. 'Tea?' he offers.

Kanya forces herself to remain polite. 'You're very kind.'

Yashimoto motions to the windup girl, and she stands and

leaves the room. Unconsciously, Kanya relaxes. The creature is . . . unsettling. And yet now that she is gone, silence stretches between them as they wait for the translator to return. Kanya feels seconds ticking away, minutes being lost. Time, time, time moving. Storm clouds gathering and here she sits, waiting for tea.

The windup girl returns, kneels beside them at the low table. Kanya forces herself not to speak, not to interrupt the girl's precise whisking and steeping of the tea, but it is an effort. The windup girl pours, and as Kanya watches the creature's strange movements, she thinks she sees a little of what the Japanese desired from their engineered servants. The girl is perfect, precise as clockwork, and contextualized by the tea ceremony, all her motions take on a ritual grace.

The windup carefully does not observe Kanya in return. Does not say anything about her being a white shirt. Does not observe that in another context Kanya would happily mulch her. She ignores Kanya's Environment Ministry uniform entirely. Exquisitely polite.

Yashimoto waits for Kanya to sip her tea, then sips himself. Sets his tea deliberately on the table. 'Our countries have been friends always,' he says. 'Ever since our Emperor made a gift of tilapia to the Kingdom in the time of your great scientist King Bhumibol's time. We have always been steadfast.' He looks at her significantly. 'I hope that we can help you in this matter, but I wish to emphasize that we are friends of your country.'

'Tell me about windups,' Kanya says.

Yashimoto nods. 'What do you wish to know?' He smiles, motions at the girl kneeling beside them. 'This one, you can see for yourself.'

Kanya keeps her expression impassive. It is difficult. The creature beside her is beautiful. Her skin is sleek, her movements surprisingly elegant. And she makes Kanya's skin crawl. 'Tell me why you have them.'

Yashimoto shrugs. 'We are an old nation; our young are few. Good girls like Hiroko fill the gap. We are not the same as the Thai. We have calories but no one to provide the labor. We need personal assistants. Workers.'

Kanya carefully makes no show of disgust. 'Yes. You Japanese are very different. And except for your country, we have never granted this sort of niche—'

'Crime,' Jaidee supplies.

'—exemption,' she finishes. 'No one else is allowed to bring in creatures like this one.' She nods unwillingly at the translator, trying to hide the disgust in her voice. 'No other country. No other factory.'

'We are aware of the privilege.'

'And yet you abuse it by bringing a military windup—'

Hiroko's words cut her off, even as Kanya continues to speak. Hiroko instead picks up the vehement response from her owner.

'No! This is impossible. We have no contact with such technology. None!'

Yashimoto's face is flushed, and Kanya wonders at his sudden anger. What sort of cultural insult has she unwittingly delivered? The windup girl continues her translation, no trace of emotion on her own face as she speaks with her owner's voice. 'We work with New Japanese like Hiroko. She is loyal, thoughtful, and skilled. And a necessary tool. She is as necessary as a hoe for a farmer or a sword for a samurai.'

'Strange that you mention a sword.'

'Hiroko is no military creature. We do not have such technology.'

Kanya reaches into her pocket and slaps down the picture of the windup killer. 'And yet one of yours, imported by you, registered to your staff, has now assassinated the Somdet Chaopraya and eight others, and disappeared into thin air, as if she is some raging *phii.* But you sit before me and tell me that it is impossible for a military windup to be here!' Her voice rises to a shout, and the windup girl's translation finishes at a similar intensity.

Yashimoto's face stills. He takes the picture and studies it. 'We will have to check our records.'

He nods to Hiroko. She takes the photo and disappears out the door. Kanya watches Yashimoto for traces of anxiety or nervousness, but there are none. Irritation, she sees, but no fear. She regrets that she cannot speak directly with the man. Listening to her words echo into Japanese, Kanya wonders what surprise is lost when the windup girl delivers them. What preparation Hiroko provides for his shock.

They wait. He silently offers more tea. She refuses. He does not drink anymore himself. The tension in the room is so thick that Kanya half expects the man to leap to his feet and cut her down with the ancient sword that adorns the wall behind him.

A few minutes later, Hiroko returns. She hands the picture back to Kanya with a bow. Then speaks to Yashimoto. Neither of them betray any emotion. Hiroko kneels again beside them. Yashimoto nods at the photograph. 'You're sure this was the one?'

Kanya nods. 'There is no question.'

'And this assassination explains the increasing rage in the city. There are crowds gathering outside the factory. Boat people. The police have driven them away, but they were coming with torches.'

Kanya stifles her nervousness at the increasing frenzy. Everything is moving too fast. At some point, Akkarat and Pracha will be unable to back off without losing face and then everything will be lost. 'The people are very angry,' she says.

'It is misplaced anger. She is not a military windup.' When Kanya tries to challenge him, he looks at her fiercely and she subsides. 'Mishimoto knows *nothing* of military windups. Nothing.

Such creatures are kept under strict control. They are used by our Defense Ministry, only. I could never possess one.' He locks eyes with her. 'Never.'

'And yet—'

He continues to speak, with Hiroko translating, 'I know of the windup you describe. She had fulfilled her duty—'

The windup girl's voice breaks off even as the old man continues speaking. She straightens and her eyes flick to Yashimoto. He frowns at her break in decorum. Says something to the windup. She ducks her head. '*Hai.*'

Another pause.

He nods at her to continue. She regains her composure, finishes translating. 'She was destroyed according to requirements, rather than repatriated.' The windup's dark eyes are on Kanya, steady, unblinking now, betraying nothing of the surprise she evinced a moment before.

Kanya watches the girl and the old man, two alien people. 'And yet she apparently survived,' she says finally.

'I was not the manager at the time,' Yashimoto says. 'I can only speak to what I know from our records.'

'Records lie, apparently.'

'You are correct. For this, there is no excuse. I am ashamed of what others have done, but I have no knowledge of the thing.'

Kanya leans forward. 'If you cannot tell me how she survived, then please, tell me how it is that this girl, capable of killing so many men in the space of heartbeats could come into this country. You tell me she is not military, but, to be direct, I'm having difficulty believing that she is not. This is a gross breach of our country's agreements.'

Unexpectedly, the man's eyes crinkle with a smile. He picks up his tea and sips, considering the question, but the mirth does not leave his eyes, even as he finishes his tea. 'This I can answer.'

Without warning, he flings his cup at Hiroko's face. Kanya starts to cry out. The windup girl's hand blurs. The teacup smacks into her palm. The girl gapes at the cup in her hand, as surprised, apparently, as Kanya.

The Japanese man gathers the folds of his kimono around himself. 'All New Japanese are fast. You have mistaken the question to ask. How they use their innate qualities is a question of their training, not of their physical capabilities. Hiroko has been trained from birth to pace herself appropriately, with decorum.'

He nods at her skin. 'She is manufactured to have a porcelain skin and reduced pores, but it means she is subject to overheating. A military windup will not overheat, it is built to expend considerable energy without impact. Poor Hiroko here would die if she exerted herself like that over any significant amount of time. But all windups are potentially fast, it is in their genes.' His tone becomes serious. 'It is surprising though, that one has shaken off her training. Unwelcome news. New People serve us. It should not have happened.'

'So your Hiroko here could do the same thing? Kill eight men? Armed ones?'

Hiroko jerks and looks at Yashimoto, dark eyes widening. He nods. Says something. His tone is gentle.

'*Hai.*' She forgets to translate, then finds her words. 'Yes. It is possible. Unlikely, but possible.' She continues, 'But it would take an extraordinary stimulus to do so. New People value discipline. Order. Obedience. We have a saying in Japan, 'New People are more Japanese than the Japanese."

Yashimoto places a hand on Hiroko's shoulder. 'Circumstances would have to be extraordinary to make Hiroko into a killer.' He smiles confidently. 'This one you seek has fallen far from her proper place. You should destroy her before she can cause any more damage. We can provide assistance.' He pauses. 'Hiroko here can help you.'

Kanya tries not to recoil, but her face gives her away.

'Captain Kanya, I do believe you're smiling.'

Jaidee's *phii* is still with her, perched on the prow of the skiff as it cuts across the Chao Phraya's wide mouth on a stiff breeze. Spray blows through his form, leaving him unaffected, even though Kanya expects him to be drenched each time. She favors him with a smile, allowing her sense of well-being to reach out to him.

'Today, I did something good.'

Jaidee grins. 'I listened to both ends of the conversation. Akkarat and Narong were very impressed with you.'

Kanya pauses. 'You were with them as well?'

He shrugs. 'I can go almost anywhere, it seems.'

'Except on to your next life.'

He shrugs again and smiles. 'I still have work here.'

'Harassing me, you mean.' But her words have no venom. Under the warm light of the setting sun, with the city opening before her and waves splashing against her boat's hull as they cut across the water, Kanya can only be grateful that the conversation went so well. Even as she was talking to Narong, they were issuing orders to their people to pull back. She heard the radio announcement go out. They would meet with the December 12 loyalists. The beginning of a stand-down. If the Japanese had not been so willing to take the blame for their rogue windup, it might have been different. But reparations were already being offered and Pracha was exonerated by the copious documentation the Japanese offered, and for once, all things were turning out well.

Kanya can't help but feel a measure of pride. Wearing the yoke of two patrons has finally paid off. She wonders if it is *kamma* that places her so that she can bridge the gap between General Pracha and Minister Akkarat for the good of Krung Thep. Certainly, no one else could have pierced the barriers of face and pride that the two men and their factions had erected.

Jaidee is still grinning at her. 'Imagine the things our country could accomplish if we were not always fighting one another.'

In a burst of optimism, Kanya says, 'Maybe anything is possible.'

Jaidee laughs. 'You still have a windup to catch.'

Involuntarily, Kanya's eyes go to her own windup girl. Hiroko has folded her legs under her and gazes out at the city that is rapidly approaching, watching with curious eyes as they thread between clipper ships and sailing skiffs and kink-spring patrol boats. As if sensing Kanya's gaze, she turns. Their eyes lock. Kanya refuses to drop her gaze.

'Why do you hate New People?' the windup asks.

Jaidee laughs. 'Can you lecture her about niche and nature?'

Kanya looks away, glances behind her to the floating factories and drowned Thonburi. The *prang* of Wat Arun stand tall against the blood red sky.

Again the question comes. 'Why do you hate my kind?'

Kanya eyes the woman. 'Will you be mulched when Yashimoto-sama returns to Japan?'

Hiroko lowers her gaze. Kanya feels obscurely embarrassed that she seems to have hurt the windup's feelings, then shakes off the guilt. It's just a windup. It apes the motions of humanity, but it is only a dangerous experiment that has been allowed to proceed too far. A windup. Stutter-stop motion and the telltale jerk of a genetically engineered beast. A smart one. And dangerous if pushed, apparently. Kanya watches the water as she guides her craft across the waves, but still she watches the windup out of the corner of her eye, viscerally aware that this windup contains the same wild speed of the other one. That all these windups have the potential to become lethal.

Hiroko speaks again. 'We are not all like this one you hunt.'

Kanya turns her gaze back on the windup. 'You are all unnatural. You are all grown in test tubes. You all go against niche. You all have no souls and have no *kamma*. And now one of you has—' she breaks off, overwhelmed at the enormity, '—destroyed our Queen's protector. You are more than similar enough for me.'

Hiroko's eyes harden. 'Then send me back to Mishimoto.'

Kanya shakes her head. 'No. You have your uses. You are good proof, if nothing else, that all windups are dangerous. And that the one we hunt is not a military creature. For that, you will be useful.'

'We are not all dangerous,' she insists again.

Kanya shrugs. 'Mr. Yashimoto says you will be of some help in finding our killer. If that's true, then I have a use for you. If not, I would just as soon compost you with the rest of the daily dung collection. Your master insists that you will be useful, though I can't think how.'

Hiroko looks away, across the water to her factories on the far side.

'I think you hurt her feelings,' Jaidee murmurs.

'Are their feelings any more real than their souls?' Kanya leans against the tiller, angling the little skiff toward the docks. There is still so much to be done.

Abruptly, Hiroko says. 'She will seek a new patron.'

Kanya turns, surprised. 'What do you mean?'

'She has lost her Japanese owner. She has now lost this man who ran the bar she worked for.'

'She killed him.'

Hiroko shrugs. 'It is the same. She has lost her master. She must find a new one.'

'How do you know?'

Hiroko looks at her coldly. 'It is in our genes. We seek to obey. To have others direct us. It is a necessity. As important as water for a fish. It is the water we swim in. Yashimoto-sama speaks correctly. We are more Japanese than even the Japanese. We must serve within a hierarchy. She must find a master.'

'What if this one is different? If this one doesn't?'

'She will. She has no choice.'

'Just like you.'

Hiroko's dark eyes sweep back to her. 'Just so.'

Is there a flicker of rage and despair in those eyes? Or does Kanya simply imagine it? Is it something Kanya assumes must be lurking deep within, an anthropomorphizing of a thing that is not and never will be human? A pretty puzzle. Kanya returns her attention to the water and their imminent arrival, checks the surrounding waves for other craft she will have to jostle with for slip space. She frowns. 'I don't know those barges.'

Hiroko looks up. 'You keep such close watch on the waters?'

Kanya shakes her head. 'I used to work the docks, when I was first inducted. Spot raids, checking imports. Good money.' She studies the barges. 'Those are built for heavy loads. More than just rice. I haven't seen . . .'

She trails off, her heart starting to pound as she watches the machines wallow forward, great dark beasts, implacable.

'What is it?' Hiroko asks.

'They aren't spring-driven.'

'Yes?'

Kanya pulls at her sail, letting the breezes of the river delta yank at the small boat, cutting away from the oncoming craft.

'It's military. They're all military.'

38

Anderson can barely breathe under the hood. The blackness is total, hot with his own breath and suppressed fear. No one explained why he was being hooded and marched out of the flat. Carlyle was awake by then, but when he tried to protest their treatment, one of the Panthers clipped his ear with a rifle butt, letting blood, and they'd both fallen silent and allowed the hoods to be drawn over their heads. An hour later, they were kicked to their feet and herded down to some kind of transport that rumbled with exhaust fumes. Army, Anderson guessed, as he was shoved aboard.

His broken finger hangs limply behind his back. If he flexes his hand the pain becomes extreme. He practices a careful breathing under the hood, controlling his fears and speculations. The close dusty fabric makes him cough, and when he coughs, his ribs send spikes of pain deep into his core. He breathes shallowly.

Will they execute him as some kind of example?

He hasn't heard Akkarat's voice in some time. Hasn't heard anything. He wants to whisper to Carlyle, to see if they are being kept in the same room, but doesn't feel like being clubbed again if it turns out there's a guard in the room with him.

When they were let down from the vehicle and dragged into a

new building, he had been unsure if Carlyle was even there. And then they were in an elevator. He thinks they descended into some sort of bunker, but it is ghastly hot in the place where they kicked him down. The place is stifling hot. The hood's fabric itches. Of all the things he wishes, he wishes he could scratch his nose where sweat trickles and then damps the fabric, leaving it itching. He tries to move his face, tries to get the fabric away from his mouth and nose. If he could just get a breath of clean air –

A door clicks. Footsteps. Anderson freezes. Muffled voices above him. Suddenly hands grab him and yank him to his feet. He gasps as they jostle his broken ribs. The hands drag him along, guiding him through a series of turns and stops. A breeze kisses his arms, cooler, fresher air, some kind of air vents. He gets a whiff of the sea. Thai voices mutter around him. Footsteps. People moving. He has the sense that he is being led down a corridor. The steady arrival and recession of Thai voices. When he stumbles, his captors jerk him upright again and shove him onward.

At last, they stop. The air is fresher here. He feels the wind of circulation systems, hears the ratchet of treadles and the high whine of flywheels. Some kind of processing center. His captors push him to stand straight. He wonders if this is how they will execute him. If he will die without seeing daylight again.

The windup girl. The goddamn windup girl. He remembers the way she flew from the balcony, plunging into darkness. It wasn't the look of a suicide. The more he thinks about it, the more he is convinced that the look on her face was one of supreme confidence. Did she really kill the Queen's protector? But if she were the killer, how could she have been so afraid? It doesn't make sense. And now everything is wrecked. Christ, his nose itches. He sneezes, sucks dusty hood air, and starts coughing again.

He doubles over, coughing, ribs screaming.

The hood is ripped off his face.

Anderson blinks as light spears his eyes. He sucks gratefully at the luxury of fresh air. Slowly straightens. A large room, full of men and women in army uniform. Treadle computers. Kinkspring drums sitting in the room with them. Even an LED wall screen with views of the city as if they are in one of AgriGen's own processing centers.

And a view. He was wrong, he didn't go down. He went up. High above the city. Anderson reorients his confused perceptions. They're in a tower somewhere, an old Expansion tower. Through the open windows he can see across the city. The setting sun glazes the air and buildings a dull red.

Carlyle is there, too, looking dazed.

'My goodness, you both smell terrible.'

Akkarat, standing nearby. Smiling with a certain sly humor. The Thais are said to have thirteen kinds of smile. Anderson wonders what sort he is looking at now. Akkarat says, 'We'll have to get you a shower.'

Anderson starts to speak, but another fit of coughing overwhelms him. He sucks air, trying to get his lungs under control, but keeps coughing. The cuffs dig into his wrists as he convulses. His ribs are a mass of pain. Carlyle doesn't say anything at all. He has blood on his forehead. Anderson can't tell if he fought his captors or if he's been tortured.

'Get him a glass of water,' Akkarat says.

Anderson's guards push him against a wall, shove him down until he's seated. This time he narrowly avoids jostling his broken finger. Water arrives. A guard holds the cup to Anderson's lips, letting him drink. Cool water. Anderson swallows, absurdly grateful. His coughing subsides. He makes himself look up at Akkarat. 'Thanks.'

'Yes. Well. It seems we have a problem,' Akkarat says. 'Your story checked out. Your windup is a rogue, after all.'

He squats down beside Anderson. 'We have all been victims of bad luck. They say in the military that a good battle plan can last as long as five minutes in real fighting. After that, it comes down to if the general is favored by fate and the spirits. Bad luck, this. We must all adjust. And now, of course, I have many new problems that I must adjust to as well.' He nods at Carlyle. 'You both, of course, are angry at your treatment.' He grimaces. 'I could offer my apologies, but I'm not sure that it would be enough.'

Anderson keeps his expression steady as he looks Akkarat in the eye. 'If you hurt us, you'll pay.'

'AgriGen will punish us.' Akkarat nods. 'Yes. That is a problem. But then, AgriGen is always angry with us.'

'Untie me, and we forget all this.'

'Trust you, you mean. I worry that this is not wise.'

'Revolutions are a rough business. I don't hold a grudge.' Anderson grins, feral, willing the man to believe. 'No harm, no foul. We still want the same things. Nothing's been done that can't be undone.'

Akkarat cocks his head, thoughtful. Anderson wonders if he's about to get a knife in the ribs.

Abruptly, Akkarat smiles. 'You are a hard man.'

Anderson stifles a flutter of hope. 'Just practical. Our interests are still aligned. No one benefits with us dead. This is still a small misunderstanding that we can undo.'

Akkarat considers. Turns to one of the guards and requests a knife. Anderson holds his breath as it comes close, but then the blade is slicing between his wrists, setting him free. His arms flood with tingling blood. He works them slowly. They feel like blocks of wood. Needle pricks follow. 'Christ.'

'It will take a little while for your circulation to recover. Be glad we were gentle with you.' Akkarat catches sight of the way

Anderson cradles his injured hand. Smiles with embarrassment and apology. Calls for a doctor before going over to Carlyle.

'What is this place?' Anderson asks.

'An emergency command center. When it was determined that the white shirts were involved I moved our operations here, for security.' Akkarat nods at the kink-spring drums. 'We have megodont teams in the basement sending up power. And no one should know that we had this center equipped.'

'I didn't know you had something like this.'

Akkarat smiles. 'We are partners, not lovers. I do not share all my secrets with anyone.'

'Have you caught the windup yet?'

'It's only a matter of time. Her likeness is now posted everywhere. The city will not permit her to live amongst us. It is one thing to bribe a few white shirts. Another to attack the palace.'

Anderson thinks back to Emiko, to her huddled fear. 'I still can't believe that a windup could do something like that.'

Akkarat glances up. 'It is confirmed by witnesses, and by the Japanese who constructed her. The windup is a killer. We will find her and execute her in the old way, and we will be done with her. And the Japanese will be made to pay reparations unimaginable for their criminal carelessness.' Abruptly he smiles. 'On this at least, the white shirts and I agree.'

Carlyle's hands come free. Akkarat is called away by an army officer.

Carlyle pulls off his gag. 'We friends again?'

Anderson shrugs, watching the activity around them. 'As much as anyone in a revolution can be.'

'How you doing?'

Anderson touches his chest gingerly. 'Broken ribs.' He nods at his hand where the doctor is splinting his finger. 'Busted finger. Think my jaw's okay.' He shrugs. 'You?'

'Better than that. I think my shoulder's sprained. But I wasn't the one who introduced the rogue windup.'

Anderson coughs and winces. 'Yeah, well, lucky you.'

One of the army people is cranking a radio phone, gears ratcheting. Akkarat takes a call.

'Yes?' He nods, speaks in Thai.

Anderson can only catch a few words, but Carlyle's eyes widen as he listens. 'They're taking the radio stations,' he whispers.

'What?' Anderson scrambles to his feet, wincing, pushing aside the doctor still working on his hand. Guards lunge in front of him, blocking him from Akkarat. Anderson calls over their shoulders as they shove him back against the wall. 'You're starting? Now?'

Akkarat glances up from his phone, finishes his conversation calmly and hands the receiver back to his communications officer. The winding man settles back on his haunches, waiting for the next call. The flywheel hum slows.

Akkarat says, 'The Somdet Chaopraya's assassination has brought out a great deal of hostility for the white shirts. Protests outside the Environment Ministry. Even the Megodont Union is involved. People were already angry at the Ministry's crackdowns. I have decided we will capitalize on this.'

'But we don't have our assets in place,' Anderson protests. 'You don't have all your army units down from the northeast. My strike teams aren't supposed to be ashore for another week.'

Akkarat shrugs and smiles. 'Revolutions are a messy business. It is better to take the opportunities that come before us. Still, I think that you will be pleasantly surprised.' He turns back to his hand-cranked radio phone. The steady whir of the flywheel fills the room as Akkarat talks to people under his command.

Anderson watches Akkarat's back. The man, once so obsequious in the presence of the Somdet Chaopraya, is now in charge.

He issues orders in a steady stream. Every so often the phone buzzes again for attention.

'This is crazy,' Carlyle murmurs. 'Are we still in it at all?'

'Hard to say.'

Akkarat glances over at them, seems about to say something, but instead he cocks his head. 'Listen,' he says. His voice has become reverent.

A rumble rolls across the city. Through the command post's open windows, light flares briefly, like lightning in a storm. Akkarat smiles.

'It's starting.'

39

Pai is waiting for Kanya in her office when she comes bursting in. 'Where are the men?' she asks, panting.

'They were formed up in the bachelor's housing.' He shrugs. 'We came back from the village when we heard things were—'

'Are they still there?'

'Maybe some of them. I heard Akkarat and Pracha were going to negotiate.'

'No!' She shakes her head. 'Get them, now.' She's rushing around the room, grabbing extra spring gun clips. 'Get them formed up and armed. We don't have much time.'

Pai stares at Hiroko. 'Is that the windup?'

'Don't worry about her. Do you know where General Pracha is?'

He shrugs. 'I heard he inspected our walls and then he was going to speak with the Megodont Union about the protests—'

She grimaces. 'Get the men formed up. We can't wait anymore.'

'You're crazy—'

An explosion shakes the ground. Outside, trees crackle as they crash to the ground. Pai leaps to his feet, a look of shock on his face. He runs to the window and stares outside. A warning klaxon starts to sound.

'It's Trade,' Kanya says. 'They're already here.' She grabs her spring gun. Hiroko is preternaturally still, standing with her head cocked as though she is some sort of dog, listening. And then she turns slightly, her attention leaning forward, anticipatory. Another series of explosions rock the compound. The entire building shudders. Plaster crackles off the ceiling.

Kanya rushes out of her office. Other white shirts stream out with her, those few who were working evening shifts, or who hadn't yet been assigned to patrol and containment on the docks and anchor pads. She dashes down the hall, followed closely by Hiroko and Pai, and charges outside.

The night has the scent of jasmine blossoms, sweet and strong, along with the smell of smoke and the tang of something else, something she has not smelled since military convoys rolled across the ancient friendship bridge, over the Mekong and on toward the insurgents in Vietnam ...

A tank smashes through the outer walls.

It is a metal monster, taller than two men, jungle-mottled and belching smoke from its furnace. Its main gun fires. The muzzle flashes and the tank heaves back on its treads. Its turret swivels, gears clanking, choosing another target. Masonry and marble shower down over Kanya. She dives for cover.

Behind the tank, war megodonts rush through the gap. Their tusks glint in the darkness, their riders are all in black. In the dimness, the few white shirts who have come out to defend the compound stand out like pale ghosts, easy targets. The whine of high-capacity springs comes from atop the megodonts and then the chatter of disks slashing all around her. Concrete chips rain down. Kanya's cheek opens. Suddenly she is lying on the ground, buried under the weight of Hiroko, who has shoved her down as more spring gun disks slash the air and crackle against the walls behind her.

Another explosion. The noise fills her whole head. She realizes that she is whimpering. Sounds have suddenly become distant. She's shaking with fear.

The tank rumbles into the center of the courtyard. Rotates. More megodonts pour through, their feet tangled in a wave of shock troops also rushing the gap. It's too far away to even make out which general has decided to betray Pracha. Scattered small arms spit from the upper stories of the Ministry buildings. Screams echo, Ministry people dying. Kanya pulls out her spring gun and takes aim. Beside her, a records clerk takes a disk and falls. Kanya holds her pistol carefully, fires a shot. Can't tell if it hits her man or not. Fires again. Sees him fall. The mass of troops flowing toward her is like a tsunami.

Jaidee appears at her shoulder. 'What about your men?' he asks. 'Are you going to sell yourself so easily and neglect those boys who rely on you?'

Kanya pulls the trigger again. She can barely see. She is crying. Men are spreading across the courtyards, squads leapfrogging under covering fire.

'Please, Captain Kanya.' Hiroko begs. 'We must run.'

'Go!' Jaidee urges. 'It's too late to fight.'

Kanya lets her finger off the trigger. Disks chatter around her. She rolls and scrambles for the doorway, lunges back into the relative safety of the building. Scrambles to her feet and runs for the exit at the opposite side of the building. More shells hit. The building shakes. She wonders if it will collapse before she makes the far side.

Memories from her childhood flood her as she jumps bloody bodies, following Hiroko and Pai. Memories of destruction and horror. Of coal-burning tanks roaring through villages, screaming down the remaining paved roads of the provinces in long columns before plowing out across rice paddies. Tanks running hard and fast for the Mekong, their treads tearing up the earth on their way to defend the Kingdom from the first surprise incursions of the Vietnamese. Black smoke roiling in their wake as they went to hold the border. And now the monsters are here.

She bursts through the far side of the Ministry and into a firestorm. Trees burning. Some sort of napalm strike. Smoke roils around her. Another tank smashes a distant gate, coming faster than any megodont. It is difficult for her mind to process how quickly they move. They are like tigers, streaking across the grounds. Men fire their spring guns, but they are nothing against the iron shells of the tanks; they are not built for warfare. The chatter of weapons fire rattles along with bright flashes of light. Silvery disks chatter all around, bouncing and slashing. White shirts run for cover, but they have no place to go. Red blossoms on white. Men are disassembled by explosions. More tanks pour through.

'Who are they?' Pai screams.

Kanya shakes her head dumbly. The armored division ravages through the burning trees of the Environment Ministry's grounds. More troops are pouring in. 'They have to be from the northeast. Akkarat is making his move. Pracha has been betrayed.'

She yanks at Pai, points him toward a slight rise and the shadows of unburned trees, pointing toward where the Phra Seub Temple may still be standing. Perhaps they can escape. Pai stares, but doesn't move. Kanya yanks him again and then they are off and running across the grounds. Palm trees crash down in their path, crackling and flaming. Coconuts rain green around them along with shrapnel bursts. The screams of men and women being torn apart by the well-oiled military machine fill the air.

'Where now?' Pai yells.

Kanya doesn't have an answer. She ducks as wood splinters

shower her and dives behind the partial cover of a fallen burning palm.

Jaidee flops down beside her and grins, not even sweating. He peers over the top of the log, then glances back at Kanya.

'So. Who will you fight for now, Captain?'

40

The tank surprises them all. One moment they are riding a pair of cycle rickshaws down a nearly empty street, the next, a roaring fills the air and a tank bursts into the intersection ahead. It has a loudspeaker that squawks something, perhaps a warning, and then its turret spins in their direction.

'Hide!' Hock Seng shouts as they all try to scramble off their bikes. The tank's barrel roars. Hock Seng hits the ground. A building face collapses, showering them with debris. Clouds of gray dust billow over him. Hock Seng coughs and tries to get up and crawl away but a rifle chatters and he throws himself flat again. He can't see anything in the dust. Answering small arms fire crackles from a nearby building and then the tank is firing again. The smoke clears slightly.

From an alley, Laughing Chan waves for Hock Seng. His hair is powdered gray and his face is coated with dust. His mouth moves but no sound comes out. Hock Seng tugs at Pak Eng and they scramble for safety. The hatch of the tank pops open and an armored gunner appears, firing with a spring rifle. Pak Eng goes down, his chest blossoming red. Peter Kuok ducks into an alley and Hock Seng glimpses him running. Hock Seng dives flat again and worms himself into the rubble. The tank fires again, rocking back on its treads. More small arms fire chatters from somewhere down the street. The man in the turret flops forward, dead. His rifle slides down the tank's armor. The tank engages and spins on its treads, clanking. Garbage and leaflets swirl around it. It lurches toward Hock Seng and accelerates. Hock Seng lunges aside as the tank crashes past, showering him with more debris.

Laughing Chan stares after the retreating vehicle. He says something but Hock Seng's ears are still ringing. He waves for Hock Seng to join him again. Hock Seng staggers upright and stumbles into the *soi's* relative safety. Laughing Chan cups his hands around Hock Seng's ear. His shout is a whisper.

'It's fast! Faster than a megodont!'

Hock Seng nods. He's shaking. It appeared so suddenly. So much faster than anything he has ever seen. Old Expansion technology. And the men driving it seemed mad. Hock Seng looks around at the rubble. 'I don't even know what they were doing here. There's nothing to secure,' he says.

Laughing Chan suddenly begins to laugh. His distant words tunnel past the ringing in Hock Seng's ears. 'Maybe they're lost!'

And then they are both laughing, and Hock Seng is almost hysterical with relief. They sit in the alley, resting and trying to catch their breath and giggling. Slowly, Hock Seng's hearing returns.

'It's worse than the Green Headbands.' Laughing Chan says, looking out at the street wreckage. 'At least with them, it was personal.' He makes a face. 'You could fight them. These ones are too fast. And too crazy. *Fengle*, all of them.'

Hock Seng is inclined to agree. 'Still, dead is dead. I would rather not face either.'

'We'll have to be more careful,' Laughing Chan says. He nods at Pak Eng's body. 'What should we do about him?'

'Do you want to carry him back to the towers?' Hock Seng asks pointedly.

Chan shakes his head, grimacing. Another explosion rumbles. From the sound of it, it's no more than a few blocks away.

Hock Seng looks up. 'The tank again?'

'Let's not wait to find out.'

They set off down the street, keeping to doorways. A few others are out in the open, looking toward the rumbling explosions. Trying to see where the noises are coming from, to see what is happening. Hock Seng remembers standing on a similar street only a few years before, the scent of the sea and the promise of the monsoon bright in the air the day the Green Headbands started their cleansing. And on that day, too, people had looked up like pigeons, heads swiveling toward the sound of slaughter, suddenly aware that they were in danger.

Ahead, unmistakable, the chatter of spring guns. Hock Seng motions to Laughing Chan and they turn into a new alley. He's too old for this foolishness. He should be reclining on a couch, smoking a bowl of opium while a pretty fifth wife massages his ankles. Behind them, the rest of the people on the street are still standing out in the open, still staring toward the sounds of battle. The Thais don't know what to do. Not yet. They have no experience with true slaughter. Their reflexes are wrong. Hock Seng turns into an abandoned building.

'Where are you going?' Laughing Chan asks.

'I want to see. I need to know what's happening.'

He climbs. One stairwell, two stairwells, three, four. He's panting. Five. Six. Then out into a hall. Broken doors, stifling close heat, the smell of excrement. Another explosion rumbles distant.

Through an open window, tracers of fire arc across the darkening sky and boom in the distance. Small arms snap and chatter in the streets like Spring Festival fireworks. Smoke pillars rise from a dozen points in the city. *Nagas* coiling, black against the setting sun. The anchor pads, the sea locks, the manufacturing district ... the Environment Ministry ...

Laughing Chan grabs Hock Seng's shoulder and points.

Hock Seng sucks in his breath. The Yaowarat slum blazes, WeatherAll shanties exploding in a spreading curtain of flame. '*Wode tian.*' Laughing Chan murmurs. 'We won't be going back there.'

Hock Seng stares at the burning slum that had been his home, watching with horror as all his cash and gems turn to ash. Fate is fickle. He laughs wearily. 'And you thought I wasn't lucky. We'd be roasted like pigs by now, if we had stayed.'

Laughing Chan makes a mock *wai* at him. 'I will follow the lord of the Three Prosperities into the nine hells.' He pauses. 'But what do we do now?'

Hock Seng points. 'We follow Thanon Rama XII, and then—'

He doesn't see the missile strike. It's too fast for any human being's eyes. Perhaps a military windup would have time to prepare, but he and Laughing Chan are thrown off their feet by the shockwave. A building collapses across the street.

'Never mind!' Laughing Chan grabs Hock Seng and drags him back toward the safety of the stairwells. 'We'll work it out. I don't want to lose my head for the sake of your view.'

Newly cautious, they slip through the darkening streets, working their way toward the manufacturing district. The streets are becoming more deserted as the Thais finally learn there is no safety in the open.

'What's that?' Laughing Chan whispers.

Hock Seng squints into the gloom. A trio of men crouch around a hand-cranked radio. One of them has an antenna in his hands that he holds over his head, trying to get reception. Hock Seng slows to walk, then urges Laughing Chan across the street to them.

'What news?' Hock Seng puffs.

'Did you see that missile hit?' one of them asks. He looks up.

'Yellow cards,' he murmurs. His companions exchange glances as they catch sight of Laughing Chan's machete, then smile nervously and start to shy away.

Hock Seng sketches a clumsy *wai*. 'We just want the news.'

One of them spits betel nut, still watching suspiciously, but he says, 'It's Akkarat, on the air.' He gestures for them to listen. His friend lifts the antenna again, pulling in static.

'—stay indoors. Do not go outside. General Pracha and his white shirts have attempted to topple Her Royal Majesty the Queen herself. It is our duty to defend the realm—' The voice crackles out of reception and the man begins fiddling with the knobs on the wireless again.

One of them shakes his head. 'It's all lies.'

The one doing the tuning murmurs a disagreement, 'But the Somdet Chaopraya—'

'Akkarat would kill Rama himself if he saw a benefit.'

Their friend lowers the antenna. The radio hisses static and the transmission is lost entirely as he speaks. 'I had a white shirt in my shop the other day, and he wanted to take my daughter home with him. A 'gift of good will,' he called it. They're all monitor lizards. A little corruption is one thing but these *heeya* will—'

Another explosion shakes the ground. Everyone turns, Thais and yellow cards together, trying to fix on the location.

We're like little monkeys, trying to understand a huge jungle.

The thought frightens Hock Seng. They're piecing together clues, but they have nothing to provide context. No matter how much they learn, it can never be enough. They can only react to events as they unfold, and hope for luck.

Hock Seng tugs Laughing Chan's arm. 'Let's go.' The Thais are already hurriedly gathering the radio and ducking back into their shop. When Hock Seng looks back again, the street corner is entirely empty, as if the moment of political discussion hadn't existed at all.

The fighting worsens as they near the manufacturing district. The Environment Ministry and the Army seem to be everywhere, warring. And for every professional unit on the street, there are others, the volunteers and student associations and civilians and loyalists, mobilized by political factions. Hock Seng pauses in a doorway, panting, as explosions and rifle fire echo.

'I can't tell any of them apart,' Laughing Chan mutters as a group of university students carrying short machetes and wearing yellow armbands runs past, headed for a tank that's busy shelling an old Expansion tower. 'They're all wearing yellow.'

'Everyone wants to claim loyalty to the Queen.'

'Does she even exist?'

Hock Seng shrugs. A student's spring gun blades bounce off the tank's armor. The thing is huge. Hock Seng can't help being impressed that the Army has successfully loaded so many tanks into the capital. He supposes the Navy and its admirals provided assistance. Which means General Pracha and his white shirts have no allies left. 'They're all crazy,' Hock Seng mutters. 'It doesn't make any difference who is who.' He studies the street. His knee is hurting, his old injury making him slow. 'I wish we could find some bicycles. My leg . . .' He grimaces.

'If you were on a bike, shooting you would be as easy as shooting a grandmother on a stoop.'

Hock Seng rubs his knee. 'Still, I'm too old for this.'

Rubble showers them from another explosion. Laughing Chan brushes debris out of his hair. 'I hope this is worth the trip.'

'You could be back in the slums, roasting alive.'

'That's true.' Laughing Chan nods. 'But let's hurry. I don't want to keep testing our luck.'

More dark intersections. More violence. Rumors flying on the streets. Executions in Parliament. The Trade Ministry in flames. Thammasat University students rallying on behalf of the Queen. And then another radio broadcast. A new frequency, everyone says, as they all huddle around the tinny speaker. The announcer sounds shaken. Hock Seng wonders if there is a spring gun at her head. *Khun* Supawadi. She was always so popular. Always introduced such interesting radio plays. And now her voice trembles as she begs her countrymen to stay calm while tanks rush through the streets, securing everything from the anchor pads to the docks. The radio's speaker crackles with the sound of shelling and explosions. A few seconds later, explosions rumble in the distance like muffled thunder, a perfect echo of the ones on the radio.

'She's closer to the fighting than we are,' Laughing Chan says.

'Is that a good sign, or a bad one?' Hock Seng wonders.

Laughing Chan starts to answer but a megodont's screams of rage interrupt, followed by the whine of spring guns unleashing. Everyone looks down the street. 'That sounds bad.'

'Hide,' Hock Seng says.

'Too late.'

A wave of people pours around the corner, running and screaming. A trio of carbon-armored megodonts thunders behind them. The massive heads sweep low, slashing from side to side, their tusks slash through the fleeing people with attached scythe blades. Bodies split like oranges and fly like leaves.

From atop the megodonts, machine gun cages open fire. Flickering silver streams of bladed disks pour into the packed crowd. Hock Seng and Laughing Chan crouch in a doorway as people flee past. The white shirts in their midst fire their own spring guns and single-shot rifles as they run, but the disks are entirely ineffective against the armored megodonts. The Environment Ministry isn't equipped for this sort of warfare. Ricocheting ammunition flurries around them as the machine guns chatter. People collapse in bloody writhing piles, howling agony as the megodonts trample over them. Dust and smoke and musk choke the street. A man is flung aside by a megodont and slams into Hock Seng . Blood gouts from his mouth, but he is already dead.

Hock Seng crawls out from under the corpse. More people are forming up and firing at the megodonts. Students, Hock Seng thinks, perhaps from Thammasat, but it's impossible to tell who they are loyal to, and Hock Seng wonders if even they know who they are fighting.

The megodonts wheel and charge. People pile up against Hock Seng, trying to get out of the way. Their mass crushes him. He can't breathe. He tries to cry out, to clear space for himself, but the crush is too great. He screams. The weight of desperate fleeing people presses down upon him, squeezing out the last of his air. A megodont sweeps into them. It backs and charges again, tearing into the clot of people, swinging its bladed tusks. Students throw bottles of oil up at the megodonts and hurl torches up after, spinning lights and fire—

More razor disks rain down. Hock Seng cowers as the guns sweep toward him, spitting silver. A boy stares into his eyes, yellow headband slipped down over his bleeding face. Hock Seng's leg blossoms with pain. He can't tell if he's shot or if his knee is broken. He screams in frustration and fear. The weight of bodies pushes him to the ground. He's going to die. Crushed under the dead. Despite everything, he failed to understand the capriciousness of warfare. In his arrogance he thought he could prepare. Such a fool . . .

Silence comes suddenly. His ears are ringing, but there's no more weapons fire and no more trumpeting megodonts. Hock Seng takes a shuddering breath beneath the weight of bodies. All around him, he hears only moans and sobbing.

'Ah Chan?' he calls.

No answer.

Hock Seng claws his way out. Others are dragging themselves free of the massacre as well. Helping their wounded. Hock Seng can barely stand. His leg is awash with pain. He's covered with blood. He searches through the bodies, trying to find Laughing Chan, but if the man is in the pile, he is covered in too much blood and there are too many bodies and it is too dark to pick him out.

Hock Seng calls for him again, peering into the mass. Down the street, a methane lamp burns bright, shattered, its neck spurting gas into the sky. Hock Seng supposes it could explode at any moment, ripping through the methane pipes of the city, but he can't muster the energy to care.

He stares around at the bodies. Most of them are students, it seems. Just foolish children. Trying to do battle with megodonts. Fools. He forces down memories of his own children, dead and piled. The massacres of Malaya, writ on Thai pavement. He pries a spring gun from a dead white shirt's hands, checks its load. Only a few disks left, but still. He pumps the spring, adding energy. Shoves it into his pocket. Children playing at war. Children who don't deserve to die, but are too foolish to live.

In the distance, the battle rages still, moved on to other avenues and other victims. Hock Seng limps down the street. Bodies lie everywhere. He reaches an intersection and hobbles across, too tired to care about the risk of being caught in the open. At the far side, a man lies slumped against a wall, his bicycle lying beside him. Blood soaks his lap.

Hock Seng picks up the bicycle.

'That's mine,' the man says.

Hock Seng pauses, studying the man. The man can barely keep his eyes open, yet still he clings to normalcy, to the idea that something like a bicycle can be owned. Hock Seng turns and wheels the bicycle down off the sidewalk. The man calls out again, 'That's mine.' But he doesn't stand and he doesn't do anything to stop Hock Seng as he swings a leg over the frame and sets his feet on the pedals.

If the man complains again, Hock Seng doesn't hear it.

41

'I thought we weren't going to move for another two weeks,' Anderson protests. 'We don't have everything in place.'

'Plans must change. Your weapons and funding are still quite helpful.' Akkarat shrugs. 'In any case, having *farang* shock troops in the city would not necessarily smooth the transition. It's possible that this accelerated timetable is best.'

Explosions rumble across the city. A methane fire is burning, bright and green, yellowing now as it finds dry bamboo and other materials. Akkarat studies the burn, waves to the man with the radio phone. The private cranks at the power as Akkarat speaks quietly, issuing orders for fire teams to be dispatched to the blaze. He glances at Anderson, explains. 'If the fires get out of control, we won't have a city to defend.'

Anderson studies the spreading fire, the gleam of palace *chedi*, the Temple of the Emerald Buddha. 'That fire's near the city pillar.'

'*Khap*. We can't allow the pillar to burn. It would be a bad omen for a new regime that is supposed to be strong and forward-looking.'

Anderson goes and leans on a balcony railing. His hand, splinted now, still throbs, but with the bone reset by a military doctor, it feels better than it has in hours. A swaddling layer of morphine helps keep the pain at bay.

Another arc of fire crosses the sky, a missile that buries itself in the distance, somewhere in the Environment Ministry compound. It's hard to believe the forces that Akkarat has mustered for his ascension. The man had far more power at his disposal than he let on. Anderson pretends nonchalance as he asks the next question.

'I assume this accelerated schedule won't affect the specifics of our agreement.'

'AgriGen remains a favored partner in the new era.' At these soothing words, Anderson relaxes, but Akkarat's next sentence yanks him alert. 'Of course, the situation has changed somewhat. After all, you were unable to bring certain promised resources to bear.'

Anderson looks at him sharply. 'We had a timetable. The promised troops are en route, along with more weapons and funding.'

Akkarat smiles slightly. 'Don't look so concerned. I'm sure we'll work something out.'

'We want the seedbank still.'

Akkarat shrugs. 'I understand your position.'

'Don't forget that Carlyle also has the pumps you'll need before the rainy season.'

Akkarat glances at Carlyle. 'I'm sure separate arrangements can be made.'

'No!'

Carlyle grins, glances from one to the other, then holds up his hands as he backs away. 'You all work this out. It's not my argument.'

'Just so.' Akkarat turns back to the arrangements of the battle.

Anderson watches, eyes narrowed. They still have leverage on this man. Guarantees of fertile, latest generation seedstock. Rice that will resist blister rust for at least a dozen plantings. He considers how best to affect Akkarat, to bring him back into alignment, but the morphine and exhaustion of the last twenty-four hours are wearing on him.

Smoke from one of the fires drifts across them, sending every-one into coughing fits before the wind shifts again. More tracer fire and shells arc across the city, followed by the distant rumble of explosions.

Carlyle frowns. 'What was that?'

'Probably the Army's Krut Company. Their commander refused our friendship offer. He'll be shelling the anchor pads on behalf of Pracha.' Akkarat says. 'The white shirts don't want to allow a resup-ply. They'll also go after the seawalls if we let them.'

'But the city would drown.'

'And it would be our fault.' Akkarat grimaces. 'In the December 12 coup, the dikes were barely defended successfully. If Pracha feels he is losing – and by now he must know he is – then the white shirts may try to take the city hostage to force a more favorable surrender.' He shrugs. 'It's a pity we don't already have your coal pumps delivered.'

'As soon as the shooting stops,' Carlyle says, 'I'll contact Kolkata and ship them out.'

'I would have expected no less.' Akkarat's teeth gleam.

Anderson fights to keep the scowl off his own face. He doesn't like their friendly banter. It's almost as if their earlier captivity is forgotten, and Carlyle and Akkarat are old friends. He doesn't like the way Akkarat seems to have separated Anderson's own interests from Carlyle's.

Anderson studies the landscape, mulling his options. If he just knew the location of the seedbank, he could order a strike team to move in and take it in the confusion of this urban war …

Shouts filter up from below. People milling in the streets, all of them looking toward the havoc, all of them curious what this war-fare bodes for them. He follows the gaze of the confused throng. Old Expansion towers stand black amongst the fires, bits of remnant glass windows twinkling merrily with the blazes all around. Beyond the city and the fires, the black ocean ripples, a sheet of darkness. From high up, the seawalls seem curiously insubstantial. A ring of gas lights, and then nothing beyond except hungry blackness.

'Can they really breach the dikes?' he asks.

Akkarat shrugs. 'There are weak points. We had planned to defend them with additional Navy personnel from the south, but we think we can hold.'

'And if you don't?'

'The man who allows the city to drown will never be forgiven,' Akkarat says. 'It cannot be allowed. We will fight for the dikes as if we are the villagers of Bang Rajan.'

Anderson watches the burning fires and the sea beyond. Carlyle leans on the railing beside him. His face glimmers in the light. He has the satisfied smile of a man who cannot lose. Anderson leans over. 'Akkarat might have influence here, but AgriGen is everywhere else.' He locks eyes with the trader. 'Remember that.' He's pleased to see Carlyle's smile falter.

More gunfire echoes across the landscape. From high up, the battle lacks visceral power. It's a battle of ants fighting over piles of sand. As if someone has kicked two nests together to test the clash of trivial civilizations. Mortars rumble. Fires twinkle and flare.

In the distance, a shadow descends from the black night overhead. A dirigible, sinking toward the city blazes. It floats low over the fires and suddenly a portion of a blaze winks out as a deluge of seawater pours from its belly.

Akkarat watches, smiling. 'Ours,' he says.

And then, as though the fire is not snuffed, but actually airborne, the dirigible explodes. Flames roar around it, pieces of its skin blazing and peeling off, fluttering away as the whole great beast sinks toward the city and crashes to pieces on the buildings.

'Christ,' Anderson says, 'you sure you don't want our reinforcements now?'

Akkarat's face remains impassive. 'I didn't think they would have time to deploy missiles.'

A massive explosion rocks the city, green gas burning bright, rising at the skyline's edge. A cloud of flame, roiling and expanding. Unimaginable pounds of compressed gas going up in a roaring green mushroom.

'The Environment Ministry's strategic reserve, I think,' Akkarat comments.

'Beautiful,' Carlyle murmurs. 'Fucking beautiful.'

42

Hock Seng shelters in an alley as tanks and trucks rumble down Thanon Phosri. He shudders at the thought of the fuel burning. It has to be much of the Kingdom's diesel stock, all of it going up in a single orgy of violence. Coal smoke fills the air as stoked tanks surge past on clanking treads. Hock Seng crouches in garbage. Everything he planned has fallen apart in this moment of crisis. Instead of waiting and moving north as a careful unit, he left his valuables to burn for the sake of one long-shot risk.

Quit complaining, you old fool. You would have roasted, your purple baht and your yellow card friends all together, if you hadn't left when you did.

Still, he wishes he'd had the forethought to bring at least some of that carefully squirrelled insurance. He wonders if his karma is so broken that he cannot ever truly hope to succeed.

He peers into the street again. The SpringLife offices are within view. Best of all, there are no guards present. Hock Seng allows himself a smile at that. The white shirts have their own troubles now. He wheels the bicycle across the street, using it as a crutch to keep him upright.

Inside the compound, it looks as though there was brief fighting. A trio of bodies lie against a wall, seemingly executed. Their yellow armbands have been pulled off and tossed in the dust beside them. More foolish children playing at politics—

Movement behind him.

Hock Seng turns and jams his spring gun into his stalker. Mai gasps as his gun barrel buries itself in her guts. Mewls with fear, eyes wide.

'What are you doing here?' Hock Seng whispers.

Mai stumbles back from his gun. 'I came to look for you. The white shirts found our village. People are sick there.' She sobs. 'And then your house burned.'

For the first time he sees the soot and cuts covering her body. 'You were in Yaowarat? In the slums?' he asks, shocked.

She nods. 'I was lucky.' She fights back a sob.

Hock Seng shakes his head. 'Why come here?'

'I couldn't think of any other place . . .'

'And more people are sick?'

She nods, fearful. 'The white shirts questioned us, I didn't know what to do, I told—'

'Don't worry,' Hock Seng sets a soothing hand on her shoulder. 'The white shirts won't trouble us anymore. They have their own problems.'

'Do you have—' She stops. Finally says, 'They burned our village. Everything.'

She is a pathetic creature. So small. So vulnerable. He imagines her fleeing her destroyed home, seeking refuge in the only place left to her. And then finding herself in the heart of warfare. A part of him wants to be rid of her burden, but too many have already died around him, and he is obscurely pleased for her company. He shakes his head. 'Foolish child.' He motions her into the factory. 'Come with me.'

A furious stink envelopes them as the enter the main hall. They both cover their faces, breathing shallowly.

'The algae baths,' Hock Seng murmurs. 'The kink-springs have stopped running the fans. Nothing is being vented.'

He climbs the steps to the office, shoves open the door. The room is close and hot and reeks as badly as the manufacturing floor from the long days without air flow. He pushes open shutters, letting in night breeze and city burn. Across the roofs, flames flicker, sparking in the night like prayers going up to heaven.

Mai comes to stand beside him, her face illuminated in the irregular glow. A gas lamp is burning freely down on the street, broken. They must be burning all over the city. Hock Seng is somewhat surprised that no one has cut off the gas lines. Someone should have done it already, and yet still this one flares, bright and green, reflecting on Mai's face. She is pretty, he realizes. Slight and beautiful. An innocent trapped amongst warring animals.

He turns from the window and goes to squat before the safe. Studies its dials and heavy locks, its combinations and levers. Expensive to manufacture something with so much steel. When he had his own company, when the Tri-Clipper ruled the South China Sea and the Indian Ocean, he had one like it in his offices, an heirloom, salvaged from an old bank when it lost liquidity, straight from the vault and carried into Three Prosperities Trading Company with the help of two megodonts. This one sits before him, taunting him. He must destroy it at its joints. It will take time. 'Come with me,' he says.

He leads her back down to the factory floor. Mai hangs back when he wants to go into the fining rooms. He hands her a lineworker's mask. 'It should be enough.'

'You're sure?'

He shrugs. 'Stay, then.'

But she follows him anyway, back to where they store the curing acid. They walk gingerly. He uses a rag to push aside the fining room curtains, careful to let nothing touch him. His breath is loud inside the mask, ragged sawing. The manufacturing rooms are disarrayed. White shirts have been here, inspecting. The stink of the rotting algae tanks is intense, even through the mask. Hock Seng breathes shallowly, forcing himself not to gag. Overhead, the drying screens are all black with withered algae. A few streamers dangle down, black emaciated tentacles. Hock Seng fights the urge to duck from them.

'What are you doing?' Mai pants.

'Looking for a future.' He spares her a small smile before he realizes she can't see his expressions through the mask. He digs gloves out of a supply cabinet and hands her a pair. Gives her an apron as well. 'Help me with this.' He indicates a sack of powder. 'We're working for ourselves, now. No more foreign influences, yes?' He stops her as she reaches for the sack. 'Don't get any on your skin,' he says. 'And don't let your sweat touch it.' He guides her back up to the offices.

'What is it?'

'You shall see, child.'

'Yes, but—'

'It's magic. Now go get some water from the *khlong* out back.'

When she returns, he takes a knife and carefully slices into the sacking. 'Bring me the water.' She pulls the bucket close. He dips into the water with his knife, then runs it through the powder. The powder hisses and begins to boil. When he takes the knife out, it's half gone, melted into nothing, still hissing.

Mai's eyes go wide. A viscous liquid pours off the knife. 'What is it?'

'A specialized bacteria. Something the *farang* have created.'

'Not acid, though'

'No. It's alive. In a way.'

He takes the knife and begins to scrape it along the face of the safe. The knife disintegrates completely. Hock Seng grimaces. 'I need something else, something long, to spread it with.'

'Put water on the safe,' Mai suggests. 'Then pour on the powder.'
He laughs. 'Clever child.'

Soon the safe is soaking. He prepares a paper funnel and lets the powder stream through in a tiny fountain. Wherever it touches the metal face it begins to boil. Hock Seng steps back, horrified at the speed of the stuff. Fights the urge to wipe his hands. 'Don't get any on your skin,' he mutters. Stares at his gloves. If there is a trace of powder on them and they are wetted ... His skin crawls. Mai is already backed away to the far side of the office, watching with terrified eyes.

Metal pours off the face, eaten and discarded iron, peeling away in sheaves, layers of it flaking away as if blown by autumn winds. The bright leaves of melting iron land on teak flooring. They hiss and spread. The flakes burn on, creating a lattice of broken seared wood.

'It doesn't stop,' Mai says, awed. Hock Seng watches with increasing unease, wondering if the yeastlike stuff will eat away the floor below and send the safe crashing down into the manufacturing lines. He finds his voice. 'It is alive. It should lose its ability to digest, soon.'

'This is what the *farang* make.' Mai's voice is frightened and awed.

'Our people have made such things as well.' Hock Seng shakes his head. 'Don't think the *farang* are so much as all that.'

The safe continues to disintegrate. If only he had been brave before. He could have done this when there wasn't a war boiling outside the window. He wishes he could go back in time to his former frightened paranoid self, so worried about deportation, about angering foreign devils, about preserving his good name, and simply whisper in that old man's ear that there was no hope. That he should steal and run, and it could not turn out worse.

A voice interrupts his thoughts. 'Well, well. Tan Hock Seng. How nice to see you here.'

Hock Seng turns. Dog Fucker and Old Bones, along with six others, are standing in the doorway. All of them carrying spring guns. They're scratched and sooted from the warfare of the streets, but smiling and confident.

'We all seem to have been thinking along the same lines,' Dog Fucker observes.

An explosion lights the sky, casting orange across the office. The rumble of destruction trembles through Hock Seng's soles. It's hard to tell how far away it was. The shells seem to fall randomly. If there is intelligence guiding them, it's not for them to understand. Another rumble, this one closer. The white shirts, defending the levees, most likely. Hock Seng fights an urge to flee. The cracking of the iron-digesting bacteria continues. Leaves of metal waft to the floor.

Hock Seng tests the waters. 'I'm glad you're here. Help me, then. Come on.'

Old Bones smiles. 'I think not.'

The men shoulder past Hock Seng. All of them larger than he. All of them armed. All of them uncaring of his and Mai's presence. Hock Seng staggers as they bump him aside.

'But it's mine,' he protests. 'You can't take it! I told you where it was!'

The men ignore him.

'You can't take it!' Hock Seng fumbles for his gun. Suddenly a pistol presses against his skull. Old Bones, smiling.

Dog Fucker watches with interest. 'Another killing will make little difference on my rebirth. Don't test me.'

Hock Seng can barely control his rage. A part of him wants to fire anyway, to steal away the man's smug expression. The safe's metal continues to bubble and hiss, falling away, slowly revealing his last object of hope. The *nak leng* all watch Hock Seng and Old Bones. They're loose, smiling. Unafraid. They haven't even lifted their pistols. They simply watch, interested, as Hock Seng points his pistol at them.

Dog Fucker grins. 'Go away, yellow card. Before I change my mind.'

Mai tugs at Hock Seng's hand. 'Whatever it is, it isn't worth your life.'

'She's right, yellow card,' Old Bones says. 'This is not a fight you can win.'

Hock Seng lowers his pistol and allows Mai to pull him away. They back out of the office. The Dung Lord's men watch with small smiles, and then Hock Seng and Mai are going down the stairs and out into the factory, and from there into the rubbled streets.

In the distance, a megodont screams in pain. The wind gusts, carrying ash and political pamphlets and the scent of burning WeatherAll. Hock Seng feels old. Too old to still be striving against a fate that clearly wishes him destroyed. Another whisper sheet tumbles past. The headline screams of windup girls and murder. Amazing that Mr. Lake's windup could cause so much trouble. And now everyone in the city is hunting for her. He almost smiles. Even if he's a yellow card, he's not as disadvantaged as that sorry creature. He probably owes her thanks. If it hadn't been for her and the news of Mr. Lake's arrest, he supposes he would be dead by now, burned in the slums with all his jade and cash and diamonds.

I should be grateful.

Instead, he feels the weight of his ancestors pressing down upon him, crushing him with their judgments. He took what his father and grandfather before him had built in Malaya and turned it to ash.

The failure is overwhelming.

Another whisper sheet flutters up against the factory wall. The windup girl again, along with accusations against General Pracha. Mr. Lake was obsessed with that windup girl. Couldn't stop fucking her. Couldn't resist bringing her to his bed at every opportunity. Hock Seng picks up the whisper sheet, suddenly thoughtful.

'What is it?' Mai asks.

I am too old for this.

But still, Hock Seng feels his heart beating faster. 'I have an idea,' he says. 'A possibility.'

A new absurd flicker of hope. He cannot help it. Even when he has nothing, he must strive.

43

A tank round explodes. Dirt and woody debris showers Kanya's head. They've abandoned the Ministry buildings – giving ground is what Kanya has called it, but in truth it's a rout – running as fast as they can from the oncoming tanks and megodonts.

The only thing that has saved them so far is that the army seems intent on securing the main campus of the Ministry, and so its strength remains gathered there. Still, she and her men have encountered three commando units coming over the south walls of the compound and they have cut Kanya's platoon in half. And now another tank, just as they were about to slip out a secondary exit. The tank smashed through the gate and blocked their escape.

She has ordered her men into the forest groves near Phra Seub's temple. It is in shambles. The carefully tended garden has been trampled by war megodonts. Its main columns have been burnt by a fire bomb attack that swept through the dry teak of the forest like a raging demon, shrieking and roaring, so now they shelter in ash and stumps and smolder.

Another tank shell drops into their hillside position. More commandos slip around the tank, break into teams and dash across the compound. It looks as though they're heading for the biological laboratories. Kanya wonders if Ratana is working there, if she even knows of the warfare above ground. A tree shatters beside her as another tank round explodes.

'They know we're up here, even if they can't see us,' Pai says. As if to emphasize his words, a hail of disks whines overhead, embedding themselves in the burnt forest trunks, gleaming silver in the black wood. Kanya motions to her men that they should pull back. The other white shirts, all their uniforms carefully smeared now with soot and ash, scamper deeper into the guttering forest.

Another shell drops below them. Burning teak splinters whine through the air.

'This is too close.' She gets up and runs, Pai dogging her. Hiroko streaks past, takes cover behind a black fallen log and waits for them to catch up.

'Can you imagine fighting that?' Pai gasps.

Kanya shakes her head. Already the windup has saved them twice. Once by spying out the shadow movement of commandos coming toward them, the second time pushing Kanya down a moment before a rain of spring disks shredded the air above her head. The windup's eyes are sharp where Kanya's are not, and she is blisteringly fast. Already, though, she is flushed, her skin dry and scalding to the touch. Hiroko is not built for this tropic warfare, and even though they pour water on her and try to keep her cool, she is fading.

When Kanya catches up, Hiroko looks up at her with fever-bright eyes. 'I will have to drink something soon. Ice.'

'We don't have any.'

'The river then. Anything. I must return to Yashimoto-sama.'

'There's fighting all along the river.' Kanya has heard from others that General Pracha is at the levees, trying to repel the landing Navy boats. Fighting his old ally, Admiral Noi.

Hiroko reaches out with a scalding hand. 'I cannot last.'

Kanya searches around her, seeking an answer. Bodies are every-where. It's worse than a plague, the men and women ripped by high explosives. The carnage is immense. Arms and legs, a foot separated and flung into a tree branch. Bodies piled and burning. Napalm hissing. The clank of tanks rumbling through the com-pounds, the burn of coal exhaust. 'I need the radio,' she says.

'Pichai had it last.'

But Pichai is dead and they aren't sure where the radio has gone.

We aren't trained for this sort of thing. We were supposed to stop blister rust and influenza, not tanks and megodonts.

When she finally finds a radio, it is from a dead hand that she takes it. She cranks the handset. Tests the codes that the Ministry uses for discussing plagues, not warfare. Nothing. Finally she speaks in the clear. 'This is Captain Kanya. Is there anyone else out there? Over?'

A long pause. The crackle and static. She repeats herself. Again she repeats. Nothing.

And then, 'Captain? This is Lieutenant Apichart.'

She recognizes the assistant's voice. 'Yes? Where is General Pracha?'

More silence. 'We don't know.'

'You aren't with him?'

Another pause. 'We think he's dead.' He coughs. 'They used a gas.'

'Who is our ranking officer?'

Another long pause. 'I believe it is you, ma'am.'

She pauses, shocked. 'It can't be. What about the fifth?'

'We haven't heard.'

'General Som?'

'He was found in his home, assassinated. Also Karmatha, and Phailin.'

'It's not possible.'

'It is rumor. But they have not been seen, and General Pracha believed it when we received word.'

'No other captains?'

'Bhirombhakdi was at the anchor pads, but all we see is fire from there.'

'Where are you?'

'An Expansion tower, near Phraram Road.'

'How many do you have with you?'

'Maybe thirty.'

She surveys her people with dismay. Wounded men and women. Hiroko lying against a dead shorn banana tree, face flushed like a Chinese paper lantern, eyes closed. Perhaps dead already. Fleetingly she wonders if she cares about the creature or . . . Her men are all around her, watching. Kanya takes in their pathetic ammunition. Their wounds. So few of them.

The radio crackles. 'What should we do, Captain? ' Lieutenant Apichart asks. 'Our guns don't do anything against tanks. There's no way for us—' The channel crackles with static.

From the direction of the river, a deep explosion rumbles.

Private Sarawut climbs down from a tree. 'They stopped shelling the docks.'

'We're alone,' Pai murmurs.

44

It's the silence that wakes her. Emiko has passed the night in a blurry sprawl, periods of sleep broken by the rumble of high explosives and the whine of high-capacity springs unleashing. Tanks clank down the streets burning coal, but much of it is distant, battles fought in other districts. On the streets bodies lie abandoned, casualties of the riot, now forgotten in the larger conflict.

A strange silence has settled over the city. A few candles twinkle in windows where people keep midnight watch on the ravaged city, but nothing else is lit. No gas lights in the buildings or on the streets. Total blackness. It seems that either the city's methane has run out, or someone has finally shut off the mains.

Emiko pulls herself out of the garbage, wrinkling her nose in disgust at the discarded melon rinds and banana peels. Against the flame-orange sky, she can see a few columns of smoke, but nothing else. The streets are empty. There is no better time for what she plans.

She turns her attention to the tower. Six stories above, Anderson-sama's apartment waits. If only she can get to it. At first, she had hoped to simply speed through the lobby and find her way higher, but the doors are locked and guards patrol within. And she is now too well-known to risk an attempt at direct entrance. But she has an alternative.

She is hot. Terribly hot. A green coconut that she found and smashed early in the night is a wistful memory now. She counts the balconies again, one after the other, rising above her. Water is up there. Breezes. Survival and a temporary hiding place, if she can make it.

A rumble comes from the distance, then a crackle like fireworks. She listens. Best not to wait any longer. She scrambles for the lowest balcony. It is cased in iron bars, as is the one above. She pulls herself up the face of the first and second balconies, using the easy handholds of the bars to climb.

She stands at last on the open third balcony, panting with the effort. She feels dizzy with the heat building within her. Below her, the alley cobbles beckon. She looks up at the balcony lip of the fourth floor. She gathers herself and jumps ... and is rewarded with a good handhold. She pulls herself up.

On the fourth balcony, she perches on its railing, staring up at the fifth. The heat of her exertion is building. She takes a breath and jumps. Her fingers catch. She dangles in the open air. She looks down and immediately regrets it. The alley is far below, now. She slowly pulls herself up, gasping.

The apartment within is dark. No one stirs. Emiko tests the iron lattice of the security gate, hoping for a lucky entrance, but it is locked. She would give anything to drink water now, to pour it over her face and body. She studies the security gate's construction, but there is no way for her to break in.

One more jump.

She returns to the balcony's edge. Her hands are the only part of her that seem to sweat like a normal creature's, and now they are as slick as oil with her body's moisture. She wipes them again and again, trying to make them dry. The intense flush of too much exertion is swallowing her. She scrambles up onto the balcony's lip, balances. Dizzy. She crouches, steadying herself.

She leaps.

Her fingers scrabble at the balcony rim, then slip. She crashes back, slamming across the lower railing. Her ribs explode with pain as she flips over and smashes into potted jasmine vines. Another blossom of pain flares in her elbow.

She lies whimpering amongst shattered pottery and night jasmine perfume. Blood gleams black on her hands. She can't stop whimpering. Her whole body is shaking. She's burning up with the exertion of climbing and jumping.

She pushes herself up awkwardly, cradling her damaged arm, expecting people to come charging out at her, but the apartment beyond the gate remains dark.

Emiko staggers to her feet and leans against the balcony rail, looking up at her goal.

You foolish girl. Why do you try so hard to survive? Why not just jump and die? It would be so much simpler.

She peers down into the black alley below. She doesn't have an answer. It is something in her genetics, as deeply ingrained as her urge to please. She hauls herself up again onto the railing, balancing awkwardly, cradling her throbbing arm. She looks upward, praying to Mizuko Jizo the windup bodhisattva to give her mercy.

She jumps, reaching one-handed for salvation.

Her fingers catch . . . then slip away.

Emiko lashes out with her bad hand and catches hold. Her elbow's ligaments tear away. She yelps as the bones separate, then crack wide. Sobbing, breath sawing in and out of her throat, she scrabbles for the railing with her good hand. Seizes a handhold. She lets her broken arm fall and hang limp.

Emiko dangles one-handed, high above the street. Her arm is nothing but flame. She whimpers quietly, preparing to wound herself once again. She lets out a ragged sob and then reaches up once again with her ruined arm. Her hand closes on the railing.

Please. Please. Just a little more.

She lets her weight settle onto the arm. White pain. Emiko's breath saws ragged in her throat. She hauls a leg up, feeling with her foot, scrabbling for a toehold, finally it hooks on the iron. She pulls herself up, teeth gritted, sobbing, refusing to let go.

Only a bit more.

The barrel of a spring gun presses against her forehead.

Emiko opens her eyes. A young girl grips the pistol in trembling hands. She stares at Emiko, terror-stricken. 'You were right,' she whispers.

An old Chinese man looms behind her, his expression shadowed. They peer over the balcony precipice, watching Emiko as she dangles. Emiko's hands begin to slip. The pain is almost unbearable now.

'Please,' Emiko whispers. 'Help me.'

45

The gas lights in Akkarat's operations center gutter out. Anderson straightens in the sudden darkness, surprised. The fighting has been desultory for some time, but all across the city it is the same. Krung Thep's gas lamps are winking out, green points of light smothered down the thoroughfares, one by one. A few zones of conflict still flicker yellow and orange with burning WeatherAll, but all the green is gone from the city. A black blanket covers it, almost as complete as that of the ocean beyond the levees.

'What's happening?' Anderson asks.

The dim glow of computer monitors is all that still lights the room. Akkarat comes back inside from the balcony. The operations room buzzes with activity. Emergency hand-cranked lantern LEDs come to life, spattering light around the room, illuminating Akkarat's smiling face. 'We've taken the methane works,' he says. 'The country is ours.'

'You're certain?'

'The anchor pads and the docks are secure. The white shirts are surrendering. We've gotten word from their commanding officer. They will be laying down their weapons and surrendering unconditionally. The word is going out over their coded radio now. A few will fight on, but we have the city now.'

Anderson rubs at his broken ribs. 'Does that mean we can leave?'

Akkarat nods. 'Of course. I will detail men to escort you back to your homes in just a little while. The streets will still take a bit of time to settle.' He smiles. 'I think you will be very happy with the new management of our Kingdom.'

A few hours later they're being ushered into an elevator.

They plunge to street level and find Akkarat's personal limousine waiting. Outside, the sky is just starting to lighten.

Carlyle stops on the verge of climbing into the car, staring down the thoroughfare to where the yellow edge of dawn is thickening. 'Now that's something I wasn't expecting to see.'

'I thought we were dead.'

'You seemed cool enough.'

Anderson shrugs gingerly. 'Finland was worse.' But as he climbs into the car, he has another coughing fit. It goes on for half a minute, wracking him. He wipes blood off his lips as Carlyle stares.

'Are you all right?' Carlyle asks.

Anderson nods as he gingerly pulls the door closed. 'I think I'm busted up inside. Akkarat used a pistol on my ribs.'

Carlyle studies him. 'You sure you haven't caught something?'

'Are you kidding?' Anderson laughs, which makes his ribs hurt. 'I work for AgriGen. I'm inoculated against diseases that haven't even been released yet.'

The car accelerates away from the curb with an escort of kinkspring scooters swarming around the coal-diesel limo. Anderson settles himself more comfortably in his seat, watching as the city slides past beyond the glass.

Carlyle taps a leather armrest thoughtfully. 'I'll have to get me one of these. Once the trade starts flowing, I'm going to have a lot of money to spend.'

Anderson nods, distracted. 'We're going to need to start shipping calories right away. Famine relief. I want to commission your dirigibles immediately, as a stopgap. We'll bring U-Tex in from India. Give Akkarat something to crow about. Benefits of open markets, all that. Lots of good press from the whisper sheets. Get things cemented.'

'You can't just enjoy the moment?' Carlyle laughs. 'It's not often you escape a black hood, Anderson. The first thing we do is go find some whiskey and a rooftop, and watch the damn sun rise over the country we just bought. That's what we do first. The rest of the crap will all wait for tomorrow.'

The limousine makes a turn onto Phraram I Road and their escort forges ahead of them, hurtling across the rapidly lightening city. They come down off a flyway and detour around a rubbled Expansion tower that has been entirely toppled in the fighting. A few people are scavenging in the wreckage, but no one is armed.

'It's over,' Anderson murmurs. 'Just like that.' He feels tired. A pair of white shirt bodies lie half-off the curb, rag-doll limp. A vulture stands beside them, edging closer. Anderson touches his ribs gingerly, suddenly glad to be alive.

'You know someplace we can buy that whiskey?'

46

The old Chinese man and the young girl crouch away from her, watching carefully as she guzzles water. Emiko was surprised when the old man allowed the girl to help her crawl over the balcony's edge. But now that she is safe, he keeps his spring gun trained on her and Emiko understands that he is not motivated by charity.

'Did you really kill them?' he asks.

Emiko gingerly lifts her glass and drinks again. If she didn't hurt so much, she could almost enjoy the fact that they are afraid of her. With water, she feels vastly improved, even with her right arm lying limp and swollen in her lap. She sets the glass on the floor and cradles her wounded elbow close. She breathes shallowly through the pain.

'Did you?' he asks again.

She shrugs slightly. 'I was fast. They were slow.'

They are speaking Mandarin, a language she hasn't used since her time with Gendo-sama. English, Thai, French, Mandarin Chinese, accounting, political protocol, catering and hospitality... So many skills she doesn't use anymore. It took a few minutes for her memories of the language to surface but then it was there, like a limb that had atrophied from long neglect, and then miraculously turned out to be strong. She wonders if her broken arm will heal as easily, if her body still holds surprises for her.

'You are the yellow card secretary from the factory,' she says. 'Hock Seng, yes? Anderson-sama told me that you ran away when the white shirts came.'

The old man shrugs. 'I came back.'

'Why?'

He grins without humor. 'We cling to whatever flotsam we have.'

Outside, an explosion rumbles. They all look toward the sound.

'I think it's ending,' the girl murmurs. 'That's the first one in more than an hour.'

Emiko thinks that with the two of them distracted, she could probably kill them both, even with her shattered arm. But she is so tired. Tired of destruction. Tired of slaughter. Beyond the balcony, the city smokes against a lightening sky. An entire city torn to ribbons over ... what? A windup girl who couldn't keep her place.

Emiko closes her eyes against the shame of it. She can almost see Mizumi-sensei frowning disapproval. She's surprised that the woman still holds any power over her at all. Perhaps she will never be free of her old teacher. Mizumi is as much a part of her as her wretched pore structure. 'You want to collect the reward for me?' she asks. 'Wish to profit from catching a killer?'

'The Thais want you very badly.'

The apartment's locks rattle. They all look up as Anderson-sama and another *gaijin* stumble through the door. Dark bruises decorate the foreigners' faces, but they're laughing and smiling. They both stop short. Anderson-sama's eyes flick from Emiko to the old man, to the pistol that now points at him.

'Hock Seng?'

The other *gaijin* backpedals and slips behind Anderson-sama. 'What the hell?'

'Good question.' Anderson-sama is studying the scene before him, pale blue eyes evaluating.

The girl Mai makes a reflexive *wai* to the *gaijin*. Emiko almost smiles in recognition. She too knows that knee-jerk urge to show respect.

'What are you doing here, Hock Seng?' Anderson-sama asks.

Hock Seng gives him a thin smile. 'You aren't pleased to capture the killer of the Somdet Chaopraya?'

Anderson-sama doesn't respond, just looks from Hock Seng to Emiko and back again. Finally he asks, 'How did you get in here?'

Hock Seng shrugs. 'I did, after all, find this flat for Mr. Yates. Presented the keys to him myself.'

Anderson-sama shakes his head. 'He was a fool, wasn't he?'

Hock Seng inclines his head.

With a chill, Emiko sees that this confrontation can only turn against her. The only person here who is disposable is herself. If she is quick, she can simply strip the pistol from the old man's hand. Just as she took the pistols from those slow bodyguards. It will hurt, but it can be done. The old man is no match for her.

The other *gaijin* is slipping out the door without another word, but Emiko is surprised to see Anderson-sama does not retreat as well. Instead, he eases into the room, hands held up, palms out. One of his hands is bandaged. His voice is soothing.

'What do you want, Hock Seng?'

Hock Seng backs away, keeping space between himself and the *gaijin*. 'Nothing.' Hock Seng shrugs slightly. 'The killer of the Somdet Chaopraya, righteously punished. That is all.'

Anderson-sama laughs. 'Nice.' He turns and settles carefully into a couch. Grunts and winces as he leans back. Smiles again.

'Now, what do you really want?'

The old man's lips quirk, sharing the joke. 'What I've always wanted. A future.'

Anderson-sama nods thoughtfully. 'You think this girl will help you get that? Get you a nice reward?'

'The capture of a royal assassin will surely earn me enough to rebuild my family.'

Anderson-sama doesn't say anything, just stares at Hock Seng with his cold blue eyes. His gaze turns to Emiko. 'Did you kill him? Really?'

A part of her wants to lie. She can see in his eyes that he wants that lie as well, but she can't force the words out. 'I am sorry, Anderson-sama.'

'And all the bodyguards, too?'

'They hurt me.'

He shakes his head. 'I didn't believe it. I was sure Akkarat set it all up. But then you jumped off the balcony.' His unsettling blue eyes continue to watch her. 'Are you trained to kill?'

'No!' She recoils, shocked at the suggestion. Rushes to explain. 'I did not know. They hurt me. I was angry. I didn't know—' She has an overwhelming urge to kowtow before him. To try to convince him of her loyalty. She fights the instinct, recognizing her own genetic need to roll over on her back and bare her belly.

'So you're not an assassin, trained?' he asks. 'A military windup?'

'No. Not military. Please. Believe me.'

'But still dangerous. You tore the Somdet Chaopraya's head off with your bare hands.'

Emiko wants to protest, to say that she is not that creature, that it was not her, but the words won't come out. All she can do is whisper, 'I did not take off his head.'

'You could kill us all if you wanted, though. Before we even knew you were coming. Before Hock Seng could even lift his pistol.'

At these words, Hock Seng whips his spring gun back to point at her. Pathetically slow.

Emiko shakes her head. 'I do not wish it,' she says. 'I only wish to leave. To go north. That is all.'

'But still, you're a dangerous creature,' Anderson-sama says. 'Dangerous to me. To other people. If anyone saw me with you, now.' He shakes his head and grimaces. 'You're worth far more dead than alive.'

Emiko readies herself, prepares for the excruciating pain that will come. First the Chinese, then Anderson-sama. Maybe not the little girl—

'I'm sorry, Hock Seng,' Anderson-sama says abruptly. 'You can't have her.'

Emiko stares at the *gaijin*, shocked.

The Chinese laughs. 'You will stop me?'

Anderson-sama shakes his head. 'Times are changing, Hock Seng. My people are coming. In force. All our fortunes will be changing. It won't just be the factory anymore. It'll be calorie contracts, freight shipping, R&D centers, trade negotiations ... Starting today, everything changes.'

'And this rising tide will raise my ship as well?'

Anderson-sama laughs, then winces, touching his ribs. 'More than ever, Hock Seng. We'll need people like you more than ever.'

The old man looks from Anderson-sama to Emiko. 'What about Mai?'

Anderson-sama coughs. 'Stop worrying about small things, Hock Seng. You're going to have an almost unlimited expense account. Hire her. Marry her. I don't care. Do what you like. Hell, I'm sure Carlyle would find a place for her too, if you don't want her on your own payroll.' He leans back and shouts out into the hall. 'I know you're still out there, you coward. Get in here.'

The *gaijin* Carlyle's voice calls in. 'You're really going to protect that windup?' He peers around the corner, cautious.

Anderson-sama shrugs. 'Without her, we wouldn't even have

had an excuse for the coup.' He gives her a crooked smile. 'That must be worth something.'

He looks again at Hock Seng. 'Well? What do you think?'

'You swear this?' the old man asks.

'If we break faith, you can always report her later. She's not going anywhere soon. Not with everyone on the lookout for a windup assassin. We all benefit, every one of us, if we come to agreement. Come on, Hock Seng. This is an easy call. Everyone wins, for once.'

Hock Seng hesitates, then gives a sharp nod and lowers his gun. Emiko feels a sudden flood of relief. Anderson smiles. He turns his attention to her and his expression softens. 'Many things will be changing now. But we can't let anyone see you. There are too many people who will never forgive. You understand?'

'Yes. I will not be seen.'

'Good. Once things calm down, we'll see about getting you out of here. For the moment, you'll stay here. We'll splint up that arm. I'll get someone to bring in a case of ice. Would you like that?'

The relief is almost overwhelming. 'Yes. Thank you. You are kind.'

Anderson-sama smiles. 'Where's that whiskey, Carlyle? We need a toast.' He gets up, wincing, and comes back with an array of glasses and a bottle.

As he sets the glassware down on a small end-table, he coughs.

'Goddamn Akkarat,' he mutters, and then he coughs again, a deep hoarse sound.

Suddenly he doubles over. Another cough wracks him and then more follow in a wet rattling series. Anderson-sama puts out a hand to steady himself but instead jostles the table. Tips it.

Emiko watches as the glasses and whiskey bottle slide toward the edge of the table, spill off. They fall very slowly, glinting in the light of the rising sun. They're very pretty, she thinks. So clean and bright.

They shatter across the floor. Anderson-sama's coughing spasm continues. He collapses to his knees amongst the shards. He tries to get up, but another spasm seizes him. He curls over on his side.

When the coughing finally releases him, he looks toward Emiko, blue eyes staring out from sunken hollows.

'Akkarat really cracked me up,' he rasps.

Hock Seng and Mai are backing away. Carlyle has an arm over his mouth, frightened eyes peering over the crook of an elbow.

'It's like the factory,' Mai murmurs.

Emiko crouches down beside the *gaijin*.

He suddenly seems small and frail. He reaches for her, clumsy, and she takes his hand. Blood spackles his lips.

47

The formal surrender occurs on the open parade grounds before the Grand Palace. Akkarat is there to greet Kanya and accept her *khrab* of submission. Already AgriGen ships are in the docks, unloading U-Tex rice and SoyPRO onto the docks. The sterile seeds of the grain monopolies – some to feed people now, some to go to Thai farmers in the next planting cycle. From where she stands in the parade grounds, Kanya can see the corporate sails with their red wheat crest logos billowing above the levee rim.

There was a rumor that the young Queen would oversee the ceremony and cement the new government under Akkarat, and so the throngs are larger than would be expected. But at the last moment, word came that she would not, after all, attend, and so they all stand in the heat of the dry season that has gone on too long already, sweating and sweltering as Akkarat steps up on a dais while monks chant. He swears oaths as the new Somdet Chaopraya to protect the Kingdom in this unsettled state of military law, then he turns and faces the army and civilians and remaining white shirts under Kanya, all arrayed before him.

Sweat trickles down Kanya's temples but she refuses to move. Even though she surrendered the Environment Ministry into Akkarat's hands, still she wishes to present it in the best, most disciplined light, and so she remains at attention, sweating, with Pai in the front rank beside her, his face schooled into careful immobility.

She catches sight of Narong standing a little behind Akkarat, watching the proceedings. He inclines his head to her and it is all she can do not to scream at him, to shriek that all of this destruction is his fault. Wanton and pointless and avoidable. Kanya grits her teeth and sweats and drills her hatred into Narong's forehead. It's stupid. The one she hates is herself. She will formally surrender the last of her good men and women to Akkarat and see the white shirts disbanded.

Jaidee stands beside her, watching thoughtfully.

'You have something you want to say?' Kanya mutters.

Jaidee shrugs. 'They took the rest of my family. In the fighting.'

Kanya sucks in her breath. 'I am sorry.' She wishes she could reach out. Touch him.

Jaidee smiles sadly. 'It is war. I always tried to explain that to you.'

She wants to answer but Akkarat beckons for her. Now is the time for her abasement. She hates the man so. How is it that her youthful rage can be so undone? She swore as a child she would destroy the white shirts, and yet now her victory has the reek of the Ministry's burning grounds. Kanya climbs the steps and performs her *khrab*. Akkarat allows her to remain prostrate for a long time. Above her, she can hear him speaking.

'It is natural to grieve a man such as General Pracha,' he says to the multitudes. 'Though he was not loyal, he was passionate, and for that, if nothing else, we owe him a measure of respect. His last days were not his only days. He labored on behalf of the Kingdom for many years. He worked to preserve our people in times of great uncertainty. I will never speak against his good work, even if, at the end, he went astray.'

He pauses, then says, 'We, as a Kingdom, must heal.' He looks down at them all. 'In the spirit of good will, I am very happy to announce that the Queen has accepted my request that all the combatants who fought on behalf of General Pracha and his coup attempt are granted amnesty. Unconditionally. For those of you who still wish to work at the Environment Ministry, I hope that you will continue to work there with pride. We face all manner of hardships, and we cannot know what our future holds.'

He motions to Kanya to stand and walks across to her.

'Captain Kanya, though you fought against the Kingdom and the palace, I grant you both a pardon and something more.' He pauses. 'We must reconcile. We, as a kingdom and nation, must reconcile. Must reach across to one another.'

Kanya's stomach tightens, she feels sick with disgust at the whole proceeding. Akkarat says, 'As you are the highest ranking member of the Environment Ministry, I now appoint you to its head. Your duty is as it was. Protect the Kingdom and Her Royal Majesty the Queen.'

Kanya stares at Akkarat. Behind him, Narong is smiling slightly. He inclines his head, showing respect. Kanya is speechless. She *wais*, deeply shocked. Akkarat smiles.

'You may dismiss your men, General. Tomorrow we must once again rebuild.'

Still speechless, she *wais* again, then turns. Her first attempt at an order comes out as a croak. She swallows and give the order again, her voice cracking. Faces, as surprised and uncertain as her own feels, stare at up at her. For a moment, she fears that they know her for a fraud, that they will not obey. Then ranks of white shirts turn as one. They march away, uniforms flashing in the sunlight. Jaidee marches with them. But before he does, he *wais* to her as if she truly is a general, and this hurts more than anything that has come before.

48

'They're leaving. It's done.'

Anderson lets his head fall back on the pillow. 'We've won then.'

Emiko doesn't respond; she's still looking out toward the distant parade grounds.

Morning light burns through the window. He is shivering. Freezing and grateful for the onslaught of sun. Sweat pours off of him. Emiko lays a hand on his forehead and he's surprised to feel that it is cool.

He looks up at her through his haze of fever and sickness. 'Is Hock Seng here yet?'

She shakes her head sadly. 'Your people are not loyal.'

Anderson almost laughs at that. He pushes ineffectually at his blankets. Emiko helps him strip them away. 'No. They're not.' He turns his face to the sun again, soaking it up, allowing it to bathe him. 'But I knew that.' He would laugh more, if he weren't so tired. If his body didn't feel as if it was breaking apart.

'Do you want more water?' she asks.

The thought doesn't appeal. He's not thirsty. Last night, he was thirsty. When the doctor came at Akkarat's order he could have drunk the ocean, but now, he is not.

After examining him, the doctor went away, fear in his eyes, saying that he would send people. That the Environment Ministry would have to be notified. That white shirts would come to work some black containment magic upon him. All that time Emiko hid, and after the doctor went away, she waited with Anderson through the days and nights.

At least, he remembers her in fractured moments. He dreamed. Hallucinated. Yates sat with him for a time on his bed. Laughed at him. Pointed out the futility of his life. Peered into his eyes and asked him if he understood. And Anderson tried to answer but his throat was parched. No words could force their way out. And Yates laughed at that as well, and asked him what he thought of the newly arrived AgriGen Trade Representative coming to take his niche. If Anderson liked being replaced any better than he had. And then Emiko was there with a cool cloth and he was grateful, desperately grateful for any sort of attention, for her human connection ... and he had laughed weakly at the irony.

Now he looks at Emiko through bleary vision and thinks about debts he owes, and wonders if he will live long enough to pay them.

'We're going to get you out,' he whispers.

A new wave of shivering takes him. All through the night, he was hot, and now, abruptly he is cold, shaking with the freezing feel, as if he has returned to the Upper Midwest and freezes in those still cold winters, as if he looks out at snow. Now he is cold, and not thirsty at all, and even a windup girl's fingers feel icy against his face.

He pushes weakly at her hand. 'Is Hock Seng here yet?'

'You're burning up.' Emiko's face is full of concern.

'Has he come?' Anderson asks. It is intensely important that the man come. That Hock Seng be here, in the room with him. Though he can barely remember why. It is important.

'I think he will not come.' she says. 'He has all the letters he needed from you. The introductions. He is already busy with your people. With the new representative. The Boudry woman.'

A cheshire appears on the balcony. It yowls low and slips inside. Emiko doesn't seem to notice or care, but then, she and it are siblings. Sympathetic creatures, manufactured by the same flawed gods.

Anderson watches dully as the cat makes its way across his bedroom and molts through the door. If he weren't so weak, he would throw something at it. He sighs. He's past that, now. Too tired to complain about a cat. He lets his gaze roll up to the ceiling and the slow whirl of the crank fan.

He wants to still be angry. But even that has gone. At first, when he discovered that he was sick, when Hock Seng and the girl had pulled back, alarmed, he had thought they were crazy. That he hadn't been exposed to any vectors, but then, looking at them, at their fear and certainty, he had understood.

'The factory?' he'd whispered, repeating the girl Mai's words, and Hock Seng had nodded, keeping his hand over his face.

'The fining rooms, or the algae baths,' he murmured.

Anderson had wanted to be angry then, but the sickness was already sapping his strength. All he could summon was a dull rage that quickly burned away. 'Has anyone survived?'

'One,' the girl had whispered.

And he had nodded, and they had slunk away. Hock Seng. Always with his secrets. Always with his angles and his planning. Always waiting . . .

'Is he coming?' He has a hard time forcing the words out.

'He will not come,' Emiko murmurs.

'You're here.'

She shrugs. 'I am New People. Your sicknesses do not frighten me. That one will not come. Not the Carlyle man either.'

'At least they're leaving you alone. Kept their word, there.'

'Maybe,' she says, but she lacks conviction.

Anderson wonders if she's right. Wonders if he is wrong about Hock Seng as he was wrong about so many things. Wonders if his every understanding of the place was wrong. He forces away the fear. 'He'll keep faith. He's a businessman.'

Emiko doesn't answer. The cheshire jumps onto the bed. She shoos it away, but it jumps up again, seemingly sensing the carrion opportunity he represents.

Anderson tries to raise a hand. 'No,' he croaks. 'Let it stay.'

49

AgriGen people march off the docks. Kanya and her men stand at attention, an honor guard for demons. The *farang* all stand and squint at the tropic sun, taking in the land they have never before seen. They point rudely at young girls walking down the street, talk and laugh loudly. They are an uncouth race. So confident.

'They're very self-satisfied,' Pai mutters.

Kanya startles at hearing her own thoughts voiced aloud, but doesn't respond. Simply waits while Akkarat meets these new creatures. A blond, scowling woman called Elizabeth Boudry is at their head, an AgriGen creature through and through.

She has a long sweeping black cloak as do others of the AgriGen people, all of them with their red wheat crest logos shining in the sun. The only satisfying thing about seeing these people in their hated uniforms is that the tropic heat must be awful for them. Their faces shine with sweat.

Akkarat says to Kanya. 'These are the ones who will be going to the seedbank.'

'Are you sure about this?' she asks.

He shrugs. 'They only want samples. Genetic diversity for their generipping. The Kingdom will benefit as well.'

Kanya studies the people who used to be called calorie demons and who now walk so brazenly in Krung Thep, the City of Divine Beings. Crates of grain are coming off the ship and being stacked on megodont wagons, the AgriGen logo prominent on every one.

Seeming to sense her thoughts, Akkarat says, 'We've passed the time when we can hide behind our walls and hope to survive. We must engage with this outside world.'

'But the seedbank,' Kanya protests quietly. 'King Rama's legacy.'

Akkarat nods shortly. 'They will only be taking samples. Do not concern yourself.' He turns to another *farang* and shakes hands with him in the foreign style. Speaks with him using the *Angrit* language and sends him on his way.

'Richard Carlyle,' Akkarat comments as he returns to Kanya's side. 'We'll have our pumps, finally. He's sending out a dirigible this afternoon. With luck we'll beat the rainy season.' He looks at her significantly. 'You understand all this? You understand what I'm doing here? It is better to lose a little of the Kingdom than everything. There are times to fight and times to negotiate. We cannot survive if we are entirely isolated. History tells us we must engage with the outside world.'

Kanya nods stiffly.

Jaidee leans over her shoulder. 'At least they never got Gi Bu Sen.'

'I would rather give them Gi Bu Sen than the seedbank,' Kanya mutters.

'Yes, but I think that losing the man was even more irritating to them.' He nods at the Boudry woman. 'She was quite enraged. Shouted, even. Lost all her face. Paced back and forth waving her arms.' He demonstrates.

Kanya grimaces. 'Akkarat was angry, too. He was after me all day, demanding to know how we could have allowed the old man to escape.'

'A clever man, that one.'

Kanya laughs. 'Akkarat?'

'The generipper.'

Before Kanya can plumb more of Jaidee's thoughts, the Boudry woman and her seed scientists approach. An ancient yellow card Chinese man approaches with her. He stands ramrod straight, nods to Kanya. 'I will be translating for *Khun* Elizabeth Boudry.'

Kanya makes herself smile politely as she studies the people before her. This is what it comes to. Yellow cards and *farang*.

'Everything is change.' Jaidee sighs. 'It would be good for you to remember it. Clinging to the past, worrying about the future ...' He shrugs. 'It's all suffering.'

The *farang* are waiting for her. Impatient. She guides them down into the war-damaged streets. Somewhere in the distance, off near the anchor pads, a tank booms. Perhaps a cell of holdout students, people not under her control. People beholden to different sorts of honor than she. She waves to two of her new underlings, Malivalaya and Yuthakon, if she remembers correctly.

'General,' one of them starts, but Kanya scowls at him.

'I told you, no more generals. No more of that nonsense. I am a captain. If captain was good enough for Jaidee, then I won't name myself higher.'

Malivalaya *wais* apology. Kanya orders the *farang* into the comfort of the coal-diesel car, and then they are whispering through the streets. It is a luxury that she has never experienced, but she forces herself not to exclaim at Akkarat's suddenly exposed wealth. The car slides through the empty streets, making its way toward the City Pillar Shrine.

Fifteen minutes later, they emerge from the car into burning sun. Monks lower their heads in courtesy to her, acknowledging her authority. She nods back, feeling sick. In this, King Rama XII placed the Environment Ministry above even monks.

The monks throw open gates and lead her and the rest of the

entourage down below, down into the cool deeps. Airtight doors swing up, filtered air under positive pressure wafts out. Perfectly humid air, chilly. She forces herself not to clutch her arms to her as the cool increases. More vault doors open, revealing interior corridors, powered by coal-burning systems, triple fail-safed.

Monks in saffron wait politely, stepping away from her to ensure that she doesn't come in contact with them. She turns to the Boudry woman. 'Don't touch the monks. They have taken vows not to touch women.'

The yellow card translates into the *farang's* squawking language. Kanya hears a snort of laughter behind her but forces herself not to react. The Boudry woman and her generipper scientists all chatter excitedly as they work their way deeper into the seedbank. The yellow card translator doesn't bother to explain their weird exclamations, but Kanya can guess most of it from the delighted expressions.

She leads them deeper into the vaults, to the cataloging rooms, all the time thinking on the nature of loyalty. Better to give up a limb than to give up the head. The Kingdom survives when other countries fall because of Thai practicality.

Kanya glances back at the *farang*. Their greedy pale eyes scan the shelves, the vacuum-sealed containers of thousands of seeds, each one a potential line of defense against their kind. The true treasure of a kingdom, laid out before them. The spoils of war.

When the Burmese toppled Ayutthaya, the city fell without a fight. And now, again, it is the same. In the end, after all the blood and sweat and deaths and toil, after the struggles of seed saints and martyrs like Phra Seub, after the sale of girls like Kip to Gi Bu Sen and all the rest, it comes down to this. *Farang* standing triumphant at the heart of a kingdom betrayed once again by ministers uncaring for the crown.

'Don't take it so badly.' Jaidee touches her on her shoulder. 'We all must come to terms with our failures, Kanya.'

'I am sorry. For everything.'

'I forgave you a long time ago. We all have our patrons and our loyalties. It was *kamma* that brought you to Akkarat before you came to me.'

'I never thought it would come to this.'

'It is a great loss.' Jaidee agrees. Then he shrugs. 'But even now, it doesn't have to be this way.'

Kanya glances over at the *farang*. One of the scientists catches her eye, says something to the woman. Kanya can't tell if it is mocking or thoughtful. Their wheat crest logos gleam in the flicker of electric lighting.

Jaidee raises an eyebrow. 'There is always Her Majesty the Queen, yes?'

'And what can that accomplish?'

'Would you not prefer to be remembered as a villager of Bang Rajan who fought when all was lost, and held the Burmese at bay for a little while, than as one of the cowardly courtiers of Ayutthaya who sacrificed a kingdom?'

'It's all ego,' Kanya mutters.

'Maybe.' Jaidee shrugs. 'But I'll tell you true: Ayutthaya was nothing in our history. Did the Thai not survive the sack of it? Have we not survived the Burmese? The Khmers? The French? The Japanese? The Americans? The Chinese? The calorie companies? Have we not held them all at bay when others fell? It is our people who carry the lifeblood of this country, not this city. Our people carry the names that the Chakri gave us, and it is our people who are everything. And it is this seedbank that sustains us.'

'But His Majesty declared that we would always defend—'

'King Rama did not care an ounce for Krung Thep; he cared for us, and so he made a symbol for us to protect. But it is not the city, it is the people that matter. What good is a city if the people are enslaved?'

Kanya's breathing has become rapid. Icy air saws in and out of her lungs. The Boudry woman says something. The generippers yawp in their awful tongue. Kanya turns to Pai.

'Follow my lead.'

She draws her spring gun and fires it point blank into the *farang* woman's head.

50

Elizabeth Boudry's head jerks back. Blood sprays Hock Seng in fine mist, spattering his skin and newly tailored clothes. The white shirt general turns and Hock Seng immediately drops to his knees, making a *khrab* of obeisance beside the collapsed body of the foreign devil.

The blond creature's surprised dead eyes stare out at him as he prostrates himself. Spring gun disks chatter across the walls, people are screaming. Suddenly there is silence.

The white shirt general yanks him to his feet and shoves her spring gun into his face.

'Please,' Hock Seng whispers in Thai. 'I am not their kind.'

The general's hard eyes study him. She nods sharply, and shoves him aside. He huddles against a wall as she begins barking orders to her men. They quickly drag the AgriGen bodies aside, then coalesce around her. Hock Seng is surprised at how quickly the unsmiling woman musters her troops. She goes to the monks of the seedbank. Makes her own *khrab* of respect and begins speaking quickly. Even though she performs a *khrab* to their spiritual authority, there can be no doubt that she is the one who is the master of the place.

Hock Seng's eyes widen as he hears what she is planning. It's terrifying. An act of destruction that cannot be allowed ... and yet, the monks are nodding and now people are streaming out of the seedbank, all of them working quickly. The general and her men begin throwing open doors, revealing rack after rack of weaponry. She begins assigning teams: the Grand Palace, Korakot Pump, Khlong Toey Seawall Lock ...

The general spares a glance at Hock Seng as she finishes dispatching her people. The monks are already taking seeds down from the shelves. Hock Seng cringes at her attention. After what he has heard, she cannot intend to let him live. The bustle of activity increases. More and more monks stream in. They stack the seeds cases carefully. Rank after rank of seeds coming down from the shelves. Seeds from more than a hundred years ago, seeds that every so often are cultured in the strictest of isolation chambers and then carried back to this underground safe, to be stored again. The heritage of millennia in the boxes, the heritage of the world.

And then the monks are streaming out of the seedbank, carrying the boxes on their shoulders, a river of shaven-headed men in saffron robes, bearing forth their nation's treasure. Hock Seng watches, breathless at the sight of so much genetic material disappearing into the wilds. Somewhere outside, he thinks he hears monks chanting, blessing this project of renewal and destruction, and then the white shirt general is looking at him again. He forces himself not to duck his head. Not to grovel. She will kill him. She must. He will not grovel and piss himself. At least he will die with dignity.

The general purses her lips, then simply jerks her head toward the open doors. 'Run, yellow card. This city is no longer a refuge for you.'

He stares at her, surprised. She jerks her head again and the shadow of a smile touches her lips. Hock Seng *wais* quickly and climbs off his knees. He hurries through the tunnels and out into hot open air, the river of saffron-robed men all around him. Once they reach the temple grounds, the monks disperse through various gates, separating into smaller and smaller groups, a diaspora bound eventually for some pre-arranged place of distant safety. A secret place, far from calorie company reach, watched over by Phra Seub and all the spirits of the nation.

Hock Seng watches for a moment longer as the monks continue to pour from the seedbank, and then he runs for the street.

A rickshaw man sees him and slows to a stop. Hock Seng leaps in.

'Where to?' the man asks.

Hock Seng hesitates, thinking furiously. The anchor pads. It is the only certain way to escape the coming chaos. The *yang guizi* Richard Carlyle is probably still there. The man and his dirigible, preparing to fly for Kolkata to retrieve the Kingdom's coal pumps. There will be safety in the air. But only if Hock Seng is fast enough to the catch the foreign devil before he untethers the last anchor.

'Where to?'

Mai.

Hock Seng shakes his head. Why does she torment him now? He owes her nothing. She is nothing, in truth. Just some fishing girl. And yet against his better judgment he allowed her to stay with him, told her he would hire her as a servant of some sort. Would keep her safe. It was the least he could do . . . But that was before. He was going to be flush with money from the calorie companies. It was a different sort of promise, then. She will forgive him.

'The anchor pads,' Hock Seng says. 'Quickly. I don't have much time.'

The rickshaw man nods and the bike accelerates.

Mai.

Hock Seng curses himself. He is a fool. Why does he never focus on the most important goal? Always he is distracted. Always he fails to do what would keep him alive and safe.

He leans forward, angry with himself. Angry at Mai. 'No. Wait. I have another address. First to Krungthon Bridge, then to the anchor pads.'

'That's in the opposite direction.'

Hock Seng grimaces. 'You think I don't know it?'

The rickshaw man nods and slows. He turns his bike and aims it back the way he came. He stands on his pedals, getting up to speed. The city slides past, colorful and busy with cleanup activity. A city completely unaware of its impending doom. The cycle weaves through the sunshine, shifting smoothly through its gears, faster and faster toward the girl.

If he is very lucky there will be enough time. Hock Seng prays that he will be lucky. Prays that there will be enough time to collect Mai and still make the dirigible. If he were smart, he would simply run.

Instead, he prays for luck.

Epilogue

The destroyed locks and sabotaged pumps take six days to kill the City of Divine Beings. Emiko watches from the balcony of the finest apartment tower in Bangkok as water rushes in. Anderson-sama is nothing but a husk. Emiko squeezed water into his mouth from a cloth and he sucked at it like a baby before he finally expired, whispering apologies to ghosts that only he could see.

When she first heard the colossal explosions at the edge of the city, she did not guess at first what was happening, but as more explosions followed and twelve coils of smoke rose like *naga* along the levees it became clear that King Rama XII's great floodwater pumps had been destroyed, and that the city was once again under siege.

Emiko watched the fight to save the city for three days, and then the monsoons came and the last attempts at holding back the ocean were abandoned. Rain gushed down, a vast deluge sweeping out dust and debris, sending every bit of the city swirling and rising. People swarmed from their homes with their belongings on their heads. The city slowly filled with water, becoming a vast lake lapping around second-story windows.

On the sixth day, her Royal Majesty the Child Queen announces the abandonment of the divine city. There is no Somdet Chaopraya now. Only the Queen, and the people rally to her.

The white shirts, so despised and disgraced just days before, are everywhere, guiding people north under the command of a new Tiger, a strange unsmiling woman who people say is possessed by spirits and who drives her white shirts to struggle and save as many of the people of Krung Thep as possible. Emiko herself is forced to hide as a young volunteer in a white uniform works the halls of her building offering assistance to anyone who needs food or safe water. Even as the city dies, the Environment Ministry is rehabilitated.

Slowly, the city empties. The lap of seawater and the yowl of cheshires replace the call of durian sellers and the ring of bicycle bells. At times, Emiko suspects that she is the only person living. When she cranks a radio she hears that the capital has decamped north to Ayutthaya, once again above sea level. She hears that Akkarat has shaven his head and become a monk to atone for his failure to protect the city. But it is all distant.

With the wet season, Emiko's life becomes bearable. The flooded metropolis means that there is always water nearby, even if it is a stagnant bathtub stinking with the refuse of millions. Emiko locates a small skiff and uses it to navigate the city's wilderness. Rain pours down daily and she lets it bathe her, washing away everything that has come before.

She lives by scavenge and the hunt. She eats cheshires and catches fish with her bare hands. She is very quick. Her fingers flash down to spear a carp whenever she desires it. She eats well and sleeps easily, and with water all around, she does not so greatly fear the heat that burns within her. If it is not the place for New People that she once imagined, it is still a niche.

She decorates her apartment. She crosses the wide mouth of the Chao Phraya to investigate the Mishimoto factory where she had once been employed. It is shuttered, but she finds remnants of her past and collects some of them. Calligraphy torn and left behind, Raku *chawan* bowls.

A few times, she encounters people. Most of them are too occupied with their own problems of survival to bother with a tick-tock creature more glimpsed than seen, but there are a few who prey on a lone girl's perceived weakness. Emiko deals with them quickly, and with as much mercy as she knows how.

The days pass. She becomes comfortable entirely in her world of water and scavenge. She is so comfortable, in fact, that when the *gaijin* and the girl find her, scrubbing her laundry from atop a second-floor apartment rail, they surprise her utterly.

'And who is this?' a voice asks.

Emiko draws back, startled, and nearly falls from where she perches. She jumps down and darts splashing into the safety of the abandoned apartment's shadows.

The *gaijin's* boat bumps up against the rail. '*Sawatdi khrap?*' he calls. 'Hello?'

He's old, mottled skin and bright intelligent eyes. The girl is lithe and brown with a soft smile. They both lean against the balcony railing, peering into the dimness from their boat. 'Don't run away little thing,' the old man says. 'We are quite harmless. I can't walk at all, and Kip here is a gentle soul.'

Emiko waits. They don't give up, though. Just continue to peer in at her.

'Please?' the girl calls.

Against her better judgment, Emiko steps out, wading carefully in the ankle-deep water. It has been a long time since she has spoken with a person.

'*Heechy-keechy,*' the girl breathes.

The old *gaijin* smiles at the words. 'New People, they call themselves.' His eyes contain no judgment. He holds up a limp pair of cheshires. 'Would you like to dine with us, young lady?'

Emiko motions toward the balcony rail where she has tethered her own day's catch just under water. 'I do not need your help.'

The man looks down at the string of fish, then up at her with new respect. 'I suppose you don't. Not if your design is the one I know.' He invites her closer. 'You live near here?'

She points upstairs.

'Lovely real estate. Perhaps we could dine with you this evening. If cheshire is not to your taste, we would certainly enjoy a bite of fish.'

Emiko shrugs, but she is lonely and the man and girl seem harmless. As night falls, they light a fire of kindled furniture on her apartment's balcony and roast the fish. Stars show through gaps in the clouds. The city stretches before them, black and tangled. When they are finished eating, the old *gaijin* drags his wounded body closer to the fire while the girl attends him.

'Tell me, what is a windup girl doing here?'

Emiko shrugs. 'I was left behind.'

'Ourselves, as well.' The old man exchanges smiles with his friend. 'Though I think our vacation will be ending soon. It seems we are to return to the pleasures of calorie detente and genetic warfare, so I think that the white shirts will once again have uses for me.' He laughs at that.

'Are you a generipper?' Emiko asks.

'More than just that, I hope.'

'You said you know about my ... platform?'

The man smiles. He beckons his girl over to him and runs his hand idly up her leg as he studies Emiko. Emiko realizes that the girl is not entirely what she seems; she is boy and girl, together. The girl smiles at Emiko, seeming to sense her thoughts.

'I have read about your kind,' the old man says. 'About your genetics. Your training ...

'Stand up!' he barks.

Emiko is standing before she knows it. Standing and shaking with fear and the urge to obey.

The man shakes his head. 'It's a hard thing they have done to you.'

Emiko blazes with anger. 'They also made me strong. I can hurt you.'

'Yes. That's true.' He nods. 'They took shortcuts. Your training masks that, but the shortcuts are there. Your obedience . . . I don't know where they got that. A Labrador of some sort, I suspect.' He shrugs. 'Still, you are better than human in almost all other ways. Faster, smarter, better eyesight, better hearing. You are obedient, but you don't catch diseases like mine.' He waves at his scarred and oozing legs. 'You're lucky enough.'

Emiko stares at him. 'You are one of the scientists who made me.'

'Not the same, but close enough.' He smiles slightly. 'I know your secrets, just as I know the secrets of megodonts and TotalNutrient wheat.' He nods at his dead cheshires. 'I know everything about these felines here. If I cared enough, I might even be able to drop a genetic bomb in them that would strip away their camouflage and over the course of generations turn them back into their less successful version.'

'You would do this?'

He laughs and shakes his head. 'I like them better this way.'

'I hate your kind.'

'Because someone like me made you?' He laughs again. 'I'm surprised you aren't more pleased to meet me. You're as close as anyone ever comes to meeting God. Come now, don't you have any questions for God?'

Emiko scowls at him, nods at the cheshires. 'If you were my God, you would have made New People first.'

The old *gaijin* laughs. 'That would have been exciting.'

'We would have beaten you. Just like the cheshires.'

'You may yet.' He shrugs. 'You do not fear cibiscosis or blister rust.'

'No.' Emiko shakes her head. 'We cannot breed. We depend on you for that.' She moves her hand. Telltale stutter-stop motion. 'I am marked. Always, we are marked. As obvious as a ten-hands or a megodont.'

He waves a hand dismissively. 'The windup movement is not a required trait. There is no reason it couldn't be removed. Sterility ...' He shrugs. 'Limitations can be stripped away. The safeties are there because of lessons learned, but they are not required; some of them even make it more difficult to create you. Nothing about you is inevitable.' He smiles. 'Someday, perhaps, all people will be New People and you will look back on us as we now look back at the poor Neanderthals.'

Emiko falls silent. The fire crackles. Finally she says, 'You know how to do this? Can make me breed true, like the cheshires?'

The old man exchanges a glance with his ladyboy.

'Can you do it?' Emiko presses.

He sighs. 'I cannot change the mechanics of what you already are. Your ovaries are non-existent. You cannot be made fertile any more than the pores of your skin supplemented.'

Emiko slumps.

The man laughs. 'Don't look so glum! I was never much enamored with a woman's eggs as a source of genetic material anyway.' He smiles. 'A strand of your hair would do. You cannot be changed, but your children – in genetic terms, if not physical ones – they can be made fertile, a part of the natural world.'

Emiko feels her heart pounding. 'You can do this, truly?'

'Oh yes. I can do that for you.' The man's eyes are far away, considering. A smile flickers across his lips. 'I can do that for you, and much, much more.'

Acknowledgments

Without a number of supporters, *The Windup Girl* would have been a poorer effort. A heartfelt thanks goes out to the following people: Kelly Buehler and Daniel Spector, for hosting, tour guiding, and crash space in Chiang Mai while I was doing research; Richard Foss, for flywheels; Ian Chai, for kindly interceding and fixing glaring problems with Tan Hock Seng; James Fahn, author of *A Land on Fire*, for his expertise and insights into Thailand's environmental challenges; the gang at Blue Heaven – particularly my first readers Tobias Buckell and Bill Shunn – but also Paul Melko, Greg van Eekhout, Sarah Prineas, Sandra McDonald, Heather Shaw, Holly McDowell, Ian Tregillis, Rae Carson, and Charlie Finlay. I doubt I would have found my way to the book's conclusion without their wisdom. I'd also like to thank my editor Juliet Ulman, who helped identify and solve critical problems with the story when I was completely stymied. Bill Tuffin deserves a special note of thanks. I was lucky enough to get to know him when this book was still in its infancy, and he has proven to be both a rich source of cultural information in Southeast Asia and a good friend. And finally, I want to thank my wife Anjula, for her unflagging support over many many years. Her patience and faith are unmatched. Of course, while all these people helped bring out the best in this book, I am solely responsible for its errors, omissions and transgressions.

On a separate note, I would like to mention that while this book is set in a future version of Thailand, it should not be construed as representative of present-day Thailand or the Thai people. I enthusiastically recommend authors such as Chart Korbjitti, S. P. Somtow, Phra Peter Pannapadipo, Botan, Father Joe Maier, Kukrit Pramoj, Saneh Sangsuk and Kampoon Boontawee for far better windows into the Thai Kingdom and its many aspects.

extras

www.orbitbooks.net

about the author

Paolo Bacigalupi was brought up in Colorado, living for a short time in a commune with his parents. He majored in East Asian Studies in Ohio, then worked in China as a consultant helping foreign companies enter the Chinese market. Bacigalupi returned to the United States to work for a web development company and more recently worked for a biweekly environmental newspaper. He now writes critically acclaimed, award-winning short stories in addition to novel length fiction, and lives in Western Colorado with his wife and son.

Bacigalupi's debut novel *The Windup Girl* has been one of the most highly regarded SF novels of recent years, winning the Hugo Award, the Nebula Award, the John W. Campbell Memorial Award and the Locus Award for best first novel. It was also named by *Time Magazine* as one of the Top 10 Books of 2009. Bacigalupi has also won the Theodore Sturgeon Award for SF short story writing.

You can find out more about this talented author and his books at www.windupstories.com

Find out more about Paolo Bacigalupi and other Orbit authors by registering for the free monthly newsletter at www.orbitbooks.net

interview

Let's start with the question that all interviews with you should start with: how the hell do you pronounce your name?
I have no idea. Bunch o'galoshes. That's the best description I've heard. Yeah, it's Paolo BATCH-i-ga-LOOP-ee. [. . .] It's 'baci' as in 'kiss', so 'kiss of the wolf' is the loose translation for it.

And at what age did you finally learn how to spell your last name?
Three. My mother had to spell it a lot for other people, so it became a bit of a singsong chant to me.

The Windup Girl has been your big break, and you've been winning awards left and right.
It feels like I just woke up in some kind of fairy-tale. I wrote four novels that never sold, and I kept trying and banging my head against the wall so many times, that when I finally sold *The Windup Girl* and knew it was gonna come out, I really didn't have any expectations at all. I figured, it's a science fiction novel, and we know science fiction novels don't do very well.

Does it change things for you when you're at the keyboard? Now that you're Hugo-and-Nebula-winning-author Paolo Bacigalupi.
The things that have really gotten confusing to me is how you

balance the desires of your publishers to produce things on a schedule, and people are always sort of giving you ideas on what you should follow up with, or how you should proceed next, and things like that. You know, career things that are then impinging on and messing around with the question of just, what am I interested in writing?

So I've gone through a couple of gyrations with that, where it's been a little confusing for me, just trying to get back to the centre of, well, these are the things I'm really interested in. This is the kind of story that I feel like telling right now. And getting more comfortable with the fact that that might not necessarily be what people assume is coming next from me. I think that's the part that's a little confusing for me. I think inherently – a little bit – I'm a bit of a pleaser and I want people to like me and be nice, and to not ruffle feathers and just make everybody happy and stuff. It's a personality flaw.

One of the consequences of this is that I just threw an entire book away. I'd written it out to eighty or ninety thousand words and I just threw it away, because it's not what I love.

That's a lot of discipline, to bin that many words.
My wife says that I'm nuts, actually. It's one or the other. You can just tell when it doesn't work.

In many ways, though, it's not just a science fiction novel, right? Most of the technology you describe, at least in terms of non-biological technology, is older than what we have now.
Yeah, it's more like throwback technologies. When I say science fiction, I think of classic *Foundation*, I think of rocket ships. But there's this other tradition of science fiction, which is sort of the stealth version. It's the stuff you see with Aldous Huxley or George Orwell, where you're extrapolating about who are we, where are we

going, what our society looks like, and I feel very connected to that strain of science fiction writing.

Your work tends to focus on environment issues, often projecting a somewhat pessimistic outlook toward the future. What is the driving force behind this? And is your upcoming work in the same vein?

Most of the news about the state of the environment is pretty ugly. This is frightening for me personally, but actually motivational for me artistically. Environmental science is telling us a lot about our future and what it could look like, whether we're talking about global warming (the current poster child for the environment) or a loss of genetic diversity in our food supplies, or the effects of low-dose chemicals on human development. The surfeit of bad trends pushes me to set my stories in worlds which are often diminished versions of our own present. Mostly, I write these versions of the future because I'm worried about what seems to be happening, and I'm worried that we as a society aren't particularly interested in changing our ways. Certainly the next couple novels you'll see from me will be set in fairly ravaged futures. I'm trying to find ways to tell compelling and engaging human stories within those futures, but yeah, the future looks a bit bleak to me.

One of the interesting things about *The Windup Girl* is that it all comes back to responsibility. Responsibility to one's self, or to karma or, in Anderson Lake's case, to 'calorie company' AgriGen. How did that come about?

It's interesting, because a lot of people find those characters unlikable, and I've always loved those characters. I think of them as different versions of myself. And I have empathy for people who make difficult or what we might say are unethical or cruel decisions. It's not so much that people are bad, it's just that under strain, people break and our ideals break. When you build an entire world where everybody's under strain, there's something there that's very powerful to me. People doing the best they can under hard circumstances.

FACT: the solution to all of the world's environmental issues is bioengineering photosynthetic humans. As a speculative author, what's the first consequence that comes to your mind?

At first, I think, death of the meat industry, but really, we don't need to eat meat now, so there's no reason we'd stop eating it just because we don't need it. Ditto for the rest of the ag industry. But there is the possibility of foodie culture becoming an even more rarefied and elite object, something for aesthetes. On the other hand, if we're all photosynthesising, maybe that causes mass equatorial migration, so we can maximise our children's health and access to sunlight, so the sun-deprived north wages war on the equatorial zones for better sunlight territory. I think Alaska basically depopulates. Of course, then the question really is: can we only photosynthese? Or is it supplemental energy? Maybe the effect is that we keep eating just like always, but we're also photosynthesising, and so we GET REALLY OBESE and just lie around as giant green lumps on lawn chairs, soaking up free sun food and doing nothing else at all. Come to think of it, if we photosynthese, it would also mean a change in our food spending, so grocery stores and convenience marts would disappear ... which would mean that stoners with the munchies would be completely out of luck. But as long as we're engineering ourselves to have chlorophyll, maybe we could add in THC, and sit around clipping our hair and toenails and smoking it. And if we photosynthese, does that mean we go around naked all the time, or at least wearing transparent clothing so we can absorb as much sunlight as possible? Maybe because we're photosynthesising we'll do more work outside. So our laptops will have to get rid of these damn glossy screens that have become so popular. And then we'll sit around outside, sucking up sun, getting fat and green and surfing the net.

Wow! So what are your writing habits like? Do you have any peculiar writing habits that somehow work for you but everyone else would find quirky (and/or insane)?
Not really. I like to have a good selection of tea on hand. I write at a standing desk, which has helped me be much more productive and solved some back problems, but mostly all my quirky habits have to do with procrastination and avoidance rather than with work. I'm slowly trying to stamp those out.

Finally, every writer has a favourite word. What's that unique word that tries to find its way into everything you write?
F***

But then I have to take it out.

if you enjoyed
THE WINDUP GIRL

look out for

MR SHIVERS

by

Robert Jackson Bennett

Chapter One

By the time the number nineteen crossed the Missouri state line
the sun had crawled low in the sky and afternoon was fading into
evening. The train had built up a wild head of steam over the last
few miles. As Tennessee fell behind it began picking up speed, the
wheels chanting and chuckling, the fields blurring into jaundice-
yellow streaks by the track. A fresh gout of black smoke unfurled
from the train's crown and folded back to clutch the cars like a
great black cloak.

Connelly shut his eyes as the wave of smoke fl ew toward him and held on tighter to the side of the cattle car. He wasn't sure how long he had been hanging there. Maybe a half hour. Maybe more. The crook of his arm was curled around one splintered slat of wood and he had wedged his boots into the cracks below. Every joint in his body ached.

He squinted through the tumble of trainsmoke at the other three men. They hung on, faces impassive. One of them called to the oldest, asking if it was soon. He grinned and shook his head and laughed.

Ten miles on Connelly felt the train begin to slow and the countryside started to take shape around him. The fields all seemed the same, nothing but cracked red earth and crooked fencing. Sometimes there were men working in the fields, overalled and with faces as beaten as the land. They watched the train's furious procession with a country boy's awe. Some laughed and called to them. Most did not and watched their coming and going with almost no acknowledgment at all.

The old man before him hitched himself low on the train, eyes watching the wheels as one would a predator. He held up three fingers, waved. Then two. Then one, and he dropped from the side of the train.

Connelly followed suit and as he rolled he saw the churning wheels no more than three feet from him, hissing and cackling. He slid away until he came to rest in a ditch with the others. They stood and beat the dust and grit and soot from their faces. Then they crouched low in the weeds and waited until the train's passage was marked only by a ribbon of black smoke and a roar hovering in the sky.

'Think they coming back?' whispered one of the young ones. 'Coming back to look for us?'

'Boy, what are you, an idiot?' said the old man. 'No train man is going to double back looking for trouble. If we're off then we're off. Done.'

'Done?'

'Yeah. Count your limbs and teeth and start using your feet. Maybe your head, too, if you feel like it.' He scratched his gray hair and grinned, flashing a crooked mouthful of yellowed teeth.

They shouldered their packs and began heading west, following the tracks.

'Should have held on longer,' said one of the men.

'Ha,' said the grayhair. 'If you did that then I guarantee you wouldn't be looking so hale and hearty right now. Don't want to get caught, caught by the freight boss. He'd whale you raw.'

'Not with him, I'd reckon,' the man said, nodding toward Connelly, who was a head taller than the others. 'What's your name?'

'Connelly,' he said.

'You got any tobacco?'

Connelly shook his head.

'You sure?'

'Yeah.'

'Hm,' he said, and spat. 'Still think we should've held on longer.'

They took up upon an old county road. As they walked they kicked up a cloud of dust that rose to their faces, turning their soot-gray clothes to raw red. The land on either side was patched like a stray's coat, the hills dotted with corn lying flat as though it had been laid low by some blast. Roots lay half submerged in the loose soil, fine curling tendrils grasping at nothing. In some places growth still clung to the earth and men grouped around these spots to pump life into their crop. As Connelly passed they looked up with frightened, brittle eyes and he knew it would not last.

The two younger men paced ahead and one said, 'Why don't these dumb sons of bitches leave?'

'Where they going to go?' asked the other.

'Anywhere's better than here.'

'Looks like home to me. This seems to be my anywhere and it ain't much better.'

'Things'll turn different in Rennah,' the other said. 'You just watch.'

The grayhair dropped back beside Connelly. 'You headed to the same place? Rennah, you headed there?'

Connelly nodded.

The grayhair shook his head, swatted the back of his neck with his hat. 'Your funeral. Nothing going to be there, you know that?' He leaned closer to confide a whisper. 'These fellas is just suckers. They flipped that ride 'cause they heard there's work here, but there ain't. Further down the line, I say. Maybe south, maybe west. Eh?'

'Not going for work,' said Connelly.

'What? What the hell you going for, then?'

Connelly bowed his head and pulled his cap low. The old man let him be.

The sun turned a deep, sick red as it sank toward the earth. Even the sky had a faint tinge of red. It made a strange, hellish sight. It was the drought, everyone said. Threw dirt up into the sky. Touched the heavens with it. Connelly was not so sure but could not say why. Perhaps it was something else. Some superficial symptom of a greater disease.

He counted the days as he walked and guessed it had been more than two weeks since he had left Memphis. Then he counted his dollars and reckoned he had spent a little over three. He was spending at far too high of a rate if he wanted to go much farther. And he would have to go farther. The man had a week's head start on him at least. It was unlikely that he'd even be in Rennah. But he had been there once and that was all Connelly needed.

Closer, he said to himself. I'm close. I'm very close now.

'Town's up that way,' said one of the men, pointing to a few lines of smoke on the horizon.

The old man eyed the spindle-like lines twisting across the sunset. 'That ain't the town,' he said.

'No?'

'No. Those are campfires.'

The men looked at each other again, this time worried. Connelly was not surprised. He knew they had expected it, whether they said so or not. For many it was the same as the town they had just left.

Connelly caught its scent before he saw it. He smelled rotten kindling and greasy fires and cigarette smoke, excrement and foul water. It was a plague- stink, a battlefield-reek. Then he heard the cacophony of dogs barking and children crying, a junkyard song of pots and pans and old engine parts and drunken melodies. Then finally it came into view. They shaded their eyes and looked at the encampment before them, saw jalopies lurching between canyons of shuddering tents, people small as dots milling beside them. A wide smear of gray and black among the white-gold of the fields. There had to be at least a hundred people there. At least.

'Jesus,' said one of the men.

'Yeah,' said another.

'Can't see there being much work here.'

'I reckon not, no.'

'Told you so,' said the grayhair softly. 'Told you so.'

Connelly and the men parted ways as they approached. The men walked on and came to the camp's ragged border. Some of the people had tents and some had cars and some had nothing at all but still mingled around these tattered constructs like refuse caught washing downstream. They watched the new strangers approach, too tired to hold any real resentment. The men split up and wandered in and were caught among the webs of the encampment, filtering through the grubby people to find some spot to sit in or a fire to stand by. They sat and made talk and waited for night and the following dawn. By now it was routine.

Connelly did not join them. He walked around the camp and into town.

Chapter Two

The town couldn't have been more than five hundred people, at most. Yet the essentials were there: a main street, a post office, a general store, and finally a saloon at the end of the street.

Connelly peered through the yellowed windows of the bar. Dusty bottles were lined up behind an old wooden countertop. Men sat in sweat-soaked shirts with their hats pulled low, staring into their drinks with eyes like muddy ice.

He walked in carefully, stepping like the floor could collapse at any moment. All the men looked at him, for his size caught the eye. He removed his cap and stuffed it in his pocket and sat down at the bar. The others relaxed as he did, seeing that underneath all the miles of travel he was still a man, though no doubt one who had been roughing it for the past months. His hair had grown long and a beard crawled at the edges of his jaw. He could have been thirty, or forty, or even fifty, as his skin was tanned and dark and bore deep lines from the sun.

'What can I get you?' asked the bartender.

'Whisky,' Connelly said.

'Ten cents.'

'All right.'

Neither one moved.

'You don't have whisky?' asked Connelly.

'We have whisky. You have ten cents?'

Connelly reached into his satchel and took out a thin wallet and a dime and slid it over.

'Sorry,' said the bartender, taking it. 'Got to do that. Lots of folks come in here, order, then run out.'

'Wasn't anything.'

The bartender poured and placed the glass in front of him. Connelly took the glass and drank it in a single swallow.

'Long time getting here?' asked the bartender.

'Here is just another stop on the road,' he said.

An ancient old man stood up and came and sat beside Connelly. He ordered as well, hands trembling. Then he turned to Connelly and studied him, his face fixed in a terrible awe.

'What you doing there, grampa?' asked the bartender cautiously.

The old man did not answer. Instead he said, 'West.'

'What?' said Connelly.

'West. You're going west, ain't you?'

'If that's where I'm going, yeah,' said Connelly.

'You are,' he said. 'You are. I can tell. I seen enough people heading west to know when one's going that way. And you are.'

'Okay.'

'You shouldn't, you know. You shouldn't.'

'I could go back south or north right after you get done talking to me.'

'No. You won't. Certain men, the way they look at things and the way they walk, they're drawn to the west, to the far countries. Even if they turn aside and walk for days on end, soon enough they'll find themselves facing sunset again.'

'A lot of people are moving west right now.'

'True. That's true. But they should not go.'

Connelly fiddled with his glass, ignoring him.

The old man said, 'They say the sun kisses the land out there, like a lover. That may be so. I been out there. For years, I been out there. And if that's so then the sun's love is a terrible, harsh thing. Where it's placed its kiss nothing grows, all is burned away, everything is scorched and nothing lives and your heart is the only one of its kind that beats for miles and miles. And all is red. Where the sun and the horizon and the sands meet, all is red.'

'Is it?'

'Yes,' said the old man. 'You should not go. You should turn around. Stop looking. And go.'

'You leave me the hell alone,' Connelly said.

'Listen,' the old man pleaded. 'Listen to me. I been out there. I seen the great, red hunger, and where it walks everything aches. From the stones to the skies, everything aches. It's broken land, there. It is broken and lost, like those who live there, and they cannot go back. You should not go out there. You should not.'

The bartender scowled. 'Get out of here, you damn crazy fool. Stop worrying my customers and get the hell out of here.'

'Go back to your home,' said the old man.

'I don't have a home,' said Connelly. 'Not anymore.'

'But you still could have another,' said the old man. 'In the west there is no hope of that. Such things are forfeit there.'

'Get out. Now,' said the bartender. 'I won't ask you again. If you stay here for one more second I'm going to whale you, I don't care how old you are.'

The old man stepped down from the seat and staggered out onto the sidewalk. He mumbled to himself, played with the buttons on his overalls, and shambled away.

'I apologize for that,' said the bartender. 'Damn old coot. He's always causing trouble. I don't think he even lives here. He just drinks when he can and sleeps in whatever alley he finds. There's more and more of them. They're almost like dogs.'

'Another whisky,' said Connelly.

The bartender poured, gave him the glass, and watched again as Connelly drank in one swallow.

'Well, you don't spend like an Okie and you don't drink much like an Okie, either,' said the bartender.

'Probably 'cause I'm not an Okie.'

'Oh?'

'No.'

'Where you from?'

'Back east.'

'Ha. People who're east ought to stay east, I'd say.'

'You going to give me another earful like the old man?'

'No. I just don't see why you'd want to come here. Nothing to come for. No one wants to stay here. *I* don't want to stay here. Folks are all heading west or south or wherever they can go that isn't here. Anywhere there's green ground and work.'

'I'm not looking for work.'

'What are you doing here, then?'

'I'm looking for a man,' said Connelly quietly.

'Oh?'

'Yeah. He came this way. Took a train, hitched his way here. I'm looking for him.'

'Why are you looking for him?'

'Got some questions for him.'

'What sort?'

Connelly didn't answer.

The bartender grunted. 'I don't want any trouble.'

'I don't mean to give you any,' Connelly said.

'Ain't that what they all say.'

'You may have seen him.'

'I see a lot of men. Too many of late.'

'You would remember him,' said Connelly. 'He was scarred, on his face.'

'Any working man is liable to be scarred.'

'He had a bunch of them, all over his face. Three big ones, here and here,' he said, and drew one finger from each edge of his mouth along the cheeks, back to the angle of the jaw. Then once more, around the socket of his left eye.

The bartender turned to watch. His mouth opened slightly in surprise and he looked away.

'You seen him,' said Connelly.

'I haven't.'

'You have.'

'I said I haven't and I meant it. I haven't.'

'Then why'd you almost fall over on yourself when I asked?'

'I didn't. Just . . . You ain't the only one looking for him,' he said.

Connelly's eyes opened wide and he sat forward. 'What do you mean?'

'I don't want trouble,' said the bartender. One hand reached under the bar. Almost certainly searching for some hidden cudgel.

Connelly sat back down. 'I just want to know what's going on,' he said.

'I don't rightly know,' the bartender said, and sighed. 'Three men come in here, just a day or two ago. Came in, asked if I'd seen a man with a scarred face. 'Like he's got a big mouth. Big,' they said, and they drawed on their own faces just as you done now. I hadn't seen him, not a man with scars as such, and I told them the same as I told you.'

'Who were they?'

'I don't know. How the hell should I know? Don't know you, either. I don't know you from Adam.'

'What else did they say?'

'They didn't say anything else. They just come in here, ask, then when I said no they just go on out.'

'Where'd they go?'

'To the camp, I guess. Back out to that camp outside, with all the other people who pitched out there. I guess they came in on the train,' he said, and eyed Connelly once more. 'Much like you.'

'Where are they camping?'

'You got a hell of a lot of questions for a guy who only drank two whiskies.'

'I just want to know. That's all I want. Please.'

'Little bit northwest of here, I think. At the old tree. Bent tree, big dead tree. You can't miss it.'

Connelly thanked him for the drink and walked out.

Outside the sun had fallen until its light was a pale pink halo in the distance. Pools of shadows swept down out of alleys and ditches and into the streets. Miserable fires glowed in the darkness, like mad fireflies or failing stars. Connelly wound through the streets and the camp and out to the hills on the other side of the town.

As he walked through the weeds and the stones he looked but saw no other encampment. Just the growing dark and the faint outline of the country. The chatter of cicadas rose and fell, punctuated by the chirps of the nighthawks circling far overhead. As he mounted the next knoll he saw the greasy spark of a small fire not far away and above it the twisted skeleton of an ancient tree. He stood watching the flame and began to ascend. When he heard the mutter of quiet talk he stopped.

He took off his cap and used it to dab at the sweat on his brow. He knelt to think and as he did the voices ceased. Then a hoarse shout came: 'If you're going to come out then come out. We can't wait on you all day.'

Connelly hesitated, then tramped up the hill. He saw three men standing before the fire looking down on him, their faces almost masked in the dark. One, the shouter, was very tall, and while not as tall as Connelly just as broad. His face was aged and hoary and was half hidden by a grisly, raw beard. The one beside him was shorter and more slender, his face narrow and handsome and somewhat amused. The third was short and portly. His eyes were runny and frightened and unkempt hair grew around his chin and upper lip. He wore a ragged bowler hat that he could not stop touching and he stayed back farther than the other two.

'The camp is back that way,' said the leader. 'Plenty of room there.'

'I didn't come here to throw down a mattress,' said Connelly.

'Then what did you come here for?'

'To ask a question.'

'A question, eh? If you want to ask, then ask.'

'I came looking for someone.'

'Oh?'

'Yes. A . . . a man. A scarred man. Cheeks all tore up.'

They did not answer, did not move or tense or twitch. They stood as statues crowning a hill, eyes placid and blank, faces dark.

'Heard you were looking for him, too,' said Connelly. 'Came to . . . to see. Just to see.'

The men still did not speak, nor did they glance among themselves to confer. They remained quiet for far longer than any man had the right to.

'Why are you looking for him?' said Connelly. 'What's he done? What's he done to you? Who . . . who is he?'

'The camp is back that way,' said the leader, this time quieter. 'Plenty of room there.'

Connelly looked at them a moment longer, waiting for some answer or at the very least some sign of knowledge. They gave him nothing. He walked back down the hill to the camp. When he glanced back they were still standing, still watching him, unmoving as though part of the hill itself.

It was late when Connelly made it back to the grounds and he could not navigate among the jalopies and the shabby homes.

He picked out the bank of a small stream not far from the camp. Then he unrolled his bedding and threw it down and lay there, looking up at the stars and listening to the worried mutterings of the other travelers. He took out a pint of whisky and drew deeply from it. He grimaced as it went down, then took another draw and watched the sky die and the moon rise above him.

On the cusp of sleep he whispered to himself: 'Molly. Molly, I'm close. I'm closer than ever now.'

He slept, but not for long. He awoke less than an hour later, his heart beating and his mind screaming, awoken by some nameless animal instinct that told him he was no longer alone.

His eyes snapped open and he sat up and heard a gruff, low shout. Something crashing through the brush to his right. Then a figure barreled through the weeds at him, arm held high, something gold and glittering clutched in its fingers.

Connelly reacted without thinking and threw his arm up to catch the blow. His elbow met with the man's lip and the man grunted and something sprayed Connelly's cheek, hot and wet and thick. His attacker stumbled and collapsed, clutching his face. Another voice cried out in the darkness, 'Georgie, Georgie! What you done to my Georgie!' A second man came running out, ready to tackle Connelly, but Connelly outweighed the man easily and tossed him to the ground. He straddled him and struck him once, twice, around the face. He tried to weigh down the man's struggling but still he cried out, 'Georgie! Say something! Say something!'

Fingers dug into the flesh at Connelly's neck and the other hand clawed at his armpit. Connelly groped in the dark and found the pipe that had served as the first's weapon and brought it down, again and again. The man yelped and fell silent, his body seizing up and his knees rising to touch his face. Behind Connelly the first attacker struggled to his feet. He roared drunkenly and though Connelly could not see him his ears sought the sound and brought the pipe to it. With a sharp crack the man fell limp and did not move again.

Connelly stood over them, breathing hard, his arm aching and his blood beating so hard and fast he felt it would erupt out of his veins. Yards away voices were shouting, calling out, 'What was that? What the hell's going on out there?' Connelly looked at the shapes of the bodies in the dark, not knowing if they were alive or dead, unable to hear any breathing over the rush in his own ears. He hurled the pipe into the stream and felt his hand and knew it was covered in blood, perhaps his or perhaps another's.

He gathered up his satchel and his bedding and ran downstream, across the water and over stones. The keening of birds and insects filled his ears. He threw himself down next to a fallen old oak and looked over the top. He could see nothing, no eyes in the starlight, no hands or glint of metal. Someone shouted, calling to another. He held his breath, then picked himself up and began running again.

He ran until his legs failed and he collapsed beside the stream, lungs and knees on fire. He washed his hands and face, cupped his hands and drank deeply and tried to ignore the coppery taste that he knew was blood, then drank again.

'You sure beat the hell out of those gentlemen,' said a voice.

He looked up. Across the stream was the leader of the three men, his hoary face floating above the silvery water and his eyes alight with satisfaction. Before him he held on to a thick walking stick, chin high. He leaned forward on it thoughtfully.

'What?' said Connelly.

'Those men. I saw. They jumped you as you slept. Trying to roll a drunk, I believe. And you beat them. I'll not turn you in,' he said as Connelly began to move. 'I don't think you could run much further, regardless.'

'You saw me?'

'I came down here to refill my canteen. Yes, I saw. Not many men could go from sleep to fighting off two men.'

There were more shouts from downstream. Connelly whipped his head to look. The other man did not.

'If you find the scarred man, what will you do?' the man asked.

'What?' said Connelly.

'If you find the scarred man, what will you do? What do you want of him?'

'They're coming.'

'Yes. They are. I have nothing to run from, so let them come. They may not know you to be innocent in this affair, however.' He leaned into his staff. 'If you were to find this man, what would you do, sir?'

Connelly looked at him, then down at the water. He could barely make out his own reflection. It was faceless, formless.

'Kill,' said Connelly. 'I'd kill him.'

The man nodded, satisfied. 'Then cross. Come with me. You can stay by our fire. If they come I will say you have been there all along, and avoid any unpleasantness, should God allow it.'

He turned and began walking uphill and soon disappeared into the undergrowth. Connelly heard the bark of dogs to the east, then hoisted his satchel over his head and crossed, wading through the water and up to the fire on the hill.